CW00546836

GOLDEN HEART

ALSO BY KATHERINE GENET

The Wilde Grove Series

The Gathering

The Belonging

The Rising

The Singing

Wilde Grove Series 2: Selena Wilde

Follow The Wind

The Otherworld

Non-Fiction

Ground & Centre

Golden Heart

KATHERINE GENET

Wych Elm Books

Copyright © 2023 by Katherine Genet

All rights reserved.

No part of this book may be reproduced in any form or by any electronic or mechanical means, including information storage and retrieval systems, without written permission from the author, except for the use of brief quotations in a book review.

Wych Elm Books

Otago, NZ

www.wychelmbooks.com

kate@wychelmbooks.com

ISBN: 978-1-99-117792-6

For Barbara, my mother,
who told me to focus, and to tell the truth.

1940-1987

1

Here is the way it was.

The way it had to be then, so it could be now.

In the midst of the ancient forest, the priestesses and their helpers come together, their breath barely a breeze in the leaves, hardly a step to hear above the calling of the birds.

For the birds are singing of this gathering, spreading the news amongst those with feathers, fur, and scales.

Amongst those with branch and leaf.

Amongst those of stream and breeze.

Amongst those too who shine, barely visible now unless the eye is wide open, but there all the same, their steps matching those of the women and men, pacing them as they move up the hillside to the place where they will settle, build their shelters.

Light their fires.

Make their circle of stones.

Sing the world to keep turning.

. . .

BRYN'S HORSE TOILED UP THE SLOPE, WATCHING HIS STEPS FOR there were roots under the springy ground and the myriad of flowers that brought colour to the forest floor. Wiping her brow, Bryn let herself glance ahead, at the swaying back of the woman who led the way.

They must, she thought, be almost there.

The journey had started in the last cycle of the moon, and now it was well into the new. When she and the priestess had camped the night before, wrapping their shawls tight about them to ward off the cooling night air, Bryn had lain upon the ground and gazed up at the moon as she'd sailed above them, bright and swelling as the stars swirled around her.

She'd listened to Awel's low singing, letting it wash over her, sweeping the homesickness away as the older priestess sang of the night and the owl who flew high in the sky, seeking the dazzling moon, only to come tumbling down, out of breath and dazed, and the woman who picked her up from the ground and breathed life and healing back into the owl's broken body, and who ever after danced with owl feathers in her hair and wings upon her arms.

Bryn had fallen asleep then, and dreamt of flying, not as an owl, but with her own wings, spread wide over the sea, the moon at her back, her shadow upon the water, and as always, delight in every light hollow bone of her body. She glided, dipped a wing to turn, sought the breath of the wind upon which to soar and opened her beaked mouth to cry out with joy.

Yes. They were almost there. Bryn saw the knowledge in

the sudden excitement in the air around Awel and she touched a hand to the stone her mother had given her, and which hung yet on a cord around her neck. The stone was polished from the sea's tumbling, and her mother had held the hole in it up to her eye, then nodded.

'To remind you,' she had said, and Bryn heard her mother's voice crack where it never had before, in all the singing, prompting, even the chastising.

'To remind you that your task now is to learn to see.'

'WHAT DO YOU WANT TO DO?' EBONY ASKED.

Rue had the phone clamped between her shoulder and ear as she pulled her sneakers on. 'I want to go to the beach.'

'The beach?' Ebony was faintly disappointed. But then, she didn't know why – was there a single decent thing they could do the day before Rue left for Wilde Grove?

She shook her head. No. There was not.

'Yeah.' In her bedroom, Rue straightened. 'I don't know which one, though. There's something I want to find.'

Rue's statement perked Ebony up a little. 'Are you planning us an adventure?' She turned and leaned against the back of her house. She'd been about to stare glumly at the backyard where her mother was in the greenhouse trying to talk the spinach into growing through the winter, but now she nodded, her mood lifting. 'What will we be looking for at the beach? And which beach?'

Rue held her phone and shook her head. 'I don't know

which beach – I want your opinion on that. I'm looking for one of those stones with a hole in the middle of it. You know the sort I mean?'

'A hag stone,' Ebony said. 'Also known as a Druid stone and a serpent stone.'

'A serpent stone?' Rue paused. 'You mean, like a dragon?'

'Well, dragons were often described as serpents, but a serpent could just be a snake as well.'

Rue shook her head. Ebony was a fount of esoteric knowledge. 'What's that got to do with a stone, though?'

Ebony laughed and a sneaky autumn wind gusted around the side of the house, flattening her hair against her cheek and driving her inside to get a hat and jacket. 'This is where it gets a bit gross,' she said. 'Apparently a serpent's stone is made of their hardened saliva, and the hole is made by their tongue.'

'Yep,' Rue agreed. 'That's kind of disgusting. Why's it called a Druid's stone, then?' Perhaps this would make a little more sense in the context of her dream. She shivered slightly at the memory of her dream, at the way Selena had gazed at her when she'd related it to her after greeting the day.

It had been Selena's idea to find a holey stone. Or a holy stone, Rue thought, remembering the way she'd pressed her hand to it in the dream. It had been precious to whoever she'd been then.

Bryn.

She'd been someone named Bryn.

Rue was determined to see if she could find one. To see if she could discover the magic of it. For surely Bryn had been wearing it because it had magic in it.

'I'll tell you on the bus or something,' Ebony said. 'Just get your butt down here. The day's half over already.' She shoved a few essentials one-handed into her backpack. 'We'll go to Aramoana. I'll call Sophie and Suze as well.'

'Aramoana?' Rue wrinkled her nose. 'I've never been there. Isn't that where that guy shot all those people?'

Ebony snorted. 'That was years ago now, and definitely not why we're going there.' She threaded her arms into her jacket and went outside, the phone still jammed against her ear. She waved goodbye to her mother and went down the driveway. 'There are heaps of shells washed up along the beach there. Those ones that look like unicorn horns, right?'

'I'm not after a unicorn horn.'

Ebony laughed. 'You sure? They're supposed to be able to cure sickness, purify water, and their horn is a powerful antidote to poison.'

Rue shook her head, but she had a wide grin on her face. 'You are a deep and endless repository of weird facts.'

'Yup,' Ebony agreed. 'It's one of the things you love about me.' She pursed her lips. 'Not too late to take me on your trip with you.'

Rue's heart sank. 'You know I want to,' she said.

'Yeah,' Ebony sighed. 'Maybe next time, eh?'

'Definitely.'

'I FORGOT TO TELL YOU THE OTHER REASON WHY ARAMOANA,' Ebony said as they walked down onto the beach.

Rue was tugging her hat down over her ears. The wind wasn't bad on the beach, fortunately, but the air was getting wintery, and the sky overhead had darkened from blue to grey during the bus trip.

'What's the other thing, then?' Sophie asked. She'd become more interested in Ebony's weird ideas since she'd decided to become a folklorist.

Ebony pointed. 'That.'

Rue looked up, then stopped walking and stared. 'What is that?' She shook her head. 'Is it natural?'

Ebony nodded and glanced at Rue in triumph. 'You wanted a hag stone, right?' She looked at the rock formation that reared from the cliff and over the beach about halfway along the stretch of sand. 'Although I guess, in this circumstance, it's probably more appropriate if we call it a Druid's stone.' She nudged Rue in the side with her elbow and grinned. 'Am I right?'

'You're right.'

'Yep. Told you I was right.'

Rue gazed up at the jutting rock, picking up her pace towards it. There was a hole in the middle of the rock, forming a natural window to the sky.

It was a very large holey stone.

'Can you climb up there?' Suze asked, zipping up her jacket against the cool day.

Ebony danced a small jig, kicking up sand under her boots. 'Yes,' she said, coming to a solemn stop and nodding. 'Yes, my dear friends, you can.' She tamped down the urge to grin and kept her expression serious. 'And when you slip through it, legend says that you will be cured of all ills.' She raised an impish eyebrow. 'And if you pass backwards seven times through the hole, then you'll soon be pregnant.'

Suze turned and looked at her, sceptical. 'Really? I don't think so.'

Ebony relaxed and shrugged. 'Okay, so that's actually said about the one in Cornwall, in the United Kingdom, but hey, who's to say it's not the same with this one?' She gazed up at it. 'Of course, the one in Cornwall is part of a Bronze Age stone circle, and not a natural formation like this.' She squinted. 'But it looks a bit like a love heart, right?'

'I'm going through it,' Rue said. 'Or at least up to it. And I'm not going to get pregnant; I think we can count on that.'

'Yeah,' Ebony said. 'None of us will be getting with child for we are currently without men.'

Rue paused, grinning at Suze who rolled her eyes, and let Ebony's words fall unanswered to the sand. 'There's really one in where? Cornwall?'

'There are standing stones with holes in them all over the place in the UK and Ireland.' Ebony sighed wistfully. 'I want to visit them.'

'You can come with me,' Sophie said, gazing up at the giant rock formation. 'There are bound to be fascinating stories attached to the stones there.' Her eyes shone as she considered it.

Rue glanced at her friends, then looped an arm over Ebony's shoulders. 'We will,' she said. 'One day we'll all visit them. What do you say to that?'

'I say hell yeah.' Ebony's smile was wide, and her eyes were dancing again. 'Let's climb the cliff and thread ourselves through this hole, right?'

'Can you fit through it?'

'It's bigger than it looks from here. You can stand up in it.'

. . .

THE SCRAMBLE UP THE CLIFF LEFT THEM OUT OF BREATH, OR perhaps it was just that close up, the hole in the rock was large and even more magical than it had looked from the ground far below. The girls stood crowded shoulder to shoulder on the path in front of it, looking through at the sky.

'Wow,' Rue breathed.

'I know,' Ebony answered.

'I've never climbed up here,' Suze said.

Sophie shook her head in awe. 'It's amazing,'

'I dreamt last night,' Rue said, because she hadn't told them about it yet.

'I was Bryn again. There was a woman with me. A priestess. She was singing.' Rue blinked. 'Something about owls, I think. We were on a long journey somewhere.'

Sophie perked up. 'Can you remember anything else about the song?'

Rue frowned, not looking at the rock anymore, but inside herself where the dream still echoed. 'An owl and the moon,' she said. 'The owl tried flying to the moon?' She pressed her lips together and shook her head. 'It fell down, or something, and a woman picked it up, nursed it back to health and then was an owl herself?' She shook her head again. 'I don't think I've got it right.'

'Where were you going?' Ebony asked.

Rue wrapped her arms around her middle and hugged herself, staring at the hole in the rock. 'To Wilde Grove, I think.' She shifted slightly. 'Except it wasn't Wilde Grove then, of course. I don't know what it was called, but I was travelling there to be a priestess.'

Ebony turned and looked at her, then shook her head.

'When?' she demanded. 'When was this?'

Rue shrugged. 'Dunno,' she said. 'Maybe near the beginning?'

'The beginning of the Grove?' Suze asked.

Rue nodded. Selena had thought so.

'I was wearing a stone on a string around my neck,' Rue continued. 'It had a hole through it, and it was really precious to me.' She nipped a tooth at her lip. 'To Bryn, I mean. Her mother had given it to her.'

'That's why you want to find one?' Suze asked.

Rue nodded. 'Selena says to bring things back from your dreams like this, if you can.'

'Yeah,' Ebony said. They'd been in on that lesson. On most of the lessons, actually. She wished once more that she was going to Wilde Grove with Rue. 'We'll look down on the beach. There should be some. I've heard that they're pretty easy to find on the beaches here.'

Rue nodded but she was looking at the great hole through the rock right in front of them again. 'I'm going to go through it,' she said, and let her arms drop and dangle loosely while she took a breath. 'I reckon this could count as one of Selena's liminal spaces, don't you?'

Ebony looked through the hole. 'Definitely.'

Suze and Sophie nodded in agreement.

Tipping her head to the side, Rue blew out a breath. 'We'll have to, you know, expand our senses, right?'

'Yeah. Just don't take a tumble on the other side.' Ebony stood on her tippy toes and looked. 'I don't think there's anywhere to stand on the other side. I think we can only stand inside the hole.'

'Okay,' Rue said, automatically adjusting her expectations. 'That's fine, right? It can be a window instead of a doorway.' She shrugged. 'We can just look.' A glance at Ebony. 'Want to do it together?'

A nod from Ebony and they drew breath simultaneously, used to doing this exercise now. They'd learnt it at the beginning when Selena had taught them how to make their staves, and from when she'd taken them to help the spirit pass on from Sophie's house. It was a basic skill, Selena said, although not necessarily an easy one.

Rue felt like she was drifting. As though she wasn't quite inside her head anymore, but was in all of her skin, her blood, bones, and wafting in the salty breeze just outside herself as well. She glanced at Ebony, saw her friend's glowing pale eyes, the smile on her lips, and nodded. Ebony returned the gesture, and they scrambled forward together.

The hole was big enough for them to stand beside each other, one arm around the other's waist, their other arms outstretched, fingers locked onto the rocky surface of the inner circle.

They saw the beach and the sky, and the seagulls on the other side of the hole, and Rue closed her eyes for a moment, looking inside as well, then flicking her eyes back open and seeing her hand lift a stone and she peered through it.

The stone was a reminder of a different way to see. Her mother had pressed it into her hand before saying goodbye, waving her off, standing in front of the hut Bryn had lived in her whole life, tears streaming down her face, her mouth stretched wide in a proud, radiant smile.

Ebony's arm clamped tighter around Rue's middle then

loosened as Rue came back to herself and nodded.

'I'm all right,' she said.

'What did you see?' Ebony asked, turning her head back to the view and closing her eyes, feeling the cold air against her face with a sudden surge of happiness. This was the life, she thought, feeling a tug of her own, a slight shifting sideways, and the press of a sudden impression. A face, a sprigged dress, blue steps.

The images vanished as she gasped.

'I saw Bryn,' Rue said, patting the rock that encircled them and twisting carefully around to step back down to the narrow pathway where Sophie and Suze waited. 'She was saying goodbye to her mother, and that's when her mother gave her the stone.' She landed with bent knees and reached a hand up for Ebony to steady herself with. 'It was meant to show her the...Otherworld, I guess.'

Ebony jumped down beside her. 'This is real, right?'

'You're asking that?' Rue laughed. 'You're the biggest believer in all this that I know.'

Sophie looked at Ebony, noticed her expression. 'Did you see something?'

'Just for a moment,' Ebony said. Then shook her head. 'I mean, it was real brief.'

'What was it? What did you see?'

'Just a face, for a moment, and a bit of this girl's dress.' Ebony frowned. 'And some steps.' She shook her head, then shrugged. 'Blue steps.'

'But that's awesome,' Rue said. 'Selena told us we'd start getting impressions and stuff if we kept doing the exercise.'

'Yeah.' Ebony took a breath then blew it out in a puff. 'I

12

really did see something, didn't I? Wow. That is so cool. I wonder who she was?'

'Our turn,' Suze announced and looked at Sophie. 'Ready?'

Sophie nodded back and they climbed into the hole in the rock and stood there looking down the beach, arm in arm.

'You can see for miles,' Suze said.

Sophie nodded, watching the ocean stretch out to the horizon. 'We're just kind of small, really, aren't we?'

Suze nodded. 'Yeah, but lucky too, right? We get to enjoy all this.'

Sophie closed her eyes for a moment, thinking about Rue seeing Bryn, and even Ebony catching a glimpse of something. She let herself relax in the way that Selena had taught them and felt the rock rough against the hand that gripped it, and Suze's warmth next to her on the other side. For a moment, everything swung around her – the whole world turning and everything endless. She opened her eyes and was glad to be even one small piece of it.

Rue led the way back down the rocky path and landed back on the beach with a thump of her sneakers. 'We've got to keep trying,' she said. 'Then we'll see more.'

She swivelled to look out at the sea. The tide had turned while they were climbing the cliff and now the waves were inching higher up the beach.

'I wish you were coming with us,' she said to her friends.

'Nah, it's only a few weeks,' Ebony said. 'It's okay.' She glanced at Suze and Sophie. 'We'll manage without you for a bit.'

The other two girls nodded.

'I'm going to hang out a bunch with Dandy anyway,'

Ebony said. She's agreed to teach me to read the tarot.'

Rue nodded, looked at her friends. 'Keep an eye on Clover for me too, will you? You know, go over, and play with her and stuff. That way I'll know she'll be all right.'

3

'Ambrose!' Selena shook her head. 'Teresa. You are both a blessed sight.'

'Selena,' Ambrose said. 'We have missed you terribly!'

Teresa nodded, glad to see her friend again so soon.

Selena smiled at them, alarmed at the tears that had sprung to her eyes. She wrapped Teresa in an embrace, then put a hand on Ambrose's shoulder, and drew him into a hug. 'You have been well?' she asked when she finally let him go.

'Very,' he said, his heart filled with gladness at the sight of Selena. 'And you are looking wonderful.' His eyes crinkled with his smile, and he turned to Rue standing slightly behind Selena. She gazed back at him.

'Welcome,' he said. 'I'm Ambrose. Selena and Teresa have told us all so much about you.'

'Yes,' Selena said, still smiling. 'This is Rue.'

Rue hugged Teresa, very glad to see her again, then gazed at the fair-haired man and felt her cheeks glow red.

He was very handsome. And a member of the Grove. Another bona fide member of Wilde Grove. She cleared her throat, Teresa's arm still wrapped around her.

'Hello,' she said.

Ambrose tipped his head and smiled. 'I'm very pleased to be able to meet you finally, and I know you've had such a long trip.'

'Are you taking us to Wilde Grove now?' Rue asked, her cheeks heating some more while she kicked herself mentally, glancing at Teresa, mortified. Of course, he was there to take them to the Grove. Did she think they were just going to stay at the airport for the whole month?

Teresa gave her a squeeze. 'We certainly are,' she said.

Ambrose beamed at her. 'Everyone there is waiting to see you. Do you like owls?'

Rue frowned in confusion. 'I guess so,' she said. 'Do you have owls there?'

'Clarice has,' Ambrose said. 'An owl, anyway. She's very keen to show her to you.'

Teresa laughed. 'Expect her to want to show you as soon as we arrive.'

Rue swallowed. Selena had told them about each person at the Grove. About Morghan and Grainne. And Clarice, who was ten, or almost eleven. But she'd never mentioned an owl.

'Clarice has an owl?' Selena asked as they walked out of the airport to Ambrose's car, her brows raised.

Ambrose grimaced. 'It was something that just sort of happened after you left,' he said. 'I was, well, talking to her about a man who trains raptors, and about how he had rescued an owl...and it just escalated from there.'

Selena laughed then shook her head. 'I can't wait to see everyone.'

THE DRIVE TOOK A COUPLE HOURS, RUE LISTENING WITH HALF an ear to Selena and Ambrose's conversation up front, and looking out the window as she sat beside Teresa in the back, feeling both excitement and nervousness. What would everyone be like, she wondered? Would Morghan like her? She glanced up at Ambrose's flop of fair hair, the way his shoulders and arms looked slim but strong, then looked quickly away, back out the window.

She watched the scenery go by, thinking then about Bryn, wondering at the dreams she'd had of her, wondering if Bryn had walked or lived near any of the places they were passing. It was possible, she decided, sitting a little straighter in the seat and squeezing her eyes open and shut trying to get rid of some of the gritty fatigue in them.

She was going to Wilde Grove, Rue thought. They were going there because of her. Because of her dreams.

Her dreams of Bryn.

She'd not known what to say when Selena had told her she wanted to take her to Wilde Grove – just for a visit, if Andy would let them go. Rue had been astounded, and immediately in contact with her father, begging him to let her take the trip, just for a few weeks.

He'd agreed, but only that she could go. Not Clover as well.

Then there was the fuss over passports, and the discussions about whether it would be better to wait until school was out for the year.

Rue had argued against that one with everything she had. The school year wasn't even halfway through, she'd said. That meant waiting months before they could go. Rue said it wouldn't matter to skip a couple weeks.

Tara hadn't liked it when she'd said that, Rue remembered, missing her suddenly. She'd frowned at Rue and argued strenuously that the whole trip should wait until the end of the year when Rue would have a whole six weeks off school.

But eventually, it had been decided. They'd go during the next school holidays, even though they were only two weeks long. Rue would take two weeks off school, which she'd have to catch up on when she got back.

A month, she thought now, marvelling at the stone cottages they were passing. Only a month. It wouldn't be long enough.

Although long enough for what, Rue wasn't quite sure.

She was going to the Grove because of the dreams, because of Bryn, but Selena admitted she wasn't sure what would happen when they got there.

'I only follow the thread,' she'd said. 'I don't always know where the thread leads.'

GRAINNE STEPPED OUT OF THE HOUSE AND ONTO THE driveway, her smile widening as she heard the car pull up. By the time Selena was getting out of the passenger's side, Grainne was laughing, her arms spread wide.

'Selena!' she said, wrapping her arms around her and breathing her in. 'You have been sorely missed.'

'As have you, Grainne,' Selena answered, smiling into Grainne's familiar face. 'You are looking very well, however.'

'I have been feeling very well.' Grainne turned her attention to Rue standing awkwardly beside the car. She beamed at her.

'Welcome to Wellsford,' she said, then swept a hand at the house. 'And welcome to Hawthorn House, your home away from home. We are honoured to have you here.'

Rue wondered why Grainne was welcoming them to Wellsford, rather than Wilde Grove, but she had no intention of asking the woman whose eyes were an astounding golden green in a face covered with reddish freckles. But still, she wondered, glancing at Teresa who merely smiled back at her. Wilde Grove was in Wellsford, obviously, but how did it work? Was it a place? Selena spoke of it as though it was, and Hawthorn House, where Selena had used to live as Lady of the Grove was part of it.

But Wilde Grove was more than an estate, Rue thought. Much more.

She was determined to learn how much more.

'Thank you,' she said, feeling a little as though she were dreaming. 'The house is beautiful.' Rue gazed at it, then glanced at Selena. 'This was where you used to live?'

Selena reached out and touched Rue's shoulder. 'Yes,' she said. 'Right up until I went looking for you and Clover.'

Rue gazed up at the building. 'It's so beautiful. I would never have wanted to leave.'

Selena laughed and put an arm around Rue's shoulders. 'I never thought I was going to, until I did. And look what I ended up with.'

But Rue shook her head, still gazing around, flabbergasted. 'I don't know how you could leave this behind, even so.'

'It was my path, Rue,' Selena said.

'And it brought you two together,' Grainne added, Teresa and Ambrose nodding beside her. 'That counts for a lot.'

Rue drew in a breath, closing her eyes. She could smell the woods, she thought. They smelt differently than she was used to. For a moment, images swam before her closed eyes and she tried to reach for them, but they slipped out of reach, back into the realm of dreams. Dancing, she thought. Dancing with the trees.

She shook herself slightly and smiled self-consciously. 'I just can't believe I'm here.'

'Selena tells me you've been here before, apparently,' Grainne said, watching the young woman with frank interest. She was very used to the idea of walking with past lives, and couldn't help but wonder why Rue's was pushing through so strongly to the present.

Still, that was why the girl had come here to Wilde Grove, after all. To discover the reason behind it.

Grainne knew there would be a reason. It was fascinating, she thought, how things worked, how the world was organised. This girl had been born so far away, and yet...

And yet, Grainne thought, glancing at Selena and nodding. She could well understand why Selena was bringing her back to the Grove.

Rue was from here. The Grove was her history, and perhaps – for who knew? Grainne could not always tell what would come – her future as well.

When Rue's gaze finally returned from taking in the sight of the house, Grainne stepped over and hugged Rue, then held her at arm's length and openly examined her, still smiling. 'Selena's told us so much about you,' she said. 'I'm very glad to be meeting you.'

Rue swallowed and resisted the urge to put her fingers to the spot where Grainne had touched her arm. Her legs trembled slightly. The way Grainne had looked at her...Rue closed her eyes for a moment. There'd been a lot of speculation in that look.

And yet, Rue didn't feel as though she'd been judged, like a fish on the end of someone's line, to see if she was the right sort, the correct length and weight, or if she was best thrown back. She'd felt interest in Grainne's look, interest and a wondering. Rue drew in a quiet breath and let it out slowly.

'Where's Morghan?' Selena asked.

'She's with one of her clients, unfortunately,' Grainne answered. 'She wanted to be here, and I'm sure she'll hurry back as soon as she can.'

Selena nodded. 'Yes,' she said. 'She told me she was working at the hospice now, and privately with people too, helping them pass over.'

Grainne nodded and laughed. 'She needed something to do with those prodigious gifts of hers, now that I don't require them anymore.'

Rue listened to the conversation and wondered what Grainne meant. How had she needed Morghan's ability to help people die peacefully? Rue decided there was no way she was going to ask, though. Even if she could get her tongue unstuck. Grainne made her feel tongue-tied and shy.

'Let's get you settled, shall we?' Ambrose said, a suitcase in each hand.

'For certain,' Grainne echoed. 'And Mrs Parker and I have made some refreshments for you, to help you settle in.' She looked at Selena. 'I'm glad you're staying here at Hawthorn House with us. There's plenty enough room for you, and I would feel rather odd, with you coming back but not being at the big house.' She laughed and shook her head, looked over at the others.

'Do you remember the trouble we had, getting Morghan to move in?'

Teresa smiled. 'She would still be at Blackthorn House if you hadn't taken matters into your own hands.'

Grainne looked back at Selena. 'It was hard for her, your going.'

Rue shifted on her feet. Her heart thudded in her chest at the thought of meeting Morghan. She wasn't quite sure why – after all, could Morghan Wilde be that different than Selena?

She glanced at Selena, who was saying something to Grainne, and turning to follow her and Ambrose and Teresa into the house.

Selena, when she closed her eyes and felt around for it, was motherly, safe, and so very much loved.

The love was old too, Rue thought, standing in the driveway suddenly unaware that the others had gone inside and she was still standing there.

The love was so very old. She shifted her thoughts to Morghan, and another feeling drifted towards consciousness.

It was love but coloured with something else too. Rue squeezed her eyes shut tighter and reached for it. Respect, perhaps? Awe.

She didn't know. Swimming back to the present, Rue opened her eyes with a shock, and shook her head.

Someone was watching her.

Rue blinked at the girl, who stared back at her, her eyes pale and searching, twigs in her hair.

And on her shoulder, a great owl, face round, eyes golden.

'Everyone's gone inside,' the girl said. 'What were you doing?'

Rue fumbled for words, didn't find any.

'Perhaps you were falling asleep,' Clarice said. 'Mum said you'd be tired when you got here. That you're coming from the other side of the world.'

Rue stared at her. 'Is that an owl?' she asked.

'Her name's Sigil,' Clarice said. She glanced at the house. 'She's not supposed to be allowed inside – we have an owlery for her – but sometimes I smuggle her into my room.'

Grainne reappeared at the door. 'Oh, there you are. Rue, has Clarice introduced herself?'

'She's introduced her owl,' Rue said and relaxed into a sudden grin. 'It's amazing – having your own owl.'

Clarice nodded gravely. 'Uncle Ambrose got her for me.'

'Yes,' Grainne said. 'He was very naughty, wasn't he?'

Clarice shook her head and lifted a hand to pat the bird who stood perched on her shoulder as if this were the most normal thing in the world.

'May I pat her, do you think?' Rue asked. She shook her head. 'Clover would adore this.'

'Clover's your sister, isn't she?' Clarice asked, turning

slightly so Rue could reach Sigil. 'Why didn't she come with you?'

'She's only three,' Rue said, gingerly touching the owl's feathers. They were soft, and this took Rue by surprise. The owl turned her head and looked at Rue, great round eyes blinking slowly.

'She still could have come,' Clarice insisted.

Rue was embarrassed. Her father had insisted that Clover not go too, and Selena had decided that Clover would be just fine staying home with Tara, Dandy, and Damien. And Natalie, who was at the house all the time. She'd said that maybe it was even better that way, that this trip was for Rue. They could always go again when Clover was older. Rue had flushed and not known what to say when Selena had announced her decision.

She'd felt honoured, and guilty.

'Her feathers are so soft,' she said to Clarice. 'Can she fly?'

'Of course,' Clarice said, then closed her mouth at her mother's narrow eyed look and nodded instead. 'She goes hunting in the evenings. She's supposed to be sleeping in the owlery now, but I wanted her to meet you.'

Rue smiled. 'She's wonderful,' she said. 'What's an owlery?'

Clarice brightened. 'You wanna see?' She looked at Grainne. 'Can I show her?'

'Rue would probably like to wash and have something to eat,' Grainne said.

But Rue shook her head. 'I'd love to see the owlery,' she said. 'If that's okay?'

'Oh,' Grainne laughed. 'Go on, then.'

Rue followed Clarice around the big house, bemused. Just wait, she thought, until she told Ebony and the others about the girl who looked more Fae than human, and her owl.

She shook her head. This trip was already promising to blow her mind.

4

EBONY LOOKED OVER THE SPREAD ON THE TABLE AND NODDED her head slowly. 'Yes,' she said. 'I think I'm going to have to.'

Natalie sat down and pressed the dish of roasted vegetables on Dandy. 'What are you going to have to do?'

Ebony spooned the rich, fragrant casserole onto her plate. 'I'm going to have to adopt you all,' she said, then waved her fork in Dandy's direction. 'I don't have a grandmother. I've been very deprived.' Then she narrowed her eyes at Damien, Natalie, and Tara. 'And I'm sorry to have to say this, but my uncles and aunts aren't nearly as interesting as you three.'

Clover piped up. 'Wha 'bout me, Eb'ny?'

Ebony nodded her head at Clover. 'Going to have to adopt you too.' She looked down at her plate again and sniffed. 'Seriously though. Thanks everyone, for inviting me to dinner.'

Damien laughed and made a show of checking with the others. 'I didn't invite Ebony, did you Natalie? Tara? Dandy?'

He grinned over the table at the teenager. 'You invited your-self, but that's cool – we're glad to have you.'

'The more the merrier,' Dandy said.

'It's very strange, with Selena and Rue gone,' Natalie said, then shrugged. 'I mean, I know I'm not here all the time or anything, but still.'

Tara nodded and set Clover's plate in front of her.

'This is only the second evening they've been away,' Dandy said, somewhat dryly.

'Yeah, but still,' Ebony said. She speared a potato. 'Selena has kind of a big presence. She sort of draws you to her without even trying.' She stared at the potato, pressing her lips together. 'What do you think it means, Rue having those dreams?'

'That's what they've gone back to the Grove to find out,' Dandy said.

Ebony shook her head. 'But why is she, do you reckon?' She took a bite and chewed thoughtfully. 'Why do we even forget our past lives, do you think?' she asked, then shook her head. 'I mean, think about it – wouldn't it make more sense to remember, at least a bit?'

'I 'member,' Clover announced.

Tara looked at her, wide-eyed. 'What do you remember?'

Clover gave an extravagant shrug then grinned. 'I 'member Rue,' she said.

'From another life?' Ebony asked.

Clover nodded and picked up her fork. 'She was my mama.'

There was silence for a long moment.

'Do you remember when this was?' Damien asked casually.

Clover looked at him, her blue eyes squinting as she thought. 'Don' know,' she said. 'Long time ago?' She popped some potato into her mouth.

After a beat, Ebony shook her head. 'I still think it would make more sense to remember our past lives,' she said.

'In what way?' Natalie asked. She glanced over at Damien, glad he'd invited her down to eat with them.

'Well, we might learn a bit more from history if we remembered being part of it,' Ebony said. She set her fork down. 'I mean, think about it, right? If I was a…a..' She cast around for a suitable example. 'Say I was a black slave in my last life, you can bet a big shiny pot of gold that I wouldn't be a racist arsehole in the next life, would I?' Her eyebrows rose as she speculated upon what she said. 'In fact, there would never be slavery, would there? Because we'd remember being different sorts of people, and so have more respect for them. Do you think we're even supposed to forget?'

It was Dandy who shook her head. 'Lots of children have past life memories, like Clover here, and then they fade as the kiddie grows older. I think forgetting is something that happens naturally.'

Natalie shook her head. 'I couldn't imagine remembering my past lives. What would that be like? It's hard enough just living this one. Think how many memories you'd have – I'm sure it would be intolerable.'

'But our soul remembers,' Dandy said, enjoying the conversation. She'd never felt so alive and stimulated as she had since meeting Selena and the rest of the gang.

'So it's what, being in these bodies that makes us forget?' Damien asked.

'Must be,' Ebony agreed. 'But what I want to know, is why? Is it some evolutionary thing, or is it a mistake? Like, a wrong turn or something?'

'Are you sure we've even lived past lives?' Natalie asked tentatively.

'I think so,' Ebony said emphatically. 'And I want to know what I was in my last life.'

'Why?' Tara asked. 'Why can't you concentrate on this one?'

Ebony stared at Tara's houseplants while she thought about this. 'I will be concentrating on this one,' she said at last. 'After all, this is the one I'm living, right?' She lifted her shoulders in a shrug. 'But like with Rue, sometimes the past has a meaning for right now, don't you think?'

'I agree,' Dandy said. 'For Rue, at least. But it might not be the same for the rest of us.'

Ebony shook her head. 'But Rue's not special.' She winced. 'I mean, she is, but she's no different from any of the rest of us. Not really. So, what if you learnt a heap of cool shit...' Ebony stopped talking at Dandy's look.

'Sorry,' she said. 'I meant stuff. What if you learnt a whole lot of cool and useful stuff in some of your other lives; wouldn't that be handy to have now, during this one?'

'What if you were an awful person in your last life?' Natalie asked.

'Wouldn't you kind of be an awful one in this life too, then?' Ebony said. 'I mean, unless you whaddoyoucallit? Come to your senses or something?' She sniffed. 'Realised the error of your ways, I mean.'

'I've often wondered about this,' Dandy said, looking interestedly past the food on the end of her fork, lips pursed. 'Whether we choose how we're going to be before we come back.' She frowned slightly, working out how to explain her thinking. 'As in, someone drawn to power without caring how they get it, who they hurt in the process, do they decide before they even come here, are born, that this is how they're okay being?'

'That's kind of like asking if it's a nature or nurture thing, right?' Damien said. 'Although taking it even further.'

'Except when people talk about nature versus nurture,' Dandy said, 'they're talking about genetics and what? Environment, I suppose. We're taking it further than that, with nature being...' She paused, considering. 'The essential temperament of the soul?' She shook her head. 'I have trouble believing that a whole soul could become that corrupted.'

It was Damien's turn to shake his head. 'But yeah, the values and so on could get corrupted, right? Selena says that some souls flock together between lives, their characters determining who they hang out with.'

'So,' Ebony said triumphantly. 'If that's the case, then totally yeah, that soul could decide he was going to come back and be as big a bastard as he was the last time around.' She pulled a face. 'Sorry Dandy.'

'He'd probably be looking forward to it,' Tara added.

'Well,' Natalie said into the pause that came as everyone thought about this. 'I don't need to know what my past life was like to decide what I want to be like in this one.'

'No,' Ebony agreed slowly. 'But what if we started something a long time ago, and it's our goal to continue that work?' She looked over at Dandy for confirmation. 'That's sort of what might be happening with Rue, right?' She nodded. 'And it could be the same with the rest of us. I'm just saying it would be handy to know what long game we're playing.'

Dandy put her knife down and reached over the table to touch Ebony's forearm. 'What you're really looking for is your purpose, Ebony dear,' she said.

'Aren't we all?' Damien said.

'The world flows,' Dandy said. 'Stepping into its current shows us our purpose.'

'You sound like Selena,' Natalie said with a nervous laugh. 'Why do we have to have some grand purpose, anyway?' Her shoulders tightened. 'I'm okay with having lowly little dreams.'

'Your dreams aren't lowly,' Damien said. 'And at least you have dreams. Look at me – I'm just drifting.'

Dandy shook her head. 'That's not the way it is. What it comes down to is this question: are you going to live in a way that polishes your soul, or tarnishes it?' She picked up her cutlery again.

'Life isn't a movie, you know. You don't have to have some big, overriding purpose. You just have to do everything in a way that polishes your soul and shines on those around you.'

She took a bite of Tara's marvellous casserole, raised her eyebrows at everyone at the table and nodded, smiling. 'And while you're at it, you try to remember to experience as much joy as possible.'

'OKAY,' EBONY SAID. 'I'M READY.'

Dandy laughed. 'It's getting late. Oughtn't you be heading home?'

'Damien said he'd give me a lift in an hour, and Mum doesn't mind. I already told her I wouldn't be back super early.'

Dandy nodded, smiling at Ebony's enthusiasm. She'd become quite fond of Rue's friend, and having her around made the absence of Selena and Rue just that bit easier. 'All right, a quick, introductory lesson, then.'

'Please, please, please,' Ebony said fervently and dramatically. 'Mum won't let me touch her cards. Or even look over her shoulder at them. I want to learn everything.'

'Everything?'

Ebony ticked them off on her fingers. 'Tarot – obviously. Mediumship, dowsing, psychometry. What else?' She shook her head. 'All of it. And I want to get a past life regression done.'

'A what who now?'

'A past life regression. There's someone in town who does them. He's a hypnotherapist.'

Dandy looked dubious for a moment. 'If you're getting that, then I want you to let me go with you.'

Ebony looked at Dandy, surprised. 'Sure,' she said. 'But why?'

'Going into trance makes you vulnerable, I think. Particularly if you're going that far back. And I don't know this hypnotherapist person, and you're still young. Best to have someone with you.'

Her answer made Ebony nod. 'Sounds reasonable. You've got a deal. I don't know if I'll get it done anyway. He charges like, over a hundred dollars for it.'

'That's a lot.'

'Yeah.' Ebony looked down at the deck of cards in Dandy's hands. 'So, the tarot, right?'

Dandy nodded, then laid out the first twenty-one cards in rows on the coffee table in front of them. 'These are the major arcana, okay?'

'Okay,' Ebony replied, nodding. She knew that from seeing her mother lay them out.

'And what these cards illustrate is the journey we all take from forgetfulness to remembrance.'

'Forgetfulness to remembrance?'

Dandy nodded, gazing down at her cards. They were soft and worn from years of use. 'I probably wouldn't have said it like that except for what we were talking about during dinner.'

'What would you have said before?'

Dandy wrinkled her nose, thinking. 'Well, it's several things, really. These cards describe archetypes which we must recognise and learn from if we are to gain anything resembling wisdom and self-knowledge, and they also plot the bigger cycle of life from birth to death, and also the cycles of the natural world, from spring to winter and around again.' She paused, sighed.

'They're about being human, really, especially when you add in the rest of the cards. They're about being human and reaching for more than that, too.'

'Seeking our souls,' Ebony said quietly.

Dandy looked at her. 'Yes,' she said. 'I think that's exactly it.'

'I want my own pack,' Ebony decided, looking at the cards, at the names of them, the symbols that seemed to dance around the illustrations. 'Can I get my own, do you think?'

'I think you'll need to,' Dandy answered, 'if you want to learn them properly.'

That made sense. 'I'll go down to Beacon tomorrow,' Ebony said, satisfaction welling up inside her. It was hard, not going to Wilde Grove with Rue, but this was okay. This was good, starting to learn the tarot with Dandy. And the conversation they'd had sitting around the table at dinner, that had been good too.

She'd find her own path, Ebony thought. Or keep walking it, since she'd decided even before meeting Rue and everyone that she was going to make a living doing something esoteric.

She looked up at Dandy. 'Will you come with me?' she asked. 'Help me choose?'

There were at least a dozen different decks at Beacon, the local witchy shop. She'd never be able to figure out which one would be the best one to start with.

'Sounds like a date,' Dandy said, beaming at Ebony's enthusiasm.

Ebony grinned back.

Dandy pointed a finger to the card at the beginning of the top row. 'The Fool,' she said. 'The first card, and why? Because we're all fools when we start out. We've forgotten ourselves. We don't know who we are, or where we're going. Even worse, sometimes we think we do know both things.'

Ebony frowned at the card. She didn't want to think of herself as a fool.

'But the fool is also exactly who we need to be,' Dandy said. 'With a big, open heart, and a desire to move, to find out, to face the world and learn it; the fool is setting off on an adventure.'

Ebony relaxed. She was determined that her world at least, would be an adventure.

Now she was beginning her exploration of it.

Already she couldn't wait for Rue to come back so they could compare notes.

5

Awel led Bryn into the cluster of buildings, and the trees that ringed the encampment shook their branches in a sudden wind so that the rustle of their leaves sounded like bells upon the wind.

Bryn felt a shiver inside and when she glanced up at the trees and the sky between them, it was for a moment as though she floated in the blueness on her wings, looking down.

She could see the thatches of the buildings, the paths worn between them, and clustering around her body standing there upon the ground, a group of women, the hair upon their heads shining in Bryn's vision.

'So,' Mother Wendyl said, hands on her hips, her voice satisfied. 'You are arrived safely under the Goddess's blessing.'

Bryn closed her eyes, and when she blinked them open, she was standing upon the ground, inside the circle of priestesses. She glanced at Awel, who nodded encouragement, then drew strength enough to meet the Mother Priestess's gaze.

It was forthright and frank, assessing.

Bryn bent her neck in a bow. 'Mother,' she said.

And how strange it was to greet another with this title. Would this woman be a mother to her, then? Not like the one who had birthed and suckled her, for certain.

But when Bryn lifted her head, Wendyl's face was kind, creased into lines that spoke of both love and laughter.

'You are welcome here, Bryn, daughter of Dwywai, and now daughter of the Goddess herself. Welcome to the Forest Grove, the Lady's Sanctuary.'

Bryn cleared her throat, glanced about her again, then looked back at the older priestess. 'Thank you for your welcome,' she said, trying not to stumble nervously over her words. 'I am honoured to be chosen by the Goddess to serve her here with you.'

Wendyl's face broke into a wide, cheerful smile. She nodded. 'When Awel told me you had agreed to your mother's wish for you to have a place here, I was greatly pleased.'

Bryn glanced uncertainly at Awel, who was her aunt. 'I still do not know how Awel got news of me to you,' she blurted.

Wendyl laughed again. 'That my dear, is just one of the many things you will learn here amongst us.'

The other women nodded their heads.

'That's what Awel told me,' Bryn said, and swallowed down the lump in her throat.

Wendyl gazed at the girl, then clapped her hands together. 'We are thirteen again,' she said. 'Which is a lot of introductions when you have been travelling all day.' She

37

nodded to one of her priestesses. 'Mairenn, would you show Bryn to her new quarters, please, and help her get settled.' She turned back to the newest of her charges. 'Mairenn will show you around and I will see you again when you are refreshed. Then will be soon enough to discuss the coming days.'

Bryn's mouth went dry. She knew that to become one of the priestesses here she would have to go through some sort of initiation, but Awel had been stubbornly silent upon the matter, saying only that it differed for each of them and thus she had nothing to say on the matter.

She nodded, letting her gaze rest on the blue swirls that patterned Wendyl's cheeks. Without realising, she lifted a hand to her own face, soft and unmarked.

'Yes,' Wendyl said, nodding. 'But it will be some time before you gain the markings of the Goddess upon your skin.'

Bryn dropped her hand as though scalded but Wendyl stepped closer to her and pressed a thumb to the middle of Bryn's forehead.

'You are blessed by the Lady of All, and we are in turned blessed by your presence here with us.'

Bryn's skin tingled, even after the older priestess had taken her thumb away. She resisted the urge to touch the spot on her forehead and nodded dumbly instead.

'Go with Mairenn.'

The rest of the women in the loose circle nodded, whispered greetings, reaching out softly to touch Bryn on the arm or the shoulder before turning to pad silently away, back to whatever task they'd been at when Awel and Bryn had arrived.

Awel turned and walked with Wendyl, her head bending low as she murmured to the priestess.

'Come,' Mairenn said, her voice light like birdsong. 'You'll be sharing sleeping quarters with me and two others and we've been impatient to meet you.'

Bryn fell in beside Mairenn, who didn't look to be much older than her own seventeen summers.

'How long have you been here?' she asked shyly.

Mairenn's laugh was delighted. 'Forever, so it seems, but only three turns of the Wheel.'

They arrived at one of the wooden framed houses and Mairenn swept an arm at the doorway. 'After you,' she said.

Bryn hesitated on the doorstep a moment, feeling the sudden knowledge that once she stepped into the shadows of the building, things would forever be changed.

But wasn't that a silly thought? Hadn't things changed when she had stepped foot in the small settlement, Awel's slender back in front of her?

For that matter, hadn't it begun well before that? Before even her mother had given her the holy stone to hang around her neck?

Bryn touched the stone now and knew it was true.

It had begun with the dreams of flying. And when had they been born?

When she was still little more than a babe in her mother's arms.

Bryn nodded and ducked through into the sleeping hut. For a moment, when Mairenn followed her, filling the doorway and shutting out the sunlight, Bryn was blinded, blinking in the sudden dimness.

Then Mairenn stepped past her, and Bryn could see again.

'This is where I sleep,' Mairenn said, then pointed to another pallet against the side of the room. 'And Brigit here, and next to her is Kennocha. We have made you a fresh bed.'

Bryn looked down at the bed, sheeted with clean linens and covered with furs. 'It's perfect,' she said with feeling, for she had spent the last many nights sleeping directly upon the dirt, only her long shawl to pad her rest.

'The chest at the end is for your use,' Mairenn added, sitting down upon her own bed and tucking her knees up, gazing at Bryn over the top of them. 'You did not bring much with you,' she remarked.

Bryn shook her head. 'Only what I could carry,' she said. 'Awel told me I would not need much, that everything would be provided for me here.'

'And so it is true,' Mairenn agreed, watching as Bryn unwrapped her parcel of belongings and set them into the chest. 'One of your first tasks will be to weave and sew your own dress.'

Bryn looked over at her in interest. 'Awel said I would only need to bring my shifts.' She paused, for she had not imagined that she would have to make the blue outer garment that the priestesses wore before she could put it on.

Mairenn shrugged. 'It is a holy task.' She shifted the subject, broaching what she'd been wanting to ask since first seeing Bryn.

'Can you really fly?'

Surprised, Bryn went still, linen shift in her hands. She

stared at the other girl, then licked her lips, dropping her gaze.

'Since I was a babe,' she said. 'At first I thought they were just dreams, or that everyone could.'

'But then you realised you were special.' Mairenn's eyes were round and bright against her dark skin. She had the blood of the old people in her.

Bryn looked down at her hands. Her skin was dark too, the bloodline of the old ones running through her mother's family. Those who had been last to pick up the axe that cleared the forests first for crops, then pastures.

But that had been generations ago now, and thus the need for the Lady's Sanctuary, the Forest House.

'I'm not special,' Bryn said, lifting her head to look at the other girl. 'No more than you or any of the others.'

A smile spread across Mairenn's face. 'True enough,' she said. 'We all learn the old ways here.' She paused. 'Which is your bird?'

Bryn took a breath before answering, feeling for a moment the familiar feathers under her hands. 'The sea wanderer,' she said.

Mairenn's brows rose. 'But they only come to land to breed,' she said, impressed. 'No wonder you like to fly.'

Bryn grimaced an embarrassed smile. 'What about you?' she asked.

But Mairenn laughed. 'I am a deer runner,' she said and stuck her legs out straight. 'Flight is not for me so much, but these legs, they can run.'

Bryn's shift was forgotten in her lap. 'You run with the deer? I thought none did that anymore.'

'You will learn to here,' Mairenn said, feeling flush and

generous. 'We all learn, although not all of us are fleet and can keep up.' She blinked. 'But we are all the Lady's priestesses, so of course we do this.'

Bryn was silent. All she'd ever done, really, was fly. Her heart quickened at the thought of running with the deer. 'I will really learn this?' she asked, her voice little more than a whisper.

'We all do,' Mairenn said, rising to her feet. 'Come, let me show you around.'

6

RUE SLIPPED OUT OF BED EARLY, UNABLE TO MAKE HERSELF GO
back to sleep. Her body was still on New Zealand time, and
that clock said it was definitely not an hour to be sleeping.

The house was silent in the first flush of dawn and Rue
glanced at the closed door to Selena's room before padding
down the stairs and looking out to the terrace. After a
moment's hesitation, she stepped outside.

It smelt differently here, she thought, lifting her face to
the softness of the air and breathing it in. More woody
perhaps than she was used to, particularly when it was
spring. Dunedin in the spring smelt riotously of flowers.

Here, Rue smelt trees, leaves, soil. The sky was light-
ening in the east, touching the tips of the trees, leaving the
rest in dark velvet shadows. She looked back inside the
house, listening for sounds of Selena, or anyone else,
moving around, but heard nothing behind its thick walls.

Rue snicked the door closed quietly behind her and
stepped out onto the paved terrace that ran between the two

wings of the house, taking in the big planters with their ornamental trees. She walked down the wide stone steps and looked confusedly at a narrow path that led into the darkness of the lawn. She would follow that in just a moment, she thought.

But first she turned around and looked at the house.

Hawthorn House.

Rue, the warm spring dawn pressing around her, strained her neck looking up at the house.

Yes, she decided, it was probably much the same size as their house in Dunedin. Windswitch. Selena hadn't wanted to name it after a tree, and seeing Hawthorn House, Rue felt maybe she knew why now. There was no replacing this place. She shook her head.

Hawthorn House was beautiful, and so much older than Windswitch.

How many Grove priestesses had lived here, she wondered? Selena and how many before her?

Rue lowered her head and turned to look out over the lawn, at the path that led from the terrace. She hoped no one would mind her wandering about out here while everyone slept.

She hadn't met Morghan yet. Only Grainne and Ambrose. And Teresa again, of course. The Palmers as well. Selena had been so glad to see them, and everyone else.

The lawn was damp with dew and Rue's steps pressed prints into the grass.

She followed the cobbled path that had caught her attention. It unspooled in the rising light, and she smiled in sudden delight when it ended in a perfectly round pond. Or well. Or something.

It couldn't be a well, she thought, crouching down to have a look. It was a perfect circle of water, but flush with the lawn. A well would have sides, and a lid to stop people falling in. This was surely just a shallow pond.

The rising sun touched the water and Rue rocked back on her heels, gasping as the water lit up in a sudden deep, swirling rainbow of colours.

There was something underneath the water, just a few centimetres down. Rue reached out a cautious hand, dipping her fingers in with a sharp indrawn breath at the chill.

SHE TOUCHED METAL. WROUGHT IRON, SHE THOUGHT, letting her fingers follow the ornate scrolls of the design.

It spanned, she decided, the entire breadth of the pond. Possibly, probably, to stop anyone falling in. A child, she guessed. Like Clover. After all, this wasn't a duck pond at a park, this was at a home, where a kid could go running about out of sight in the blink of an eye.

Rue straightened, her eyes fixed on the water, then blinked, frowning. Her breath harshened. She licked her lips, a sudden feeling catching hold of her, a presentiment...

There was a soft noise beside her, and Rue looked up, still caught in the feeling that had come over her as she'd stared into the water, thinking. Thinking what? About a child, that was it. A child in danger.

'What have you seen?' the figure beside her asked.

Rue stared at the woman, then shook her head. 'I need... I need to call home,' she said. 'I need to check on my sister.' She turned her head, looked distractedly at the sun. It was just coming morning here, but at home it would be late afternoon, early evening...

She climbed to her feet, put out a hand. 'I need to use the phone. Clover...' She blinked. 'Something's happened to Clover.'

Turning, Rue went to push blindly past the woman, the only thing on her mind getting to a phone, calling home. Something had happened to Clover.

'There is a phone in my study,' Morghan said, calling to her. 'I will show you.'

Rue swung around, eyes wide and wild in her face. She gaped at Morghan, trying to make sense of the woman's words, then nodded as they fell into place.

'Quickly,' she said.

Morghan nodded, glanced once more with interest at the well, then spun to retrace her steps back into the house. The girl was on her heels.

She led Rue into the room that had once been Selena's ritual room and now was a home office. Morghan picked up the phone, held it out to Rue.

'The country code is 64,' she said.

Rue snatched up the handset, dialled with a hand that was shaking, then pressed it against her ear, listening to the tone over her gasping breath, waiting for it to ring through.

She closed her eyes.

The phone was in the kitchen back at home. Rue imagined it ringing, going unanswered because something awful was happening, because there was no one there to answer it because they were all bending over Clover's limp body.

A hand touched her back, lightly, between the shoulder blades. 'Slowly. Breathe more slowly.'

Rue shuddered but did as she was told, pulling air into her lungs in slow motion.

Then there was a voice on the other end of the line.

Someone had answered!

'Hello?' Rue's voice was strangled, and she gulped at the air again. 'Tara?'

'It's Natalie. Is that you, Rue?'

Rue blinked. Why did Natalie sound so happy? She twisted around, leaned against the desk and squeezed her eyes shut.

'I thought,' she said, then tried again. 'I thought something had happened.'

'Happened?' Natalie's voice was clear. 'Nothing's happened – everything's okay here. Were you worried about something?'

Rue swallowed, her throat dry. 'Clover,' she said. 'Is Clover okay?'

Natalie's laughter made Rue feel off-balance. She'd been so sure...for a moment...that something...something had happened.

Something to do with a child running off, tumbling down. Into the well?

There was the sound of the phone being fumbled, then Clover's voice made Rue's legs collapse. She fell onto the chair beside the desk.

'Rue? That you, Rue?'

'Clover,' she gasped in relief, the phone tight in her grip. 'Clover are you all right?' Rue sucked in a breath. 'I thought...'

'Not me now, Rue,' Clover said, her voice dreamy from the other end of the telephone line. 'Not me I am now.'

Rue rubbed a trembling hand at her forehead. 'You're okay.' It was a statement this time.

'I'm good! Damien read me three stories, Rue. Three of them!'

Rue could feel her heart slowing. 'You've had your bath?'

It hadn't been Clover, then. Just some weird, what, glitch, or something?

She glanced up at the woman standing near her, seeing her properly for the first time.

'Nope. Haven't even had dinner yet, Rue. Is early still.'

Rue dropped her gaze. 'Okay. I want you to be extra careful at bath time tonight, okay?'

There was a pause before Clover answered and when she did, it was with that faraway voice again.

'Is okay, Rue,' Clover said. 'Is not me now. Is me long time ago. I fine.'

'All right,' Rue said on a sigh, some of the tightness in her chest loosening. 'I love you, Clover Bee.'

'I love you too, Rue,' Clover said. Then her voice fell to a whisper. 'Is okay, Rue. Is just your dreamin'.'

'Are you sure, Clover?'

'I sure. Now I gotta go, 'kay? Nat'lie and Damien an' me going to the shop for ice cream.'

'Ice cream?'

'Yup. To go with the puddin'.'

Rue put the phone down a minute later and shook her head, darting a look at the woman who could only be one person.

Morghan.

'Sorry,' she said, feeling gangly and awkward under Morghan's clear, interested gaze. 'I guess I got, confused, or something.' Rue cleared her throat, embarrassed. This wasn't how she had wanted to meet Morghan. Not skulking around the garden as the sun came up, and then having some weird...something.

'What did your sister say?'

Rue blinked.

'You were worried that something had happened to her. What did she say?'

'Um.' Rue drew in another shaky breath and let it out slowly. 'She said it wasn't her now.'

'Now?'

'She said it was my dreaming.'

Morghan nodded. 'I understand.'

Rue's eyes widened. 'I don't know what happened. I was just looking at the water and I got this terrible feeling.' She shook her head.

'You've been here before,' Morghan said. 'Perhaps you caught a memory of it.' She smiled slightly. 'The well can be powerful like that.'

Rue rubbed her palms against her jeans. Getting dressed, she'd looked at the dresses she'd made for the trip and then felt too self-conscious to put one on.

'But it was Clover,' she said. 'I was sure it was Clover.'

'Perhaps she has been here before too.'

Rue straightened, but her arms folded protectively over her chest. There was a lump in her throat and when she spoke, her voice was scratchy.

'Is this – has this sort of thing happened to you too?'

Morghan tipped her head to the side, thinking about it. 'Yes,' she said. 'It has. Our ancestors often include those whom we were in the past. And there is much they can

49

teach us.' Morghan paused, thinking, remembering her own history. 'And that perhaps we can teach them.'

Rue couldn't find her voice. She stared at Morghan, at the serious grey eyes and the long plait of dark hair than hung over one shoulder. Finally, she dropped her gaze.

'But something had happened – I felt it. Something had happened to Clover.' She swallowed painfully. 'Or whoever Clover was, I suppose.'

Morghan nodded, straightened. 'Come,' she said. She turned for the door and stepped out into the dimness of the house.

Rue stared after her for a moment, surprised, then followed.

They went back outside.

'I'm sorry I was wandering about,' she said.

Morghan didn't slow her pace but looked over her shoulder with a quick smile. 'I too am an early riser,' she said.

Rue hurried her steps to catch up. She cleared her throat. 'I usually get up with Selena to greet the day.' She shrugged. 'And you know, my body is still on New Zealand time. It thinks it's afternoon, I guess.'

Morghan nodded stepped into the woods that ringed the lawn like a crowd of onlookers. Rue looked around at the trees that backed gracefully away into the shadows.

'Our bush back home doesn't look like this,' she said, recognising some of the trees from her trips around and through the botanic gardens.

Morghan reached out and touched the trunk of an ash with affectionate fingers. 'They are beautiful, are they not?'

Rue nodded, eyes wide as she gazed about in the light-ening morning. 'No wonder Selena sometimes calls herself Lady of the Forest.'

Morghan glanced at Rue and felt a sudden knot in her throat. She touched her chest where her heart gave a sharp pang.

How must it be to walk as a Lady of the Forest when your woods were no longer there? She hoped, secretly and quietly, that she would never be given a task that would require her to leave her beloved home.

Rue was looking at her curiously now and Morghan let the frank gaze sweep over her. Her lips curled suddenly in a smile.

'Have we even introduced ourselves?' she asked.

'You're Morghan,' Rue said promptly, then dropped her gaze, suddenly shy. 'You can guess who I am, of course.'

'Your name is Rue,' Morghan said as they walked the path that climbed the hill slightly. 'An interesting choice of name.'

Rue lifted her shoulders in a shrug and watched her feet as she walked beside Morghan along a track that was well-worn. Morghan, she thought, must come this way all the time.

'I thought it sounded sad,' she said, and her cheeks flushed with a sudden heat. 'I went through a, you know, goth phase.' She paused for a moment before speaking again. 'And I was sad. But Selena told me that Rue is actually a strong plant with protective properties.' She blinked, her eyes stinging slightly. 'And I like that better, now.'

She lifted her chin at the same time as they broke free of the trees, and she gasped at what she saw.

'Wow.'

7

'Wow,' she said again. 'It's like that Diana Gabaldon novel, Cross Stitch.' She peeled her eyes from the stone circle and glanced at Morghan who stood beside her letting her look. 'Have you read it?'

Morghan shook her head.

'The main character, she goes to look at a stone circle and falls through one of the stones into the past.' Rue took a tentative step forward. 'I got the book out of the library a while ago.'

Rue turned and looked at Morghan. 'Can I – can I go and touch them?'

Morghan smiled at her. 'Of course you may.' She was about to say something about falling through into the past – quite the possibility, she knew, if not the same way it probably happened in the book Rue had mentioned, but then she stopped herself and watched instead. It was refreshing to see the young woman's awe as Rue stepped into the small circle and goggled at the stones.

'I suppose you've never seen standing stones before,' Morghan said.

Rue shook her head, placing her palm against the tallest stone, which was only her own height, maybe a little higher. For a moment, the stone seemed to vibrate under her hand, and she pulled away, then, more gingerly, put it back against the rough stone.

It was quiet underneath her sensitive fingers.

'We definitely don't have these at home,' she said. 'I've only ever seen pictures.'

Rue moved around the circle, touching the stones one by one. 'How old are they?' she asked.

'Around five thousand years,' Morghan answered, still content to watch Rue's wonder.

Rue shook her head, back at the first stone again. 'What were they for?'

'We no longer know,' Morghan said. 'It's been lost to the mists of time.'

Rue dropped her hands and simply stood there, staring at the stones. 'I wish we could find out,' she said in a voice that was barely more than a whisper. She glanced over at Morghan. 'Do you use this circle for anything now?'

The grass was shorter around and between the stones.

Morghan nodded. 'We hold most of our rituals out here. It feels right.'

Rue took a long, deep breath, and smiled at the stones. 'That's what they did in the book I was telling you about too. A group of women from the village came and danced at the stones.'

'They seem to like us dancing here.'

Rue laughed. 'I can kinda believe that.' She huffed out a

breath and turned towards Morghan. 'Thank you for bringing me here to see this.'

'Actually,' Morghan replied. 'I brought you here for the flowers.' She gestured over the far side of the circle, at the trees.

Rue spun about and shook her head. 'How could I have missed these?'

'You were busy with the stones,' Morghan smiled. She crossed the circle and stopped at the edge of the trees, gazing at the bluebells.

'They're so beautiful,' Rue breathed, coming to stand beside her.

'Yes,' Morghan agreed. 'They are. And we will gather a stem or two in a moment.'

Rue raised her eyebrows. What would they need some bluebells for? She didn't know why, really, but Morghan didn't strike her as the type to go in for flower arranging.

She looked back at the carpet of blue flowers. The sun was higher in the sky now and it was full dawn, the light reaching into the shadows of the old woodland to light upon the flowers, making them glow.

She could pick armfuls, she thought, and put them in every room. It wouldn't even make a dent in this great drift of flowers.

She pulled her attention back to Morghan, who had turned to a big tree that grew close to the circle, its branches reaching out over the stones.

'What are you doing?' she asked before she could stop herself.

'This is Grandmother Oak,' Morghan said. 'It would be rude to come this way and not acknowledge her.'

Rue edged around beside Morghan, who was taking something out of the small bag she wore slung around her waist and holding it pinched between her fingers.

'What's that?' she asked, all shyness forgotten in her wonder and absorption of the moment.

Morghan passed the small twist of dried herbs to Rue. 'Hold that for me.'

Rue looked down and recognised what she held. 'Teresa makes these,' she blurted. 'But bigger.'

'She does indeed,' Morghan said. 'And these are herbs from her garden.' She drew a small box from her pouch and took out a match. 'I like to make these tiny bundles to use as offerings.'

'Offerings?'

'You must have seen Selena do this,' Morghan said, lighting the match and holding the flame to the tip of the dried herbs.

Rue held the burning twist.

'Shake it now so that the flame goes out and it only smokes.'

'Selena probably does this when she's on her own,' Rue said. 'She's taught us to do other things, though.'

'I'm sure she has,' Morghan said. She let Rue hold the smouldering herb bundle and then dipped a thumb into a small bowl of water at the roots of Grandmother Oak. Straightening, she drew with her wet thumb the sign of the Wheel on the old tree's trunk.

'From sky to root,' she said. 'From age to age.'

Rue watched, swallowing, the herbs fragrant and smoking between her fingers.

Morghan took the herbs gently from her and loosened

the hawk feather from her belt. She wafted the smoke with it, up over the bark of the big old tree, then, closing her eyes, over herself.

Eyes open again, she turned with a smile to Rue, and fanned some of the smoke over her also.

'The blessing of air, earth, fire, and water over you, Grandmother,' she said, looking back to the tree and lowering her head in a small bow of acknowledgment. 'And your blessings upon us.'

She let the smoke drift for a moment longer, then pinched the fire out of the small herb bundle, holding her fingers over it until it no longer burned and was safe to replace in her small bag. She tied the feather back in place and lifted her head at last to smile upon Selena's girl.

'Now,' she said. 'Let's do what we came here for, shall we?'

Rue nodded dumbly, having no idea what they'd come here for, but willing already to go wherever Morghan wanted her to, and do whatever she wished.

She'd been so casual, Rue thought. The way she'd just done what? Blessed the tree, and themselves?

As though to do so was entirely normal.

'Are you all right?' Morghan asked her.

Rue nodded again, licked her lips. 'I just, I guess I just suddenly realised that this is where Selena comes from.' She took a breath. 'Really comes from, you know?' She thought of Windswitch, the shrine to the spirit of the house, the rocks they'd placed at the corners of the property, the offerings at the altar near the goldfish pond, all of it.

It was all wonderful. Just as wonderful as this. Rue gazed

around, seeing the bluebells and the ancient woods, the stone circle.

But this was where it had all come from.

Rue shivered a little at that thought and swallowed, her throat clicking dryly.

'Sorry,' she said. 'I'm just. I don't know. Overwhelmed to be here, I guess.'

Morghan laid a hand on her shoulder for a brief moment and smiled. 'Come, let us do this last thing, then, and you can go back to the house, get some breakfast. I'm sure Selena will be up by now.'

Rue nodded, dazed. She looked into Morghan's clear gaze. 'What are we going to do?' she croaked.

'You are going to pick a stalk of bluebells,' Morghan answered.

'Okay.' Rue turned to the flowers.

'They will be an offering,' Morghan said. 'Whisper your thanks as you take them.'

Rue glanced back at Morghan, then nodded and walked over to the flowers, crouching down and selecting one.

'May I?' she asked, her throat still dry. 'To be an offering,' she whispered, not yet knowing what the offering was for, or who it was going to be given to. 'Thank you for letting me.'

She paused for a moment, her hand on the flower stalk, as though giving it a moment to disagree, to tell her no, but there was no objection.

None that she could tell.

She snapped the stalk and rose, the vibrant blue flowers hanging for all the world like bells from the stalk.

Rue looked up and smiled at Morghan. 'I've never seen

these before,' she said. 'I feel like they'd really ring like bells if I shook them.'

Morghan laughed. 'Perhaps they would, and someone in another world would hear them.'

Rue, delighted with the notion, shook the flowers in her hand and imagined them ringing out in another world. For all she knew, they really did.

'Is that possible?' she asked. She wished that Clover was with her because Clover could probably have heard the flowers ring.

'I'm sure it is,' Morghan answered, then turned and walked back across the circle to the path on the other side.

Rue hurried to catch up with her.

'Where are we taking them?' she asked.

Morghan nodded. 'To the well.'

'The well?'

Whatever Rue had expected, it hadn't been that, and she gave an involuntary shiver at the memory of the weirdness that had happened there earlier, as the sun had been barely risen.

'Why?' she asked.

'It is a sacred well,' Morghan replied.

Rue frowned. 'What makes it sacred?'

'It rises from deep within the belly of our mother earth.' She glanced at Rue. 'And water holds memory and knows how to sing.'

Silently, Rue considered this. She felt off-kilter, as though she'd stepped truly into another world. She'd thought she was used to it, used to hearing things from another perspective, when Selena would speak, saying things just like this.

That water holds memory.

That the earth was their mother.

She shook her head slightly and looked down at the bluebells in her hand, then around at the trees between which the path wound.

'I feel like I've stepped into a dream,' she said.

Morghan, walking deliberately along the trail, drawing some of the earth's energy into her with every step, nodded.

'I felt the same way when I came here,' she said.

Rue looked at her. It was hard to imagine, she thought, Morghan not ever being here. They'd only just met, Rue knew, but Morghan seemed so much part of the woods, the stone circle, the house and well, that it was hard to picture her anywhere else.

'You're like something from another world,' she said, and her cheeks coloured as soon as the words had spilled out.

Morghan turned and looked at her, then smiled. 'I am just as you are,' she said, then looked back where they walked. 'As we all are.'

Rue heard her words and cradled them inside her mind, turning them over, puzzling at them. She looked at Morghan again and wanted to speak, ask what she'd meant, but something welled up from deep inside her and she held her tongue.

Instead, she tucked the words away to keep as a precious thing, and straightened a little. Perhaps it was an echo from her past that reached her here, under the growing light of the day, her first in Wilde Grove, but she felt that the place was suddenly familiar to her.

Familiar and much loved.

They reached the lawn and Morghan didn't hesitate, walking across it to the well.

Rue wanted to ask questions. Why was the well built like that, flush to the ground? Why, when she looked into it, did it seem to have so much colour in it, almost as though it were oil, not water?

And perhaps a hundred other questions.

But she kept her mouth closed, and the day unfolded around her, real and surreal. Familiar and unfamiliar.

'I feel like I'm walking in her footsteps,' she finally murmured.

'Your ancestor's?' Morghan stood at the rim of the well, gazing into the depths of the water.

Rue nodded, standing beside Morghan and suddenly nervous again. What had happened when she had looked into this water before?

Had she really seen something? Felt it?

Had it really been an echo of the past?

She asked Morghan this.

'I think so,' Morghan answered.

Rue nodded. 'Have you lived here before, do you think?'

Morghan glanced at the young woman, then lifted her head and looked around – at the house, at the trees, on the other side of which sat tucked the village of Wellsford.

'Yes,' she said finally. 'I believe so. Probably more than once, when I consider it.'

'Do you remember any of them?' Rue knew she should probably quit asking so many questions, so they could get on and do whatever they were here to do, but she wanted to know.

She wanted, she realised with a start, to know everything that Morghan could teach her. She wanted to soak up the other woman's knowledge like she was a sponge. Draw it into herself and carry it around.

Rue looked back at the water and wondered. Was this just her wanting this so badly? Or was it the other too, Bryn, the one who was so close and yet so far back in time?

'I do, yes,' Morghan said after a long pause.

Not caring that the knees of her jeans would grow damp, Rue sank down to the ground, kneeling at the edge of the well, staring at the water. She could see the reflection of the sky now, as though there was no division between water and sky, as though they were just parts of one thing.

For a moment, she wobbled, thought she was going to tumble down into the water, up into the sky.

Morghan crouched beside her, putting a restraining hand on Rue's shoulder. 'Stay here for now,' she said, her voice low, firm.

Swallowing, Rue turned and looked at her, blinking. 'I almost fell in,' she said, and there was a slight quaver to her voice.

Astonishingly, Morghan smiled. 'Most of us do,' she said. 'The first time we gaze into this wellspring.'

Rue rocked back and shook her head. 'Is that why there's an iron, like, safety net just under the surface?'

But Morghan shook her head. 'That is there for safety purposes, certainly. But those of us who tumble in, do so in spirit, rather than body.'

Rue stared at her, then frowned down at the water. 'I don't understand.'

Morghan was silent, giving Rue time.

'You mean, I was imagining it?' Rue asked at last.

'No.'

'I still don't understand, then.'

'You are more than your body, are you not?' Morghan said.

Rue nodded. 'Mind and body and spirit.'

'It is not only during dreams that the spirit can fly free,' Morghan said.

Rue narrowed her eyes. She was leaning slightly forward over the water again. The wellspring, as Morghan had called it, was a perfect circle, rimmed with neatly fitting stones.

'Why did you stop me, then?' she asked finally.

Morghan looked down into the water and thought about the answer to that. Why had she stopped the girl?

It was Rue who answered for her. 'Because of what I felt before, right? The feeling that something was wrong – that something had happened with Clover.' She nodded to herself. 'I might have gone back there, and I don't know if I'm ready for that.'

Morghan said nothing for a long moment, then sighed softly.

'Let us give your offering to the spirit of this spring,' she said. 'Give your thanks to her for holding the memories and the songs of the world.

Rue paused, then nodded. She laid the stalk of bluebells upon the surface of the water and drew a deep breath.

'Spirit of this holy well,' she breathed, letting her fingers dip into the water. 'My gratitude for your long memory and your songs of lifetimes.'

She closed her eyes for a moment, then got to her feet and stood beside Morghan.

8

EBONY WAS PRACTICALLY QUIVERING WITH ANTICIPATION AS she walked up the driveway to the house. She wished fiercely that Rue and Selena were still there, or even better, that she'd been able to go to Wilde Grove with them.

She reached the house and hoped she wasn't too early. But Dandy wouldn't mind. Old people didn't need so much sleep, wasn't that right? Ebony was sure that Dandy would be an early riser.

She smiled at a woman ducking out the door and hurrying away down the drive, her head bent, arms wrapped tightly around herself as though something inside her was hurting. Ebony glanced back at her and shook her head. The woman had completely ignored her.

Shrugging, Ebony pushed the door open and stepped inside, taking deep, appreciative breaths. Selena's house always smelt so good.

Herbs and baking. Ebony's stomach rumbled and she envied the kids Tara looked after. They were going to have something extra good for morning tea, if the warm, fragrant scent from the kitchen was anything to go by.

There wasn't anyone in the kitchen, however, so Ebony stepped out into the big hallway, nodded at the statue of the house spirit, and followed the sound of voices into the second living room that was now a full on playroom.

'Eb'ny!' Clover came barrelling across the room and flung herself at her sister's best friend.

'Heya, Clover Bee,' Ebony said, grinning down at her and tickling her for good measure. 'You going to make a ruckus with your friends?'

Tara, holding a young lad in her arms, rolled her eyes, then grinned. 'We're going to make things with Play-Doh today, aren't we? And do some puzzles and build a giant tower with blocks.'

'An' draw some pictures,' Clover added. She hadn't lost any of her enthusiasm for drawing. 'Josh is sad today.' She grinned up at Ebony. 'I goin' to draw him a picture to cheer him up!'

Ebony nodded at her. 'That sounds like a great idea,' she said, then looked over at Tara, her brows lifted in a question.

Tara grimaced and patted the boy on his back. 'This is Josh, and he is a bit sad today, isn't he?'

'Was that his mum who I saw just leaving?' Ebony asked.

Tara nodded and sat down on the couch with Josh still in her arms. Since she'd plucked him out of his pushchair, he'd been clinging to her like a little barnacle.

'Because she didn't look very happy either.' Ebony walked with Clover over to the kiddie-sized table laid out with paper and crayons. Another little girl about Clover's age was already sitting there, tongue poking out in concentration as she drew something that might have been a dog.

Or a dragon.

'They not happy,' Clover said, sitting down and looking for the yellow crayon. 'Josh's daddy has a loud voice.'

Ebony turned and stared wide-eyed at Tara again. Then looked at Clover. 'Just a loud voice?' she asked. 'Not big fists as well?'

'Ebony!' Tara was shocked.

But Ebony shook her head. 'It's gotta be asked, though, doesn't it? And we have our own little seer here, so we can.'

'We can what?' Dandy asked, coming into the room and smiling at the sight of the children.

'Ask Clover if that kid's dad is being violent,' Ebony said, pointing with her chin at the boy in Tara's lap. 'Has he gone to sleep?'

Tara looked down at Josh, who was only eighteen months old and a small, delicate child. 'Yes,' she said.

'Odd time for a nap, isn't it?' Ebony asked.

'Depends entirely on what time he got up this morning,' Dandy said wryly, speaking from experience.

Clover had found the yellow crayon and was drawing a big sun in the corner of her paper. 'Josh's dad don't hit him,' she said. 'Nores him.'

'Nores him?' Tara asked.

'Yup.' Clover finished the sun, then looked over at her friend Danielle's picture. 'I like your cat,' she said.

'Wait,' Ebony said. 'What does 'nores' mean?'

But Clover just shrugged and sorted through the crayons.

Ebony looked at Tara. 'Well, noring him is probably better than hitting him, right?'

Tara nodded, still frowning, but then her face brightened momentarily. 'Ignores him. That's what she's saying.' She looked down at the sweet boy in her lap and hugged him. 'Poor wee thing.'

'His mum looked a bit ragged,' Ebony said, speaking more softly, now that she knew that the kid wasn't going to be sporting bruises under his natty little shirt and trousers.

Tara nodded. 'She's a really lovely person, but I get the feeling she's a bit overwhelmed. She brings Josh here and always looks like she'd rather stay here with him.' Tara smiled sadly at the image of Josh's mother Rachel looking around in wonder at the house and the freshly baked bread.

And the atmosphere in the place probably had something to do with it too, Tara thought. Windswitch House had a particular feel to it – everyone who came inside commented on it, how it made them feel calm and happy.

'Maybe that's because her husband has a big voice.'

Dandy nodded, looked at Tara. 'Perhaps we should try talking to her later. Let her know she's not alone. She's awfully young, isn't she?'

Tara sighed, pressed a kiss to Josh's soft hair. 'I don't know exactly, but nineteen or twenty, I think.'

Ebony shuddered. Considering Josh's age, that was far too close to her own for comfort. She turned to Dandy, hopping her mind back to the main item on her agenda. 'You set to go to Beacon?'

Dandy laughed, then shook her head. 'Oh, all right then. I wondered why you were here so bright and early.'

'Gotta get the worms, Dandy,' Ebony said solemnly. 'Early birds get the worms, it's a well-established fact.'

Danielle looked up from her picture. 'Worms are yuck,' she said. 'Blech.' She pulled a face as though she knew for a fact how they tasted. For all Ebony knew, looking down at her, the kid did. She was pretty sure she herself had eaten at least one or two worms when she'd been just a little guy.

'WHAT'S IT LIKE?' EBONY ASKED AS SHE AND DANDY GOT OFF the bus and walked to Beacon.

'What's what like?' Dandy asked absently. She was thinking of young Josh, who had still been sound asleep in the cot when they'd left. She should have taken a closer look at the lad. And she'd tell Tara from now on, she decided, that she oughtn't accept the kids in the morning without them being awake – even if it meant being woken up for the hand-over.

There were just too many things that could go wrong, and too many less than stellar reasons for a kiddie to be so sleepy.

'What's it like giving a reading for someone?' Ebony asked, looking around at the street that was already busy in the autumn sunshine. It was good not to have to be in school, she thought, stretching and grinning.

Dandy shook herself out of her thoughts at the question and wrinkled her nose. She liked Ebony; the girl's vim and vigour amused her, and underneath all that excess of enthusiasm, she was a smart and thoughtful girl.

But goodness, Ebony was nothing but question after question.

'It's usually less interesting than you think it will be, and often sadder.'

Ebony turned wide eyes towards her. 'What? Why's that?'

Dandy tipped her face slightly to the morning sun, letting it warm her old skin and sink down inside to her bones.

'People don't usually come to get their cards read unless there's something already on their mind.'

'Ah,' Ebony said, thinking she'd caught on already. 'And usually that's what – problems with money or love, I bet.'

'Hmm.'

'That doesn't sound very interesting at all,' Ebony decided, disappointed.

'It would be better if you didn't see the same problems over and over.' Dandy led them around the corner and into the dimness of the small, almost hidden mall. Beacon was at the back, next to the tattoo shop on one side, and a second-hand bookshop on the other. 'Broken hearts and lost jobs.'

Well, Ebony thought, wrinkling her nose over this news, maybe she wouldn't aspire to giving readings for others, then.

But she had to do something else, she reckoned. Dealing with haunted houses and helping spirits pass over didn't strike her as likely to be a full-time job, or even something that would financially support her part-time.

Unless she lived in, like the UK or somewhere where there were haunted castles left, right, and centre. She wrinkled her nose again. Those places probably wanted to keep their ghosts. As tourist attractions and the like.

Dandy pushed open the door to Beacon and Ebony followed her through, right on her heels.

'Hi Meg,' Dandy called to the woman standing, and looking rather dismayed, in front of the shelves of crystals, a duster in her hand.

Meg turned and her face lit up before frowning. 'Dandy,' she said. 'It's not your day to read, is it?'

Dandy shook her head and gestured to Ebony. 'Bringing this one to choose her first deck.' She looked at the girl at her side. 'Ebony, this is Meg, the owner of Beacon.'

'Hello,' Ebony said and shook her head. 'Amazing shop, it must be a blast to own it.'

But Meg rolled her eyes and held up the duster. 'Not when you're the one who has to dust all these things and your allergies are trying to kill you.'

'What happened to Alyssa?' Dandy asked, peering around the shop as though the girl in question was hiding behind the essential oils.

Meg shook her head. 'She had to go back home for a while; her father's sick.'

'Oh, I am sorry to hear that,' Dandy said, and she was. She liked Alyssa, and health was such an important thing. She blessed every day she still woke up with nothing more than a few aches and pains.

'I'll do the dusting for you,' Ebony blurted. Then didn't bother looking abashed. 'I can help out until you find someone else – or just help out altogether.'

Meg stared at Dandy's young friend, then narrowed her eyes. 'Aren't you a school kid?'

Ebony shook her head. 'Not actually.' She ignored the surprised look Dandy was giving her and ploughed on. 'I mean, I have been at school, of course, but it's the holidays now, and I'm looking for a job. I may not even go back to school. You know, after the holidays.'

'What are you talking about?' Dandy asked. 'This is the first you've said about anything like this.'

Ebony shifted on her feet. 'I want to start working.'

'Hmm.' Dandy shook her head slightly. Ebony had that stubborn edge to her voice that warned that this conversation would best be dropped now and picked up again later.

But Meg looked musingly at the teenager. 'School holidays,' she said. 'They've just started, right?'

Ebony nodded. 'Today's the first day of them. Two weeks.' She nodded at the duster. 'I really can help you,' she said. 'I can start right now, even.'

Meg's heart lifted at the thought. She turned to Dandy. 'Someone you can vouch for?'

Dandy looked at Ebony and shook her head, but she was grinning. 'Enthusiastic, determined, and underneath the exuberance, quite sensible.'

Ebony's smile was wide. 'That's me,' she said. 'Add to that, super keen to learn everything about everything you sell in here, plus really good at talking to people.'

Meg nodded, and she passed the duster to Ebony. 'Start now?'

'This very minute,' Ebony said seriously, taking the duster as though she'd just been given the keys to the kingdom. 'Really?'

'Sure,' Meg said. 'Why not? I need someone, and if Dandy gives you her blessing, who am I to argue?' She nodded. 'It will give me some breathing space to find someone to replace Alyssa.'

Ebony opened her mouth to say she could do that – be the permanent replacement – but a glance at Dandy made her close her mouth and shrug.

There'd be time to convince Meg to take her on full time.

The shop bell tinkled behind them and the three of them swivelled around without thinking to look at who had stepped into the shop.

Rachel froze, eyes wide like a rabbit in headlights, then shuffled backwards. She swallowed, blew out a harsh breath of air. 'Sorry,' she said and was about to turn and reach blindly for the door handle, asking herself what on God's green earth she thought she was doing. But she stopped herself, stayed put. She wanted this, she reminded herself.

It was time to make changes.

Be more like Tara. That was what she wanted.

'Is the shop open?' she asked.

Dandy smiled at her. 'Rachel? Goodness yes, come on in.'

Ebony nudged Dandy. 'Is that Josh's mum?' she asked in a low whisper. 'I saw her leaving the house this morning.'

Dandy nodded, patted Ebony's arm, and strolled over to where Rachel stood, a little pale under the bright lights, as though she'd steeled herself to come into the shop. Dandy smiled more widely at her. She might have had to talk herself into opening the door to Beacon and coming in, Dandy thought, but the girl was doing well, looking defiantly about herself.

'Rachel,' she said, 'how lovely to see you here.'

Rachel tried to smile at Dandy, but it came out more like a grimace. She could tell by the way it felt on her face.

'Hello Dandy,' she said shyly. 'Tara said you worked here.'

Dandy nodded. 'It's Meg's shop,' she said, gesturing to Meg, who had come to greet the new customer. 'I just do readings here.'

'Is there something particular you came in for?' Meg asked. 'I'd love to be able to help you.'

Rachel nodded, tried to speak, winced.

'It's all right,' Meg said. They occasionally got nervous ones in the shop. Those who had been brought up to see a place like Beacon as the devil's work, or who had had something terrible happen and needed some reassurance.

'Are you interested in the crystals, perhaps?' she asked. 'We've a lovely selection. Perhaps one on a chain, so you can wear it around your neck? A carnelian – they're wonderful for courage and confidence, and so pretty as well.'

Further back in the shop, Ebony lifted up the duster and began swiping it at the crystal balls arranged in order of size and colour on the shelf. She kept her head slightly turned so she could listen to Meg and Dandy talking to the woman. Why was Josh's mother so jumpy?

Rachel managed a smile for Meg, took heart at being able to do that, and looked at Dandy.

'That's what I came here for,' she said. 'A reading. With the tarot cards.' She swallowed and almost groaned in frustration. She was there, she wanted what she'd come in for, why then did part of her insist on wanting to turn tail and flee? A reading wasn't going to bring the devil to chase her down.

Although she could imagine what Mike would say about it. He'd look at her like she'd grown a second head, and tell her, ever so gently, that he was worried about her mental health.

'Oh,' Meg said, her face falling. 'Dandy's just visiting this morning. Our readers aren't here at this time of the day. You'll have to come back in the afternoon.'

But Dandy put a hand on Meg's arm and smiled widely at Rachel. 'You're in luck,' she said. 'I'll be happy to do a reading.' She shrugged lightly. 'I usually do my readings here on Thursdays, but we can bend the rules a bit, can't we, Meg?'

Meg looked at Dandy in surprise, saw she was serious, then turned to the young customer. 'Well,' she said. 'There we go – Dandy is our most experienced reader; you'll be in wonderful hands.'

Rachel took a breath, let it out.

'Good,' she said. 'Thank you so much.'

9

Dandy smiled and glanced at Meg. 'I didn't bring my cards.'

'That's no problem,' Meg said. 'Take what you need from the shelves.' The decks were expensive, and she might live to regret this, she thought, but on the other hand, Dandy wouldn't have offered the reading without a good reason. And this woman had such a look of both terror and determination that Meg was almost ready to take her into the reading room and lay the cards out herself.

'Come this way,' Dandy said, and held out a hand to usher Rachel to the small room at the back of the shop where the readings were done. 'I saw Josh this morning,' she said. 'Poor wee thing looked as if he'd had a wakeful night.'

Rachel fell on the familiar topic with relief. 'He's teething,' she said. 'I think we were up half the night.'

'Oh, I remember my boy's teething, all right,' Dandy said, shaking her head. 'He was a real misery-guts with it. No wonder Josh was tired this morning.'

Rachel nodded, but her nerves had started up a wild fluttering, and she couldn't answer.

'Rachel's a lovely name, by the way,' Dandy told her, giving Ebony a small nod as they walked past. 'I had an aunt named Rachel, wonderfully eccentric and romantic woman, she was.'

Rachel winced. 'I'm not eccentric,' she said. 'I wish I was though,' she said somewhat wistfully. 'It sounds brave.'

'I like to think we all have a little of the eccentric in us,' Dandy said, and opened the door to the reading room. 'If you'd like to make yourself comfy for a moment, I'll just get what I need.' She pursed her lips. 'Can I make you a cup of tea?'

Normally, she didn't offer refreshments, but Rachel looked as though she needed a bit of something. The girl's lips were white from pressing together. Perhaps a cup of tea would put her more at ease. The chamomile would be a good choice.

Rachel squeezed her eyes shut trying to find her resolve again. She twisted the handles of her handbag in her hands and that helped. The handbag had been Susan's, of course. Everything she owned had been Susan's first.

There, she thought, there was the small spark of anger, of rebellion. She needed that.

Nodding, she sat down at the table. 'A cup of coffee would be good, if you have it,' she said. 'Thank you.'

Dandy smiled at her. 'Only tea, I'm afraid. Wait here, I'll only be a minute.'

She withdrew and closed the door gently, then made a beeline for the case of tarot cards.

'I can't believe you're going to find out what the deal is,'

Ebony hissed in barely concealed delight, sidling up to her. 'It's her husband, I bet it is.' She shook her head as though she knew. 'It's always the husband.'

'Perhaps,' Dandy said. 'But it's not good to make assumptions, and she's a person who needs help, so maybe tone down the glee a little.'

Abashed, Ebony grimaced. 'You're right. Sorry. I hope we can help her.'

'We?' Dandy's brow rose as she scanned the selection of decks. She didn't know most of them, and wished she'd had the foresight to bring her own. Maybe she should ask Meg if there was just a plain pack of playing cards available.

But Rachel, she thought, looked like she needed something a little more in-depth than the playing cards could give.

'I'll go make her a cup of tea,' Ebony said. 'Do you think Meg has chamomile?'

Dandy couldn't help her smile. 'I know she has. And that would be lovely.'

'What deck are you going to use?' Ebony asked before moving off.

'This one.' Dandy said, pulling down the Waite deck. 'Stick to the tried and tested, I think.' She pointed toward the door with her chin. 'You get that tea.'

Ebony was torn between getting the tea and tagging along with Dandy who was moving off now to the bowls of polished stones.

'Where's the tea making stuff?' she asked when she found Meg, having decided finally that she'd be best doing what she'd offered to.

Meg passed her a pretty cup and saucer, scented tea

steaming. 'Here,' she said. 'She looked like she could do with it.'

Ebony agreed and took the tea, knocking lightly on the door before letting herself in and looking around in interest before popping the hot tea down on the table in front of Rachel.

'There you go,' she said, and was about to add that she had seen her that morning, dropping Josh off, when she thought better of it, and simply backed out of the room instead. Dandy would be proud of her, she thought.

Dandy, at the door, was proud of her. She thought she had a very good idea of how much Ebony was itching to say something.

'Thank you, Ebony,' she said and closed the door firmly behind herself.

'This is a pretty room,' Rachel said. 'It reminds me of your house. You all live there together, don't you? Tara said so.'

'It is a pretty room, isn't it?' Dandy replied, looking briefly around. It was small, and the narrow window looked out into an alley, but Meg had covered it with a cheerful piece of lace, and there were silk flowers in a vase and ivy – also fake but still attractive – climbing up the wall to drape over the top of the window. It was a very sweet little space.

'And yes,' she added. 'We do share the house, and a very pleasant arrangement it is, too.'

Rachel nodded, gnawing on her bottom lip. 'Is it like, a boarding house? I mean, do you rent rooms?'

She wondered if there might be a room available.

Dandy shook her head, peeling the cellophane from the

tarot deck and after a moment, tucking the rubbish in her pocket.

'No,' she said. 'It's a private house.' Dandy looked over at Rachel and thought she caught the disappointment on her face. 'Are you looking for somewhere to live?' she asked.

Rachel looked down at her hands, at her fingernails, short, nicely trimmed. Mike did her nails for her. At first, she'd thought that was sweet, loving, but now she wasn't sure.

And it was Susan's nail polish too, of course.

'Um,' she said.

Dandy slid the cards from the box. They were slippery, smelling of ink.

'You don't have to answer that, of course,' she said. 'I shouldn't have asked.' She shuffled the cards.

Rachel watched as the cards flew in Dandy's hands. She shook her head slightly. 'You're very good at that.'

Dandy raised her eyebrows. 'At shuffling?' She laughed. 'I've been doing it for sixty years now, would you believe?' She paused a moment. It was always enjoyable handling a new deck. 'Have you had your cards read before, Rachel?' she asked.

Rachel lifted her cup and sipped at the fragrant tea, then put it down again. It was chamomile, and she really didn't like chamomile tea. It was what Susan had drunk all day long.

'No,' she said, answering Dandy's question. 'I grew up in the Peebs.'

'The Peebs?'

Rachel hunched over a little. 'People of the Exclusive Brethren.'

'Oh,' Dandy said, understanding dawning. 'When did you leave?'

'Almost three years ago,' Rachel said, and it felt good to tell this woman this tiny bit of her story. For a moment, everything seemed unreal, and she wondered again what she was doing here in this back room of a shop like this.

But Tara said that Dandy gave wonderful readings. Really helpful.

Goodness knows, she thought, she needed help.

'That must have been difficult. You would have been so young,' Dandy said, holding the cards in hands that had stilled now. 'Don't they ban you from contact with your family when you leave?'

Rachel blinked, nodded. 'Everyone disowned me.' She tried a laugh. 'My parents have never met Josh. If they saw me on the street, they'd cross the road and pretend they didn't know me.'

Dandy reached over and took Rachel's hand for a moment, held it. She wanted to ask why Rachel had left, been removed from her family, but decided against asking. It would be taken for what it was – prying.

'Did you know anyone on the outside?' she asked instead. 'When you left?'

Rachel looked down and didn't answer for a moment. 'I had an older cousin,' she said at last. 'She and her husband took me in.' Rachel shifted in her seat. She had to will herself not to bolt from the room. 'Look,' she said, her voice wire tight. 'Maybe this was a bad idea.'

'No,' Dandy said. 'I'm sorry. I was being nosy.' She smiled and nodded. 'Let's get some of these cards on the table for you, shall we?'

Rachel hesitated, hands going to grip the bag that sat in her lap, the bag she still thought of as her cousin's. Then she thought of the three twenty-dollar notes carefully folded and hidden in the zippered compartment where she kept her spare tampons and where she knew Mike would never look.

She straightened and nodded. It had taken her a month to put aside that amount of money, and this was what it was for.

Perhaps she'd get the answers she needed.

Watching her, Dandy nodded. 'All right then,' she said. 'Now, I know this might seem a little strange, but this is just the way I do things, okay? I get better cards if we do this little exercise first.'

Rachel's eyes were round and slightly damp. But she nodded.

Dandy smiled reassuringly and passed Rachel the small, smooth carnelian she had picked out. If anyone needed a dose of courage, it was Rachel, she'd decided. She'd only met Rachel in passing a few times, and never really had a conversation with her, but Tara, she knew, was increasingly fond of Josh's mother.

For a moment, Dandy was reminded of Natalie, back when she and Selena had first met her, and that made her smile wider.

Natalie was a bright light wherever she went now, full of dreams and plans for her own cake making business. Just as she ought to be.

'I want you to sit with your feet flat on the floor for a minute, Rachel,' Dandy said.

Rachel nodded, risked a breath, and looked across the

table. The stone Dandy had given her was warming in her palm and it was so pretty. She wondered if she would be allowed to keep it.

'It's Rae,' she said, tightening her fingers around the stone. 'I think I want to be called Rae. I like it.' She blinked, hunched tighter for a moment. 'It feels like the name of someone who enjoys life, and less like the name of a sucker.'

Dandy's eyes widened in surprise. 'Is that how you feel?' she asked. 'Like a sucker.'

'Oh, it's not just how I feel,' Rachel said. 'It's what I am.'

Dandy nodded. 'And who has sucked you in?'

Rachel snorted, a bitter and pained sound. 'Who hasn't?'

'Your husband?'

Rachel took a breath, looked defiantly at Dandy. 'Especially him.' She dropped her gaze to the polished stone again, then held it up. 'I like this,' she said. 'What is it?'

'It's called carnelian,' Dandy told her. 'One of the first stones to be used in Egypt, that we can tell. It's known these days for being a stone that helps you build your self-esteem, especially if you've suffered some sort of setback, which, of course, most of us do at some stage.'

Rachel made that strangled, snorting sound again. 'You could say I've had a setback,' she said. Then sighed.

On impulse, Dandy reached over the table and held Rachel's hand. She kept Rachel's fingers in hers for a good long moment, just holding them silently.

'Let's do the exercise, then take a look at your cards and decide what you want to do,' Dandy said finally, withdrawing her hand after a last squeeze.

Rachel closed her eyes for a moment. 'What makes you think I need to decide what I want to do?'

Dandy looked at her. 'Don't you?'

Rachel sighed, delved into a pocket for a tissue. She wiped her eyes, then blew her nose and nodded apologetically.

'You must think I'm an idiot,' she said.

'I don't think anything of the sort.'

Something in Dandy's voice made Rachel tuck the tissue away and sit straighter. She nodded.

'I'm ready.'

Dandy smiled.

'Right,' she said. 'Push your chair out from the table a little and sit with your feet flat on the floor, hands loosely on your lap.'

Rachel arranged herself, letting herself do as she was told.

'Now, if you can,' Dandy continued, 'close your eyes – you can open them at any time if you get uncomfortable – and listen to your breathing for a moment. Slow it down until you are breathing deeply and slowly.'

Rachel closed her eyes and took an obedient breath, but it was more like a sigh. She peeped at Dandy, but the older woman was sitting serenely, her eyes closed.

Rachel shut her own eyes again and found her breath, sucking in a deep lungful of air and letting it out in a big sigh again. She swallowed.

'It's all right,' Dandy said. 'Let the sighs out.'

'I don't know why I'm sighing,' Rachel whispered. She screwed her eyes shut tighter and tried again.

'It's because your body is tight and tense,' Dandy told her. 'You're very stressed.'

Rachel pressed her lips together. She was stressed. She could feel it in her body, in her muscles, which seemed to be quivering even though she wasn't doing anything, and even in her skin, which seemed stretched tight and terribly sensitive. She took a deep breath, tried to let it out slowly.

'That's the way,' Dandy said, sitting quietly in her own chair. 'That's really good.'

Rachel's eyes filled again, and she squeezed the tears away. Really, she thought, she should know better than to be taken in by someone being kind and understanding.

But Dandy wasn't Mike.

They weren't the same at all.

She tried another breath, let it out with only a small hitch of the chest.

Dandy waited for Rachel's breathing to even out then nodded. 'Now, we're going to use our imaginations,' she said.

Rachel felt herself tense up again. Her imagination was what had gotten her into all this mess in the first place.

But this was different, she reminded herself. She wasn't seventeen anymore, wasn't excruciatingly naive, a dreamer. She was grown up now. A mother. She thought of Josh, breathed again, tried to relax.

If she couldn't do it, she'd just pretend.

'Imagine now,' Dandy said, 'that you are holding a ball of shining silver light. Cup your hands and hold this ball of light on your lap. It's so bright that you can see it even with your eyes closed, but it isn't hot; it doesn't burn.'

She paused a moment to give Rachel time to imagine.

'The light from this shining ball goes right through your skin,' she said.

'It shines right through your skin and fills your chest. It shines down through your lap and your legs. It shines up through your head until your head is filled with it. It shines all around you and through you and you are holding it, just gently holding this shining ball in your lap. It feels good, holding this shining, silvery ball, as though you are holding a star, right there in your lap.'

She was quiet for a minute, opening her own eyes to watch the young woman opposite, noticing the tension lines around Rachel's eyes smoothing out, the furrowed brow relax.

'That's good,' she said. 'Now let the ball become entirely light and press it through your skin into your body under your ribs where it can stay, soft and gentle now, where you can still turn your attention to it whenever you want to, and feel its silvery light grow and flow through you.'

She paused again, and Rachel's hands turned and flattened against her ribcage under her breasts as though she really were pressing the ball of light inside her.

'That's perfect,' Dandy said. 'Take another breath now, and you can open your eyes again, come back to this room and this table.'

Rachel sighed again, softly this time, and opened her eyes. 'I didn't do it right,' she said.

'You didn't?'

Rachel shook her head. Picked up the carnelian stone and held it up for Dandy to see. 'The light was this colour. Do you think that matters?'

Dandy smiled, shook her head. 'I don't think that

matters at all.' She reached across the table on impulse and closed Rachel's fingers around the stone. 'I think that's even better,' she said. 'You imagined the light the colour you needed, the one that would bring you strength and confidence.'

She nodded at Rachel. 'I love that you let it be the colour that came naturally.'

10

'COME,' MORGHAN SAID. 'LET'S GO AND SEE IF SELENA IS UP.'

Rue looked up at the brightening sky and nodded. 'She's usually up with the dawn.'

They walked across the lawn and toward the house without speaking. Rue sneaked some surreptitious glances at Morghan, taking in her profile, the thick braid of hair, the long dress that buttoned down the bodice, then had an open skirt that showed Morghan was wearing trousers under it.

Rue frowned, finally. 'Do you think we've met?' she asked. 'In some other lifetime, I mean?'

Morghan looked at her. She knew that the girl had been glancing at her, examining her.

'It's very possible,' she said. 'Perhaps even likely.'

Rue nodded. 'Do you think we might remember?'

'We might,' Morghan agreed. 'If it is useful and timely.'

'Is that how it works, then?' Rue puzzled on it. 'So, I'm

remembering my past self – Bryn, who lived here – why, do you think?'

'I don't know,' Morghan answered, and she smiled at Rue. 'That's what you're here to find out.'

They stepped up onto the terrace to find Selena there, watching them, a smile blooming on her face.

'Morghan,' she said.

'Selena!' Morghan hurried the last few steps to embrace Selena. 'I'm so sorry I wasn't there yesterday to meet you. I didn't get in until so late.'

Selena was holding Morghan by the shoulders now, looking her over, face glowing with pleasure. 'Grainne and Ambrose told me all about this wonderful new work you are doing,' she said.

Morghan leaned forward and kissed her on each cheek then looked over at Rue. 'And I have met the work you have been doing.'

Selena laughed, drawing Rue into their small circle with a tug of her hand. 'This is not work but pleasure,' she said.

Rue flushed with the complement and leaned in slightly towards Selena. Something welled up inside her, filling her chest. It was gratitude, she realised.

'Thank you so much for bringing me here, Selena,' she said in a voice barely above a whisper. 'It's a magical place.' She straightened, her eyes widening. 'I saw the stone circle,' she said. 'Morghan took me to it this morning.'

'Ah,' Selena nodded and squeezed Morghan's hand. They stood, the three of them, in a circle, hands in each other's. 'And what did you do there?'

Rue's face clouded. 'I picked some bluebells to give as an offering at the well.' Her throat worked as she swallowed.

'Something happened this morning, Selena – when I looked in the well.' Her frown deepened. 'I thought...I felt like something had happened to Clover.'

Selena stiffened, glanced at Morghan, whose face was clear, relaxed as she listened. Obviously, it hadn't been anything too bad that had happened.

Rue was shaking her head. 'Morghan let me use the phone to call home, but Clover was just fine. She told me that it wasn't her now.'

'Not her now?' Selena repeated. 'What does that mean?'

It was Morghan who answered. 'We think she meant that it was a past life memory that caught Rue's attention.'

Selena was silent for a moment, then nodded thought- fully. 'That makes sense, that Clover was here also. I hope we made the right decision not to fight to bring her.' She shook her head and spoke again before Rue or Morghan could react. 'We did. Clover is too young, and bringing her here – who knows what might happen?' She laughed suddenly. 'I'm already chasing that child all over the Wildwood.'

She looked at Rue. 'This is your time here, to explore your history and see what message it has for you.' Selena tightened her grip on Rue's hand for a moment. 'You must not be afraid of what you see and remember. Clover is at home, with those we love taking good care of her.'

Rue nodded. 'I know,' she said. 'Tara and Dandy and Damien would never let anything happen to her. She's probably not even missing me. She didn't sound like she was, when I spoke to her.' Rue smiled. 'They were on their way out to get ice cream.'

'Shall we go inside for some tea?' Morghan asked.

'That sounds a lovely idea,' Selena said. 'You two have already been wandering the paths.' She paused, smiled. 'I shall be with you shortly, I think. I'd like to greet the day.'

'Shall I come with you, Selena?' Rue asked.

Selena patted her hand. 'No, sweetheart. I think I'd like a minute on my own to say hello to my old home.'

Rue nodded. 'Of course,' she said, then looked down from the terrace to the garden and beyond that, the woods so different to the bush back at home. 'I don't know how you left this place, Selena,' she said impulsively. 'I've only been here a little while and I love it so much already.'

'Oh Rue,' Selena said, smiling broadly. 'I needed to meet you and Clover. I have no regrets about leaving.'

Rue's cheeks coloured. Selena had said that as though meeting her and her sister had been important for her as well as them. She ducked her head, throat suddenly thick with emotion.

'Come on,' Morghan said, drawing Rue to the door. 'Let's go and put the kettle on, shall we?'

SELENA WATCHED RUE AND MORGHAN ENTER THE HOUSE, their dark heads close together although Morghan's was now the darker since Rue had stopped colouring her own. She hoped Rue would feel comfortable enough in the next few days to wear the dresses she'd been so excited to make for the trip.

Then, she put her thoughts of the others away and turned back to look out over the property that had used to be her home. It felt strange now to think of it like that, she realised. She'd been away how long?

KATHERINE GENET

Not quite six months, but already it felt like a dream to be back here. Selena stepped down onto the lawn and followed the stone channel down to the well. She bent down to dip her fingers in the water and touched them to her forehead.

'Bless me, water of the sacred spring. I have been away and now am returned.'

Not for long though, she reminded herself. Four weeks they'd earmarked for this trip so that Rue wouldn't miss too much school. Not that the girl had been very concerned about that.

A smile curved Selena's lips. Rue and Ebony – both girls' interests lay quite definitely outside school. And Ebony, bless her, had coped very well with being left behind. Selena knew that Ebony would have given her right arm to come to Wilde Grove with them. Selena had actually considered the possibility, before ultimately deciding against it.

Rue needed the space to discover the link she had with Wilde Grove. And Ebony, wonderful as she was, took up a lot of space wherever she went.

Selena shook her head and laughed. Here she was, back in her heart's home, and all she could think about was her new family. She took a deep breath, and the air that filled her lungs was warm with spring and scented with forest and water.

She bowed her head to the water in the well, where Rue's offering of bluebells floated, then let her feet lead her across the lawn to the trees. She would walk the old paths for a while.

The trees greeted her with rustling whispers and gathered her in under their branches in an embrace of leaves. She smiled up at them, reached out and pressed her fingers to their bark, letting herself drift between them, her mind clear, thinking of nothing but those amongst whom she walked.

Up in the branches, the birds were waking with the day also, and whistled and sang and Selena smiled at their familiar sounds, so different to the ones she'd grown used to.

'No tui here,' she murmured, then let herself sink again into a wordless joy at being back where she'd walked almost every day of her life.

And here was the stone circle, and Selena stood looking at it, finding herself thinking about how it must have been for Rue to see it for the first time.

For this they most definitely didn't have back at home.

Selena huffed out a quick breath. Every thought she had, it seemed, took her back to her new home across the ocean, instead of revelling in being here, where she'd been born. She shook her head, a small smile on her face, realising what this meant.

She had moved on. Sometime in the last five months, she'd acclimated to her new home, then embraced it, then became part of it.

This stone circle was now where Morghan danced. Selena looked back at the path behind her. This was now where Morghan walked. She was Lady of the Grove now.

And Selena's place was elsewhere.

Selena moved into the circle and walked slowly from stone to stone, touching them lightly, greeting them, for whatever had happened in the last few months, these stones were old friends.

'Grandmother Oak,' she said, moving to the grand old tree and bowing her head in greeting. 'You're looking very beautiful in your springtime finery.'

She placed her hands flat against the tree and closed her eyes, letting the old lady's solidity seep up and inside her. Very little fazed Grandmother Oak. She had seen the months and years pass, changing her clothing with the seasons, the lessons of springing forth and dying back in the song of her sap. She had stood here and watched generations of women and men come up the pathway to dance at the stones, to lift their faces to sun and moon, and she had watched them grow old and die and return to earth and sky, just as one day she herself would.

Selena listened to the old matriarch's song, until it swam in her blood, and she was slightly dizzy when she opened her eyes.

'Bless me, Mother,' she whispered. 'That I may be filled with your fortitude, your wisdom, and your song for all the days of my life.'

Grandmother Oak whispered a greeting to her, a blessing, and Selena sighed, stood, and reached into the small bag she wore. Her fingers sifted through the assortment of items and drew out at last a pockmarked pebble.

'A gift from across the sea,' she said. 'From land formed from an ancient volcano, rock born from fire, made smooth from the ocean.' She pressed a thumb against the small reddish-brown stone, then her palm against the oak tree's trunk.

'My love for you and your people, Grandmother Oak,'

she whispered, and placed the pebble on the ground between Grandmother's roots, next to the bowl of water.

She straightened and smiled at the bluebells carpeting the ground back into the woods.

'Ah,' she said. 'How long it's been since I saw your lovely faces!'

These did not grow on the other side of the world either. There, the forest was completely different.

Selena shook her head. There she was again, her thoughts drawn unbidden to her new home.

'It is my home,' she said to the bluebells, no small amount of wonder in her voice. She repeated it, a revelation that made her heart thump in her chest.

'It is my home.'

Drawing in a deep breath of fragrant air, Selena turned to the stone circle and stepped into its embrace. She lifted her hands to the sky and tipped back her face.

'I, who was once Lady of this Grove,' she called. 'Let me now be a beacon in my new home.'

She lowered her hands and stood there, closing her eyes, remembering the vision the Queen had shown her and Morghan, all those months ago.

'Shining lights of this world and all worlds,' she murmured. 'My heart gleams with this light. My soul glows with love for this world and them all. I dance the song of the Wheel, across continents and oceans, across years and centuries. My light does not diminish, but glows brightly in any darkness. I am a beacon, Lady of light, full of the light of the stars, the quickening in darkness, the comfort from all fear, the safe place of the soul.'

Selena paused, feeling her whole body humming with

her prayer, her spirit strong, making her skin prickle as she flexed her spirit so that it brightened, became a living flame of light.

'I shine,' she breathed. 'I am a shining beacon, one of many who will light this world.'

Selena opened her eyes, and for a moment, the stones swung around her, the trees behind them swaying in her vision, and then she blinked, and the stones took on their solid, planted shape again, and the trees settled back upon their roots.

Selena smiled at them all, then turned and stepped out of the circle to head back to Hawthorn House and a hot cup of tea.

After breakfast, she thought, she'd call home. Talk to everyone there, see how they were getting on.

11

'Rue,' Grainne said. 'You poor thing, you're exhausted.'

Rue grimaced. She didn't want to be tired, and certainly didn't want to give in to it and leave the circle of women sitting by the fire chatting. She opened her eyes wider and shook her head.

'I'm fine,' she said. Then yawned hugely.

'You're still jet-lagged,' Grainne said. 'It's late enough – why not turn in so tomorrow you can be fresh as a daisy?'

Selena nodded. 'I think I'll do just the same. I'm still not used to being in the wrong time zone.' She blinked, hearing what she'd just said, then laughed. 'I really have adopted life Down Under, haven't I?' She shook her head, and nudged Rue on the sofa beside her. 'Time for both of us to go to our beds, I think. We've been sitting here yawning for the last twenty minutes.'

Rue nodded in defeat and got to her feet. 'I'll see you all in the morning,' she said, then looked hopefully at

Morghan. 'Will you...' She cleared her throat then started over. 'Will you be up early again?'

Morghan smiled at her. 'I'm always up early,' she said. 'Would you like to join me in greeting the day?'

Rue glanced at Selena, suddenly uncertain, but Selena only smiled and nodded, and Rue turned back to Morghan.

'I'd like that very much,' she said, her cheeks growing suddenly hot from the fire.

'Then please do,' Morghan said. 'I shall wait for you.'

Rue nodded and a wide smile escaped. 'I'm so glad we came here,' she said. 'Good night, everyone.'

Selena watched Rue slip out of the room and heard her tread on the stairs to her room. She looked over at Morghan.

'She's taken a shine to you,' she said.

Morghan nodded. 'We bonded over the well this morning, I think.'

'I was going to spend the time with her while we were here,' Selena said. 'But I think perhaps, if you would, she would enjoy following you.'

Grainne touched Morghan on the shoulder. 'What a wonderful idea,' she said. 'One day you'll have to teach someone to follow in your footsteps, after all. This will be the perfect practice.'

Morghan caught Grainne's fingers and held them. She considered the matter. 'It will be quite some time before Clarice is old enough,' she said, musing upon it. 'I think I'd be glad to spend time with Rue.' She looked over at Selena. 'If you really don't mind, of course?'

'One of us has to do it,' Selena said with a smile. 'And no, I don't mind at all if you take the lead on this.' She nodded at Grainne. 'Teaching is different to learning and Grainne is right – it will be good practice.'

'She will have to spend time with Ambrose, too, I think,' Morghan said. 'He is beside himself that she is having memories of such an early life spent here in the Grove.'

RUE STOOD AT HER BEDROOM WINDOW LOOKING OUT AT THE darkness of the woods. The moon was three days past full, but the night was clear and there was light enough for her to see the sloping grounds and the trees that stood lined along the edge of the lawn.

Somewhere in there, she thought, was a stone circle. A genuine circle of standing stones. It didn't matter to her that the stones weren't particularly large, or the circle particularly grand; the fact that it was there was enough.

Rue thought about Grandmother Oak, and the way that Morghan had greeted the tree. That was how she wanted to be, she decided. She wanted to be someone who talked to trees like that, who gave them gifts and spoke to them as though they were real people.

Of course, she'd already been doing this at home. But somehow, it seemed all the more real doing it here, knowing the trees had been named.

The well was down there too, and Rue looked at it, seeing the darkness of its eye in the silvered lawn. She shivered, remembering the terrible panic that had clutched at her when she'd bent over the edge of the water that morning.

'Something to do with Clover,' she murmured to the

night. 'But not Clover as she is now.' Rue took a breath, let it out slowly. 'Not my Clover.'

Someone else's Clover? The girl she kept dreaming of. The young priestess Bryn. Was Clover her sister too?

It was possible, Rue thought, and she leant her forehead against the cool glass then yawned. Bedtime, she decided. Especially if she was going to join Morghan again in the morning.

Rue climbed into bed, drawing the blankets up over her shoulders and hoped that Selena wouldn't mind if she went with Morghan tomorrow.

Perhaps Selena would come too, she thought, then drifted down into sleep.

BRYN DUCKED HER HEAD AND ENTERED THE TEMPLE, EYES CAST downwards, keeping her awareness on her breath, concentrating on it so that her thoughts would not be tempted to rattle away inside her head.

The flames in the small hearth flickered in the dimness, and Bryn knelt beside them and bowed her head to Wendyl, then to the Goddess seated in the chair.

She knew it wasn't the real Goddess, but only an image made from clay, but she was as awed as the first time she had set eyes on the Deer Mother.

Wendyl had strewn the fire with sacred herbs and sat with her eyes closed and Bryn gazed at her for a moment, knowing that while Wendyl's body sat stolidly upon the ground, her spirit likely roamed the woodlands, following the Goddess's byways.

Bryn left the temple without disturbing Wendyl, and

went into the adjoining room, taking her place at one of the two looms there. She smiled at Kennocha in greeting, then turned her attention to working the loom, letting her fingers reacquaint themselves with the task, while her mind kept quiet, as she concentrated instead on the sacred business of warp and weft and making cloth.

All acts of creation were precious to the Mother, Wendyl had told her when first seating Bryn at the loom, there to weave the cloth for her first robe as a priestess.

All acts of creation belonged to the Goddess, Wendyl said. This was why the looms were in the room next to the temple.

'As you weave the cloth,' Wendyl said, her eyes bright and smile soft, 'so do you weave the singing of the world and become part of it.'

Bryn had been disappointed at first. But perhaps it was the influence of the other priestesses, or Mother Wendyl's teaching, but she soon realised that sitting at the loom was a sacred act, that in fact, every action was so.

Bryn watched her fingers lift and drop the threads, and she watched the cloth grow, and was aware of her body sitting upon the stool, and her fingers manipulating the threads, and of the second loom in the room, where Kennocha hummed slightly as she worked, her fingers nimble, her gaze almost unfocused.

The smoke drifted in from the temple room and Bryn inhaled it slowly, letting her mind relax into her hands and the room. She could feel the sunshine outside as well, and part of her greeted her kin and took on her wings and she lifted herself into the blue sky and surfed the high currents of air.

The cloth grew longer, and the shuttle passed over and under and over and under and Bryn concentrated on it both lightly and deeply, feeling the thread under her fingers, the loom under her hands, the dirt under her stool, the wind under her wings.

Rue slept and dreamt of weaving and flying and when she woke in the morning, she was sure she could still feel the silk of the breeze as it lifted and carried her, and the scent of the herbs burning upon the temple fire.

She lay in bed, not daring to move in case she lost the thread of the dream. That made her smile, for she had been weaving thread – that's what the dream had been about. Finally, she took her journal from the table beside the bed and wrote the dream down as quickly as she could.

'Good morning,' Morghan said as Rue appeared on the terrace beside her.

Rue smiled at her. 'Good morning,' she said. Morghan was dressed much the same as the morning before, but this time she'd put her hair up in a twisted bun at the back of her head. Rue looked down at her own clothes. She'd put on one of her dresses, modelled off the ones Selena had brought with her to New Zealand and worn for their solstice and equinox celebrations.

'You look lovely,' Morghan said. 'Selena tells me you make your own clothes.'

A cloud of warmth spread through Rue at the comment. Selena had told Morghan that?

She nodded. 'I made this one to be like something Selena has.'

'I like it very much,' Morghan said.

Rue nodded, wanting to ask who made Morghan's clothes, but she remembered her dream instead. 'I dreamt of weaving,' she said.

Morghan's eyebrows rose. 'Weaving?'

Rue's gaze turned inward. 'I was Bryn,' she said and cleared her throat. 'The priestess, you know – way back whenever.' She paused. 'She went into this house she thought of as the temple, but it was just you know, a regular building made with sticks or whatever they used back then.'

Sticks, she thought. Woven together, or something like that.

'And anyway, there was a statue of something that she thought of as the Goddess, and a fire going, with herbs burning in it.'

Morghan looked at her, listening, and nodded.

Encouraged, Rue continued. 'But after a moment, she went into the next room or building, and there were two looms, and she sat down at one to weave.'

Rue frowned. 'The weaving was a sacred act, but why would that be?' Before Morghan could say anything, she answered her own question. 'Bryn thought that every act of creation, whether you were weaving or making anything else, was a sacred act.' Rue looked up at Morghan. 'Do you think she was right?'

'Yes,' Morghan said. 'I do, as long as it is done with a peaceful mind and a grateful heart.'

Rue nodded. That made sense, she thought. And she would definitely remember that when she did her sewing.

Morghan turned her gaze from Rue to the morning rising around them.

'Let's walk,' she said.

'Where are we going?' Rue asked.

'To the stream that runs through the land here. It's where I like to greet the day.'

It was Rue's turn for her eyebrows to rise. 'The stream?' she asked.

Morghan glanced at her and smiled. The morning was clear, with that sharp crispness that meant springtime to Morghan. She listened a moment to the birds singing their wake-up songs, then answered Rue.

'I like water near me,' she said. 'Selena, as you may know, is drawn to the element of air, but for me, it is water to which I have the most affinity.'

Rue thought about this. 'What about me?' she asked. 'Which one do I have an affinity to, do you think?'

'I don't know. You'll have to find out.'

'How, though?' Rue asked. 'How do I find out?'

'By meeting each one and seeing,' Morghan replied.

Rue ducked her head and thought about this. They passed the wellspring, where her bluebells still floated, and went on into the woods.

Was it water, Rue pondered? Did she have an affinity – she liked the word – to water? Or was it perhaps air, like Selena? She lifted her face to the breeze, as if to taste it and concentrated on the feeling of it against her skin.

She didn't feel anything.

'How do you know, though?' she asked. 'I mean, how do you know which element is your...whatever?'

'Your strongest ally?' Morghan touched the trunk of one of the younger trees and whispered a greeting and blessing in her mind.

'Yeah,' Rue said. 'That.'

'By spending time with them,' Morghan said. 'I would think that's really the only way to do it.'

'Is that how you discovered yours was water?'

'I should say so, yes. I found myself drawn more often to the stream, or the well, or the ocean.' Morghan nodded at Rue and took the way that led in the direction away from the path to the stone circle.

12

RUE STOOD UNCERTAINLY BESIDE MORGHAN, TRYING NOT TO keep looking at her as she waited for them to do something. The stream gurgled and trilled over the stones and between the roots, and Morghan seemed to be lost in thought staring at it. Rue wondered if she ought to clear her throat or something, remind Morghan that they were supposed to be doing...something. Anything really, other than just standing there.

But Morghan lifted her head finally and smiled at Rue. 'Hearing the water helps me think and be centred,' she said.

Rue nodded. 'I'm a bit like that too,' she said. 'But I think best when I'm lying in the grass in the sun.'

Morghan tipped her head to the side. 'I wonder if it's the earth or the sun that helps you contemplate.'

Rue looked at the water, and the stream was very pretty, and she liked the sound it made, and she especially liked the way the rising sun touched the wavelets and made them sparkle.

'I don't know,' she said. 'Does it matter?'

'It helps, I think,' Morghan replied. 'For when you really want to get deep into your practice.'

'I want to get deep into my practice,' Rue replied, suddenly very, very earnest. This was what she had come here for, and what she'd say, if anyone asked her.

She spread a hand out and indicated the woods and stream, and more. 'This is what I want to do.' She gave a wincing shrug. 'I mean, I know I have to work and everything as well, earn a living and all that, but this – this is how I want to live.' She paused. 'And shine. This is how I want to live and shine.'

Morghan looked at her and smiled. 'Your words make me feel glad,' she said. 'So, in view of that, let us make a start, shall we?'

Rue swallowed. Nodded. Wondered briefly if she really knew what she was getting herself in for, then decided that didn't matter. She trusted Selena and she also, she realised, trusted Morghan. Just as much. Morghan was pretty amazing.

'We shall start with each then, I think,' Morghan said in a low voice, talking to herself as much as Rue. She nodded, satisfied, remembering how Selena had begun the job of teaching her.

'Each what?'

'Element. With water first,' Morghan said. 'And then the others.' She smiled. 'Water, because here we are already.'

When Morghan spoke again, Rue knew she was no longer talking to her, but to the stream itself. She nodded quietly, noting to herself that she was used to this as Selena did it. Selena often spoke to trees, and the sun, and the earth and ocean as if they were living things that could all hear and answer her.

Rue guessed that really, they all were. And perhaps, for all she knew yet, they could.

'I bring my good greetings to you, running water,' Morghan said. 'The sun touches you on the dawning of a new day and I am here to listen to your song, and add my own to your tune.'

Morghan hummed then, and sang a short chant of sounds that seemed for a moment to weave in and out of the streams rushing trill.

Rue glanced at her, then closed her eyes, let herself sink into the moment, into the sounds and smells of the stream and woods and the light breeze that lifted her hair and cooled her neck.

BRYN SAT DOWN ON THE STREAM BANK AND SANK HER FEET into the lazily running water. She sighed. The water felt cool and good on her hot skin. She stood, lifted off her robe and, leaving it on the grass, waded in her short shift out into the middle of the stream, glancing back at the bank to make sure no one had followed her there with the same thought of refreshment on this hot day.

But she was alone. Later, she'd come back here, with Kennocha or Brigit, to do the laundry, but for these precious moments, she was alone. Her smile widened at the thought. Alone, she definitely was not.

'Greetings to you, my little stream,' she said. 'I hear your song during my dreams at night. Will you remember me when you reach the sea, little stream?'

The water gurgled and laughed as it swept around her calves and Bryn bent down and dipped her fingers into the water.

Bryn listened to the sound of the stream then straightened slowly. She'd heard something that was not just the voice of the water as it flowed over rock and around root.

A high, light tinkling sound, and Bryn's breathing became shallow. She knew what that sound was, what it meant.

She wanted to rush to step out of the stream, to hurry to the bank and pull her dress back over her head so that at least she wouldn't be standing half naked with water dripping from her fingers.

But there was no time, for they were already there, standing on the far bank, the Shining Ones.

Bryn had heard many stories of them, of course, and Brigit had whispered that Wendyl and the other older priestesses even made a habit of visiting them in their Fair Lands, the way to which was in the woods surrounding the Grove, down the tunnel between the roots of the great wych elm that grew on one of the least travelled paths. Bryn shuddered, knowing that one day she too would pass that way to make her alliance with their Queen.

But right now, Bryn kept her chin lowered, eyes on the water swirling around her feet, suddenly too cold even with the hot sun dappled upon her head.

She could not lift her face to look at them.

'You are one of the priestesses?'

The voice sounded like sunlight and wind and Bryn closed her eyes and nodded before turning slowly to look at the Fae people standing on the bank.

She found her voice. 'I am,' she said, for not to answer would be an unforgivable rudeness.

They were three. And how apt was their title of the Shining Ones. For shine they did, their foreheads broad, their expressions at ease. They were taller than Bryn and her fellow priestesses. Taller even than Finn, one of the men, who was reaching finally his full height and towering over his uncle already.

But one of them held something in their arms, and Bryn couldn't help her gasp when she realised that it was a child. She panted a moment, then lowered her head in respect.

'I am Bryn, priestess of the Forest Grove.' She blinked, looking again at the water. 'I am at your service.'

'This child is a foundling,' the Shining One told her, and the one holding the child bent, standing it on its feet upon the grass. 'We would bid you to take her in.'

Bryn, looking at them now, her mouth hanging open in shock, blinked, struck dumb. Then she sucked in a sharp breath of air, coming to her senses.

'Take her now,' the Shining One said, and tipped their head in a shallow bow at Bryn, before the three of them turned and stepped back into the woods behind them.

Bryn stood gaping in the middle of the stream, staring at the shimmer of air where the Shining Ones had stood, and then she shook her head and turned her attention to the child.

It was a girl, Bryn thought, mostly because the Fae had called the child *she*. But her features were fine and plump, her hair as brown as Bryn's own, a dark waterfall down her back. She looked back at Bryn with eyes as brown and warm as a cow's and her mouth beneath them was a pink flower bud.

Bryn glanced behind the girl, but the Shining Ones were gone, not a trace left, not even a tremble in the air.

She huffed a breath, shook her head, turned her lips up in a smile.

'What am I doing?' she said. 'Come, little one, let's get you to see Mother Wendyl, now, shall we?'

Bryn splashed across the width of the stream and on the bank, the child, surely not more than four turns of the seasons old, opened her arms and reached for her.

MORGHAN WAS LOOKING AT HER WHEN RUE OPENED HER EYES, blinking them several times before glancing around to see that she was lying on the grass beside the stream.

'What happened?' she asked, strangely groggy, as though she'd woken from a sudden, deep sleep.

'Yes,' Morghan said. 'I would like to know.'

Rue sat quickly up, realising that she'd been resting practically in Morghan's lap.

'Sorry,' she said. 'I...I fell asleep?'

It was a question because she wasn't sure. She felt like she'd been dreaming.

'It was so real,' she said. 'A very vivid dream.'

'What did you see?' Morghan asked. Selena had, of course, told her about Rue's dreaming of the young priest-ess. This was the whole reason they'd come to Wilde Grove.

But Rue shook her head. 'I've never just fallen asleep in the middle of doing something before.'

Morghan shifted slightly, giving Rue more space. 'It was

not just sleeping, I think,' she said. She lifted a hand and indicated the woods around them. 'You've known this place before – very well, I am thinking. Your life here is very present for you.'

Rue stared at Morghan. She shook her head slightly. 'But why?'

'That is the question, is it not? And what Selena has brought you here to answer.'

Rue tucked her chin down as she thought about it, then she nodded. 'It was so real though,' she said, almost whispering. Then she looked suddenly at the other bank of the stream and scrambled to her feet.

'They were over there,' she said.

Morghan stood beside her. 'Who were over there?'

Rue shook her head, but not because she didn't know or couldn't remember, but because it was so bright in her mind, as though she had been the one to live through it, not someone else.

'I was standing in the middle of the stream,' Rue said. She looked at Morghan, then back at the water, nodding again. 'It was a hot day, and I'd come – Bryn had come – to the stream to cool off.' Rue's voice was full of wonder. 'She was thinking about having to come back and do the laundry at the stream later.'

Rue frowned then and glanced questioningly at Morghan. 'They washed their clothes in the stream?'

'Most probably,' Morghan answered.

Rue shook her head. 'Wow,' she said and drew in a deep breath. 'She was standing there, and then there were people on the other bank.' Rue closed her eyes and looked at what she'd seen through Bryn's gaze. 'They were different though, and Bryn was almost afraid of them.' Rue squeezed her eyes shut. 'She called them the Shining Ones.'

Morghan stood straighter. 'The Fae,' she said and nodded at Rue's enquiring look. 'The Shining Ones – the Fae.' She smiled slightly. 'They still live here.'

Rue's eyes couldn't have widened any further. 'They still live here? What do you mean?'

'The priestesses of the Grove have had a long history of association with the Fae here, and still do.'

'But they weren't human,' Rue gasped.

'Nor are trees or streams or birds or foxes,' Morghan observed calmly.

Rue looked around as though expecting the figures she'd seen as Bryn to suddenly step back from between the trees.

'But where do they live?' she asked. 'Bryn thought something about...' Rue frowned, trying to make sense of Bryn's thoughts. 'About going through the roots of a tree, or something?'

'There are many ways into the Fair Lands,' Morghan said. 'So that sounds about right.'

Rue shook her head, but a smile was widening on her face. 'This is amazing,' she said. 'Wait until I tell Ebony. She's going to flip.'

'Ebony?'

'My best friend,' Rue explained. 'She's really into all this too. She wants to be a priestess as well.' For a moment, Rue's face turned wistful. 'She really wanted to come here with me.'

Morghan nodded, answered softly. 'Perhaps she can, next time.'

Rue looked out over the stream, her attention already moving back to the vision she'd shared with Bryn.

Or, she considered, that Bryn had shared with her.

That thought, for some reason she didn't understand, made her shiver.

'They brought a child,' she said.

'A child?' Morghan asked.

Rue nodded. 'Yes.' She squinted at the memory a moment. 'A foundling. That's what they called her. A foundling. It was a little girl. They wanted me...I mean Bryn, to take her to live with the priestesses.'

Morghan digested this information, then wondered if Rue would realise who this child was likely to be.

But Rue was shaking her head. 'I can't believe that happened,' she said. She turned around and looked at Morghan. 'What do we do now?'

That was a good question.

'We continue with our greeting to the day,' Morghan said. She smiled. 'A strong practice will guide us through this.'

Rue nodded slowly. She wasn't exactly, a hundred percent sure what Morghan meant, but she thought she could see that it would be kinda...rude... to run off having only half done the morning prayers.

'And after that?' she asked anyway.

'After that,' Morghan said. 'We will have breakfast, then visit Ambrose.'

13

Tara opened the door, a smile of welcome on her face for Rachel. She bent down and grinned at Josh tucked up in his winter jacket and boots.

'Hi Josh,' she said. 'Come to have some fun?' She looked up at Rachel. 'How are you today? Isn't it cold out!'

Rachel's face glowed with two high spots of colour.

'Are you all right?' Tara asked. There was something feverish about Rachel's face. 'You're looking a bit peaky – you're not coming down with something, are you?' Tara smiled again. 'Gosh,' she said. 'What are we doing standing about out here? Come in, both of you, and let's start the day.'

Tara led them inside and looked Rachel over again as she got Josh out of the pushchair and his jacket.

'Would you like a cup of tea?' Tara asked her impulsively. She was getting better at trusting her intuition, and her intuition was right now telling her that something was going on with Rachel.

Something big.

'Do you have time?' she asked, picking Josh up and giving him a squeeze.

Rachel hesitated, then nodded. 'Yes, okay,' she said. 'That would be nice.'

Something about her voice had Tara raising her eyebrows. 'Is everything okay?' she asked.

The words that Rachel had been rolling around all morning – for the last couple days, in fact – spilled out of her mouth before she could stop them. 'I'm leaving Mike,' she said.

They sounded so much more certain when she heard them out loud. She put a hand over her mouth, horrified.

'What?' Tara paused on her way to the kettle. She put Josh down and watched him toddle over to the small basket of toys she kept out of the way in the kitchen. 'Today?' she asked.

Rachel took a deep breath and sat down at the table. She knotted her hands together. 'Do you know why I was thrown out of the Peebs?' she asked.

Tara stared at her for a moment, then resumed the journey to the teapot. They'd definitely need something to go with this conversation.

'No,' she said. 'I don't think you've ever told me.'

She knew Rachel had never told her.

'I wanted to be a dancer,' Rachel said.

Tara's mouth curved up in a smile and she flipped the electric jug on. 'But that's wonderful.'

'Not when your family is Exclusive Brethren,' Rachel said.

Tara shook her head. She didn't know much about the

sect Rachel had been part of. 'But why? Dancing is a beautiful thing to want to do.'

'No.' Rachel turned to look at Josh, who was sitting on the floor now, turning the pages of a board book and chattering to himself. He loved being in this house, Rachel thought. And she didn't blame him. It felt good inside Windswitch. She wanted a home that felt like this.

Was that possible?

'No?' Tara asked, pouring the tea.

Rachel shook her head. 'You're not allowed to listen to music there.'

Tara brought the teapot over to the table. They could stay and chat for a few minutes. Danielle was already there, in the playroom with Clover and Dandy.

'What do you mean?' she asked. She couldn't imagine not being able to listen to music.

But Rachel was shaking her head. 'No music,' she said. 'No dancing. No radio, no television. Just boring old newspapers, and really only the men read those.'

Tara stared at her, shocked. 'No nothing?'

'No nothing,' Rachel said. 'It's called *"preserving the people from the world."*' She took the cup Tara gave her. 'Thank you. Anyway. I got myself one of those CD Walkmans.' Her mouth quivered slightly. 'I stole it. And I stole the CDs to listen to, as well.' She looked at Tara. 'I'd never stolen anything before, never broken the rules at all, but I couldn't seem to stop myself.'

Tara didn't know what to say, so she picked up the teapot and filled their cups.

'And of course, I was found out,' Rachel said. She closed her eyes, waited for the tears to recede. She still missed her sisters. 'And eventually it was decided that I needed to leave.'

'Who decided that?'

'It felt like everyone,' Rachel said, and she stood up. Suddenly, she didn't feel like talking about it anymore. 'Sorry,' she said. 'I'd better get going. Mike will wonder where I am.'

Tara rose. 'You said you were leaving him.'

Rachel nodded. The muscles in her neck were so tight they felt like they were made from piano wire.

'Yes,' she said. 'When I find somewhere to go.' She walked over and crouched down to kiss Josh on the head.

'Love you, Joshy Boy,' she said. 'Be good for Tara, okay?' She kept her face to his hair for a moment, breathing in the scent of him, eyes closed, then stood up and nodded to Tara. 'Take care of him.'

'Always,' Tara answered, and she stood there watching as Rachel Manners let herself out.

CLOVER WAS BUILDING A TOWER OF BLOCKS WITH LITTLE JOSH, who giggled as the tower got higher and higher.

'There ya go, Josh!' Clover squealed and clapped her hands in delighted anticipation.

Little Josh, knowing his part, crowed with laugher and swiped a hand at the tower of wooden blocks, sending them tumbling to the ground. He rolled onto his back and chortled.

Tara had to laugh along with them, even though she shook her head as well, wondering why it always set off so much glee to destroy something.

But Clover was already pouncing on the blocks, rebuilding the tower.

Tara looked down at Danielle on the couch next to her. They'd been reading a story, and Danielle had her thumb firmly corked in her mouth.

'Shall we go and have some morning tea now?' Tara asked her.

Danielle's eyes widened and she nodded, pulling out her thumb and grinning. She loved Tara's morning teas. There was always something yummy.

'Come along then,' Tara called to the other two. 'Time to have a bite to eat.' She picked up Josh, marvelling as always at the fact that he weighed barely more than a twig. 'Let's feed you up, shall we?' she asked him, smiling. He wasn't as sleepy as he'd been the morning before last, and his eyes were bright enough. His teeth must have been giving him less trouble.

She walked toward the door, Josh in her arms and Danielle at her heel.

Only Clover didn't come. She was standing on the rug, a block in each hand, and a frown on her face as she gazed at something only she could see.

'Clover?' Tara asked. 'Are you all right?'

Clover didn't respond, and Tara hesitated a moment, then put Josh down on the couch and gave him one of the books. She nodded at Danielle. 'We'll go to the kitchen in just a minute, okay?'

Clover burst into tears, the red and green blocks falling from her hands.

'Clover!'

Tara knelt on the rug beside her, wincing as her knee

came down on a block. She shifted and scooped Clover into her arms.

But Clover was frozen, her face white mottling with red, mouth wide open in shock as she howled.

'Clover, sweetheart, what's wrong?' Tara asked, pulling Clover closer. But the little girl's body was rigid against her.

Behind her, on the couch, Josh started crying as well, great cries of fright. Tara glanced at him, then noticed at Danielle's lower lip was also trembling.

'It's all right, Danielle, Josh,' she said. 'Clover just got a fright, that's all.'

Danielle's lip steadied, but Josh continued howling along with Clover, and he slid off the couch and toddled over to Tara.

The door opened and Dandy poked her head in. 'Goodness me,' she said. 'What's going on in here?'

Tara shook her head. 'Can you take Josh?' she asked over the racket. 'Take him and Danielle into the kitchen for their morning tea?'

Dandy nodded immediately and came into the room to gather up the howling Josh. She took Danielle's hand and led her out of the room.

'Come on sweeties, let's go find our morning tea.'

Tara looked back at Clover, who was now taking great whooping breaths, her face stricken.

'Shh, now, sweetie,' Tara said. 'It's okay. I'm here. Just breathe nice and slow, okay.'

Clover's gaze swung wildly around the room, then fastened at last on Tara and she managed to suck in first one breath then another.

Tara stroked her forehead and Clover relaxed at last,

sinking into Tara's lap and burying her head in Tara's neck. She was crying now, her narrow shoulders shaking with the sobs, but at least, thought Tara, it wasn't that scary shocked screaming.

Tara rocked Clover on her lap, whispering sweet words, waiting for Clover to calm down.

And she did, eventually. When she finally lifted her tear-streaked face to look at Tara, her eyes were red and round and wet, and her mouth trembled.

'What happened, sweetie?' Tara asked.

For a moment, Clover thought she was going to burst into tears again, but she didn't. She thought of Rue instead, and Selena, and wished they were home.

'I miss Rue,' she whispered.

'Oh honey, I know you do,' Tara said, even though Clover had been doing just fine without her sister up until this moment. 'Did something scare you?'

'Josh,' Clover said, and her mouth stretched in agony again.

Tara put a hand on Clover's cheek and kissed her damp forehead. 'Hush,' she said. 'Josh is in the kitchen with Dandy; he's eating his muffin and is perfectly okay.'

Clover shook her head, then ducked her head down again onto Tara's shoulder. She wouldn't think about it, she decided.

If she didn't think about it, maybe it wouldn't be true.

'Can you tell me what Josh did to scare you?' Tara asked, trying to remember where Josh even was when Clover started her screaming. Hadn't Clover been still on the rug with the blocks, while she herself was holding the small boy, ready to go out to the kitchen?

Yes, Tara decided. That's exactly how it had been.

Clover pressed her lips together and shook her head. 'I want a drink,' she said instead, sniffing. 'Please may I have a drink?'

Tara stared down at her for a minute, then nodded. 'Of course. Let's go get one.' She paused. 'But Clover, you know you can tell me anything, right?'

Clover looked down at the floor, at the blocks spilled all over the rug.

'I'm firsty,' she said.

Tara was still for a moment, then nodded, plastering on a smile. Whatever had happened, Clover clearly didn't want to talk about it.

'Clover,' Tara asked, suddenly thinking of it. 'Is Rue okay?'

Clover nodded. 'I tired, Tara,' she said. 'Firsty and tired. Can I have a drink an' a nap?'

Tara stood up, lifting Clover into her arms as she did, aware that her own heart was thumping quickly and loudly in her chest. She couldn't think of any way to make Clover talk to her, though.

Something had clearly happened, and just as clearly, Clover didn't want to say what it was.

'Of course, sweetie,' she said. 'Let's get you a drink.'

'An' a nap,' Clover said.

Tara nodded against Clover's small head on her shoulder. 'Then a nap, if that's what you want.'

'I wan' a nap.'

Dandy looked up questioningly as Tara entered the kitchen, but Tara shook her head briefly, and went to the table, poured Clover a drink.

'You want this here?' she asked.

Clover straightened on Tara's hip and reached for the glass. She drank down the weak peppermint tea and gave the empty glass back to Tara before planting her head back on Tara's shoulder.

'Clover's going to have a nap now,' Tara said. 'I'll just go and tuck her in.' She looked a moment at Dandy, then carried Clover upstairs to her room.

'What was all that about?' Dandy asked when Tara came back into the kitchen. Josh was in the highchair, happily chasing raisins around the tray. Danielle was on her knees on one of the chairs, eating a muffin and drawing a picture that seemed to be of a queen or princess, going by the large golden crown that encircled the character's head.

They both had clearly gotten over the surprise of Clover's outburst.

Tara retreated behind the kitchen counter and put the jug on to reheat. She needed a cup of tea herself, now.

She shook her head. 'I don't know,' she said to Dandy.

'What did Clover say?'

'Nothing.' Tara reached for the jar of dried chamomile flowers she and Natalie had harvested from the garden and noticed her hand was shaking. She looked over at Dandy, whose face had creased into worried lines.

'It's like she decided she didn't want to talk about it.' Tara put the tea back and pressed her palms to the counter-top. 'She just said she missed Rue, then told me she was thirsty and tired.'

'What did happen?' Dandy asked.

Tara glanced over at the children, but they were both fine for the moment. She shook her head.

'I don't know. We were about to come out here for morning tea and Clover was standing on the rug where she and Josh had been playing with the blocks, and all of a sudden, she just starts this really weird screaming.'

'I heard it,' Dandy said. 'It didn't sound like she'd been hurt, though.'

'I agree,' Tara said. 'It was more like she'd had a shock. A terrible shock. She said Josh scared her.'

They were both silent for a moment, looking at the little boy who seemed perfectly well.

'She saw something,' Dandy said at last.

Tara nodded in agreement.

'SHE'S STILL ASLEEP,' TARA SAID AN HOUR AND A HALF later, coming down into the kitchen where Dandy was sitting at the table pretending to read a magazine. The kitchen was the hub of the house. 'And Josh's mother is late.'

Danielle was already picked up and on her way home. Tara only looked after the children for half a day.

Dandy closed the pages of her magazine thoughtfully. 'Josh is asleep too?'

Tara nodded. 'I had to put him down for a nap. He's in the travel cot in the playroom. I checked on him.' She sighed. 'He's fine.'

She'd stood over him for a full minute until she was sure he was still breathing normally, his little chest rising and falling under the blanket.

Now, she wished Rachel would hurry up and arrive to pick him up. If Clover had had some sort of premonition about the boy, Tara wanted him back safely with his mum as soon as possible.

'Rachel told me this morning that she was going to leave her husband.' She looked at Dandy. 'You said you'd done a reading for her at Beacon the other day.'

Dandy nodded.

'What did it say? The reading?'

Now, Dandy shook her head. 'Readings are confidential,' she said. 'But put it this way – I'm not surprised she's decided to leave him. I really don't think she is happy there.' Dandy looked at the door. 'How late is she? Did she say she was moving out today?'

Tara checked her watch and sighed. 'Only half an hour so far, but it's not like Rachel. She's always early, if anything.' She paused, replaying the morning's conversation. 'Not today, I don't think. She talked about having to find somewhere to go, first.'

'She could have been held up in any number of ways,' Dandy said, but there was an itching sensation deep inside her. Was something wrong? 'Clover's upset just has us a bit on edge, I think.'

She hoped that was just what it was and waited for the itch to go away.

Tara nodded and sat down at the table, resting her head in her palms. 'What a morning,' she said.

Twenty minutes later, there was a knock at the door, and Tara almost spilled her chair over backwards in her hurry to get up and answer it.

'Oh,' she said. 'It's you.'

Natalie blinked at her. 'Is this a bad time?' she asked. 'I can come back if it is.'

'No, no, no,' Tara said, shaking her head. 'Goodness, I'm sorry – you've got to come in, of course. I don't even think you should still be knocking.' She blinked and knew she was beginning to babble. Which is what she did when she got really nervous. 'We should give you your own key, not that the door is locked when we're home.' She held the door wide for Natalie to come in.

'What's happening, then?' Natalie asked, unloading her usual biscuit tins onto the kitchen bench. She looked over at Dandy at the table, then back at Tara. 'Something is, isn't it?' Her thoughts went to the other members of the household and for a moment her blood seemed to run cold.

'It's not Damien, or the others, is it?' she asked, her voice suddenly weak.

'No, nothing like that,' Tara said, making an effort to be calm.

Natalie's knees went weak with relief. 'Something's happened, though?'

'One of my mums hasn't turned up yet,' Tara said. 'Josh's mother. He's having a nap, and she was supposed to be here...' Tara looked at her watch again. 'Almost two hours ago.'

'Perhaps she's had an accident, or something,' Natalie said, trying not to be ashamed that she was still glad nothing had happened to Damien. Or the others.

'She doesn't drive,' Tara said. 'Josh's mum, Rachel; she always takes the bus here and back. I don't think she ever learnt to drive.' She glanced at Dandy. 'I think they only have one car, and her husband uses it.'

Dandy didn't know. But she was growing more worried about Rachel with every passing moment.

Tara was looking at Natalie again. 'Clover had this really weird turn,' she said. 'She saw something; we're convinced of it.'

'Saw something?' asked Natalie. 'Like, really saw something?'

'Had a vision,' Tara said.

14

Two hours past pick-up time, and Tara was sitting at the table with Josh back in his highchair eating a late lunch. He waved a piece of apple at her, and she smiled vaguely back at him.

Most of her attention was focused on Dandy, who was calling Rachel's house again.

Dandy looked back at her and shook her head. 'No answer,' she said.

Rachel didn't have a mobile phone.

'What about her husband?'

Rachel's husband did have a mobile phone. He just hadn't been answering it.

Dandy hung up, then dialled the husband again. Mike, his name was. Dandy listened to the call go through, thinking about the cards she'd pulled for Rachel. The thread of disquiet running through her body thrummed more loudly.

'Rachel wanted to be a dancer,' Tara said, looking

around her lovely kitchen and not seeing any of it. 'That's why she had to leave the Exclusive Brethren. She wouldn't stop dancing, and they're not allowed to dance, apparently. Or listen to music.' Tara focused on Natalie's face. 'She stole a Walkman and listened to music on that.'

'He's still not answering.' Dandy replaced the handset and looked at Tara. 'Have you ever met this Mike fella?'

Tara shook her head.

Natalie looked up. 'They're not allowed to listen to music?' She was doing what she always did when things were going wrong, and was baking a cake. Just a simple one this time, a banana cake. It would be ready to pop in the oven in a minute and then she'd have to find something else to do with her hands. She took a deep, centring breath, just the way Selena had taught her.

'I wish Selena were here,' she blurted.

Josh threw a slice of apple on the ground, and Tara bent to pick it up. She put it on the table and smiled wanly at the little boy.

'I'm sure we can manage here,' Dandy said. 'How was Rachel this morning, when she told you she was leaving her husband?'

Tara rested her forehead on a hand and thought about going to check on Clover again. She never had such long naps anymore.

'Do you think we need to take Clover to the hospital?' she asked.

Natalie's eyes widened.

Dandy shook her head. Walked over and put a calming hand on Tara's shoulder. Tara, who loved Clover and Rue as well as if she'd been their mother.

'She had a shock, dear. She's just sleeping it off. The hospital wouldn't be able to make it better.'

'But she never sleeps this long.' Tara reached for the hand on her shoulder and clasped the fingers.

'Aren't you supposed to go to hospital for shock?' Natalie asked.

Dandy shook her head. 'She's not had any injury. They wouldn't know what to do with her.' She squeezed Tara's hand. 'We know what to do for her.'

Tara shook her head. 'I don't feel like I do,' she said. 'What happened? What did she see – and why won't she tell me?'

Tara had thought that Clover knew she could tell her anything.

'Perhaps she doesn't want to go over it again,' Dandy said.

'It must have been something bad, then,' Natalie said. 'To make her not want to talk about it.'

They were silent for a long moment after that. Josh picked up the last raisin and held it up in triumph. When no one looked at him, he fed it into his mouth and ate it.

'Doesn't Rachel help her husband in his business?' Dandy asked at last.

Tara nodded. 'He runs some sort of bookkeeping business.'

Natalie gasped. 'Bookkeeping – like some sort of gambling bookie?'

'No.' Tara got up from the table and picked up a cloth to wipe Josh's face and hands. He grinned at her. 'I mean actual bookkeeping, taxes and all that. I don't think Rachel would bring Josh here if she didn't have to work with him for a few hours. With her husband, is what I mean.'

Natalie shook her head. 'Why would she have him in day care if she doesn't really want it?'

Dandy pressed her lips together. People, in her long experience, did many things they didn't really want to, but felt like they had reason to.

But Natalie had moved on. 'So, if Josh is here, then shouldn't she be at work?' Natalie scooped the cake batter into the tin.

'If she was going to tell her husband today that she was leaving him, then the day may have gone quite differently to usual,' Dandy said.

Natalie put the cake in the oven and twisted the timer on. She looked at the other women. 'You don't think something happened, do you?' she asked at last. 'That he lost his temper or something.'

Things like that happened.

Dandy looked out the kitchen window, the one that overlooked the driveway. She hoped to see Rachel scurrying up the gravel drive, apologies already on her lips, her face pale and flustered.

But the driveway was empty.

She didn't want to answer Natalie's question.

But it might explain the shock that had sent Clover to her bed.

'I spent quite a lot of time talking to her, to Rachel,' Dandy said. 'People often open up when they get their cards read. She certainly wasn't happy in her situation.'

'Did she say anything that would help us today?' Tara asked, sudden hope lighting up her face.

But Dandy shook her head.

'I'm going to go check on Clover again,' Tara said, getting up. 'Watch Josh a minute for me?'

She went upstairs and pushed Clover's door open, walking over to the bed, hoping to see Clover awake and smiling up at her.

Clover was still asleep, her cheeks round and pink and warm, a blonde curl plastered to one. She was burrowed deeply into her bright yellow comforter and Tara pulled it back slightly so that Clover wouldn't be so hot in there.

She wanted Clover to wake up, and frowned as the child slept on. Clover never slept this long during the day. She still had an afternoon nap, but it was only for an hour or so, and then she'd be back up, full of beans ready for the rest of the day.

Tara shook her head and stroked the sticky curl from Clover's cheek. She must have really seen something, Tara thought, for her to be wiped out like this.

Clover moved, stretched for a moment, then curled back up under the blankets, her eyes still closed. Tara looked at her for a moment longer, then sighed and went back downstairs.

'She's still out like a light,' she said. 'I'm worried about her. She never sleeps this long.' Tara glanced at Josh. 'She hasn't even had her lunch.'

'She'll be all right, I'm sure,' Dandy soothed. 'She will also have burnt up a lot of calories, and now she needs rest.'

Tara stared dubiously at Dandy. 'Burnt up a lot of calories? What do you mean?'

'I mean, that a psychic vision like that uses up a lot of energy.'

'Oh,' Natalie said. She hadn't thought of that.

'We'll let her sleep just a little longer,' Dandy said. 'But I'm not worried about her.'

Tara sucked in her bottom lip and bit down on it. She wanted to go back upstairs and wake Clover up, make sure she was all right.

And ask her again what she'd seen.

But she nodded and turned to Josh instead. She pulled him out of the highchair.

'I guess I'll take him back to the playroom,' she said. She looked out the window too, but Rachel still wasn't there.

'I'll give his dad another call,' Dandy said.

'Do you think we ought to call the police?' Natalie asked.

'We will if we can't get hold of his dad soon,' Dandy replied. Her voice was grim, and she punched in the numbers with a little more force than necessary, trying to quash down the thought she kept having.

That even if they did get hold of Mike Manners, that still didn't account for the whereabouts of Rachel.

She remembered Rachel's expression as the cards were dealt. A mixture of hope and fear, Dandy thought. As though she thought the cards were going to tell her it was okay to do whatever she was really thinking.

Dandy raised her eyebrows, considering that. Lots of people, women particularly, came to get their cards read because what they were really wanting was another voice to back them up, giving them permission to do what they knew already they needed to, but were afraid of for any number of reasons.

She'd thought Rachel had fallen into that camp. In fact, by the end of the session, she'd been pretty convinced that

Rachel was deciding to leave her husband. Which had been confirmed with the events of this morning. She wondered what Mike Manners was like.

And then he answered the phone, finally.

'Yes?'

For a moment Dandy was too surprised at the call being answered that she was speechless. She held up a hand to stop Tara leaving the room and cleared her throat.

'Mr Manners?' she asked.

'Yes. Who's this, please?'

'Mr Manners, your wife hasn't arrived to pick up your son from his day care.'

There was a pause on the other end.

'Mr Manners?'

'I'll be there shortly.'

Dandy looked down at the phone, replaced it slowly, thoughtfully, then looked at Tara and tried to smile. 'He's on his way over.'

'Did he say what's happened to his wife?' Natalie asked.

Dandy shook her head. 'No, he didn't say anything. Just that he'll be here shortly.'

The three women looked at each other.

'Is that weird?' Natalie asked.

'I think so,' Tara said.

'Or maybe it's not,' Dandy said. 'He has no idea who I am, after all. And he's on his way, at least.' She wrinkled her nose. 'We can ask about Rachel when he gets here.'

'I'd rather hand Josh over to his mother,' Tara said, and her grip on the child on her hip tightened.

'I don't think we have a choice about that, dear,' Dandy said. 'But we'll ask if he knows where Rachel is.'

'And we'll listen very carefully to his answer,' Natalie added.

NATALIE POUNCED ON THE DOOR WHEN SHE HEARD THE knock, nodding to the others as she pulled it open.

'Mr Manners?' she asked.

'That's me,' Josh's father said, and stepped through into the kitchen at Natalie's gesture. 'Is he all set?'

Tara picked up Josh's backpack but didn't make any move to hand it over. She was watching Josh, who had been doing an animal puzzle on the floor. He was staring up at his father as though confused.

'Do you know where Rachel is?' Tara asked. They'd agreed that she ought to question Mike Manners, since she was the one officially looking after Josh.

'She had a hair appointment,' Mike said. He smiled down at Josh. 'Guess it went longer than expected.' He glanced up at the three women. 'You know what you ladies are like when you get to things like your hair.'

Tara stared at him, barely able to believe what she'd heard. She looked over at Natalie, who gaped back at her.

'Rachel's two hours late, Mr Manners,' Tara said. 'Hair appointments don't take that long.'

Mike Manners was more handsome than she'd expected. He turned a charming smile in her direction and picked up Josh, then reached to pluck the bag out of Tara's hand. 'I guess she had some shopping to do afterwards.' He shook his head. 'She's always losing track of time. Thanks for taking care of Josh, and for calling me.' He walked over to the door and turned, nodding at them. 'We'll pay you for the extra time, of course.'

Tara was too shocked to say anything, but Dandy did.

'Will Rachel be bringing Josh back tomorrow?'

Mike nodded. 'If it's one of his mornings here, I'm sure she will.'

He disappeared out the door and Tara shook her head.

'Should I go after him?'

'And say what?' Dandy asked. 'He could be right; Rachel could have forgotten the time.'

'I don't believe that for a minute.' Tara was adamant, crossing her arms.

Dandy lifted her hands in defeat under the weight of Tara's scowl. 'Nor do I, but we also, when it comes to it, don't know otherwise either, do we?'

'Rachel has never been late picking up Josh before.' Tara's face was pale.

'But it does happen sometimes, I'm sure,' Natalie said tentatively.

'It does,' Dandy said. 'I think we're worrying more than usual because of Clover.'

They were silent after that. Tara closed her eyes and spoke finally.

'What are we thinking is going on here?' she asked.

'Nothing,' Dandy said. 'We've no reason to think anything.'

'Except we do, don't we?' Natalie said. 'You told me Clover saw something, and then Rachel didn't turn up, and I think Josh's father is lying through his teeth about Rachel being out getting her hair done.'

They were quiet again, letting that sink in.

Tara shook her head. 'But we can't make Clover tell us what she saw, if she doesn't want to.'

'No,' Dandy agreed. 'So, we'll just carry on with our day, because that's all we can do. And Rachel, hopefully, will turn up tomorrow morning, full of apologies.' She looked at Tara. 'Are you expecting Josh tomorrow?'

Tara nodded. 'What if she doesn't come?'

'Then we deal with that then.'

It was Natalie who spoke next. 'Just to be clear though – we think something might have happened to Rachel, isn't that right?'

The words sounded flat and awful, and the women stared at each other.

'I think I'll call Rachel at home later,' Tara said. 'This evening. See if she's there.'

She swallowed dryly. 'And perhaps Clover will let us know what she saw that upset her so much.' She glanced at Dandy. 'Maybe we can call Rue. She might speak to Rue.' Tara shook her head. 'I know I oughtn't, but I wish Rue and Selena were here. Selena would know if something had happened to Rachel, just by plucking it out of the air or something.'

Dandy stepped over to her and put an arm around her shoulder.

'They're not here,' she said. 'But we'll manage. It's a good idea to call Rachel later. She'll probably be home safe and sound and very sorry she was delayed. Or perhaps there was an accident and she's broken her arm or something. There are a dozen reasons why she might not have been able to make it.'

Tara nodded, but she wasn't mollified.

Because Rachel had said she was going to leave her husband. Perhaps she'd told him, and he hadn't liked it.

He'd looked like the sort who wouldn't like it, underneath all that smarm and charm.

Tara grimaced. What about Clover then?

Clover had seen something.

Something had happened, Tara was sure of it, thinking again of Clover's shocked screams. And Clover had seen it.

Something had happened that was very bad.

15

RUE WANDERED OUT ONTO THE LAWN. IT WAS AFTER DINNER and the sun was westering, touching the tops of the trees as it headed towards the horizon.

She stood looking at the trees, the well at her back, her arms prickling. Not because she was afraid – she rubbed at her arms and blew out a breath between pursed lips – but because the world was suddenly so much larger than she'd known.

And living with Clover, she'd thought it was pretty big to begin with.

There were soft footsteps and Rue smiled at Clarice.

'Where's Sigil?' she asked.

Clarice shook her head. 'This is her hunting time. She'll be out there somewhere, looking for a tasty mouse.'

Rue's eyebrows rose. 'A tasty mouse?'

Clarice nodded. 'I think mice would be very tasty to an owl, don't you?'

Rue was silent, thinking that Clarice was undoubtedly right.

'I heard Morghan and Selena talking,' Clarice said. 'She was telling how you'd slipped back and seen the Shining Ones.'

'You know about the Shining Ones?'

Clarice hopped on one leg, then went spinning around on the grass, her hair twirling out so that for a moment, in the dimming light, she looked to Rue like a star.

'The Fae like to dance,' Clarice said, coming to a stop and not at all dizzy. 'I like to dance too.'

'Wait,' Rue said. 'Are you telling me you dance with them? You're not, right?' She shook her head.

Clarice pointed to the woods. 'You can get to the Fair Lands from in there,' she said, then shrugged. 'I do it all the time.'

Rue was shocked to silence, looking at Clarice. 'What?' she said at last.

But Clarice just laughed, then looked sideways at Rue, her face sly and mischievous. 'I can show you, if you like.'

It was said as a statement rather than a question. But there was more than a hint of a challenge in Clarice's voice.

Rue looked away to the trees, where the velvet shadows were reaching up from the ground to tangle in the branches as the twilight deepened.

'Shouldn't you be going to bed, or something?' she asked at last.

Clarice rolled her eyes. 'I often go out into the woods after dark.'

Rue looked at her dubiously. 'Does your mother know about this?'

'Yes,' a voice answered from behind them. 'Her mother does know about this, and doesn't approve, isn't that right, Clarice?' Grainne came up behind her daughter and wrapped her arms around Clarice, dropping a kiss on her pale hair.

'She's not enticing you into the woods when she should be getting ready for bed, is she?' Grainne hugged her daughter tighter and laughed. 'Go on and get ready for bed, sweetheart.'

Clarice grumbled. 'I was going to show her the way to the Fair Lands. It isn't far.'

'It's a very long way,' Grainne corrected, 'and you've got to get to bed. It's a school day tomorrow.'

Clarice scowled. 'I wish you'd home school me,' she said to her mother, then looked over at Rue. 'Are you still at school?'

Rue nodded.

'Do you like it?' Clarice demanded.

'It's all right, I guess,' Rue said. 'I've made some good friends.'

'I haven't,' Clarice said emphatically. 'The kids think I'm weird, and they're right. I am weird, and I'd rather spend my days in the woods.' She looked up at her mother and blinked her fair eyelashes. 'Like Morghan does.'

But Grainne just stroked her daughter's hair and looked at her. 'Even Morghan went to school,' she said.

Clarice rolled her eyes then shook her head. Looking at her, Rue guessed that this was an argument she'd lost before.

Clarice turned her attention back to Rue before she

stomped off to the house. 'Tomorrow, then,' she said. 'I'll show you the way to the Fair Lands tomorrow.'

Rue flicked a glance at Grainne, uncertain what she should say.

But Clarice wasn't waiting for an answer anyway. She turned and grumbled her way back inside.

'Does she really know the way to the Fair Lands?' Rue asked. 'I mean too, is there really a way there?'

She swallowed, thinking of the figures she'd spoken to, that Bryn had spoken to, on the bank of the stream.

'I'm not sure I'd know what to do if I saw them for real,' she said. 'They're really...' She couldn't think of the right word. 'Different,' she said at last, but that wasn't right either. It wasn't enough. 'And a little bit intimidating,' she added and was more satisfied.

Grainne nodded. 'They are at that,' she said, then gazed out at the woods. 'Clarice does know the way there, however.' Her mouth curved in a smile. 'Sometimes I think that girl is half Fae herself.'

Rue frowned. 'Is that possible?'

'I don't know,' Grainne laughed. 'Probably not, except in stories. Clarice's father was just an ordinary man.'

'Well, she's not in the slightest ordinary,' Rue said, then coloured. 'I mean, not in the way she looks, or anything, but the way she is.'

Grainne nodded. 'It's all right,' she said. 'I know what you mean.'

Rue was quiet for a minute, gazing out at the woods, barely able to believe where she was. 'It's like a dream, being here,' she said, her voice low, awed, as the sky turned the colours of apricot and peach.

'Could she really show me the way there?' Rue asked. 'I mean, should I really go with her?'

'I don't know,' Grainne said. 'I think there are more important things for you to do.'

Rue's eyes widened. 'There are?' She shook her head. 'I mean, I know I'm here to learn some stuff, I guess. But I don't know all of what that is, yet.'

'I think – and Selena and Morghan do too – that you're here to learn what your dreams mean.'

For a moment, Rue was confused. 'My dreams?' She shifted, restless suddenly. 'Oh. You mean Bryn?'

'Yes. She wouldn't be reaching out to you like this without a particular reason.'

Rue nodded. 'Selena thought bringing me here would make it easier for me to find out about her.' She paused, then smiled. 'And it has already, hasn't it?'

She looked at Grainne, who seemed very beautiful in the falling night. 'Have you...have you had this sort of experience?' she asked. 'Where someone you once were has, kind of, made contact, I guess?'

Grainne nodded slowly. 'Yes,' she said. And after a moment, added, 'and Morghan too.'

Rue's heart lifted. 'So you know what it's like, then? To have these dreams, and...whatever today was.'

'I call it shifting,' Grainne said.

'Shifting?'

'Yes.' She gestured with her hands. 'When everything suddenly shifts, and you're not where you were a moment ago.' She paused. 'Or who you were.' Her lips curved in a smile. 'It happened a lot to me when I first came here.'

Rue gazed at her. She suddenly had so many questions

she didn't know which to ask first. She shook her head, overwhelmed.

But Grainne looked up at the sky. 'I'd best go say good night to Clarice. Make sure she's tucked in good and tight.'

Rue's mind skipped back to her conversation with Clarice. 'Does she really slip out at night?'

Grainne shook her head and laughed. 'I wouldn't be at all surprised.' She patted Rue on the shoulder then made her way back to the house.

Rue stood on the lawn, alone now, the twilight gathering about her like a thick cloak. She stared at the trees, then bent her head a little, straining to see if she could hear their song. Morghan had said they sang, the trees. That they were the timekeepers of the world.

That in the Otherworld all forests were one forest, and they all knew the history of the worlds, passing it down from elder to sapling in songs that took lifetimes to sing.

Rue shook her head, not knowing what to make of it, but she thought she could probably believe it. There was definitely something about trees, the way they stood planted in one spot long enough to notice everything around them.

Maybe, if she was a Lady of the Forest, like Morghan and Selena, then she would be able to hear the trees' songs too.

She turned and looked up at Hawthorn House. It was hundreds of years old as well.

Rue shook her head then looked around at the garden and lawn. Was this, she wondered, where the buildings had stood that Bryn had lived in?

It could be, she thought. It could be this very spot she stood in. Maybe that's why she'd shifted so easily.

Rue tried out the word on her tongue again, getting used to it.

'Shifted,' she murmured. Then breathed deeply, suddenly excited. She shook her head. Marvellous things were happening.

Someone from hundreds of years ago – no, thousands – was reaching out to her.

Her head swam, and a dizziness spread through her so that she listed slightly to the side.

The world was so different than she'd known, she thought, lowering herself to the ground before she fell. She stretched out, on her back, still feeling as though she were listing to the side, as though she could just fall through the years if she wanted to.

Did she want to? She thought of Bryn, reaching for the small child.

And then she fell.

Shifted.

'AND THEY JUST GAVE HER TO YOU?' WENDYL FROWNED AT Bryn, then looked again at the small child, shaking her head. It didn't look like a Fae child.

The Shining Ones wouldn't give up their own children anyway. They were a long-lived race and bore children only infrequently.

'She is a human child,' Wendyl said.

Bryn nodded, holding herself quiet for the moment. She smiled at the little girl instead, who stood staring up at the circle of priestesses gazing down at her.

'Where did they find her, though?' Awel asked. 'And why

pick her up at all and bring her here?' She looked over at Wendyl and raised an eyebrow. 'They do not usually interfere in such matters, do they?'

'No, they don't,' Wendyl said.

'And who are her parents?' Ula asked. 'Why was she not returned to them, if she needed to be given to anyone?'

Wendyl shook her head, for right now, that seemed a mystery only the Shining Ones and the Goddess herself knew. She looked sharply at Bryn.

'And they did not tell you anything more?'

Bryn shook her head. She'd already been over this, but she understood Wendyl's need to ask again. For it was a mystery.

Bryn thought back to the moment she'd been standing in the stream, enjoying the water's coolness about her legs, and the Fae had appeared, dazzling her sight.

'They said only that she was a foundling and that I should take her in.' Bryn straightened. 'That was everything and all they said. 'We would bid you to take her in, is what they said.' She paused and watched Mother Wendyl. 'We will, won't we?' she asked. 'Take her in?'

'I think we must,' Awel muttered, then raised her voice to speak to them all and Wendyl in particular. 'Do you not also agree that we are bound to do as they have bidden us?'

'It would offend our relationship with the Queen, if we did not,' Gitta, another of the elder priestesses added.

Wendyl sighed and nodded. 'You are right, of course,' she said. 'We will do as they have asked us to, whether there is more to it or not, but simply because they have asked.' She stared at the child, who looked to be a perfectly normal healthy girl, except that she'd not yet said a word. 'Awel, when you next visit the Queen, perhaps you could find a way to ask about the child.'

Awel lowered her head in acknowledgment. 'I will go soon,' she said.

'Where will the girl sleep?' Gitta asked. 'And who will caretake her?' She shook her head. 'We are not equipped here for a child.'

'I shall look after her,' Bryn said, then spoke more strongly. 'It was into my arms that she was placed, and I feel a responsibility.'

'I think it was just that you were there at the stream, and thus easily accessible, Bryn,' Mother Wendyl reproved.

But Bryn gave a small shake of her head and dared to contradict her. 'They could have come with her anywhere, right to our temple, if they pleased.' She paused, then ploughed ahead. 'But they came to the bank of the stream, where I was, and they gave her to me.'

Awel placed a restraining hand on Bryn's shoulder, but Bryn, even under its weight, did not stop.

'I would take care of her,' she said. 'Good care.'

The child stared at her with her wide eyes. She hadn't said a word since Bryn had picked her up and carried her into the Wendyl's hut and Bryn didn't know if the child could talk, but it didn't matter.

Bryn had already given the small girl her heart.

Wendyl looked at her, gaze appraising. 'It will interfere with your learning,' she said, and looked at the older priestesses instead. 'It should be one of you, who has already learnt the path of the Goddess.'

'No,' Bryn cried. 'It needs to be me. Who is to say that this is not the path the Goddess wishes for me?'

Wendyl pursed her lips together at Bryn's words, then looked to Awel. 'What think you?' she asked.

Awel still had her hand on Bryn's shoulder, and she could feel the girl's tense trembling under her touch. She sighed.

'I think we should let Bryn care for the child. She feels strongly about it.' She removed her hand and nodded. 'And she is right. The Shining Ones could have delivered the child to any of us, had they desired. There is no barrier to stop them coming to us here.'

It was true. Elsewhere in these times, the Fae did not enter anymore into the settlements of humans, there being a barrier that had fallen around them, and which the Shining Ones did not bother to cross.

But there was no such barrier about the Forest Grove. The priestesses took care to make sure none fell across the place.

'It is decided then,' Mother Wendyl said and looked at Bryn. 'The child is yours to caretake. She will live here and be taught the path of the Deer Mother, and you will be responsible for her.'

Bryn closed her eyes, then bowed her head, relief flooding through her body even while she heard the gravity in Wendyl's words.

'I shall take good care of her, Mother,' she said, and reached a second time for the child.

16

'HAS THIS EVER HAPPENED TO ANY OF YOU?' RUE ASKED, looking from Selena to Morghan to Ambrose.

They were gathered in Ambrose's house, which Rue had learnt to her bemusement was also named after a tree. She didn't know what a blackthorn looked like, however.

With Rue's question, everyone's gaze turned to Morghan, and Rue, unable to help but notice, looked at her too.

'You've had a past life reach out to you?'

'We all have,' Morghan said, with a disproving frown for Selena and Ambrose.

Rue looked immediately at Selena. 'You have too?'

Selena settled back into the chair and shifted a stack of books slightly with her foot. They were crowded into Ambrose's study, and he'd had to drag in a kitchen chair for them all to fit in the room. Rue was now perched upon it.

'They are our ancestors, just as those of our blood also are,' Selena said. 'And when you learn to walk the worlds with purpose, a guide will often come to you, to teach you – or help you remember, is more like it – and they are often another soul aspect, what we call a past self, usually one who lived during a time, or in a place, when more about the worlds was known.' She glanced at the others. 'Or at least this has been our experience.'

Rue's eyes were wide, and there was that thrumming excitement inside her again. She was coming to recognise it, because it seemed to be almost her permanent state since coming to Wilde Grove.

She thought this place was amazing.

'And this is what happened to you?' she demanded.

Selena nodded. 'Yes. Her name was Isleen. She taught me the paths of the Otherworld; where to go, and where not to go. She reminded me of all I had learnt in previous incarnations.'

Ambrose was nodding. 'We decided that she seemed likely to be a priestess here from the early Middle Ages, did we not?'

Rue's eyes rounded. 'Wilde Grove really has been going on that long?'

Morghan smiled at her. 'It has. I think sometimes it has limped along, and for most of its history, there has only been the one priestess of the old ways, but we have survived. Not only survived, but kept the old ways to the best of our abilities, adding in new stories and understandings as we go along.'

Rue shook her head, trying to take this information in. She turned to Ambrose.

'What about you?' she asked. 'Who was your guide to the...to the Otherworld?'

The question she asked made Rue think of Ebony, and how thrilled by this conversation she be, if she had come. She'd be practically jumping up and down in her seat, Rue thought, and felt a pang of homesickness for her friend.

'Mine?' Ambrose rested his elbows on his desk. He had his notebook open in front of him, and had recorded with growing excitement Rue's account of her shifting from the night before. Much valuable information would be gleaned from her story.

'I was guided in my travels by a lifetime from a completely different land,' Ambrose said. 'A medicine man from the First Nations of Canada – not that he ever told me this; it is only my extrapolation.' Ambrose paused, looking inward for a moment, a smile growing on his face. 'He taught me to dance the sacred hoop and sing love songs to bears.'

'Love songs?' Morghan asked, laughing.

'What else would they be called?' Ambrose asked her, grinning.

But Morghan just shook her head, amused.

Ambrose looked back at Rue, the smile still on his face. 'He was the first of my ancestors to bless me with his teaching. Later, I was joined by a huntress who flew an eagle.' Ambrose shook his head at the memory. 'She taught me to fly, to look and see far.'

'Wait,' Rue said. 'This eagle lady was one of your ancestors?' She shook her head. 'I mean one of your past lives? A woman?'

'We have all been the different genders in our various incarnations,' Ambrose said. He saddened. 'And many different races too, which is why I cannot understand the amount of othering that goes on in this world.'

Rue thought about that for a moment, realising she didn't need to ask Ambrose what he meant by *othering*.

She looked at Morghan and grew bold, straightening in her chair. 'Everyone looked at you, when I first asked if any of you had had your past lives reach out for you.' She took a quick breath. 'How come?'

Ambrose and Selena held their tongues, although they each could have answered the question. But it was Morghan's history, and her decision how much of it she told.

Morghan closed her eyes for a moment, thinking how best to reply. The answer fell into her lap, and she wondered why she hadn't seen the parallels before.

She looked at Rue, gaze gentle. 'Because the priestess with whom I walked, walked with me in all worlds.'

Rue frowned. 'In all worlds?'

'Yes,' Morghan said. 'I did not need to go into trance and travel to the Wildwood or the Otherworld to meet her.'

'You mean?' Rue's frown deepened as she looked for the meaning of what Morghan was saying. 'You mean you were seeing her even when you were just, like walking down the street here?'

'That's exactly what I mean.'

'But how come?'

Yes, Morghan thought. How come? That was the rub, and the point of intersection between her experience and Rue's own.

'Because she wanted something from me,' Morghan said at last, feeling Selena's and Ambrose's gazes upon her.

Rue was silent. Her skin had prickled at Morghan's

words, and she wasn't sure if that was because of her own situation with Bryn, or if it was something else, the sense that this was something big and maybe even terrible in Morghan's history. She opened her mouth to speak, then shook her head.

Which question to ask?

Outside the window of Ambrose's study, the clouds finally let loose their rain, and Rue startled at the sound of it on the roof and window. It had been threatening for the last hour, the wind rising as they breakfasted, bringing rain clouds in its wake.

Finally, she asked.

'What did she want?'

Morghan's lips curved in a small smile. 'That is a long story,' she said. 'But in essence, I think we could safely say that she wanted me to right a wrong she had done during her lifetime.'

Rue leaned back in her chair. Whatever answer she had expected, it hadn't been that. 'I thought they reached out to teach,' she said.

'And the Lady Catrin did so,' Morghan replied. 'After I had done her bidding.'

Rue glanced at the others, but they were silent. 'I don't understand,' she said, looking back at Morghan.

'Like I said, it is a long story, and a very personal one.' Morghan paused. 'But I think we have hit on something that has been niggling around the edges of my mind, now that I consider it.'

'Bryn wanting something,' Selena said, and she nodded. 'I think so, too.'

'But what does she want?' Rue shook her head. 'All that's

been happening so far, is that I've been getting these glimpses of her life.'

It was Ambrose who posed the question. 'We are wondering however, for what purpose?'

'Does there have to be a purpose?' Rue asked.

She looked across the room at Morghan, who nodded.

'I rather think there does, and that there is,' Morghan said.

Rue took this in, swallowed. 'So,' she said. 'How do we find out why I'm seeing Bryn like this?'

Morghan shook her head. 'How long do we have?' she asked Selena.

'Four weeks,' Selena said. 'Well, closer to three, now.'

'That is a very short amount of time,' Morghan said with a sigh, then smiled at Rue. 'How do you fancy a crash course in walking the worlds?'

Rue sank back against the kitchen chair and looked at Selena, who reached out and patted her hand.

On a deep breath, Rue nodded her head.

'I think I came here for that,' she said.

'How are we going to start?' Rue asked as she and Morghan walked through the woods heading back to Hawthorn House. Selena had gone the opposite direction, to visit Teresa.

Morghan looked kindly at her. 'You look apprehensive.'

'I am,' Rue said. 'I've never done this before.'

But Morghan shook her head at that. 'You've definitely done it before. Perhaps not so often in this lifetime, but Bryn would have done it as naturally as breathing.'

'Is that how she was able to see the Shining Ones?'

'It is, indeed.'

The answer made Rue swallow, nervous now that the course of action had been decided upon and she was going to be expected not just to tumble headfirst into new experiences, but to do it deliberately.

'There's no need to worry,' Morghan said, seeing Rue's face pale. 'It's only an extension of what you've already been learning with Selena. She told me that you and your friends made a staff each?'

Rue nodded and ducked her head under a low hanging branch, its twiggy fingers waving a green bunch of oak leaves at her. It was still raining, but here under the cover of the trees, only a drizzle seeped through, and the rain pitter-patted on the trees' crowns instead.

It was dim though, and for the first time since coming to Wilde Grove, Rue thought the place was a bit spooky.

'It's a shame you couldn't bring it with you,' Morghan mused. 'We shall just have to do things another way.'

Rue turned her head quickly, looking at Morghan, who looked as calm and unruffled as she always did.

'Do you ever get afraid?' Rue asked suddenly. She grimaced once the question had slipped out of her mouth. 'I'm sorry,' she said. 'That was a really personal question to ask, and I shouldn't have.'

But Morghan shook her head. 'It is a fair enough question.' She gazed off into the trees, seeing their vibrancy, their deep browns, silvers, greens, and hearing like a lullaby the deep humming of their songs.

'I think, actually, it is one of the most important questions you could ask me.'

Rue's brows shot up. 'You do?'

But Morghan only nodded and touched a hand to the straight, narrow trunk of a tree that stood beside the well-worn path. Her fingers seemed to tingle from the touch.

'I sometimes get afraid – it is hard not to,' Morghan said. 'All animals feel fright, and fear, do they not?'

Rue considered this. 'Like fright or flight, you mean?'

Morghan nodded. 'The thing with humans, though, is that we can invent fear.'

'What?' Rue was dubious. 'What do you mean, we invent it?'

'We are afraid of so much that we needn't be.' Morghan breathed deeply, filling her lungs with the scent of soil and leaf.

'There are some pretty scary things in the world,' Rue said, and looked down at her feet. She wore her boots, wet from the rain and grass. 'When I was looking after Clover by myself, I was afraid most of the time.'

Morghan looked over at her, a shining grief for Rue on her face. 'Yes,' she said. 'I can too well imagine you must have been.'

'But you're saying I invented that fear?'

'How did you deal with it?' Morghan asked instead of answering Rue's question.

Rue looked away and shrugged, then thought about the question properly.

'I just kind of kept going, I guess,' she said and rubbed her hands against the skirt of her dress. 'I just kept doing the next thing.'

Rue blinked in the dimness of the woods. 'And I kept telling myself that it was going to be okay.' A cold drop of rain fell down the back of her neck, its touch making her shiver.

'You instinctively did the exact right thing,' Morghan said. 'You kept yourself there where you were and did whatever came next. It sounds like you didn't let yourself spiral off into stories of what could go wrong.'

Rue considered this, then nodded. 'I couldn't afford to do that,' she said. 'Because then I'd start to panic and that just made everything worse.' She snorted a small laugh. 'Besides,' she said. 'Every time I gave into it, you know, Clover would pull me up.'

'She'd get you to stop?'

'Yeah. She's pretty good at reading my mind. And she'd come and put her hands on my cheeks and look real serious, and she'd tell me it was okay.' Rue paused. 'The only time I saw her get really panicked, was just before we met Selena.'

She trickled off into silence.

For a minute, they walked together along the track, neither speaking. The rain thrummed on the leaves above them, and something moved in the shadows beside the path, a rabbit perhaps.

'She had a book,' Rue said eventually, wanting to tell Morghan what had happened. Wanting to share it with her. 'Clover did. It was just a kids book you know? About a dog running away from a dogcatcher and finding a new home.'

Rue blinked rain from her eyelashes. Or perhaps they were tears.

'She kept the book even though it was supposed to go back to the library, because it had a map in it, you see. And she thought that if we followed the dog's map, then the catcher wouldn't get us.'

Rue hugged herself, wrapping her arms around her middle. They were almost back at the house, and she wanted to finish the story.

Morghan let her talk and listened quietly.

'I tried everything I could think of, to stay away from the dogcatcher – which of course, was a social worker in real life. But I couldn't in the end.' Rue dipped her chin down to her chest and another raindrop slid down the back of her neck.

'Yet you did, didn't you?' Morghan asked. 'You went to see an old friend of your mother's?'

Rue lifted her head and nodded. 'Yeah. I did. When Heather – she's our social worker – was in the other room, I sneaked out with Clover and we took off.' A slow smile blossomed across her face. 'And then we met the Lady.' Rue laughed softly. 'Clover knew Selena was coming by that time, although I had no idea what she was talking about when she was going on about a Lady coming to save us.'

'A Lady. Is that what she called Selena?'

Rue nodded. 'And she was right, wasn't she? Lady of the Grove, and all that.' Shyness suddenly overtook Rue, as she realised she was talking to another Lady of the Grove.

'Yes,' Morghan said, and looked at Rue.

'And now you're here, a priestess of Wilde Grove.'

17

'THANK YOU,' SELENA SAID, AND SAT DOWN AT THE KITCHEN table with a sigh. She looked around at the room that had turned cosy with the rain outside and the plants inside, the sweet smell of the herbs hanging from the ceiling to dry, and the paintings on the wall, done by Teresa's own hand.

'You're welcome,' Teresa said and looked pointedly at her friend. Selena looked very well, she thought, as though things were agreeing with her. Which made her next question even more pertinent. 'Why the sighing?'

Selena looked over at her good friend. 'I sighed?' She blew on her tea, then took a sip. 'I miss your blends,' she said. 'Although Tara and Natalie are coming along very well with their gardening and their herb skills.' She laughed quietly. 'Already they surpass mine.'

She fell silent and sipped her tea, sighing again.

'I'll write some recipes for you to take back with you,' Teresa said, but she had her eyes narrowed. 'Is that what's bothering you? You don't want to go back?' She shook her head, sitting down at the table opposite Selena, where she could watch her expressions properly. 'I wondered if that might happen, with returning here so soon.'

But Selena was already shaking her head. 'I don't know if you'll believe this,' she said, setting down her tea and looking across at Teresa, meeting her eyes so that her friend would know she meant what she said. 'But I'm actually having the opposite problem.'

'The opposite?'

A nod and Selena picked up her cup again for another sip of tea. It was lovely to be sitting back in the kitchen of Ash Cottage. She looked around again at the familiar things. The plants, trailing long stems and leaves from their hanging pots. The shelves of books through in the sitting room, and Teresa's art on the walls, her intricate botanical paintings. Selena had always loved visiting Teresa's home. It was on such a different scale than Hawthorn House.

Sweet. Intimate. Earthy.

'Selena?' Teresa looked at her and wonder dawned on her face. 'You miss it, don't you? You miss your new life back there.'

Selena gave a rueful laugh and dragged her attention back to Teresa. 'I do,' she said. 'I didn't expect to. I thought I'd get back here and feel resistance at having to leave it again.' She shook her head. 'But things have moved on here. Hawthorn House is no longer mine.' She paused for a moment, took another taste of tea, and considered her next words, checking to see if they were true before she said them.

'Even walking the old paths through the trees, I feel, not

as though I've become a stranger, but as though I'm just a visitor now, and that's a very odd thing.'

'You've embedded yourself in your new land,' Teresa said, sitting back and gazing interestedly at Selena. 'That must be unexpected.'

She herself had found the foreign country fascinating, particularly in its flora, but it hadn't for even a minute felt like home. She'd enjoyed her visit but she'd also been very glad to return to Wellsford and Ash Cottage.

'Yes,' Selena said, and she laughed, picking up her teacup. 'Very unexpected. I still miss everything here,' she said. 'But I'm missing it while I'm here, which is rather disorienting.'

'I don't understand.'

Selena shook her head half-heartedly. 'It's nostalgia I feel as I walk through the Grove, as I visit the stone circle, as I wander out to the well at Hawthorn House. Even while I'm doing it, I'm viewing it as part of my life I'm revisiting, rather than living it.'

She took another sip. 'I'm looking forward to going back. I wouldn't have thought it, since all I wanted the first few months there, was to return here.' She lifted her eyebrows. 'And now I'm here, all I want is to go back there.'

Teresa leant forward over the table and looked seriously at Selena. 'I'm glad for you,' she said. 'I'm glad you're feeling this way.'

Selena nodded, her mouth curving into a smile. 'It does make it easier, doesn't it?' Another small sigh. 'And I miss Clover. That girl brings a light of her own to my heart.'

'How is she?' Teresa asked, sitting back, relaxing. 'I'll bet she's missing you too. Why didn't you bring her?'

'She's very well, coming along so well.' Selena smiled. 'I thought about bringing her, but her father didn't want her to leave the country, and he still gets a say in these things. I realised though, that in the end it was good she couldn't come, because her gift is so large, so all-encompassing in who she is, that I was afraid if she were here, she would take up all the oxygen in the air, so to speak, and it's Rue who needs to be here to learn why she is dreaming of this place.'

Teresa considered this, pouring herself another cup from the pot.

'Yes,' she said. 'I can see what you mean. Clover shines so very brightly.' She tapped the rim of her cup with the ring her daughter Becca had given her for Mother's Day years ago, and thought about the weeks she'd spent in New Zealand, helping Selena move into her new life.

'How do you think she's going to manage such a gift, growing up?'

Selena was quick to shake her head. 'I don't know,' she said. 'We've discussed this, Dandy, Damien, Tara, and I.' She paused, frowning slightly. 'On the one hand, we don't want her gift to slowly seep away as she grows, although I'm of the opinion that some of that will happen anyway. But we don't want it to be squelched out of her.'

'But on the other hand...'

Selena nodded. 'On the other hand, how do you live any sort of a normal life, when you are as wide open to the worlds as Clover is?'

'Perhaps she needs to come and live here,' Teresa said. She pursed her lips. 'Look at you and Morghan – barely ever stepping into the run of normal life. She could stay here and be safe.'

Selena was silent for a while before answering. The fire in the old range rustled and outside the rain came down heavier, a thousand tacks against the roof and windows.

'Yes,' she said. 'I've thought about that too.' Selena shook her head. 'But if that's the case, and it's the best place for her, then why wasn't she born here? Why were she and Rue born on the other side of the world. They both, I'm sure – and Rue now is very obviously displaying this fact – have had past lives here, directly here in the Grove, so why begin this incarnation so very far away?'

Teresa shook her head slowly. It was a good question, and one she hadn't considered. 'I don't know.'

But Selena was thinking about the vision the Queen had shown her and Morghan. Of the pinpricks of light scattered over the earth.

The beacons.

The lights in the darkness.

Then, for the first time, she wondered how many others there were, other children like Clover and Rue.

The question, surprisingly, made her feel uneasy.

Selena shook her head, dragged her attention back to answering Teresa's question.

'We're going to take it one day at a time,' she said, the eyes of her mind still gazing at the spread of lights, of beacons. 'One day at a time, and make adjustments as we go along, as the need becomes necessary.'

Teresa nodded. She had no doubt that Selena would find the right course of action.

'Follow the path,' she murmured, smiling at her friend.

'Yes,' Selena agreed. 'The path that becomes clear only as you walk it.'

18

DANDY GOT UP EARLY, ONLY TO FIND OUT THAT TARA AND Clover were already in the kitchen making pancakes, while Ebony sat at the table sucking down a mug of coffee.

'What are you doing here?' Dandy asked.

Ebony put the cup down and shook her head. 'Came to say thanks,' she said.

'Thanks?' Dandy smiled at Clover, who was on a stool beside Tara, clutching a spatula and taking the breakfast making very seriously. Dandy slid into a chair at the table and raised her eyebrows at Ebony.

'Yep.' Ebony nodded vigorously. 'You have my gratitude for life,' she said. 'Probably even beyond this lifetime. For getting me the job at Beacon.'

'You pretty much inserted yourself into that job,' Dandy said, but she was smiling.

'I did, yes,' Ebony agreed. 'Because my mother didn't raise any fools, and that job and I are a match made in heaven.' Ebony grew serious and leaned forward over the table.

'But you telling Meg that I was reliable and all that. It made the difference.'

Tara brought the plate of pancakes over and slid a mug of tea in front of Dandy. She nodded at Ebony.

'You're really enjoying it, then?'

Clover climbed onto a chair at the table and Tara put a pancake on Clover's plate.

'I absolutely love it,' Ebony said, snagging herself one of the pancakes. Tara had made plenty.

'Absolutely love what?' Damien asked, coming into the kitchen and stopping to sniff appreciatively. 'What is this deliciousness I smell?'

'Pancakes,' Clover said, managing a smile. 'Tara an' I made 'em.'

Damien dropped a kiss on the top of Clover's head and pretended to swipe the pancake off Clover's plate.

'This one must be mine, then.'

Clover giggled. 'Tha' one's mine,' she said. 'Yours is over there.'

'Look at that,' Damien said, glad that he'd gotten Clover to laugh. She was still a little more pale than usual. 'So it is!' He went over to make himself a coffee.

'So,' he said. 'Who absolutely loves what?'

'Ebony is enjoying her job at Beacon,' Dandy said, and patted Ebony's hand across the table.

'Yeah? That a holiday job?' Damien asked.

Ebony shook her head. 'I'm trying to convince Meg, the owner, to take me on full time.'

Everyone looked at Ebony but Clover, who was slicing up her pancake into strips, a small frown back on her face.

Ebony shrugged. 'What?'

'What?' Tara asked. 'Exactly. What about school?'

'Yeah, exactly,' Ebony asked. 'What about it?' She sniffed and squirted some maple syrup onto the pancake on her plate. 'You do realise they don't teach the stuff I need to know at school, right?'

'But you're only 15,' Tara said, trying again.

Ebony shook her head. '16. I turned 16 last month. Which means I can leave if I have a job to go to.' She rolled up the pancake and sliced expertly into it before lifting her head and nodding. 'And that's what I'm going to do.'

'Your mum's okay with that?' Damien asked, then looked at Dandy. 'What do you say about it?'

Dandy shook her head. 'I'm no expert,' she said. 'I left school at 14.'

'14?' Tara's eyes widened. 'How did you do that?'

Dandy laughed. 'It was quite a few years ago. Things were different then. I left to help my mum and dad on the farm. We grew vegetables for market.'

'See,' Ebony said, jabbing at the air with her fork for punctuation. 'If there's a good reason, it's a good thing.' She set her fork down. 'I sat and passed my first level of exams last year and now I have a job that's going to teach me a lot more of the specialised stuff I need to know than school can.'

Dandy sipped her tea, looking over the rim at Ebony. 'That reminds me,' she said. 'We need to do another tarot lesson, if you still want to.'

Ebony grinned. 'You bet I do.'

There was a knock at the door, and Dandy, Tara, and Damien went silent, looking in the direction of the back door.

'It's a bit early, isn't it?' Dandy said at last in a low voice.

Everyone looked at Clover, who had frozen, head tucked down, staring at the half-eaten pancake on her plate.

Tara glanced at the kitchen clock. 'Half an hour early,' she said, and her voice was only a whisper. She cleared her throat.

'I'll answer it,' Damien said, but still he paused a moment before moving to the door.

Clover slid off her chair and ran from the room.

'What's going on?' Ebony asked.

But Dandy just shook her head. 'Go see if Clover's all right, will you?'

Ebony nodded wordlessly and went to find Clover.

'Hey little Bee,' she said, when she discovered Clover upstairs on her bed, holding her pillow in front of her like it was a shield. 'Clover, what's wrong?'

There were two high spots of colour in Clover's cheeks, and she shook her head, her mouth turned down at the corners.

'I want S'lena an' Rue,' she said.

Ebony sat down on the bed and pulled Clover into her arms. 'What's going on?' she asked, straining her ears to catch any sounds from below.

But the bedroom was too far away from the kitchen and the only thing she heard was Clover's hitching breath.

Clover shook her head, her face tucked against Ebony's chest.

'It's Josh's daddy at the door,' she said.

'Josh's daddy?' For a moment, Ebony couldn't place who Josh was, and then she realised. 'Oh, Josh is your friend, isn't he? He comes to play here with you.'

Clover sniffed and nodded.

'Well,' Ebony said. 'What's wrong with that, then? Has Josh been mean to you?'

This time Clover shook her head and when she lifted her face to look up at Ebony, her cheeks were wet with tears.

'His mama got hurt,' she said, and a big sob burst out of her.

Ebony tightened her arms around Clover. 'Hey there, it's okay. You're okay. Everything's going to be all right.'

But Clover kept shaking her head as she cried. 'She got hurt bad, Eb'ny. Real bad.'

That sounded alarming. Ebony looked toward the door, wishing she could see what was going on downstairs in the kitchen.

'What happened to her?' she asked, rocking Clover on her lap now.

'I don' know.' Clover snaked an arm out and touched the top of her head. 'It's all red here,' she said, then buried her face in Ebony's shirt and howled again.

'Hey, Clover, honey,' Ebony said. 'She's going to be okay – I bet she is. Come on, it's going to be okay.'

But Clover, filled with a red and black horror she didn't know how to contain or deal with, howled louder, and wished she was with Rue and Selena.

'I wan' S'lena!' she screamed. 'S'lena!

She scrunched her eyes shut and screamed again, this time in her head, reaching out for Selena the way she'd done once before, back when Selena was just the Lady Clover had known was searching for them.

She needed Selena now.

Selena would know what to do.

The bedroom door opened, and Tara came in, eyes wide. 'What's happening?'

'She won't stop crying,' Ebony said, bewildered. 'What's going on?'

But Tara just shook her head, mouth in a grim line, and took Clover, who wrapped her legs and arms around her and clung to her like a monkey.

'She was screaming for Selena,' Ebony said.

Tara nodded, unsurprised. 'I've got her,' she said to Ebony. 'Let me see if I can calm her down.' Clover was hot and damp against her.

'Perhaps you should call Selena,' Ebony said.

Clover lifted her head and spoke between sobs. 'I called,' she said. 'I called her like I did before.'

Tara frowned, and then the big telephone bell rang, and her eyes widened. She and Ebony stared at each other.

'That's S'lena,' Clover said and squirmed in Tara's arms. 'Wanna talk to her.'

Tara kissed Clover's damp forehead and nodded. She absolutely believed that Clover was right. 'Let's go talk to her, then,' she said.

Ebony looked askance as they left the room and went downstairs.

'What's going on?' she hissed.

But Tara just shook her head. 'In a minute, okay?'

Ebony had to be satisfied with that, and they pushed into the kitchen.

Dandy stood holding the phone. 'Selena wants to talk to Clover.'

Tara took the cordless handset and Clover grasped it.

'S'lena?' she said and coughed a sob into the phone. 'S'lena, you gotta come home.'

Ebony stood shaking her head and frowned a question at Dandy.

Dandy nodded and held up a finger. Wait.

Ebony looked over at Damien who was holding a little boy in his arms. Josh.

It was Josh, Ebony thought. Josh, whose mummy had been hurt real bad. Unthinkingly, Ebony touched her own head where Clover had touched hers. All red there, she'd said.

Had she meant red with blood?

Ebony sidled over to Damien. Clover's crying had quietened to hitching sobs and she was listening to whatever Selena was saying to her.

'Is he all right?' Ebony asked Damien, nodding at the baby in his arms.

'Yeah,' Damien said in a low voice, and bounced Josh a little. 'He's okay, just a bit tired, apparently.'

Ebony peered at Josh's face. 'He looks sad, if you ask me.'

Clover nodded into the phone. 'Kay,' she said. 'I love you, S'lena.' She nodded again and held out the phone to Dandy. 'S'lena wanna talk to you.'

Dandy took the phone and sank down onto a chair. 'Selena,' she said into the handset.

'Come on,' Tara said. 'Let's get these two into the playroom and busy.' She checked the time. 'Danielle will be getting here soon.' Her face fell. 'Oh, and another little one is starting today. Min. She won't be here until 10, however. A half day to start with.' Tara stopped talking. She knew she was babbling. Dandy, on the phone, wasn't saying much, but in a moment, she would be telling Selena what had happened, and Tara didn't think Clover needed to hear Dandy talking about her.

'You going to be all right, Tara?' Damien asked. 'Shall I call into work and say I can't make it today?' He carried Josh into the room they'd set up as the playroom. It was the big room across from the one they used as the living room.

Tara was shaking her head. 'No,' she said. 'You're needed at work, and Dandy and I will be fine here.' She sat down on the couch and looked at Clover. 'You want to do some drawing, sweetheart?'

Clover thought about it. 'No,' she said, her voice very small and sad, even to her own ears. 'I wanna make a nest and watch 'Tilda.'

Whenever she was sad, Rue made a nest for her with blankets and pillows, and they watched movies.

Rue was at Wilde Grove now, but Clover could still have her nest. And Selena, she thought, climbing off Tara's lap and curling up on the couch clutching a cushion as a pillow, said she'd see if she could come home soon.

Tara patted Clover's back and pulled down one of the throws from the back of the couch, tucking her in.

Usually, even though there was a television and video player in the room, Tara didn't let them watch anything during the day care hours. But, glancing first at Damien who was still holding Josh, she shrugged helplessly and went to plug in the video of Matilda.

Just this once wouldn't hurt.

Josh was leaning out of Damien's arms now, and Damien put him down on the couch, at the other end to Clover, and tucked him in too.

'I think they're both going to watch the movie,' he said.

Tara looked at the two children, who didn't glance back at her, their gazes fastened to the TV screen, and nodded.

She touched Damien on the arm, and he put his arm around her and squeezed her briefly.

'Shall we go and see what Selena had to say?'

19

'WHAT DID SHE SAY?' TARA ASKED, BURSTING BACK INTO THE kitchen with Damien on her heels.

Dandy shook her head. 'She's torn. Rue really needs to be in Wilde Grove, and Clover really wants her here.'

'We can take care of Clover though, can't we?' Damien asked.

'She wants Selena.' Tara covered her face with her hands then peered between them. 'This is a nightmare,' she said.

'What's going on?' Ebony demanded.

Tara stared at Ebony for a moment before blinking and shaking her head. 'That's a good question.'

Ebony touched her hair again. 'Clover said Josh's mum has been badly hurt and that there's red stuff on her head.'

Dandy lowered herself stiffly to a chair. 'Blood,' she said and looked at the others. 'Oh my Goddess, and she's such a nice young woman too. I did a reading for her, remember?'

Dandy shook her head. 'Just the other day.' She looked across at Ebony. 'When?'

'Monday morning,' Ebony said.

'We haven't seen her since yesterday morning,' Tara said. She looked at Ebony. 'She didn't come to pick up Josh in the afternoon. I had to call Josh's father and he finally came and got him.'

There was silence in the kitchen, except for the faint sounds of Matilda playing in the other room.

'So,' Ebony said. 'Josh's dad did something to his mum?'

'We don't know that,' Damien said, then looked at the time. 'Shit,' he said. 'I have to get going.' He tapped his fingers on his thigh. 'Listen, I'm going to drive past his house later, see if anything looks amiss.'

'Do you know where he lives?' Dandy asked.

'Nope, but you do, right?' He looked at Tara who nodded.

'See if you can look in the windows,' Ebony said. 'Look for signs that there was a struggle or something.'

'If he did anything, it would have happened yesterday,' Dandy said. 'He would have tidied up.'

Ebony narrowed her eyes. 'Look to see if any place looks extra clean, then. Bits of carpet or rugs missing.' She paused. 'And check the garden too, see if there's newly turned soil under the dahlias or something.'

'Ebony!' Tara was horrified.

But Ebony shook her head, unrepentant. 'We think he did something to her, don't we?'

'Maybe we do need Selena,' Damien said. 'Remember how she knew that guy was about to break into Natalie's place?'

Tara rubbed her hands together, then wrapped her arms around her waist. 'There has to be a reasonable explanation for this,' she said.

'Did you ask where Josh's mum was when you saw his dad this morning?' Ebony asked.

'Yes.' Tara nodded. 'He said she had gone to spend a few days with her sister, who has come down with something.'

'Which I highly doubt is true,' Dandy said with a sigh.

'Of course it's not true,' Ebony said with conviction. 'Remember what Clover said. She said Josh's mum has been hurt bad.'

'Rachel told me that her close family is still Exclusive Brethren,' Dandy said. 'So, she wouldn't have gone to see her sister; she wouldn't be allowed to.'

Damien glanced at the clock again and winced. He was cutting it fine to get to work on time. 'What's Exclusive Brethren?'

Ebony answered. 'It's a bunch of super conservative Christians, who don't let the women cut their hair.'

'They're a lot more than that,' Dandy added. 'They don't associate with what they call worldly things or people. They don't have televisions or computers or even radios.'

Damien scratched his head. 'Never heard of them,' he said. 'But they sound weird.' He picked up his keys from the bowl on the sideboard. 'I've got to get to work,' he said, then paused. 'You should call the police.'

'And tell them what?' Tara asked, still hugging herself.

'What you suspect.'

'They won't believe us,' Tara replied, shaking her head but moving finally, towards the electric jug. She needed another cup of tea. Something soothing this time. And then she needed to check on the kids.

But Damien was nodding. 'The one who questioned Natalie that night. She might.'

Dandy considered this. 'She could. I told her that Selena had dreamt what was happening at Natalie's, and she didn't dismiss it outright.'

'Good,' Damien said. 'Give her a call, and I'll cruise by this joker's place and have a look around.'

Ebony rose reluctantly from the table. 'Drop me off in town?' she asked Damien, then looked at the others. 'I'll come back after work to see what's happening.'

'I've got to check on the children,' Tara said after she'd listened to Damien's car start up and turn down the driveway. She looked at Dandy. 'Do you think we ought to call the police?'

Dandy thought about it for a minute, remembering the cards she'd drawn for Rachel.

Rachel, she thought, where are you? Then she sighed. She had been heartened by the cards, on the whole, and Rachel had blushed heavily through some of the reading although she'd made little comment on the cards that made her cheeks redden the most.

'I do,' Dandy said at last. 'I think we should.' She nodded at Tara. 'I'll find Sandy Rice's details and call her.'

Tara hesitated in the doorway, then nodded, and walked to the playroom.

Josh was down on the rug, his back to the TV as he played with a toy digger, making construction noises as he drove it back and forth. Tara found a smile for him, and sat down next to Clover, who was still cocooned in the blanket, only her small face peeking out.

'I watching 'Tilda,' Clover said.

'I can see that,' Tara said, and stroked Clover's curls. 'Are you feeling any better?'

Clover shook her head. 'Is S'lena comin'?'

'She's going to talk to Rue and see.'

Clover's blue eyes stared at the television screen, where Miss Honey was teaching the children.

But Clover wasn't thinking about Matilda, or Miss Honey, or even Miss Trunchbull anymore. She was frowning. 'Rue gotta stay there,' she said, then sat up and looked at Tara seriously. 'Rue gotta find Bryn and see.'

'Who's Bryn?'

Clover shook her head. 'She's Rue.'

'I don't understand.' Tara's head spun.

But Clover just gazed into the space between them, then sighed. She put her hand on Tara's knee, her small fingers splayed.

'Can S'lena come home?' she asked. Her face crumpled. 'Josh's mama keep callin' but I 'fraid to go without S'lena.'

A chill shivered through Tara's body. While she didn't know exactly what Clover was talking about, she thought she could make a pretty good guess. She took Clover by the shoulders and looked seriously at her.

'You mustn't go without Selena, do you hear me, sweetheart?' Tara shook her head. 'Not without Selena. You must wait for her.'

Clover's eyes filled with tears, and she squeezed them shut. 'Don' wanna go without S'lena. Josh's mama look bad. She hurt.'

The hairs on Tara's arms stood up. 'Is she...is she still alive?'

Clover's face crumpled even more. 'Don' know,' she whispered.

Tara gathered Clover up into her arms and rocked her there, her gaze landing on Josh, who was sitting now with the truck on his lap, a lonely little figure, head bent, hunched over on the rug.

'Josh, sweetie,' Tara said, tears filling her eyes. 'Come and have a hug too.'

Josh looked up, then got to his feet and climbed on the couch. Tara put an arm around him and drew him close.

DAMIEN HAD AN HOUR BEFORE HIS GUY WOULD BE DUE OUT OF the meeting and ready to go to the next place. Usually, Damien would sit in the car and wait, but this time he started the car again and pulled out onto the road. The guy wouldn't miss him, as long as he was back within the hour.

Tara had texted him Mike Manners' address and Damien knew exactly where it was. It would only take about ten minutes to get there. Less, now that the traffic was lighter, everyone at work already.

Damien turned into the residential street and scanned the mailboxes as he cruised past, looking for number 14. It was an old villa, and Damien brought the car to a halt on the street outside it. He paused with his hands still on the wheel, then turned the ignition off.

There was a sign on the lawn, advertising a tax consultancy business. That was awkward, he thought. Mike Manners worked from home.

For a minute, he thought about rocking up to the door and pretending he needed some help with his taxes or something, but Damien shook his head right after he'd had the thought.

He'd been in the kitchen that morning when Mike had dropped little Josh off. He'd stood beside Tara when she'd asked the man where his wife was.

Mike would recognise him for sure.

Perhaps he wasn't home, though. There was no car in the driveway. Damien reached for his phone and punched in the number on the sign.

It rang then went through to an answering machine and a humourless grin spread across Damien's face.

He wasn't there. Mr Mike Manners, small business tax consultant, wasn't home.

Getting out of the car, Damien glanced around the neighbourhood, but everything was quiet. And there were big hedges down the sides of the Manners property, so their neighbours couldn't see over.

Someone, Damien thought, liked their privacy.

He closed the door to his car and walked up the path to the house, trying to look nonchalant, like he had every reason to be there.

Instead of going to the front door, however, Damien stepped off the path and pushed down the side of the house, around to the back.

It was a dim morning, threatening rain, but none of the house lights were on. Another mark for Josh's father not being home. Damien leaned across the narrow strip of garden at the back of the house and peered in the window.

It was the kitchen, and there was a pile of dirty dishes in

the sink, and a bowl of half-eaten cereal on the highchair next to the small table. Crumbs littered the kitchen bench.

Damien pursed his lips. Other than the dishes and crumbs, there was no sign that anything had happened to Rachel Manners.

Then Damien spied something that had him squinting at it to make sure of what he was seeing. He stared at it for a solid minute, then stood back up and jogged around the house and down the path to his car.

He called home, but the phone was giving an engaged signal. Damien nodded. That was all right, he thought. He'd drive back to the office building where his guy was having his meeting, and he'd call the house again when he got there. He knew Tara only bothered with her mobile when she was going out. She didn't carry it around the house with her.

Parked back in the same spot he'd left thirty-five minutes ago, Damien unbuckled his seat belt and reached for his phone, pressing the numbers in for the house phone at home.

This time, Dandy answered.

'Hey,' Damien said. 'It's me. I went by his house.'

After five minutes, he pressed end, put the phone down and leaned back in his seat, feigning relaxation. In reality, every muscle was tense, all nerve endings alive and humming.

But there was nothing he could do. Nothing else, he thought, nodding to himself. Dandy had called the police, and she'd be speaking to them soon.

Damien looked out his rear-view mirror, but his client wasn't coming out of the office building yet.

There was nothing to do but wait.

And be very glad he'd gone to the Manners' house to look through the windows.

20

SANDY AND HER PARTNER, A NEW CONSTABLE ON THE SQUAD, sat uncomfortably at the kitchen table trying to make sense of the story they were being told.

'Wait,' she said. 'So, you've no real reason to think something has happened, you're just worried for...why are you worried?'

Dandy scowled. 'But we do have reason,' she said. 'Mike Manners told us this morning that Rachel had gone to her sister's for a few days.'

Sandy didn't have to check her notes. 'Because her sister isn't well.'

'That's right – but you see, Rachel couldn't have gone to her sister, because she's been disowned by her family.'

This made Sandy squint. 'Her sister has been disowned by her family?'

'No.' Dandy shook her head impatiently. 'Rachel has been disowned. Her family is Exclusive Brethren, and they disowned her when she left.'

Constable Chris Boyles frowned. He didn't know why Sandy was bothering with this. These women had nothing to go on.

'I didn't think we had any Brethren in Dunedin,' he said. 'Don't they stick to small towns?'

Dandy shrugged. 'I wouldn't know. Rachel moved down here to live with her cousin when she left.'

'Where did she used to live?' Chris asked. His notebook lay unopened in his hand. He glanced up at the woman who was bouncing a sad-looking kid on her hip. She was a looker, he thought, and wondered about his chances if he asked her out.

'I don't know,' Dandy said, also glancing at Tara, who shrugged helplessly. 'We don't know.'

'What about the handbag?' Tara asked. 'Rachel's handbag?'

Sandy shook her head slowly and folded her own note-book closed. 'It could be a spare,' she said. 'I have three bags I use regularly and put my stuff in whatever one I'm taking out that day with me.' She ignored Chris's smirking glance.

Tara nodded, deflated. They'd thought, she and Dandy and Damien, that they were really onto something. That they had proof that something had happened. Something other than what Mike Manners had said that morning. But, she conceded, Sandy's argument rang true.

'I have a few as well,' she admitted.

Dandy was still shaking her head. 'I still think you need to follow up on it,' she said. 'Just go there and ask for the sister's address.'

'What would I say for just cause?' Sandy asked. She sighed. 'Look. I see your point of view, just. But this kiddie's mother being late to pick him up, then his daddy coming instead, and again the next morning to drop him off, saying his wife's gone to visit her sister – there really isn't anything in that to give us a reason to go and bother him.'

Tara and Dandy looked at each other. When it was put like that, Sandy was right. There was nothing to it.

'But she can't be visiting her sister,' Dandy repeated stubbornly.

'How can we be sure?' Sandy said. 'She left the Brethren, perhaps a sister did too. Or maybe she isn't visiting her sister. Maybe she's gone somewhere else instead, and her husband, for whatever reason, doesn't feel comfortable telling his babysitter all the wheres and whys of it.'

She stood up, and Chris followed suit, glancing in Tara's direction again and wondering how he could possibly slip in an invitation out for a drink. Reluctantly, he decided there was no way he could do it, and trailed Sandy to the door.

'Give us a bell if something real happens,' he said.

'I've got to get back to the kids,' Tara said when the door was closed on the police officers. 'That was a waste of time.' She shook her head. 'Sandy was right, we've nothing to go on, not really.'

Dandy got up and took the cups to the kitchen. 'Not when we didn't tell her about the way Clover's been acting.'

Tara shook her head. 'I just couldn't, not with that man there. He already thought we were a pair of hysterical females.'

Dandy agreed with the assessment. She set the crockery in the sink and put her hand on the tap.

'Just a moment,' she said, stopping Tara. 'What did

Clover say about Rachel?'

Tara shook her head. 'Which time?' she asked. Josh had his head resting against Tara's chest and she covered his other ear as if she didn't want him to hear what they were talking about. She had no idea how much of it he would understand.

'The last time,' Dandy said.

Tara gazed around the kitchen. She'd gone to a lot of effort to make it the space she wanted. The potted plants were growing thick and luscious now, and there was the big dresser they'd kept from the previous owner, filled with jars and containers of herbs and concoctions, all of which she'd made with her own two hands.

Her gaze drifted to the urn by the fireplace, into which all of them had put something on the last turn of the seasons. Their wishes and dreams for the future, mostly.

So far, she thought, pressing her lips together, the dream and the reality weren't lining up.

'She said that...' Tara didn't want to say Rachel's name out loud, fearing that Josh, in her arms, would recognise it. 'That she was hurt bad.'

She paused, and even just thinking about what else Clover had said made her blood icy in her veins. 'And that she keeps calling, but Clover's afraid to go to her without Selena.' Tara paused. 'I asked if she was...still alive, and Clover said she didn't know.'

Dandy was shaking her head before Tara had even finished. 'I wish I'd been able to tell Selena that, but we'd finished talking by then.'

'Is she going to come back, do you think?'

'I don't know,' Dandy replied. 'How is she supposed to

decide? When both girls need her?'

Tara was quiet for a moment, listening to her thoughts and the low drone of the fridge.

'I don't think you, Damien, and I can do what Clover needs, in this situation,' she said at last. 'I don't think any of us know how; not well enough.'

Dandy sighed. She'd come to the same conclusion.

'I'll call Selena and tell her,' she said.

RUE STOOD UP. IT WAS RAINING HARD OUTSIDE NOW, THE spring storm clattering against the roof. Someone had lit the fire, and it gave the dim afternoon a pleasant, cosy look.

'We have to go back,' she said. 'I'll pack my things.'

But Selena shook her head and held up a restraining hand. 'Let's talk about this a minute more,' she said, and glanced at Morghan, who nodded slightly.

They'd already had a discussion on the matter. Come tentatively to a conclusion.

Rue sat abruptly back down and looked confusedly at Selena. 'What's there to talk about?' she asked. 'If Clover needs us?'

'We need to talk about what you need, Rue,' Grainne said gently from the seat beside her.

Rue looked at her, frowning. She shook her head. 'What do you mean, what I need?'

Shifting her weight on her feet, Morghan spoke from where she leaned against the window. 'We want you to consider the necessity of staying here and following the thread of what has been happening regarding Bryn.'

Rue didn't speak at once, and when she did, it was

slowly, understanding dawning. She looked at Morghan, then over at Selena, sitting opposite.

'You want me to stay here?' she asked.

'I want you to consider it,' Selena said.

'But Clover...'

Selena nodded, understanding. 'Clover will be all right. I will take care of her.'

'But she's my sister. I've always looked after her.'

'I know,' Selena said. 'In a little while, we'll call home, and you can speak to Clover yourself. But Tara has told me that Clover said you need to stay here.'

'But we have to go home if she's in trouble.'

'I will go,' Selena said, leaning forward and speaking earnestly. 'But perhaps you need to stay here and learn what Bryn has to tell you.'

Rue sat back, shaking her head slightly, thinking hard. 'Clover really said I should stay here?'

'That is what Tara told me.' Selena had spoken to them again, Tara and Dandy taking turns on the phone to speak with her.

'But Clover needs you?' Rue demanded.

'She's asking for me, yes.'

'But I've always taken care of her,' Rue repeated.

Grainne put her hand on Rue's arm. 'You have,' she said, her voice kind. 'But it's not just you anymore. Clover has a whole family to turn to now.'

'I feel like it should still be me,' Rue said stubbornly.

Morghan walked over and sat down. 'Selena and I feel strongly that you need to continue the work you've begun here.'

Rue's thoughts were a confused swirl. On the one hand,

she'd always looked after Clover. Always. Clover had counted on her.

But now there was everyone else looking out for Clover as well. She blinked at Selena. Selena who was willing to fly back and make sure Clover was okay.

'I should stay here without you?' she asked her.

'Yes. There's too much for you to learn, I think,' Selena said. 'And according to Tara, Clover seems to think so too.'

Rue would need to hear Clover say that herself to truly believe it. Her gaze turned to Morghan, and she felt a rush of longing to continue learning from her. They'd only just begun.

It had only been yesterday morning that they'd decided that she needed a crash course in walking the worlds.

Rue shook her head. 'What else did Clover say?'

Selena paused only a moment before replying. She shifted in the armchair and closed her eyes, letting the heat of the fire warm her skin.

'She said that Josh's mother is calling her, but she's afraid to go to her without me.'

The words sent a shiver of fright through Rue. 'What does she mean, go to her?'

Selena sighed. 'I think she means that something terrible has happened to Josh's mum, and that she is hurt and needs help, that her soul, or a shard of it is stuck somewhere.' She looked at Morghan in the chair beside her. 'Do you agree?'

'That would be my thought, with the little we know.'

Selena looked back at Rue. 'I could go and find Josh's mum spirit from here.' She pursed her lips and considered it. 'Probably,' she said. 'But it would be easier if I were there.'

Rue rubbed her face. 'Clover needs you there. She doesn't get frightened very often.'

It was true. The most frightened Rue had ever seen Clover was when the dogcatchers were after them.

'Do you think Josh's mum is dead?' she asked.

'I don't know,' Selena said quickly. 'But Tara and Dandy are worried about her.'

'And I should stay here?' Rue asked again.

'We'd make sure you're all right here,' Grainne said, speaking up. 'And you can call home every day.'

Rue nodded. Her gaze drifted back to Morghan. 'You really think I need to learn what Bryn wants?'

'I do,' Morghan replied.

Rue turned to Selena again. 'But couldn't you teach me at home?'

'Remember why we came here?' Selena said. 'This is where Bryn walked. It will be easier for you to forge that link with her if you are here.' She smiled at Morghan. 'And Morghan has a lot of experience in this particular area. She would be your best guide.'

Rue looked at Morghan, but Morghan's gaze was on Grainne before she turned and nodded at Rue.

'Selena's right,' she said. 'The link will be stronger here if you're walking the same land. It can be done otherwise if it were necessary, but this will make it easier, particularly when you have no experience.'

Rue dropped her chin and closed her eyes, a battle going on inside her.

Finally, she looked at Selena.

'I can call every day?'

21

THAT NIGHT, RUE DREAMT THAT CLOVER CAME AND SLIPPED under the covers beside her.

'Have you seen the white dragon yet, Bryn?' Clover asked.

Rue turned her dreaming eyes to her sister and gazed at her. Clover's curls glowed like a halo around her head in the moonlight from the window where the curtains were drawn to let the night look in.

'I'm Rue,' she said, then frowned. 'What dragon?'

'The white dragon,' Clover whispered. 'Close your eyes, I show ya.'

Rue knew she was dreaming, that her eyes were already closed. She must be dreaming, for Clover was 18 thousand kilometres away.

But she closed her eyes anyway and felt Clover's small, cool hand against her eyelids.

'There,' Clover whispered. 'Do you see him now?'

Rue shuddered under Clover's hand and the world tilted sideways.

Rue shook her head, for she was no longer in her bed, but standing on the top of a round hill, Clover at her side, holding her hand. Beneath them, like a monk's tonsure, was a ring of trees, but that wasn't what Rue was looking at.

What she couldn't take her eyes from.

'It's a dragon,' she breathed.

'Is our dragon,' Clover said.

It was the most beautiful thing Rue thought she'd ever seen. The night sky was a swirl of stars above it, and it seemed to gleam, its white scales and feathers like mother of pearl in the ancient light of the stars.

It lay, head resting on the ground, eyes closed as though it slept, and its tail curved protectively around its body. Clover tugged on Rue's hand.

'Come on,' she said.

Rue stumbled after her, heart thudding loudly in her chest. She pressed a hand to it, as if afraid it would break through her ribs.

'What are we doing?' she hissed at Clover.

But Clover just turned and looked at her. 'This is my friend,' she said. 'Our friend.'

Rue shook her head. She didn't have any dragons as friends.

But then she remembered that she was dreaming, and her chest loosened, and her breathing came easier again. She followed Clover willingly now, knowing she was only dreaming.

Clover dropped a kiss on the beast's great long snout and grinned at Rue, before tugging her into the protective curve of the dragon's tail and slipping down to sit with her back against its side.

'Sometimes I come here and sleep,' she said.

Rue sank down to the soft grass and touched a hand tentatively to the great white wall that was the dragon's side.

'It's warm,' she said in surprise, for she had expected the gleaming scales to be cold to her touch. She put her fingers to a spray of feathers that grew under a scale and stroked it lightly. They were silken, like a bird's.

The dragon shifted slightly, and Rue froze, but it settled again, its tail pinning them in.

But Clover wasn't worried. Rue looked at her and found she was asleep, tucked against the warm side of the dragon, curls like spun gold against its white scales.

Gingerly, Rue leaned back against the dragon's bulk, and looked up at the sky. The Milky Way snaked overhead, and Rue followed it with her eyes.

Another dragon, she thought, in flight through the sky.

RUE WOKE DAZED IN HER BED, BLINKING IN THE EARLY morning light. Her room had a window facing east, and the first touch of the rising sun crept through the uncurtained glass to tease her awake.

She looked down at the bed, remembering her dream, how Clover had climbed in beside her.

And then what? Rue closed her eyes, feeling her sleep-gummed lashes stick together.

And then the dragon, that was what.

They'd gone to sleep, she thought, both of them. Lying against the huge side of a white dragon.

But she didn't know what it meant.

Rue looked at her journal on the bedside table and knew she ought to write the dream down, while it was fresh in her mind, but she shook her head, looking at the clock and seeing the time.

Besides, she didn't think she'd forget it. Not this one.

'It felt so real,' she murmured, and pushed back the blankets, setting her bare feet on the rug beside the bed and reaching for her clothes to pull on. She'd write down the dream later. She dressed, then picked up the holey stone she'd found with Ebony and Suze and Sophie, that day on the beach.

She pressed it hard against her palm, then held it up and looked through it, out the window.

She saw trees and sky, and in her imagination, a great white dragon leaving a trail of stars as it flew.

Lowering the stone, Rue dropped its cord around her neck and let the stone lie warming against her skin between her breasts.

It was time to go and greet the day with Selena and Morghan, because later, after breakfast, Ambrose and Teresa would be driving Selena back to the airport.

SELENA HELD HER FACE TO THE RISING SUN. SHE COULD FEEL Rue next to her, the uncertain swirl of her feelings, yet when she glanced at her, Rue's face was pale but composed, her expression clear and smooth. Selena smiled to herself and when she glanced at Morghan, then Grainne and Clarice, her heart swelled with love and gratitude.

'Greetings to you, Rising Sun,' she said. 'Bringer of light and strength.'

Selena closed her eyes again. 'We ask your blessings, spirits of air, creatures of wing and feather and fast-beating hearts.'

She paused, then turned to the south. Next to her, Rue turned also, keeping her breath slow and measured, her spirit lifting and expanding in the spring-scented breeze.

Selena spoke. 'We ask your blessings, spirits of fire.' She opened her eyes once more and looked thoughtfully at Rue, continued the prayer. 'Dragon, guardian of the fire at the centre of our golden hearts, I ask your blessing.'

Rue, startled, didn't stop the image of Clover's dragon – their dragon – rising up before her, wings strong and broad, flanks bright white in the dimness of the morning. She looked at it behind her eyes and trembled.

What did the dragon mean?

She shook her head slightly and hurried to turn with the others to the west.

'Hail spirits of the west,' Selena called. 'We ask your blessings this brightening day. Spirits of water, of the depths, of the hidden mysteries of life, we beg your blessing.'

Rue thought of the well at their feet, how it went down and down into the darkness underground. She shivered slightly, wondering what was down there in that deep cold watery darkness.

Selena spoke again. 'Greetings to you, spirits of the north. Of the ground beneath our feet, that which holds us steady while the trees grow, and the bear rises from her cave. We ask your blessings.'

There was a moment of quiet between them all as they stood on the dew-heavy lawn of Hawthorn House, spirits awake and shimmering.

Morghan spoke then, her voice low and clear upon the rising morning. She looked up at the sky, where the stars were faded against the dawn.

'The Pole Star is overhead,' she said.

'We follow it through the forest,

'Bear dances with us, we can feel her hot breath on the wind.'

Morghan took a breath, letting the next words of the prayer come to her.

'We can feel her fur brushing us as she passes, lifting and placing her feet, her brown bear eyes looking at us with love.

'I am strong, she says,

'We are strong, she says,

'We dance here under the sky,

Amongst the trees,

Following the North Star.'

SELENA LISTENED, FELT THE THICK SOFTNESS OF BEAR'S PELT as she brushed past, and wiped sudden, trickling tears from her cheeks as she opened her eyes and looked upon her dearest friends and companions.

'My darlings,' she said. 'How I will miss you.' She thought of the North Star, and how it had guided her all of her life, since she had been a small child, and she shook her head, thinking then of the Southern Cross, which rose overhead each night in her new home; Damien had told her that some Māori thought it was the anchor for Māui's great canoe, and others called it an opening in the sky through which the winds blew. She liked thinking of the winds blowing through those far away stars, bringing with them the songs of the universe.

RUE TOOK A DEEP, STEADYING BREATH, THEN LET SELENA GO, doing her best to smile at her.

'I'll be okay,' she said to Selena's unspoken question. 'Just take care of Clover for me.'

Selena nodded and cupped a palm to Rue's cheek. 'I will always do so,' she said. 'To my dying breath and beyond.'

Rue nodded, sniffed, then smiled. She'd spoken to Clover the evening before and asked her what was going on. Clover had tried to tell her, but mostly she'd cried over the phone, something that had threatened to break Rue's heart.

'But you gotta stay there,' Clover had said when Rue had told her she would come home too. 'Jus' for a minute.'

When Rue had asked why she had to stay there, Clover had done her best to explain.

'You gotta find Bryn and see,' she'd said. 'I don' know what you s'posed to see, but something.'

Rue hadn't really understood, but that was the way with Clover. Rue didn't understand most of what Clover knew and said.

'Clover?' she'd asked at the last minute. 'Do you know a dragon?'

Clover was quiet a minute.

'Don't fink so,' she said.

'Huh.' Rue had said goodbye then and promised to call every day.

'I'm going to miss you,' she told Selena.

'And I will miss you too,' Selena said. 'I am so proud of you, staying here and doing this.'

Rue nodded. Other than her worry over Clover, staying at Wilde Grove was no hardship. A frisson of excitement shivered through her, and her smile widened, became true.

'Thank you for bringing me here,' she whispered.

Selena kissed her forehead. 'My blessings upon you, Rue. Learn well, and I will see you in a couple weeks.'

Rue watched Selena and Teresa get into the car, and Ambrose took the driver's seat. She waved as the car tyres crunched over the gravel and down the driveway.

'I wish she were staying,' Clarice said, startling Rue who turned and looked at her.

'I do too,' Rue said.

'You should all come over here and live with us,' Clarice said, mouth downturned. She looked up at Rue. 'Would I like your sister, do you think?'

Rue nodded. 'She would love you. And Sigil.'

Clarice thought about that. It would be fun, perhaps, to have a little sister. It wasn't going to happen, of course, and she was okay with that, but perhaps if Rue and Clover and Selena came to live with them, then she could borrow Clover to be her sister too.

'I would take her walking in the woods,' Clarice said. 'I would show her all the paths.'

'You could show me them instead,' Rue told her.

Clarice considered this. 'When?' she asked at last.

Rue pursed her lips. Morghan had said they would start their learning tomorrow, so she had the afternoon free.

'Now?'

'Do you know how to cross the borders?'

'I don't know,' Rue said. 'What borders?'

22

CLARICE STRODE AHEAD, KNOWING EXACTLY WHERE SHE WAS going. She flung her head about to check that Rue was still following.

'Are you sure about this?' Rue asked, puffing slightly. Clarice walked fast, her white hair streaming out behind her like a pale cloak.

'Of course,' Clarice said with supreme confidence. 'I go there all the time.'

Rue shook her head. She wasn't certain this was a good idea anymore. 'Do we have to walk this fast?'

That made Clarice laugh. 'No, but I don't know how else to get you there.'

'Get me where? Rue asked, coming to a stop, determined to make Clarice tell her what they were doing.

Where they were going.

Clarice stopped walking and looked at her, exasperated. 'Come on,' she said.

'Not until you tell me exactly where we're going.'

Clarice's brow wrinkled. 'We're going to the Fair Lands,' she said. 'I go there all the time. It's great.'

'I don't even know what the Fair Lands are,' Rue said, not much liking the sound of Clarice's plans.

'It's where the Fae live, of course,' Clarice told her. She shook her head. 'How come you don't know that?'

'I don't know lots of things yet,' Rue said. 'I've been busy doing other stuff.'

'Like what?' Clarice cocked her head to one side.

Rue was nonplussed. 'Like looking after Clover and going to school, I suppose.'

Clarice's face fell. 'I hate school,' she said. 'It's so boring.' She waved at the trees surrounding them. 'I would rather come out here every day.' Then she amended her statement. 'For the whole day.' She sniffed dismissively. 'Come on. Not much farther now.'

Rue followed her, thinking Clarice was as wild as the hare she had just seen hopping between the trees.

'Here it is,' Clarice said triumphantly a few minutes later, dropping to her knees and grinning up at Rue.

'What is it?' Rue asked, getting down on the ground to look at it.

'A rabbit hole,' Clarice said, then giggled. 'Like Alice's rabbit hole, I suppose, except it doesn't go to the funny place she went to.' She thought about this. 'It's still kinda wonder-land, though.'

Rue didn't comprehend any of this. She looked at the hole dug between the roots of the tree, which was some sort she didn't recognise.

'And we go down this?' she asked.

Clarice nodded.

'We would never fit through there,' Rue told her, backing away from it. 'And it's a rabbit hole. It doesn't go anywhere.'

Clarice shook her head. 'We dream we go down there,' she said, making herself explain it patiently. 'We don't go down there in our bodies.' She grimaced at the thought, then laughed. 'And it leads to the Fair Lands. I go there all the time.' Her gaze flickered. 'I'd live there all the time, if I could, and if I wouldn't miss Mum and Morghan, and Uncle Ambrose, and Teresa.'

Rue was looking more curiously at the hole between the roots now. It looked for all the world like an ordinary rabbit hole.

'How do you dream yourself down there?' she asked.

Clarice shrugged. 'You just do. You sit here, but you go down there.'

'Like, in your imagination?'

Clarice shook her head. 'In your spirit.'

A bird somewhere above them squawked, then whistled.

'I don't know how,' Rue said at last, leaning back on her heels and shaking her head.

Clarice was deflated. 'Morghan better hurry up and teach you then,' she said. 'It'd be nice to go with a friend.'

Rue sat down and looked at Clarice. 'Do you go there often?'

Clarice nodded. 'I have friends there. They don't mind me visiting.' She blinked and a smile spread across her face. 'I've even met the Queen.'

'The Queen?'

'Yup.'

'The Queen of what?' Rue asked, not used to talk of queens and such.

'The Queen of the Fae, of course.'

'What's her name?' Rue asked, intrigued. This was a bit like talking to Clover. 'Is she nice?'

Clarice pulled a face. 'I don't know her name,' she said at last. 'I don't think I've heard anyone speak it. And I think she might be nice, but I don't really know.' She shrugged her thin shoulders. 'The Fae aren't like humans. They live a long time and know a lot more about things we've forgotten.' She considered the matter. 'You should ask Morghan to introduce you to the Queen,' she said. 'If you want to meet her.'

Rue's head spun. 'Morghan knows the Queen?'

'And Selena. She does too.'

'This is the Queen of Fairies we're talking about, right?' Rue asked.

'Well, not little things with wings like you get in the picture books,' Clarice said. She shifted and sat with her legs crossed. 'The Queen and her people are tall like us.'

'I've seen them,' Rue said, wonder tinging her voice. She shook her head, things finally clicking together in her mind. 'I've seen them – when I was...dreaming...of Bryn. Except Bryn called them the Shining Ones.'

Clarice nodded enthusiastically. 'That's them,' she said. 'The Shining Ones. Where did you see them, again?'

'On the bank of the stream,' Rue said, but didn't add that this had been a few thousand years ago. It was confusing enough as it was.

'That's brilliant,' Clarice crowed. 'They don't cross into our world all that often anymore, or not so as people can see them, anyway – but you said you were dreaming, didn't you?' She nodded. 'It's easier when you're dreaming.'

'Morghan called what happened shifting,' Rue said.

Clarice nodded seriously. 'I think that's something different though. When you go to the Fair Lands, I call it dreaming, because that's what it feels like. Like I'm making myself have a dream. Morghan calls it travelling, but then, she goes a lot farther than I do.' Clarice shivered. 'I only go to the Fair Lands. You couldn't get me to go to some of the other places there are behind the borders.'

'Why?' Rue asked. 'Are they dangerous?'

'I'm only 11 years old,' Clarice said. 'Mum would not be happy if I was wandering around the Otherworld.'

It was hard for Rue to believe she was having this conversation. 'But she lets you go to see the Fae?'

Clarice shrugged. 'Sure. There's always been an alliance between the Fae here and the Lady of the Grove.' She leaned forward and splayed a hand in the dirt. 'I belong to the Grove, so I can go there too; they don't mind.'

Rue was silent, trying to make sense of what Clarice was telling her. The bird above them whistled again.

'I don't really get all this,' Rue said at last, sighing.

'You will,' Clarice said, and got to her feet, dusting off her clothes. 'Come on.'

'Where are we going?' Rue asked, alarmed.

'Back to the house,' Clarice said. 'I don't think you're ready to go down the rabbit hole yet.' She nodded sincerely. 'We'll let Morghan teach you some more, and then I'll take you.'

Rue fell silently in step beside her.

'What did they want?' Clarice asked, when they were halfway home.

'What?' Rue said, startled out of their silence. 'Who?'

'The Shining Ones. On the stream bank? You said you'd seen them. They must have been there for a reason?'

Rue remembered Bryn standing in the middle of the stream, the water running about her legs, the welcome coolness of it when the day had been so hot.

'They had a child with them,' she said. 'They wanted me to take her.' Rue paused. 'It wasn't me though. I mean, I was someone else. Someone called Bryn, who lived here a long time ago.'

Clarice nodded, puzzled over it. 'I wonder where they got the child? Was it human or Fae?'

Rue felt suddenly dizzy. What a conversation to be having!

'Human,' she said. And shook her head.

'Hmm.' Clarice skipped a few steps ahead then turned and grinned at Rue. 'I'll ask some of my friends about it when I go there later.'

'Some of your friends?' Rue hurried after her. 'Some of your...Fae friends?'

'Uh huh. They might remember.'

Rue's eyes widened. 'How long do they live?'

'I don't know. Maybe forever.' Clarice reached out and grabbed Rue's hand, held it as she skipped along. 'Maybe thousands of years?' She shook her head. 'I've never met them all, of course. Only the ones that live near here.'

. . .

Rue was hungry. She checked her watch, saw there were still hours until dinnertime, and unfolded her legs from the chair by her bedroom window with a grimace. She'd been sitting so long, they'd gone to sleep. She shook them out straight, wincing at the pins and needles that spread through them. How long had she been sitting there sewing?

But the sight of the half-made bird brought a smile to Rue's face, pins and needles or not. She touched it with a gentle finger and grinned. It was coming along really well and beginning to look like a real albatross.

When she was done making her albatross, she thought she'd make an owl for Clarice. An owl just like Sigil. She'd begun the albatross before leaving New Zealand, but she thought there must be a fabric shop somewhere around Wellsford that she could visit.

There were voices coming from the drawing room when Rue made her way downstairs, intending to visit the kitchen in search of a snack. She paused at the bottom of the stairs, knowing it was poor manners to eavesdrop, but the door was ajar, and she could hear perfectly well.

They were talking about her dragon.

Rue stood frozen, her hand on the newel post, her skin prickling. Ambrose was there, speaking to Morghan.

'It can't be like Grainne's dragon,' Morghan said.

Rue's mouth dropped open and she glanced back up the stairs, as if Grainne would appear there.

'Why not?' Ambrose answered.

Rue stepped down and padded across the hallway.

'Did it not act as a protector?' Ambrose said.

What did Ambrose mean, Rue wondered. Was Clover's dragon a protector? What did that mean?

But Morghan was speaking again. 'Selena said she saw the dragon rise over a vision of Rue, not Clover.'

'Which just means that Rue is also the protector.'

Silence stretched out after that, and Rue realised she could not stand there in the hallway, ear tipped to the sitting room door anymore. She scuttled across the way to the kitchen.

'Hello Rue,' Grainne said. 'I was just making tea for the drawing room. Do you want to join us?'

'Do you have a dragon?' Rue blurted, unable to keep the question inside her. She shook her head and clapped a hand to her mouth, mortified.

'I'm sorry,' she said. 'That's so rude of me.' She blew out a breath. 'It's just, that I heard Morghan and Ambrose talking. Morghan said that Clover's dragon can't be like yours.' Rue came to a stop and hunched over, embarrassed.

But Grainne was shaking her head, a wide smile on her face. 'That's what she said, did she?'

Rue straightened. 'I overheard them.'

'Did Ambrose agree?'

Rue shook her head.

Grainne pursed her lips and went to the cupboard for cups and saucers. She got four of them and put them on the tray with the teapot, steam drifting from its spout. From a different cupboard she brought down a biscuit tin and opened it.

'My dragon has been with me since I made him,' Grainne said, putting several biscuits on a plate. They were freshly baked. Mrs Parker, as usual, had made Morghan's favourite.

'You made him?'

Grainne nodded. 'Centuries ago, when I was a quite extraordinary person. Rather like Ambrose, actually.'

'But no one can make a dragon,' Rue said. She shook her head. 'I mean...how?'

'I don't know really. Maybe I conjured him out of thin air, or maybe I just called him to me, and he let me pretend I had knitted him together from dreams and spells.'

Rue shook her head. It was spinning again, and she almost laughed. Every day, she thought, since she'd stepped off the plane, something had happened, or been said, that threatened to short circuit everything she'd ever thought she'd known.

'You remember this?' she asked, her voice a hoarse whisper.

'In bits and pieces,' Grainne said. 'But I can feel the dragon. He has been with me ever since.'

Intrigued, Rue took a step closer. 'You can feel him?'

'In here.' Grainne patted her chest. 'He's a fierce old thing.' She lifted her eyebrows. 'And what else did Morghan and Ambrose say about your dragon?'

Rue shook her head. 'I only heard Ambrose saying that the dragon was – is, I mean – Clover's protector.' She paused. 'And that I am, too.' She swallowed. 'But I don't know what that means.'

Grainne picked up the tray. 'Dragons are very great protectors of our precious, golden hearts,' she said. 'Come on, let's go hear what they have to say.'

23

JOSH AND HIS DAD SHOULD HAVE ARRIVED ALREADY, TARA thought, checking the clock on the wall for what must have been the hundredth time. She picked up the tea towel and wiped her hands, looked over at Dandy.

'He's late,' she said. 'Yesterday he was early, but today he's late.'

Dandy just shook her head. 'Probably not used to getting Josh ready. There's a lot of work in caring for a little guy.'

'I wish he'd get here already. I'm nervous.' Tara looked at Clover, who sat at the table, a crayon in her hand. It was the red one, but she wasn't drawing anything, just staring at the blank piece of paper in front of her. Tara looked over her head at Dandy.

Dandy lowered her gaze to look at Clover. She shook her head slightly, worried about the girl. Clover hadn't been anything near her usual self.

Not since the day that Rachel hadn't turned up to collect Josh.

Dandy reached out to stroke Clover's curls. They were the only thing about Clover that still bounced. 'Are you all right, sweetie?' she asked.

Clover lifted her gaze from the paper and blinked at Dandy. She didn't say anything.

'She's barely spoken a word,' Tara said. 'I can't wait until this afternoon.'

Clover turned her head to Tara. 'S'lena comin' this aft'noon?'

Tara nodded. 'She sure is. Damien is picking her up from the airport and bringing her straight home.'

Clover nodded, then went back to staring at the piece of paper on the table in front of her. She wanted to do some drawing, which was her favourite thing in the whole world, but all she could see was Josh's mama, all red and hurt. Clover closed her eyes, her fingers tightening around the red crayon and tried to wish Josh's mama away. But she didn't budge. Just stood standing there in the tangle of trees at the back of Clover's mind where she was really hard to ignore.

Clover dropped the crayon, and it rolled across the table. She climbed down from her chair.

'Where are you going?' Tara asked her.

'I goin' to watch 'Tilda,' Clover said, and she could too. She knew how to turn the television on, and the video player. She even knew how to rewind the tape.

Dandy watched the sad little figure walk out the door to the playroom. 'She's breaking my heart,' she said.

'I know,' Tara agreed. 'Mine too.' She closed her eyes.

She'd go and set up the movie for Clover, but she was afraid to budge from where she stood, waiting for Josh's father to turn up.

She needed to speak to him this morning.

Dandy interrupted the slow-motion carousel of Tara's thoughts.

'I'll go tuck Clover into her nest and sit with her,' she said. 'I don't think she should be alone.' Dandy paused at the door. 'I'm so glad Selena is arriving today.'

Tara nodded, nervousness rising again as she listened for the sound of a car in the driveway. She cleared her throat. 'I am too,' she said.

Dandy still didn't leave. 'You remember what we decided?' Tara looked faint, she thought. 'Are you sure you don't want me to ask him?'

But Tara shook her head, her hands fisted in the tea towel. 'I'll do it,' she said. 'I'll be all right. It'll be fine.' She glanced outside. 'I just wish he'd get here already.'

Dandy slipped out of the room.

Tara tightened her grip on the tea towel. Luckily, this wasn't one of Danielle's days, and little Min wouldn't be arriving until later.

Tara wanted to speak to Mike Manners without the bustle of everyone getting dropped off at the same time.

They'd decided the night before what to do, not that it was much. Just a puny effort, really, but better than nothing.

It had been Ebony's idea. 'Make up a reason to have to speak to Rachel,' she said. 'Something about Josh that only she would be able to answer. That will give you a reason to want the phone number of where she's staying.' Ebony had shrugged. 'If he doesn't give it to you, then I reckon that signals loud and clear that he's done something to her.'

There was a crunching of gravel outside as a car pulled up, and Tara put down the cloth and sucked in a deep breath.

'I can do this,' she told herself, then opened the door and stepped outside, putting as sunny a smile on her face as she could manage.

'Hello Josh!' she said, bending over at the car window and waggling her fingers at Josh in his car seat. She straightened and tried to beam at Mike Manners. 'I hope he's been being a good boy for you, Mr Manners,' she said. 'He must be missing his mum.'

Mike shook his head. 'Do them both good to have a break from each other.'

Tara's eyebrows rose towards her hairline, and she quickly drew them back down. 'I was wondering if you have a contact number for Rachel while she's at her sister's,' Tara said, aware that she was talking too quickly now as the man opened the car door and reached in for Josh. 'Only, you see,' she continued, 'We've been organising an outing for everyone, a bit of a picnic.' She swallowed, her mouth dry.

'Getting a bit chilly for picnics, isn't it?' Mike asked, passing Josh to Tara.

'Oh,' Tara said, catching Josh into her arms. 'It's going to be at the Chipmunks indoor play arena.'

'Josh is a bit young for that, isn't he?' Mike held out Josh's nappy bag. 'That place is for bigger kids.'

'Well, I've found the younger ones love it too – they have an area there for the littler ones.' Tara drew in a breath, knowing she wasn't pulling this off near as well as she needed to. 'Anyway, I'd like to give Rachel a call, talk over the details.'

'When is it?'

'Um,' Tara stalled. 'It's for Clover's birthday,' she said, inspiration dawning finally. It was Rue's birthday coming up, not Clover's, but Mike Manners wouldn't know that.

'When is it?' Mike asked again, his face as bland as the clouded white sky.

'On the 21st,' Tara said. Another complete fabrication, but she needed a date far enough away to be believable.

Mike shook his head and opened the driver's door. 'She won't be back by then,' he said, then slipped in behind the wheel. 'See you at 12.'

Tara stood holding Josh, who snuggled into her, his cheek warm against her neck as she gazed at the retreating car in astonishment.

'What did he say?' Dandy asked when Tara brought Josh into the playroom. 'Did you get her number?'

Tara shook her head and popped Josh down on the floor in front of an array of his favourite trucks. He grasped hold of the digger with delight and held it up to her, grinning.

'That's your digger, Josh,' she said, and patted his small, sweet head.

Josh nodded and set its wheels on the ground, making vrooming noises in his throat.

Tara looked at Clover, wrapped up in the blanket, gaze fixed on the television screen where Matilda was walking once more home from the library with a little wagon full of books.

Dandy got up, twitched her head at the door. 'They'll be all right for a minute,' she said.

Tara followed her out.

'What did he say, then?'

'Well, he didn't give me a contact number,' Tara said, leaning against the wall and rubbing her face. She peered at Dandy. 'I told him we were organising an outing to Chipmunks for Clover's birthday, and he just asked when it was.' Tara shook her head and dropped her hands. 'I said it was for the 21st, which would be time enough to expect Rachel back.' She sighed, letting the air out in a huffing breath. 'He said she wouldn't be back by then and got in his car and drove away.'

Dandy had raised both eyebrows. 'Well. I wish he had given us a contact number for her.'

Tara nodded.

They were both quiet, the only sounds the TV in the next room, and Josh playing with his digger. Outside on the road, the rubbish truck grumbled along the narrow street.

'Now we know, I guess,' Tara said at last.

'As well as we can,' Dandy nodded.

THIS WOULD BE SELENA'S FIRST WINTER IN NEW ZEALAND and she could tell already that it would be damp, windy, and cold. Even so, she looked out at the city with delight.

'I would never have guessed that I would fall in love with this place,' she said.

Damien stopped at the traffic light and grinned. 'Miss us, did ya?'

His question made Selena laugh. 'I did,' she said. 'I hadn't expected that I would, but I did.'

'Bet that was a shock,' Damien said, accelerating

smoothly and following the road through the city. 'I figured it'd probably be the other way around, that you'd not want to come back.'

'I was always going to come back.'

Damien nodded. 'Yeah, of course. But Wellsford or Wilde Grove, that's your real home.'

Selena watched as they passed the old fire station, and the Cadbury factory. She breathed in the scent of chocolate and shook her head, smiling.

'I thought that as well,' she said. 'But in actual fact, when I got there, I realised how thoroughly my place of belonging had changed to this small city, and all of you.' They passed the grassy lawn in front of the museum and stopped at another light to let a light stream of university students cross the road to the campus.

'Morghan is fulfilling the role of Lady of the Grove as well as I thought she would,' Selena mused.

'She's doing a good job?'

'An excellent job. She always was a natural at it all.' Selena smiled, then drew in a breath. They were almost home.

'This is where I need to be, now,' she murmured.

'And this is where we're glad to have you,' Damien added, turning off the main road to drive the last little distance to the house.

'S'lena!' Clover jumped up and down clapping her hands as Damien pulled the car in. When it had stopped, she ran around and tugged at the passenger's side door. 'S'lena!' she squealed. 'I missed you!'

Selena opened the door and her arms, and Clover

barrelled into them. Selena sat on the seat of the car, her feet on the driveway, and held Clover close.

'I missed you too,' she whispered.

Clover sat back and looked at Selena's face. 'I was okay for a while,' she said. 'Cos I knew you were with Rue and doin' 'portant things.' She blinked and her small face crumpled. 'But then the lady got hurt and she won't stop cryin'.'

Selena wrapped her arms around Clover and drew her close, pressing a kiss to the warm curls. 'I know,' she whispered. 'I know. But I'm here now, and we can help her.'

From the warmth and safety of Selena's embrace, Clover nodded. Already, tucked inside Selena's aura, Josh's mum's cries were fading.

24

'I DON'T THINK I'M VERY GOOD AT DANCING,' RUE SAID
hesitantly, following Morghan barefoot along the early
morning path to the stone circle.

Morghan glanced back at her, a smile lighting her face.
'Everyone can dance,' she said.

Rue shook her head. She wasn't so sure. She'd never had
a CD player like the portable one that Morghan was carrying, or one of the MP3 players that everyone had, so she'd
had to rely on the TV for music.

Which she'd never really felt like dancing to.

Nerves prickled along her skin, and she rubbed at her
arms. The morning had dawned warm and fragrant after all
the rain and Rue took a deep breath scented with trees and
flowers and soil.

'Right,' said Morghan, setting the CD player down just
outside the circle and smiling at Rue. 'Here we are.'

Rue nodded, rather wishing that there they weren't. Of

all the things she'd thought Morghan might get her to do, dancing had never crossed her mind.

She looked up at the sky through the canopy of branches that curved over the circle and tried to calm herself. Morghan wasn't going to care if she was gawky and goofy. She peeked a glance at Morghan, who was still smiling at her.

Would she?

As if reading Rue's mind, Morghan shook her head then walked across the circle. 'Come,' she said. 'Let's give our thanks first to Grandmother Oak, for her faithful guardianship of this sacred spot.'

Rue nodded. Here, she felt on steadier ground. Joining Morghan in front of the venerable old tree, she reached into the small bag at her waist for a tiny twist of herbs. Grainne had given the bag to her just the day before, made by her own hands and it matched Morghan's. Rue had been almost speechless with pleasure.

Morghan had taken Rue down to Teresa's place after that, and there Teresa had been delighted to lead them into her potting shed where they'd fashioned the small bundles of herbs while the rain came again, pouring down the panes in the adjoining glasshouse.

Now, under Grandmother Oak, Morghan had a feather hooked onto her bag, which she used to fan the smoke into the tree's branches. Rue looked at it and wondered which bird it came from.

'Grandmother Oak,' Morghan said. 'We come here to honour you as those of our line have done for age upon age, both you, and your ancestors.'

Rue bowed her head and inhaled the fragrant smoke. She held up hers and let the smoke drift and mingle with Morghan's, high into Grandmother Oak's leaves, which rustled down at them.

'May your blessing be upon us,' Morghan said. 'May we live in peace together, for your life is my own.'

Rue frowned over that, puzzling out the meaning behind Morghan's words, then realised it was obvious. Without trees, the world would be uninhabitable.

Morghan put her twist of herbs in the small bowl nestled in the ground at Grandmother Oak's roots and Rue followed her lead and did the same, the herbs smouldering safely, gently.

'Good,' Morghan said, turning to Rue. 'Are you ready?'

Rue shook her head. 'No,' she said. 'The thought of dancing makes me nervous.'

Morghan put her hand on Rue's shoulder and drew her into the circle of stones. 'We dance,' she said, 'for two reasons.'

She considered that a moment. 'Three reasons,' she decided.

'What are the reasons?' Rue croaked. Morghan hadn't even turned on the music yet, and already she felt slightly sick.

'We dance because it is our job to sing the Wheel to turning, and to dance is also to sing.'

Rue wasn't quite sure that made sense.

Morghan smiled, well aware of how cryptic that sounded. She'd thought so, when Selena had brought her out here and told her the same thing.

'We dance because it is a way to honour the world.' She

raised her brows in a question and Rue nodded, although still looking dubious.

'And we dance, lastly, so that we may lose our self-consciousness.'

'How does that work?' Rue blurted before she could stop herself.

'With practice,' Morghan smiled. 'Listen,' she said. 'There are many ways to flex and strengthen our spirits, and dance is one of them. It is a prayer and a story that uses your whole body. It is also a way to open the doors of the worlds.'

'I've never wished I was in a wheelchair before,' Rue grumbled.

Morghan laughed in delight. 'I would make you dance in your seat,' she said. 'Even if all you could do was sway a little.'

Rue blew out a breath.

Morghan moved to the CD player and pressed play. The notes of a flute lifted and played upon the breeze. She nodded and went back to the circle, gave Rue a sympathetic look.

'I really have to do this?' Rue asked, her fingers knotted in the dress she wore.

'You really do,' Morghan said. 'All priestesses of the Grove are taught to dance.'

'I still don't get why, though.'

Morghan tried one more time, although she suspected that Rue would in the end, just have to realise through doing.

'Because dance allows us to both honour and lose ourselves in the spirit of the world.'

'I'm going to trip over myself,' Rue warned, wanting to

be convinced, but feeling far from it. How, she wondered, could she join in prayers and offerings to trees and Goddesses, yet feel completely out of her depth when she was asked to dance?

'Just follow my lead,' Morghan said. 'We won't do anything difficult. Just follow my lead and let the music inside you.'

Rue nodded, tried to relax. The flute was joined by a drumbeat as low and slow as the beating of her own heart. At least the music was pretty nice, she decided.

'We'll start with three big breaths,' Morghan said, standing opposite Rue, facing her. 'We'll draw our arms up, moving our hands from our chests to the sky as we breathe in.' She did the movement as she spoke, raising first her elbows, then her hands. 'And on the exhale, we'll sweep downward, bringing our arms around to the sides in a circle and bending over as we lower them.'

Rue followed Morghan's lead, drawing in a lungful of air and stretching, elbows first, then hands toward the sky.

It actually felt pretty good to stretch like that.

Morghan, bent over, spoke. 'Then on the next inhale, bring your hands up in front of your body as you rise.' She followed the words with the action, closing her eyes. 'And bring your arms down until your hands are cupped at chest level.' She looked at Rue and nodded. 'That's good. Bend your knees a little; keep them loose as we sweep up and repeat the sequence.'

Rue did it again and smiled slightly. She felt sort of sinuous and the voice of the flute shimmied around her as she moved. Elbows, then hands to the sky, reaching for the sun, she thought, then let her arms go and they floated out in a circle as she bent forward to almost touch the ground. She straightened, bringing her hands up in front of her to repeat the movement the third time.

'That's not so bad, is it?' Morghan asked.

Rue shook her head. It wasn't so bad, mostly because it wasn't at all what she'd expected.

'Now,' Morghan said, turning. 'We're going to step around in a circle, lifting and pointing our feet as we walk, and giving a little turn every now and then.' She demonstrated, letting herself hear the music again, letting everything else fall away except for the ground under her bare feet, the stones at her side, each one of which she greeted with her dance, and the trees overhead and around.

Earth, air, water, fire, she thought as she stepped around the directions, spinning and bowing at each point. When she opened her eyes to see how Rue was getting on, she smiled.

Rue was doing perfectly well.

This was not like normal dancing, Rue thought, sweeping into a little bow to one of the stones, just as Morghan had done. Well, she thought, perhaps not as gracefully, but still. She was doing it.

The music lifted, and they quickened their steps a little, and Rue lifted her arms, checking how Morghan was holding hers, and doing the same.

After a little while, Rue realised she really was dancing, and now they were crossing the centre of the circle, their fingers touching briefly as they passed each other, and Rue gasped.

She was doing it. Sure, she was watching every step, and some of her turns weren't fluid or graceful, and her lips were pressed together in concentration, but – she took a breath and let it out – she was doing it.

At last, the music faded and Morghan came to a stop, sweeping into a deep bow to Rue.

'Thank you,' she said. 'For dancing with me, for honouring earth, stone, sky.'

Rue bowed clumsily, then went red and laughed.

'You will come out here and practice every day,' Morghan said. 'You can bring the player, or I have a small one you can use that has headphones. But practice every day until you lose your self-consciousness.'

Rue nodded, but she was frowning. 'What do you mean, my self-consciousness?'

'Your awareness and anxiety over what you're doing,' Morghan explained. 'It holds you back. We must be able to relax into the moment, into being, into being completely present, our awareness not stuck in our heads feeling nervous, but expanding into our body and even further, into the world, out toward the stones, the trees, the sky.'

Rue thought she understood, but she was still frowning, even as Morghan had turned and stood with her head bowed to Grandmother Oak, silent for a moment. She went and stood next to Morghan.

'Give your thanks,' Morghan prompted.

Rue tipped her head. 'My gratitude, Grandmother,' she said, her voice low.

Morghan moved. Touched the tallest of the stones. 'And to the stones also.' She tilted her chin to the sky and closed her eyes. 'For the magic of your circle,' she said.

Rue, heart in her throat walked over to the stone and touched it. It was cool and rough under her hands, and she thought with a start that she was touching something that had been shaped and raised thousands of years ago.

Had Bryn danced between these stones, she wondered?

'For the magic of your circle,' she repeated.

25

SELENA, ON HER WAY DOWNSTAIRS, CLOVER TUCKED SILENTLY at her side, paused in front of Rue's bedroom door, hoping that she was doing well. A small smile quirked her mouth at the thought of Morghan leading her along the paths of the Grove, showing her the ways they led.

'We talk to Rue later?' Clover asked.

Selena nodded, putting a hand to Clover's curls. 'We will,' she promised.

It was already dark outside the windows, where autumn was well tucked in, spreading its blanket of leaves and dark-ness over the city. Selena touched one of the radiators in the hallway and swiftly drew back her hand. Damien had got the furnace going.

'Natalie!' she said, walking into the kitchen and seeing Natalie smiling shyly back at her. Selena opened her arms and hugged Natalie, then looked at her, laughing.

'I know in reality it's only been a little over a week since we left, but it feels like it was so much longer.' Selena patted Natalie's arm. 'How are you?' she asked.

'I'm doing well,' Natalie said. 'I'm getting more and more orders for my cakes every day, it seems.' She paused, glanced around at everyone she'd come to love so well, then nodded. 'My therapist says I'm doing well, too. I feel like I am.' Mortifyingly, tears sprang to her eyes, and she wiped them away, sniffing and laughing.

'I'm so glad,' Selena said. 'You and Bear are a formidable team.' She beamed around the kitchen, her favourite room in the house, the place where they all seemed so naturally to congregate, fortunate that it was large enough to hold them.

'Ebony,' she said in surprise. 'How are you?'

'I'm good,' Ebony grinned. 'Real good, actually – I've got a job working at Beacon, and Dandy here is teaching me to read cards as well.'

Selena moved to the table and grasped Dandy's hand as she held it up to greet her. She squeezed it and smiled widely at Ebony. The poor girl had wanted so much to go to Wilde Grove with Rue; she was glad now that Ebony had found something so satisfying to do with her time.

'I've also been trying to puzzle out what to do about Josh's mum,' Ebony said, her own smile fading, especially as she looked at Clover's small pale face.

Selena took a seat at the table and Clover climbed onto her lap. She wrapped her arms around the child.

Damien came out from behind the kitchen counter where he and Tara had been busy and kissed Selena on the cheek.

'So good to have you back,' he said, then looked over at Ebony. 'You're staying for dinner?'

Ebony lifted her face and sniffed. 'Yep,' she said decisively. Whatever they were making smelled too good to miss.

She looked back at Selena. 'What are we going to do?' she asked, pointing with her chin at Clover, who sat uncharacteristically quietly in Selena's lap, head resting on Selena's shoulder.

'What can we do?' Tara asked, bringing a bowl of salad to the table. She put her hands on her hips. 'I mean, we went to the police, but they said they wouldn't do anything.'

'Didn't they say there were no grounds to worry?' Natalie asked.

Tara nodded. 'We spoke to Sandy Rice, because we thought she might be at least a little but understanding, but she still said there weren't grounds for concern. Not officially, anyway.' Tara sighed and sat down opposite Selena, looking at Clover, who hadn't perked up, not really, even with Selena's arrival.

'I'd almost believe her, if it wasn't for Clover,' Tara said. 'And we didn't tell Sandy about Clover.'

Damien and Natalie brought the rest of the food to the table and sat down. Everyone looked silently at the spread in front of them, their appetites suddenly gone.

'Well,' Damien said at last, forking some vegetables onto his plate. 'You're back now, Selena, so at least Clover's going to be all right.'

Now everyone was moving, filling their plates, nodding in agreement.

'How are you, you know, going to fix her?' Ebony asked Selena.

'Ebony,' Tara frowned. 'Clover isn't broken.'

But Ebony just shrugged. 'Are you sure?'

Clover had squirmed onto the chair next to Selena, but she was eating with one hand splayed on the table next to Selena's plate and their chairs pushed up right against each other's.

Selena touched Clover's small hand. 'We'll think of something, won't we, sweetheart?'

Clover nodded. 'She's wanderin' the far an' wide.' She looked up at Selena. 'We go get her so she not cryin' anymore?'

'Yes,' Selena agreed. 'That's exactly what we'll do.'

'And ask her who killed her while you're at it.' Ebony nodded and chewed a mouthful ruminatively. 'Will she be able to tell you, do you think?'

'I don't know,' Selena said. 'I've never been in this position before.'

'And we don't know if she's dead,' Tara said with a shudder at the thought that poor Josh's mum might be.

'We don't know that she's not,' Ebony retorted. 'If she isn't, then I say we better hurry up and find her.' She paused to take a breath. 'When are you going to do it?' Ebony asked. She was fascinated by the whole thing; horrified by poor Josh's mum potentially being dead, but still fascinated. 'Whatever it is you're going to do?'

Selena stroked Clover's head. She wasn't very hungry, despite the delicious meal Tara and Damien had provided. 'Tomorrow, I think. After I've had a good rest.'

'Goodness, yes,' Natalie said. 'You'll be jet-lagged.'

'It is a very long plane flight,' Selena answered, shaking her head. 'One I'm not keen to make again in any hurry.'

'Twenty-four hours, isn't it?' Damien commented. 'Or near enough.'

'Which is a long time to spend in an aeroplane.'

'I don' like planes,' Clover said, piping up for the first time.

'You've never been in one,' Ebony told her.

Clover shook her head. 'Rather fly with Blackbird,' she said and giggled, glancing at Selena.

There was a surprised hush at the table, then everyone laughed, partly at Clover's joke, mostly in relief that Clover was laughing too.

'That's exactly right,' Selena said. 'Far better to fly by Blackbird than by jumbo jet.'

'You shoulda flied by Crane,' Clover said, still giggling. 'An' Rue coulda gone by albatruss.' She narrowed her eyes and pointed her fork at Ebony, standing up on her chair to do so.

No one told her to sit back down.

'Eb'ny,' Clover said. 'You can fly by sparrow. And Damien, he can wear his...' She frowned and looked at Selena. 'I don' know wha' is called.'

'Describe it to me,' Damien said.

Clover nodded, looking into the space between them.

'Is got black feathers,' she said, and turned around to present her bottom to the table. 'They white on the ends here,' she said, waving a hand at her rear. Then, sitting down again, she planted her hands to her cheeks. 'An' orange, here, and a really long beak.'

Damien gazed at her. 'It's a huia,' he said. There was a lump in his throat.

'A huia?' Natalie said. 'I've never heard of that.'

'It's extinct,' Damien told her, then shook his head. 'It was tapu – sacred, and only those with a high status in the tribe could wear its feathers.' He shook his head, dazed.

Clover nodded, then pointed at Natalie. 'I know yours,' she said. 'Is a swan.'

Natalie's eyes widened. 'A swan?'

'Black or white?' Ebony asked, wondering why she'd got a bird as plain as a sparrow. She'd have to find out if there was anything special about sparrows.

Clover frowned. She'd never seen a white swan. None of the ones Rue had ever shown her were white. 'Is black, of course,' she said.

Selena put a hand on her back and Clover looked up at her, then at Tara, who pressed her fingers to her chest and laughed nervously.

'What is it?' she asked. 'What's my bird?'

Clover looked for it. 'Is a bellbird.' She cocked her head to the side. 'Sings good,' she nodded.

There was a stunned and wondering silence at the table for several minutes after Clover had finished her pronouncements.

Natalie shook her head. 'Is she right?' she asked. 'Do we really have these birds as our kin?'

Selena ruffled Clover's hair. Clover was grinning at everyone.

'I would tend to believe Clover on this one,' Selena said. 'She has very good vision.'

Clover turned to look wide-eyed at Selena. 'You can see 'em too,' she said.

'Yes,' Selena nodded. 'But I would have to try a lot harder to than you just did.'

Clover wrinkled her nose. 'They just come to me,' she said, and then her face grew sombre once more. 'We have to find Josh's mum's birdie. She can't see him.'

'And once you've found her bird, then what?' Ebony asked, her food forgotten and cooling on her plate.

'Then she goes home,' Clover said, looking uncertainly at Selena. 'Don' she go home then? If she's...'

'Yes,' Selena said quickly. 'Then she can go home.'

Clover squinted, concentration fierce on her face. Finally, she relaxed and shook her head. 'I don' know where that is, 'xactly.' She frowned at Selena. 'Cross the river?'

'Yes, across the river or the sea to the Summer Isles.'

'What's that?' Damien asked, then added another question. 'Where's that?'

'The land of the dead,' Selena answered, then shook her head. 'And before you ask more, that's all I know. From there, where do the souls go? I don't know. Do they all go there? No, but it's probably where they need to go.'

'But we take Josh's mama there?' Clover asked, following the conversation as best she could. 'If we hafta?'

Selena cupped her hand around Clover's small head. 'Yes, my love. That's where we'll take Josh's mummy, if that's where she needs to go.'

No one said anything more for a long moment.

'I'm going to get a past life regression done,' Ebony announced finally, unable to bear the silence. She looked at

Dandy and nodded. 'I've decided. I can afford it now that I'm working.'

'A what?' Selena asked.

'A past life regression.' Ebony repeated, picking up her knife and fork again, appetite restored. 'You know, when some guy hypnotises you and takes you back to a past life.' She nodded with satisfaction. 'I think it sounds cool. I wanna know who I was.'

'You've been many people,' Selena said, frowning over the idea. 'And yet, always yourself.'

'What do you mean?' Natalie asked, fascinated despite herself. She wasn't sure she wanted to know about any past lives – she was having enough trouble with the current one, but the idea was still sort of exciting.

Selena looked across the table at her. 'I think that there are essential parts of our personalities that we keep from life to life, and in between too.'

Tara pushed her plate away. 'Do you know anyone who remembers their lives, like more than one of them?'

Selena nodded. Clover had tucked herself tight against her again, but Selena could feel that the conversation about birds had lightened her heart a little.

'I do,' she said. 'Back at Wilde Grove, both Morghan and Grainne remember several – not the entire passage of years of their lives, but the memories are significant none the less.'

'But how come?' Damien asked. 'Why do they?'

Selena smiled slightly, remembering the weeks after Grainne had first come to Wellsford seeking her brother. They had been eventful, to say the least.

'Their memories were jogged by their coming together,' Selena said. 'They have considerable shared history.'

'Is that usual?' Dandy asked.

Selena considered the question. 'I think sometimes there is another with whom we are deeply entwined, but more often there are groups of souls who incarnate together or near one another because they have formed bonds.' She pursed her lips. 'This is the lore that has been passed down in the Grove, but the true mechanics of it, I do not know.'

'Well,' Ebony said, standing up to begin clearing the plates. 'I'm looking forward to finding out more. Although if I find out that my mum was once my husband or wife, that's just going to be weird.' She grinned and carried the plates to the sink.

'I'm going with you, whenever this happens,' Dandy reminded her.

'Are there other ways to remember?' Natalie asked Selena tentatively. 'Than being hypnotised?'

'Yes,' Selena mused. 'I'm sure there are, although it's not something I've pursued, outside of learning the ways of the Otherworld through an ancestor from my own lives who came to lead me through them.'

'Rue's remembering,' Tara reminded everyone.

'Of course,' Selena said. 'Yes, she is. She began remembering in her dreams, which is common.'

'Awesome,' Damien said, getting up to help Ebony. 'I dreamt the other night I was a strong, wise rangatira – chief.' He paused, searching his memory of the dream. 'I got some living up to that to do.' Damien shook his head.

'Did you write your dream down?' Selena asked him.

'Yeah, sure did. Been writing them all down, but mostly I'm just remembering fragments, you know?'

'What's another way to remember without a regression?' Ebony asked. Maybe she wouldn't have to spend a hundred dollars to get it done.

'Travelling to the Otherworld, travelling into a dream fragment, or being triggered by a person or place,' Selena answered promptly.

'So,' Ebony said after a pause. 'Hypnosis it is.'

26

'Once,' Morghan said, 'once I spent a hundred years – or perhaps it was a thousand – as a tree.'

Rue had not been expecting this as Morghan led her deeper into the woods. 'A tree?' she asked, then: 'What sort of tree?'

Morghan looked at her and grinned. 'Good question. One that spread roots and branches wide and knew the songs well.'

Rue glanced at the trees surrounding them. She reached out and grazed her fingers against the nearest. 'I would like to hear the trees singing.'

'No sooner said than done,' Morghan replied. She led them unerringly off the path and wove between the trees and ferns until she reached a small circle of slender birches. 'Ah,' she said. 'Here they are.'

'How come they're in a circle?' Rue asked, standing in the centre and looking around at them.

'Perhaps they are dancing,' Morghan said.

Rue looked at her in surprise, then laughed. 'I suppose they could be.'

Morghan touched one of the trees lightly with her hand. 'That's what I like to think.' She paused, gazing up at their leaves. 'When I first danced and sang with the trees, it was in the Wildwood – the wooded land of the Otherworld, and it was in a circle much like this one. You can perhaps imagine my pleasure when I found these trees echoing what I had seen there.'

'There are seven of them,' Rue said, having counted.

'The Seven Sisters. That's what I've called them since,' Morghan agreed.

Nodding, Rue gazed at the trees. Here, they were deep in the woodland and the air itself seemed lazy, green, and alive with the buzzing and humming of insects, the trilling of birds.

'What are we going to do?' she asked.

'We will join them in their dance for a little while.'

Rue stopped herself from immediately asking how. Or even why. This was the sort of thing she was here to learn, she thought.

How to dance with trees.

Had Bryn learnt this same thing? She gazed around her again with new eyes. These trees looked far too young to have been around at the same time as Bryn, but perhaps their ancestors had. Perhaps she had stood in much the same place and dreamt she was a tree.

Morghan had kicked off her shoes and placed them just outside the circle of birches. Rue did the same, and the ground was soft and cool underfoot.

'You cannot be inside your head, for this exercise,'

Morghan said. She was going around the circle, touching one tree after another, greeting them.

Rue nodded. Selena talked often about not being stuck inside your head, so at least, she thought, rather relieved, she had an idea about how to do that one. She stepped over to the nearest tree and put her fingers to it, letting her mind empty, so that she greeted the tree with her heart instead.

She followed Morghan around the circle until they were both back in the middle, facing each other.

'We'll begin with the same movements we did yesterday, at the stone circle,' Morghan said. 'But instead of dancing around this circle, we will stay in place, and become trees also.'

Rue nodded, squelching the small voice that wanted to run commentary on the situation, or even worse, scoff about it before she'd even tried.

Morghan moved, lifting her arms to the sky, breathing deep and slow, smelling the scent of tree and soil, smiling as the breeze brushed up against her cheek as though in greeting, and when her fingers reached to the sky, they were twigs, laden with the bright green leaves of spring.

She let her arms float down, able already to hear the first strains of the trees' songs. At this time of the year, their voices were clearer, filled with sap and vigour, awake and alive in the world.

Come autumn, they would grow sleepy, their humming voices drowsy.

But now they celebrated being awake, roots dug deep, the soil rich and dark between them, leaf-laden branches spread wide and high, catkins hanging.

Morghan reached out to them with her spirit, letting

herself drift in the circle, until she could feel each of the Seven Sisters surrounding her, could hear their voices, the high dreaming hum of their song.

They were singing of soil and sun, of forest and earth, of the dance of air and water, of their growth from seed to sapling to slender dancer in the spring sunlight. They sang of the seasons, wheeling through the year, springing forth, standing tall, shedding their leaves and sleeping before beginning the cycle over, springing forth once more.

They sang of the history of their woodland, and Morghan joined them, tall and slender, trunk and root and leaf.

They sang of the Wildwood, the forest that is all forests, and the creatures that run, scuttle, and fly between them.

Rue stretched upwards and caught a shard of song, and she closed her eyes to reach for it. She dug her toes in the ground and they became roots, sturdy and strong in the soil, reaching for her sister trees. Her body lengthened, stretched, blood turning to sap, her mind settling into the rhythm of the song, of the sisters' glorying song of celebration.

How fine it was to be a tree! Rue waved her finely leafed fingers in the breeze and a bird alighted on them, joined in the song. Eyes closed, Rue lost track of time, became aware only of the season and the song.

When she finally came back to herself, lowering her arms and shuffling her feet, she grinned at Morghan.

'That was amazing,' she said, and there was wonder in her voice. 'I was a tree. I heard them singing – and they're dancing, I'm sure they are.'

Morghan nodded, delighted. 'What did they sing of?'

'Wow.' Rue reached for the nearest tree and flattened her palm against it. She thought she could still catch the faintest hum of song and she looked over at Morghan.

'They sing of the turning of the seasons,' she said. 'And right now, they sing of the coming swing from spring to summer, and how awake they are.'

'Yes,' Morghan said. 'That is their song. Their love song to the world, and the turning of the Wheel.'

'What can I do?' Rue asked. 'How can I thank them?' Her eyes widened and she delved into the small bag she wore again at her waist. Bringing out one of the tiny herb bundles Teresa had helped her make, she raised her eyebrows at Morghan, who nodded in agreement.

Rue lit the end of the bundle with the lighter that was also in her bag, and waited until the flames caught, then waved them out, so that the herbs smouldered, their fragrant smoke lifting to the air.

'My sister trees,' Rue said, moving instinctively from one tree to the next. 'I am grateful to you for your song and your beauty. Thank you for dancing with me.'

Morghan watched with pleasure from the centre of the circle as Rue went light-footed from tree to tree, giving them her thanks. A movement caught Morghan's eye, from off in the woods and she stilled, letting her second sight discern the figure there.

She caught Rue gently by the shoulder and turned her in the direction of the movement.

'There,' she said. 'Between those trees something is stirring. Can you discern it?'

Rue looked where Morghan pointed, and she frowned. 'I don't see anything,' she whispered.

'Take a breath,' Morghan said. 'Let it out slowly and let your spirit relax as you do. Look with that, with the whole of yourself, not just your eyes.'

Selena had been teaching her this, Rue realised, and took the breath Morghan told her to, and as she let it out, she let herself sink from her mind inside her head into her body, and past the edges of it.

Rue shook her head. 'I can sense something there, but not what it is.' She could feel a presence in the woods, between the trees, but could see nothing. She did feel a little dizzy though and reached out to clutch Morghan's arm.

'I feel like I'm going to faint.' She squeezed out the words through lips that felt thick and numb.

'You're seeing with your spirit sight,' Morghan said. 'Let's take advantage of that, shall we?' She moved her hands, putting them on Rue's shoulders, and stepped through into the Wildwood, bringing Rue with her.

For a moment Rue was too dizzy to see properly, but the sensation faded, Morghan's hands still steadying on her shoulders.

Then she reared back in fright, her breath a squeak from her lungs as she bumped into Morghan.

'Hush,' Morghan calmed her. 'He won't do you any harm.'

Rue's eyes were wide, and she shook her head. She'd never seen a snake before, and this one was thick and long and terrifying.

'How do you know?' she asked, fingers digging into Morghan's arms, which were protectively around her now.

'Because he is my kin,' Morghan said.

Prying her gaze from the snake on the ground, who had

turned his head to stare back unblinking at her, Rue looked at Morghan.

'Your kin?' she wheezed.

Her eyes shifted to the large black dog sitting on the forest floor next to Morghan and she bit back a yell of fright.

'Is that dog your kin too?' she asked, only her lips moving.

'He's not a dog,' Morghan said, and there was a hint of a smile in the words. 'Come now, stand up. Neither Snake nor Wolf is any danger to you, for they are both my kin.' She glanced upwards and saw the shadow of Hawk's wing.

It wasn't Snake or Wolf that Morghan wanted Rue to see, but the creature still waiting in the shadows of the trees. She nudged Rue and nodded towards it.

'Look there again,' she said. 'He waits for you.'

Rue's mouth was dry, but she turned and gazed into the gathering of trees.

Morghan was right. There was something there, and Rue's heart leapt. She had been right too – hadn't she felt something was there?

Now, she narrowed her eyes, then turned to Morghan in confusion.

'It's a sheep,' she said.

Morghan's wolf turned his head and looked interestedly at the animal. Rue groped for Morghan.

'Your wolf's not going to eat it, is it?'

Morghan laughed and straightened, her hand going to the great wolf at her side, fingers burying in his fur.

'He won't eat your ram,' Morghan said.

'My what?'

'Your ram.'

A ram? Her ram? Minding the snake on the forest floor beside them, Rue took a tentative step closer to the trees, before looking back at Morghan.

'My sheep?' she asked.

Morghan nodded. 'I would think so,' she said. 'Ask him.'

Rue's eyes widened. Ask the animal?

'This is my kin?' she asked Morghan instead. She'd wondered, when Selena had told her of both her kin, Crane and Hind, whether it was usual for there to be two.

Oftentimes a bird for flying, and another for walking the Underworld, Selena had said.

Rue hadn't understood then, and she didn't now either, not really, but, focused on the woolly animal beneath the tree branches, she was willing to find out.

The sheep looked up at her, his eyes inquisitive, interested.

Rue flung a glance back at Morghan. 'Can I touch him?' she asked.

Morghan's hand was still upon the shaggy neck of her wolf, and she nodded.

Tentatively, her hand shaking slightly, Rue put her fingers to the sheep's head, between the curling horns.

'You are a ram,' she whispered. 'I'm Rue,' she added. 'Are you here for me?'

The ram snorted, blowing a huff of air from his nostrils, then turned and trotted off between the trees, stopping after several steps and looking back at Rue as though waiting for her.

'Do I follow him?' Rue asked Morghan. 'I think he wants me to go with him.'

'Then that is what we shall do,' Morghan replied.

Rue nodded, glad that Morghan had said *we*, and turned to follow her new kin through the Wildwood.

27

IT WAS THE WEEKEND, SO THERE WOULD BE NO SMALL children arriving at the house to play, but Selena would have taken Clover with her to the attic room even if it hadn't been so.

'All right?' she asked, looking down at Clover, who was pale in the wan light from the late rising sun.

But Clover nodded. She was holding Selena's hand and it made her feel better. Last night, she'd even slept in Selena's bed, curled against her, and it had kept the dreams away, made Josh's mother quieter.

This morning, there were still the dark circles around her eyes that had made an appearance sometime during the week, but she felt hopeful, now that Selena was there.

'We goin' to make it better?' she asked.

'We are going to try,' Selena said, and thought of Morghan. This probably was more Morghan's thing, for it wasn't something that Selena had ever done.

In some ways, her upbringing at Wilde Grove had been

very sheltered. And when, of course, Annwyn had died, she'd sung her over as was right, but she'd never gone looking for someone stuck between the worlds.

Although, she thought now, setting Clover down on one of the big floor cushions, hadn't Clover's own mother been stuck between the worlds – hadn't Beatrix called out to her?

And hadn't she answered the call?

Selena remembered the conversation beside the wide, dark-flowing river.

Yes. She had gone there, and although this was different, it was also similar. Selena looked over at Clover and smiled reassuringly at her.

'We're going to be okay,' she said.

Clover nodded. She trusted Selena implicitly. But she wasn't looking forward to going and finding Josh's mother.

Josh's mama, she thought, was hurt, and there was blood.

It was scary.

Selena kneeled on the rug in front of Clover and took her small hands in her own.

'What we're going to do, Clover,' she said, her voice low and kind, 'is you're going to show me where to go, and then we'll bring you back here. Do you understand?'

'I don't hafta go too?' Clover asked, relief making her shoulders sag.

Selena shook her head and stroked Clover's curls. 'No,' she said. 'This is a job for me.'

'I too little,' Clover said.

'Exactly,' Selena agreed. 'You're too little.' She smiled. 'You're little and very precious to me.'

Clover nodded. 'I love you too.' She thought for a moment. 'I just gotta show you where to go?'

'Just that.'

That was okay, then. Clover thought she could do that as easily as breathing. She looked inside for a moment, and something caught her inward glance.

'Rue,' she said. 'Rue got a new kin.'

Selena sat back and gazed at Clover in astonishment and delight. 'A new kin?'

Clover nodded. 'I fink it's a sheep.'

'A sheep?'

'Yep. Real woolly.' Clover curled her hands on either side of her head. 'Has horns like this.' She frowned at Selena. 'Do sheeps have horns like that?'

'Yes,' Selena said. 'Sometimes they do. Rams especially – boy sheep.'

'Huh.' Clover went to look again, to see what Rue was doing in the Far 'n Wide, but Josh's mum rushed at her instead and she shrank back with a cry.

'Are you all right?' Selena asked. Clover fought back tears and nodded. 'Hafta help Josh's mama.' She sniffed and took a shuddering breath. 'I can't see past her no more.'

Selena got up. 'Then that's what we'll do,' she said. 'That's exactly what we'll do.'

On her big table, Selena turned on the battery powered tea lights she'd bought to use when she was there with Clover. Lighting real candles when travelling while Clover was in the room seemed like a potentially bad idea. The little electric lights weren't quite the same, but they were safer, and Selena was getting used to their light that still flickered like candles.

She picked up one of her herb bundles and lit the end of it, blew the flame out and stood for a moment, the fragrant smoke covering her.

'You ready?' she asked, turning to look at Clover.

Clover nodded but stayed seated on the cushion. Then she thought of something to ask.

'S'lena?'

'Yes, sweetheart?' Selena was moving towards the south side of the room.

'Do I have 'nother kin, too?'

Selena looked at her, pursing her lips as she thought about it.

Where, she wondered, did the dragon fit in?

'I expect you do,' she said at last.

Clover nodded. 'I fink so too. Can we find it when we done helpin' Josh's mama?'

Selena looked at Clover and her heart filled with love for her. 'Yes,' she said. 'We can, and we will. Is that good?'

'Yeah,' Clover said, shifting to get more comfortable on the cushion. 'That's real good.'

Selena watched her a moment longer, then turned back to the task in hand.

She was a little nervous, she realised, and stopped where she was to find the sensation in her body. The niggling sensation was in her lower belly, and she breathed into that spot, letting her breath fill her with light, until her spirit was bright, filling her, spilling out from her.

She walked to the south. 'Spirits of the south,' she said, holding aloft the herbs and letting the smoke rise from them. 'Mother Bear, protect and bless us in our travelling, and in our task.'

She moved to the east. 'Spirits of the east,' she said. 'Crane, with feather and wing, protect us in our travelling, and in our task.'

Selena smiled at Clover as she crossed to the west. 'Spirits of the west,' she said, breathing in the scented smoke. 'Whale, wisdom keeper of the deep, bless and protect us in our travelling, and in our task.'

North was last, and Selena closed her eyes. 'Spirits of the north, Salamander and Phoenix. Bless and protect us in our travelling and in our task.'

She paused, seeing the circle around them, the space protected and sacred, a small area of the world that now crossed borders, that nudged up against the Otherworld and the world of the dead.

Selena stepped to the centre of the room, and Clover got up off her cushion and joined her. Selena let the smoke waft over the both of them.

'We are spokes on the great Wheel,' she said, looking into Clover's wide blue eyes. 'We sing the world to weaving. We weave the world with our singing.'

The smoke purified them, and the sacred space swung around them.

'As above,' Selena said. 'So it is below. As it is within, so it is without.'

Clover looked around the room at the trees that grew around them now, their trunks strong, their branches filled with bunches of bright green leaves. Her lips trembled.

Selena moved, putting the herb bundle in the cast iron pot and setting the lid against it. Then she walked back to Clover.

'Do you see the trees?' she asked, for she had drawn the forest of the Wildwood about them.

Clover nodded.

They sat down on the cushions, and Selena took Clover's hands again in hers.

'Show me the path,' she said.

Clover looked around, and the room was gone now; there were only the trees, and on a branch in front of her, Blackbird perched, wings tucked against its sooty body, eyes bright in welcome.

'Blackbird show us the way,' Clover said, and looked to her side to check that Selena was there too.

Selena smiled down at her and nodded, took Clover's hand and squeezed it.

Blackbird hopped down onto Clover's shoulder, and she could feel his soft feathers brush against her cheek. He leaned close to Clover's ear, and she nodded.

'He whisperin' to me,' she told Selena. 'Tellin' us where to go.'

They followed Blackbird's directions, deeper and deeper into the Wildwood, and somewhere along the way, Hind stepped out of the forest to walk beside Selena.

All at once, there was a wall blocking their way. Selena stared up at it, then peered down its length. It had no end.

'She in there,' Clover whispered, shrinking back. 'This a scary place.'

Selena placed a hand on Clover's shoulder, then gathered her closer while she examined the wall.

There was something familiar about it, she thought, narrowing her eyes at the large blocks of stone, and then she nodded.

'I know where we are,' Selena said softly.

'You bin here before?' Clover whispered.

'There's an entrance far around the wall. I've been there.'

Clover shivered, even with Blackbird on her shoulder and Selena's arm around her.

'I don' like this place,' she said. 'Do I hafta go in there?'

Blackbird made a throaty dak-dak-dak noise and Clover nodded.

'Blackbird say I don' gotta.'

'Blackbird is right,' Selena said, peeling her gaze away from the lichen-covered, vine-laden wall. 'You don't have to. We'll take you home now, and I'll come back myself.'

Worry wrinkled Clover's forehead. 'You be okay?'

Selena crouched down and cupped Clover's face in her palms, pressed a kiss to her forehead.

'I will be,' she said, and glanced at Blackbird still perched on Clover's shoulder. 'I will have Hind and Crane with me, and they will guide me.'

Clover nodded, but more slowly. 'I go home now?'

'I will take you back,' Selena said.

They retraced their steps, and Blackbird flew from branch to branch whistling and trilling. Selena looked behind them, caught Hind's eye, and both stared at the wall, now a dark shadow rising almost to the height of the trees.

Selena knew how to get there, all right. She'd only been behind the wall once before, however, and that had been a great many years before, during her training, when Isleen, her guide, had led her through the Otherworld, reawakening her knowledge of the places within it.

Selena had not enjoyed her first trip there, and she

relished this one even less, for this one would have a particular purpose – to find one lost soul out of the thousands who crowded the dirty streets behind the wall.

But the hand with which she held Clover's did not tremble. Her breathing remained as measured and calm as ever. She tamped her nerves down by recalling that she walked the Goddess's path. All her training had prepared her for this, and she did not fear for herself.

They opened their eyes to Selena's attic room, and while they were gone it had begun to rain, and they both glanced up at the roof, at the din of the rain on the skylights.

'When you goin' back?' Clover asked.

'Soon, I think, but first we will take you downstairs and find Tara.'

That was good, Clover thought. For the first time ever, she didn't want to be up in the attic room with Selena. She didn't want to traipse around the Wildwood, not even to see the whales in the World Pool.

'Kay,' she said.

Selena nodded, then paused before getting up off the cushion. 'Can you still hear her?'

Clover didn't have to ask who Selena meant. She nodded. 'She still cryin'.'

There were voices coming from the kitchen and Selena made out Tara's. She sounded stressed. Selena picked up her pace.

Tara glanced at Selena and Clover as they pushed open the kitchen door and entered. Her eyes were round and frightened.

She turned back to Mike Manners.

'It's Saturday,' she repeated. 'I don't take any children on the weekends.'

But Mike was thrusting Josh at her. 'You have to. I've got work today. Everyone works on Saturdays now.'

Tara had no choice but to grasp Josh. She thought Mike would drop him if she didn't.

'Mr Manners,' Selena said. 'Perhaps it's time your wife came back from her sister's house. You heard Tara – she doesn't take children on the weekend.'

Mike Manners shook his head. Looked at Tara. 'I'll pay you double,' he said, and tried on a boyish, charming grin. 'Just today. Just give me today and I'll make other arrangements for next weekend, I promise.'

Josh tugged at Tara's hair, then pressed his cheek to hers and wrapped his arms around her. 'What about Rachel, Mr Manners?' she said. 'Why can't she look after him next weekend? I don't understand.'

But Mike shook his head, turned his mouth downwards. 'She's left.'

'She's left?' Damien asked, coming into the room, Dandy on his heels, and catching Mike's statement. 'What do you mean, she's left?'

'Left me.' Mike Manners said, blinking back the sting of tears. 'Left us.' He nodded at Josh.

Clover slipped behind Selena's legs and Dandy went over and scooped her up. 'How about we go see what cartoons are on this morning, what do you say?' She slipped out the door with her.

'Rachel wouldn't leave Josh,' Tara said, her face pale. She shook her head. 'She just wouldn't.'

'Well, I never thought so either, but guess what?' Mike

said shaking his head. 'She did. Being a mum didn't suit her, I guess.' Mike looked around at the room full of people butting into his business and rubbed at his face, forcing his expression to sorrow. 'Not every woman likes having children.'

'Rachel did,' Tara said, persisting. 'She loved Josh; she doted on him. He was the best thing in her life.' She hugged Josh to her as she spoke.

'Sure was a good actress around others, I'll give her that,' Mike said, and turned for the door. 'But at home, I had to force her to pay attention to him. And me.' He made a show of sniffing, then wrenched the door open. 'I'll pick him up at twelve.'

The door closed behind him, and Tara, Selena, and Damien stared wordlessly at each other.

28

RAM LED RUE, WITH MORGHAN ON HER HEELS, THROUGH THE paths of the Wildwood, along ways that Morghan was not familiar with. She followed without hesitation, however, excitement quickening in her chest.

Entering the Wildwood was always an adventure.

They came at last to a clearing and Rue stopped at the treeline, looking around, her mouth hanging open in surprise.

'Where are we?' she whispered to Morghan.

Morghan shook her head. 'I think it would be better to ask when.'

'When?' Rue frowned, not understanding.

'When are we?'

'Oh.' Rue looked down at the great horned sheep at her side and rested a hand tentatively on the springy wool of his neck, then looked again at what Ram had brought them to see.

'It's the same as I've dreamt it,' Rue said, letting go of a breath. 'Am I dreaming it now? Am I asleep and dreaming?'

'You are dreaming,' Morghan answered. 'Dreamwalking. We've slipped back to the past.'

Rue shook her head. 'I didn't know this was possible.'

She gazed at the buildings clustered around in front of them, recognising them from her dreams – her night-time adventures.

'This is where Bryn lives,' she whispered in awe. 'How did we get here?' Her fingers tightened in Ram's wool, knowing that he had brought them there.

Morghan looked at the buildings with interest. If only Ambrose were here with them, she thought. He would be fascinated. She gazed at them, committing them to memory to describe later for Ambrose.

She stepped into the clearing, wanting a closer look, but Rue hissed at her.

'Won't they see us?'

Morghan thought about it. 'Probably, yes, if they are adept enough.'

Rue followed her, gulping. She looked at Ram, but he stayed put, standing between the trees.

'He won't come,' she said.

Morghan looked back, saw that Rue's kin stood stubbornly where he had stopped, and she fell back reluctantly into the woods.

'I guess he wants us to stay where we are,' Rue whispered, unable to speak any louder for the fear that she would be overheard.

'Yes,' Morghan said. 'I guess he does.' She put her hand

to Wolf, but Wolf stood placidly at her side, only his ears alert, nose quivering.

'What are we here for?' Rue asked, and opened her mouth to say more, but closed it again with a snap.

A small figure appeared around the side of the nearest building.

'It's her,' Rue gasped, recognising the little girl at once. 'Morghan,' she said. 'It's her.'

'Yes. I see her.'

The small child stopped in her tracks, staring into the trees.

'Is she looking at us?' Rue asked.

Morghan shook her head. 'I think she looks past us.' She turned and peered into the dimness of the Wildwood. She thought she caught movement, but the sensation passed and there were only trees.

She turned back to look at the child, who stared still into the woods.

'What's she looking at?' Rue whispered.

'I don't know.'

The child looked back the way she'd come, then crept forward, making for the trees. Her muscles bunched for a leaping run between the trees.

But a figure appeared and scooped her up.

It was Bryn. Rue looked at her, taking a hesitant step forward as if to go to her.

Morghan put a restraining hand on her arm.

'Your kin does not move,' she said quietly. 'So we will not.'

'But isn't Bryn my kin?' Rue answered, her sight fixed on the two figures. Bryn swung the little girl around until the child smiled widely and tumbled from her arms, racing back out of sight the way she'd come.

Bryn followed her, unaware of being watched.

Rue shook her head, then looked at Morghan. 'I don't understand,' she said. 'What was the point of seeing that?'

Morghan was silent for a moment. 'I don't know,' she admitted at last.

'I wish we could go and look around,' Rue said. She looked down at the ground, not seeing it but thinking, frowning. 'The little girl,' she said. 'Something about her reminds me of Clover.'

Morghan considered that, decided it was more than possible. 'Perhaps it is Clover.'

'We've been together before?' Rue asked. 'Do you think so?'

'I would say it was highly likely.'

There was a rustling in the undergrowth as Snake moved, restless. He slithered back the way they'd come.

'Let us go,' Morghan said, noticing that Rue's Ram was turning also. 'I think you've seen what you were supposed to.'

'Me?' Rue asked, with a last look back at the small cluster of buildings. 'I was supposed to see this?'

'Yes,' Morghan said, sure of the fact. It was fascinating, she thought, how this was all unfolding.

Tomorrow, she decided, she would have Rue walk the path, call her power in.

Call Bryn to her.

Then they would see what happened.

. . .

AMBROSE STOOD NEXT TO THE UNLIT FIREPLACE IN Blackthorn House's small kitchen, lost in thought, his eyes shining.

The kettle whistled and Morghan got up with a smile and filled the teapot with the steaming water. She helped herself to the biscuit tin and brought it to the table.

'Here,' she said to Rue. 'Eat a couple of these, you'll feel steadier.' She plucked a chocolate biscuit out of the tin for herself and bit into it.

'I feel kinda seasick,' Rue said.

'Eating something will help,' Morghan said. 'Food and drink will ground you back here again.'

'I wish you'd gone further into the settlement,' Ambrose said.

'We didn't go into it at all,' Morghan replied, bringing the pot to the table and going back for mugs. 'Our kin would not budge from the sidelines.'

'I would have liked to see the arrangement of the place,' Ambrose said. 'Particularly the temple.'

'I've already told you about the temple,' Rue said. 'I dreamt it, remember?'

'Yes,' Ambrose said, rubbing his palms together. 'But is it in the centre of the buildings, or off to the side, perhaps?'

Rue couldn't see how it mattered all that much. The biscuit was making her feel better. Morghan was right, the food was grounding. She nodded as Morghan filled a mug for her with hot tea and she took a sip of it, not minding that it was scalding. She just wanted to stop the room from tipping from side to side as though it were a boat and not a house.

'The temple has like, three rooms to it,' Rue said,

remembering it. She shook her head, took another gulp of tea and wondered if it would be all right to take another biscuit. 'The weaving room or whatever you call it is to the side of it. Almost like it's part of the temple.'

'Yes,' Morghan said, sitting down and smiling at Ambrose's flushed, excited face. 'I remember you telling me that – and I remember what it made me think at the time too.' She pursed her lips, for she'd totally forgotten the lesson it had brought to mind. A lesson that could prove valuable for Rue.

For everyone, really.

'What was that?' Rue asked her, taking a second biscuit and savouring the chocolate upon her tongue.

'The reason why the weaving room would be part of the temple.'

'Ah,' Ambrose said. 'Yes. Good point.'

Rue lifted her eyebrows and waited.

Morghan chewed, swallowed and nodded. She looked across the table at Rue.

'You see,' she said. 'I do believe you're here to discover what Bryn wants you to know, but while you are here, there are other lessons to learn.'

'That will also be Bryn's purpose, I would think,' Ambrose interrupted.

'Yes,' Morghan agreed. 'I don't see how they couldn't be.'

Rue wasn't following. 'What do you mean?' She looked at Ambrose. 'What about the weaving room being part of the temple?'

'Hmm.' Ambrose reached for his mug of tea and held it cupped in his hands. He'd yet to sit down, too full of excite-

ment to settle. He bounced slightly on his toes, considering
how to put his thoughts and Morghan's into words.

'It's because weaving is like, a metaphor for weaving the
worlds, right?' Rue said, nodding because she thought she
was understanding after all.

Ambrose beamed at her. 'It is, yes,' he said. 'Cloth is
woven with fibre that has been grown and spun. We weave
too with our lives – our songs, which aren't always real
songs, but are always the actions of a life that lives in
harmony with the turning of the Wheel.'

'Weaving is a sacred act of creation,' Morghan added. 'As
should be everything we do.'

'Everything?' Rue looked dubiously at her, but Morghan
only smiled and nodded.

'The smallest, most everyday thing can become a song
to the world.'

Now Rue shook her head. 'No,' she said. 'I don't see how
that one works. Most of what we have to do in a day is
boring.'

Morghan laughed. 'That's the lesson. To bring a joyful
mindfulness to every task. The world opens to you when
you walk this way.'

Rue was silent after this, but she wasn't sure she'd ever
turn doing the dishes or cleaning the toilet into a song to
the world. It might be an act of creation in that a dirty something turned into a clean something, but it still wouldn't be
a song and would still be tedious. In fact, the more she
thought about it, the more tiresome things she could think
of that had to be done each day, and wasn't she right about
that?

She shook her head at Morghan, then grinned. 'Challenge accepted.'

LATER, IT WAS TIME TO CALL CLOVER, AND MORGHAN intercepted her on the way to the office to use the phone.

'May I come with you for a moment?' she asked.

Rue stopped, surprised. 'Do you want to talk to Selena?'

'No,' Morghan replied, shaking her head. 'I only want to show you something to try.'

'Okay, then,' Rue said, intrigued despite her worry over Clover. 'Sure.'

'Thank you.'

Morghan followed Rue into her office, and when Rue went to take a seat like she usually did when she was calling home, Morghan shook her head.

'I think I'd like you to stay standing for this,' she said.

Rue froze, then moved back out from behind the desk and nodded. 'Okay. What do you want me to do?'

'Look at the phone,' Morghan said.

Rue looked at the phone. 'Right.'

'Describe it to me.'

Rue looked at Morghan in mystified surprise. 'Describe it to you?'

'Yes. Just relax and tell me what the phone looks like.'

'Righto,' Rue said and looked back at the phone. 'Well, it's the old sort,' she said. 'With a whaddoyacallit? A rotary dial. And it's black and sort of squat.' Rue giggled. 'It's sitting on the desk like an old toad.'

Morghan raised an eyebrow and hid her smile.

Rue glanced at her. 'Why do you have such an old phone?'

'Because it still works,' Morghan said. 'Now, keep describing it to me.'

Turning her attention back to the phone, Rue shook her head. 'Okay, well, it's made of some sort of plastic, I guess, and it has a cord attaching the headset of the phone to the... body, I suppose. The cord is a curly one, corkscrew curly. It will stretch out about a metre or so if I pick up the handset and move away.' She glanced at Morghan, who nodded at her to keep going.

'All right. The black plastic on the body is sort of shiny,' Rue said. 'And not dusty, so someone comes in here and cleans.' Rue wondered for a moment if it was Morghan, making an everyday task a song, but she didn't ask. 'The dial has numbers on it, one through nine, and in the centre of the dial, there's a sticker with a handwritten phone number on it.' She looked back at Morghan, running out of things she hadn't already described.

Morghan nodded, shifted lightly on her feet. 'Now describe the wall behind you.

Rue turned in surprise. 'The wall?'

'Yes. The wall.'

'Um, well, it's about...' Rue imagined she had her dress-maker's tape with her. 'About three metres wide, and there is some artwork on it.' She looked more closely at the pictures. She'd not paid them much attention when she'd been in here before. A smile curved her lips. 'Are they Grainne's?'

'They are,' Morghan said.

Rue nodded. She'd visited Grainne in the small summer

house she used as an art studio and hung out with her for a while. 'Thought so.'

'Describe the wall,' Morghan reminded her.

'Right. Well, there are three pictures on the walls. They're encaustic art,' Rue said, remembering what Grainne had told her. 'They're made with wax and paper and stuff. One of them shows a wolf.'

Rue came to an abrupt halt in her recital and looked at Morghan. 'It's your wolf, isn't it?' Excitement rose up inside her. 'The one I saw today?' She returned her gaze to the artwork and looked more closely. 'It's your wolf, and he's looking out at us from some trees.'

She turned her attention to the next picture. 'Trees again.' She snuffled a laugh. 'Lady of the Forest. This one has a snake draped around one of the branches.' Rue took a step towards the picture, the phone forgotten for the moment behind her. 'Is that a pear tree?' she asked, confused. 'Wasn't the snake supposed to be with an apple tree?'

The pears on the tree, around whose branches Morghan's snake wound, were plump and gold, as if coloured with gold leaf under the layers of wax.

'It's not illustrating a Christian story,' Morghan said mildly.

'Oh. Right.' Rue nodded and turned to the third picture. This one also had trees, and when she glanced at the other two, she realised they were all three of the same place. 'It's like, what is it called?' The word came to her. 'A triptych, isn't it?' She nodded, and described the third painting, thinking about earlier that day, when they had stepped together into exactly these woods, and Rue had seen her sheep.

Ram, she corrected herself.

'I can't see any animal in this one,' she said, then looked more closely. 'Wait. There's a bird on this branch here – how could I have missed that?' She glanced at Morghan. 'You have a bird too? You have three animals that walk with you?'

Morghan just nodded.

'What sort of bird is it?' Rue asked, looking back at the picture. 'A hawk?'

'Yes,' Morghan said. 'Hawk flies with me, and I sometimes with her.'

Rue nodded, then shivered with delight. 'I wish my friend Ebony was here,' she said. 'She would be over the moon excited about everything we're doing.'

29

'Perhaps you can teach her some of these things when you go back to your home,' Morghan said.

'She would never let me not,' Rue answered, straightening. 'I think I've described everything on this wall.'

'Have you?'

Rue scanned it again. 'Oh. There's a cupboard in front of it? Is that what you mean?' She looked at it. 'It's kind of long, and low, with cupboard doors in the front, and on the top – there's still no dust – there's...' Rue looked at the array of things and wondered where to start.

'You want me to describe all this?'

'Yes.'

'Okay, well, at one end there are two candlesticks, they look like silver, sort of heavy looking, with square bases, and they have yellow candles in them.' She leaned forward and sniffed them. 'Beeswax, I think.'

She glanced at Morghan. 'Keep going?'

Morghan nodded.

Rue turned back to the items arrayed along the top of the cupboard. She didn't know what all this describing was for, but she was keen to find out.

'There's a bowl with some sort of herbs loose in it, and another shallow dish with what looks like water in it.'

Rue stood back. 'It's an altar,' she said. 'This is your altar.'

'It is,' Morghan said. 'One of them, anyway. Do you think, if you turned around, that you'd be able to see most of what's there in your mind?'

'Ah, yeah, probably,' Rue said, scanning the wall, the pictures, the cupboard, the altar setup. She nodded. 'Not perfectly, but still, I'd get most of it.'

'And the telephone,' Morghan said, then held out a hand when Rue went to spin about. 'Don't look at it, just imagine it.'

Rue brought up the phone in her mind. The black plastic body with a dial which went from one to nine, then a zero next to the nine, and the nine was at the bottom, the farthest around the dial.

'I can see it,' she said.

'Good. Now, turn around and go to the phone, pick up the handset and press it to your ear, listen to the dial tone.'

Rue did as she was told, even more interested now to figure out what was going on. The phone buzzed in her ear.

'Listen to the dial tone. Can you see the wall behind you?' Morghan asked. 'Without turning around. Feel it there behind you.'

Rue's eyes widened, and she brought up the image of the wall in her mind. The altar. The three pictures. Wolf, Snake, Hawk. She felt them at her back.

'Look at the phone, listen to the dial tone, be aware of the wall behind you.'

Rue nodded. The dial tone began to beep at her. She needed to dial or hang up. She listened to it instead, feeling the wall at her back, Morghan to the side, leaning against that wall, her legs crossed at their booted ankles. Rue closed her eyes for a moment, and she could feel the whole room now, as though she wasn't just in her body standing in front of the desk, but slightly outside it too, aware of everything. She opened her eyes again and looked at Morghan.

She looked down at Morghan's side, and wondered if the wolf was there, even now, looking back at her.

She thought maybe the wolf was there.

'What now?' she asked.

'Now,' Morghan said. 'Now, without leaving your aware-ness of this room, the phone, this wall, these paintings, I want you to become aware of the house around you, then I want you to find the well outside.'

No sooner had Morghan stopped talking than Rue could feel the well. She closed her eyes again, aware of the room around her, the wolf's eyes on her from the painting, from Morghan's side. And she could feel the rooms upstairs, the hallway outside the door, and outside the house, was the well, a sensation of depth and weight that was in a partic-ular spot to her left.

She blew out a breath.

'Bring your awareness back to this room,' Morghan said.

Rue reeled it in until she could feel the room snug around her again. The phone in her hand, the wall at her back.

'There are trees at the back of the room,' Morghan said. 'And your ram stands among them, looking out at you.'

Rue almost turned around, but stayed still instead, seeing the wall behind her, feeling it there, and yes, Morghan was right. The trees from Grainne's pictures were growing through the floorboards now, and Ram stood there, watching her.

'Now,' Morghan said. 'Hold all that inside and outside you as long as you can, while you make your phone call.'

She slipped from the room then, and Rue stood, the phone still to her ear, holding onto the sensation of the room around her, and the world beyond that, and Ram standing between the trees, gazing at her.

She turned slowly to the phone and put the handset down, then picked it back up and listened to the dial tone. It buzzed in her ear.

Ram lifted a hoof in the leaves behind her.

She dialled the number and heard the series of clicks as the call went through.

'Rue! I bin waitin' by the phone.'

Rue squeezed her eyes shut at the sound of Clover's voice and her grip on the room wavered.

'Clover Bee,' she said. 'I'm missing you.'

'I miss you too,' Clover said, then paused. 'You got a sheep.'

'You can see him?' Rue asked. A great sense of calm swept through her. 'Of course you can see him.'

'You brought him for me to look at,' Clover said, peering into the world around her and seeing Rue with her big woolly sheep. 'I seen him already, when I looked before. He a ram?'

'How did you know that? Rue asked and let herself spin around slowly to look at the back wall. There were the pictures, there was the altar. But, she thought, there were also the trees, and Ram. She couldn't see them there, but she could feel them.

Yes, she could do that.

And, she thought, Ram was pretty magnificent, with his horns curling around his head, and the strength in his body. Nothing just sheepish about that guy.

She turned back to the desk and focused on the phone and Clover. But the awareness of the wall and trees behind her didn't go away. Perhaps it faded a little, but it didn't go away. She cleared her throat.

'How are you doing, Clover?' she asked.

'I okay,' Clover replied. 'I asked S'lena wha' a ram is. Then we went lookin' for Josh's mama.'

Rue leaned heavily against Morghan's desk. 'You went looking for her? Where?'

'In the Otherworld,' Clover said, choosing Selena's name for it and pronouncing it carefully.

Rue pressed her palm to her mouth and shook her head before letting it drop. She gazed outside the window for a moment, where it was early evening, the day turning to gold as the sun drifted down behind the hills.

'Did you find her?'

'I took S'lena near to where she was callin', but S'lena took me back after that. She says she'll go back by herself later.'

A sudden flare of worry ignited inside Rue and Ram and the trees, and the wall behind her with the three pictures were forgotten. There was just her hand clenched around the phone and the nasty burning sensation inside her.

'Is it going to be dangerous?' Rue asked.

'Don' know,' Clover said. 'I only little, so maybe for me.'

'Can I speak to Selena, Clover? Is she there?'

There was the sound of voices then, and a pause, before Selena spoke.

'Rue,' she said. 'How are you?'

'I'm good,' Rue said. 'But I'm worried about you and Clover. What's happening?' The words tumbled from her lips. 'Are you okay? Clover told me about Josh's mum, about going to look for her, and how you wouldn't let her go the whole way.' Rue moved around the desk and sat down. Now she could see Grainne's paintings, with their eerie layers of wax, and the wolf stared back at her. She dipped her head.

'There's nothing to be too concerned about, Rue,' Selena said. 'Clover's right – I did bring her back, because she doesn't need to do any more now that she's pointed me in the right direction.'

'How come you didn't know the right direction?'

Selena laughed, and some of Rue's nervousness faded. 'Clover could hear her calling better than I could, that's all.'

'Josh's mum?'

'Yes. I'll be going back for her soon.'

'To the Otherworld?' Rue still wasn't sure how it all worked.

'Yes. There's a place there where shards of the souls of those who suffered violence often go and become lost.' She didn't add that the souls of the perpetrators often hung out there as well.

'Does that happen with everyone?' Rue shook her head. 'With everyone who, you know, gets hurt or killed?'

'I don't think it's that simple,' Selena said. 'But that's where I'll be going to look for Rachel.'

'I'm worried,' Rue said.

Selena spoke gently. 'It's going to be all right, Rue' she said. 'How are you getting on?'

Rue thought she was doing well. There were so many new things for her to practice. She'd been to the stones to dance that afternoon too, working on not being self-conscious.

It was harder than it sounded.

She looked back at the paintings while Selena got Clover back on the line, and the wolf didn't look so danger-ous, standing there looking out from the trees.

Rue thought of Morghan helping her cross – whatever it had been. The border between the worlds, perhaps, and she'd reared back in shock at the sight of Morghan's snake and wolf.

Ram wasn't standing there anymore. Rue chatted to Clover for a while longer, then said goodbye and hung up the phone. She looked at the wall, considering it, then shaking her head, she left the room.

Grainne was in the drawing room, sitting with her legs tucked up on the sofa, reading a magazine. She looked up when Rue came in and smiled.

'How is Clover?' she asked.

Rue looked around awkwardly. 'She's good,' she said. 'Is Morghan about?'

But Grainne shook her head. 'She had to go back out to see one of her clients.'

'Oh.'

Grainne patted the sofa cushion beside her. 'Come and sit down,' she said. 'Perhaps I can help with whatever is bothering you.'

Rue walked over and sat down.

30

'So,' Grainne said. 'What is it?'

Rue twisted around the ring Selena had given her for her birthday before leaving. It was a delicate gold band with a peridot crescent moon. She loved the pale green stone, loved the whole ring.

'Selena's going somewhere in the Otherworld,' Rue said, her voice rough with concern. 'Somewhere where people go who have died violently, or had something bad happen to them, or something like that.' She lifted her gaze from her ring and looked at Grainne. 'I'm worried about her. It doesn't sound like a...safe place to go.'

Grainne set her magazine aside and took one of Rue's hands in hers. 'This is because of the woman who has disappeared?'

Rue nodded. Grainne's fingers were warm, and she let the touch soothe her a little. 'Josh's mum. Josh is one of the little guys that Tara looks after. His mum never came to pick him up and his dad says she won't be back.'

'But Clover says something bad has happened to her, am I right? Selena told us about it before she left.'

Of course she had. Rue nodded. Sighed. 'Clover said she'd been hurt really badly.'

'And you're worried Selena might be in over her head?'

Rue thought about it, nodded. 'I can't help it,' she said. 'This is all still pretty new to me, and it sounds scary. Clover's been terrified.'

Grainne patted Rue's hand. 'I don't think you need to worry too much. Selena is very sensible, and she has had more training than you and I could ever know.'

Rue nodded, but the knot of concern was still in her stomach making her uneasy. 'Morghan would know, wouldn't she? If Selena would be able to safely find her way around wherever she's going? Only, it sounded dangerous.' Rue dropped her gaze. 'Are there dangerous places in the Otherworld?'

That was a good question, Grainne thought, giving it some consideration. 'I've never been anywhere dangerous, but then again, I don't go there often.'

'Has Morghan ever mentioned this place where Selena's going to go?'

'I don't know,' Grainne said. 'But when she gets back later this evening, we'll ask her. How about that?' Grainne paused. 'Perhaps she can even go with Selena – did Selena say when she would travel there again?'

'It's morning there,' Rue said and grimaced, unaware she was doing so. 'Later in the day, I guess. Maybe in a couple hours?' She paused. 'Could Morghan really go too, even though she's here, and Selena is way over there?'

'I don't see why not,' Grainne said.

'But how could they, I don't know, meet up?'

Grainne laughed. 'I don't know how they do it, I only know that they do.'

'Selena and Morghan have travelled together before?'

'They did it regularly when Selena lived here,' Grainne said.

'She never told me.'

Grainne folded Rue's fingers over in her own. 'It likely never came up,' she said. 'But they travelled together; it can certainly be done.' Grainne shook her head. 'I remember once, back when I first got here, and I was in a pretty bad state then.'

Rue's brow wrinkled. She didn't know what Grainne meant. What sort of bad state?

Grainne smiled. 'I had a very rough childhood, and the sort of way that I grew up follows you.' She shook her head slightly. 'Anyway, I was somewhat untethered when I got here.'

'Untethered?'

'Slip sliding all over the place.'

Rue still didn't understand.

Grainne considered how to explain herself. 'I came here so that Ambrose could help me with Clarice, while I threw myself headlong into dealing with everything I had gone through.' She paused, then smiled. 'We're getting off course here,' she said. 'What I was going to tell you was that one day I was wandering around feeling lost, in my mind or in the Otherworld, I don't know. I do know that Morghan talked to me – I could still hear her – and she spoke to me, told me to find a tree. Wherever I was, she said, look for a tree. If I could find a tree, she could find me.'

'And did you? Did she?'

'Oh yes,' Grainne said. 'Easy as pie. I found a tree and she found me. There's a connection between the priestesses of this place and trees, you see. Morghan told me that for her, all forests are one forest, whatever that means.' Grainne laughed. 'What one tree knows, they can all know.'

Rue was quiet a minute. 'Were you all right?' she asked. 'After that?'

'I was that day,' Grainne said. 'And I was even better after a while. After a lot of throwing myself against it all. And a little bit of being caught by Morghan as well.' She nodded. 'But that's a story for another time, perhaps.'

Rue was embarrassed. 'I'm sorry,' she said. 'I didn't mean to pry.'

'It's all right,' Grainne said. 'It was me who started telling you.' She nodded. 'But my point is that I'm sure that Selena will be perfectly all right, and if anything goes wrong, Morghan will likely know, and be able to help.'

Rue sat back against the sofa and thought about it. She looked at Grainne, noticing that her eyes were green, like her brother's.

'Do you think I will learn all this stuff?' she asked. 'I mean, I know I only have a couple weeks here, but I can learn some of it, right?'

'Morghan has already been teaching you.'

Rue snuffled a laugh. 'She's been teaching me to dance. But I don't really know why.'

'Dancing helps you get outside of your head,' Grainne explained. 'And it brings you into harmony with the song of the world.'

'Dancing makes me feel awkward and self-conscious, which Morghan says it's supposed to help me get rid of.'

'That's why you practice, until you learn to let go, so that you are just movement and song and the rhythm of the world,' Grainne said. 'So that your spirit soars and you are part of things greater than yourself.'

'Why dance though?' Rue asked. 'Aren't there other ways?'

'I'm positive there are,' Grainne said. 'But Morghan likes to dance, and it works, so there we go.'

Rue giggled, louder this time. 'She said she'd make me dance even if I was in a wheelchair and could only wave my arms around.'

'It's Beltane soon,' Grainne remarked. 'You'll be here for that. We all come together and dance then. It's rather wonderful.'

'Who comes?' Rue asked. 'Are there many who come and dance or celebrate, or whatever?'

'There are about seven or eight of us.' But this brought up another thought. 'It's your birthday tomorrow,' she said, her tone faintly accusing.

Rue dropped her gaze and shrugged. 'Yeah. I turn sixteen.' Her fingers went to the ring on her right hand.

'Why, I do believe you weren't going to mention it,' Grainne said.

Rue shook her head. 'Probably not,' she admitted.

'It's your sixteenth birthday,' Grainne said. 'It's an important day.'

'Is it though?' Rue shook her head. 'I feel like there's so much else going on. And I'm a guest here, so it's kinda weird to go around saying, hey everyone, it's my birthday.'

'Nonsense,' Grainne laughed. 'And in any case, Selena made arrangements before she left.'

Rue was confused. 'What arrangements?'

'A birthday cake, for starters. She says your favourite is chocolate?'

'I used to make it sometimes for Clover,' Rue said, her cheeks heating in a blush. 'If we had the ingredients, I'd make us cake.' She laughed. 'I'm not very good at baking, though, but Clover always liked it anyway.'

She grew silent, worry seeping into her again.

Grainne caught the change. 'You'll be able to call Clover again in the morning and speak to Selena too.'

Rue nodded, fiddled with her ring. 'It's weird though, thinking that Selena will be doing her travelling while I'm asleep.' She screwed her eyes shut tight. 'I feel like I ought to be awake, in case...in case she needs me.' Rue wound down. 'Even though I know I won't be able to do anything.' She looked at Grainne. 'Do you know when Morghan will be home? Can you get her to call Selena and speak to her? So, they can, you know, go together to this place?' Rue sighed. 'I'd just feel better if Selena wasn't going on her own. Even if she really would be all right.'

Grainne regarded Rue steadily for a moment then nodded, coming to a decision. 'How about I call Morghan now and tell her your concerns? I can leave her a message to get back to me. That way, we'll know when she's coming home, and she can talk to Selena as well, and they can work it out together.'

Rue's relief flooded through her like warm water. She sagged against the couch. 'Would you?' she asked. 'I'd feel so much better if they could do it together.'

Grainne unfolded her legs and stretched, then got up. 'I'll go and call her now.'

MORGHAN FELT THE BUZZING OF HER PHONE IN HER POCKET and pressed her hand against it until it stopped. She smoothed down the blanket over the old man and smiled up at his children.

'Perhaps you'd like to sit with your father for a while?' she said.

The son frowned, looking vaguely frightened. 'He's not going to...'

'Not in the next half hour or so, I would say. When is your other sister getting here?' Morghan looked down at old Jimmy Mason resting under the covers, his skin stretched dry and paper thin across the bones of his face. 'I feel he is waiting for her before he undertakes this journey.'

'She won't be here for another hour,' Janice, Jim's daughter said, and her face creased in a frown. 'I told her she needed to come here days ago.'

Morghan only nodded. She'd had many conversations with Jim, listening and letting him wander all down the lanes of his memory, reciting the stories of his children, his late wife. She glanced towards the corner of the room, where she could feel Joanie Mason waiting for her husband to draw his last breath.

It wouldn't be too long. Not too long after their youngest daughter arrived, Morghan thought.

She excused herself from the bedroom and went downstairs, stepping out the back door into the garden, tipping her face to slowly darkening sky.

There was a text message from Grainne on her phone, and she pressed the buttons for Grainne's number.

'Hello love,' Grainne said, answering straight away.

'Is something wrong?' Morghan bounced a little on the balls of her feet, keeping her body loose and relaxed even as she asked the question.

'No, everything's all right.'

Morghan closed her eyes, letting the warm familiarity of Grainne's voice seep through her. She smiled, waiting for Grainne to tell her what she needed.

'Rue's worried about Selena,' Grainne said.

That brought Morghan to attention, and she frowned. 'Why? Why is she worried?'

'She spoke to Clover and Selena on the phone just a half hour ago and learnt that Selena is planning to travel to some place in the Otherworld that Rue says sounds dangerous.' Grainne paused. 'Somewhere where the souls of those who have suffered violence go, she said.'

Morghan closed her eyes and the gates to the City of Lost Souls rose in her mind. 'Yes,' she said. 'I know the place.'

'Is there any danger?'

That was a good question and Morghan gave it consideration before replying.

'Some,' she said.

Grainne laughed. 'That's all right,' she said. 'You don't need to go into long, involved explanations.'

Her teasing tone made Morghan smile, but she shook her head. 'I'm sure this is nothing that Selena can't handle,' she said.

'Rue's worried. She wants you to call Selena and talk to

her about it.' There was a pause and then Grainne spoke again.

'I might have told her that it was possible for you to travel with Selena.'

31

MORGHAN SLIPPED HER MOBILE PHONE INTO HER POCKET AND gazed back up at the sky. The night was drawing in, and she listened to the birds singing the velvet darkness down.

Behind her, there was the crunching of car tyres on the driveway, and she turned in surprised gladness. Jimmy's daughter must have driven fast to get there this quickly.

Morghan let the car door open and shut before moving. She listened to the sound of footsteps, the front door opening, then closing. She'd give them a few minutes, she thought, before returning to the room where Jimmy Mason was breathing his last.

And after that, she'd return home and go with Selena on her journey to the Otherworld, to the City of Lost Souls.

'Who are you?' the new daughter asked when Morghan stepped back into the warmth of Jimmy's bedroom.

'My name is Morghan Wilde,' Morghan answered. 'My job is helping those who are dying. I've been visiting your dad for some weeks, helping him make the transition.'

The daughter – Lily of the Far Valley, Jimmy had called her, speaking always of her with exasperated affection – stared wide-eyed at Morghan, then bent back down over her father, lying her head on his chest.

'You don't need to go on being so dramatic,' Laura, Jimmy's oldest daughter said, then looked at Morghan. 'She oughtn't to be squashing him like that.'

'I'm not squashing him,' Lily said.

'Yes, you are – he's fragile, you'll be stopping his heart, lying on top of him like that.'

Lily lifted her head, rolled her eyes. 'How long?' she asked.

'Not long now,' Morghan answered. Already Jimmy's breaths were coming with long pauses between them. 'It's time to wish him well on his way,' she said.

Lily looked at her for a long minute, then nodded and turned back to her dad.

'I'm sorry I wasn't here more,' she said in a low voice. 'I should have been different, I guess.' A small smile tucked itself onto her lips. 'But then I wouldn't have been your Lily of the hills and vales, would I?' She pressed a palm to her father's cheek then leaned over and kissed him. 'Happy travels, Dad,' she said. 'I bet Mum's waiting for you.' She paused. 'And probably Kipper too.'

'Kipper!' Laura scowled, turned to Morghan. 'Kipper was Mum and Dad's cat.' She shook her head.

'It's all right, Laura,' David said. 'Let's all just sit down and be with him, yeah?'

Laura let herself be mollified and took her seat.

They listened to Jimmy's failing breathing.

Morghan stood out of the way, closing her eyes. She reached for the space she had knitted together in the room earlier, and found it once more, drew it around everyone, around the man in the bed, bathing them in a soft, soothing light and holding them there.

Jimmy's wife moved closer to the bed, smiling widely at Morghan as she passed. A black and white cat jumped onto the bedspread and kneaded the blankets.

Jimmy's Kipper, Morghan thought, and kept her eyes closed, humming softly to herself. Jimmy would be all right, she knew, even as he lifted himself from his body, going to his wife, delight on his features. Morghan watched them embrace, and Joanie, his wife, led him gently towards the light from which she'd come, Kipper winding about their ankles.

Jimmy paused on the threshold, looking back at the room, at his three children. He blew them a kiss, then winked at Morghan and followed his wife into the light and through into the next world and his next adventure.

Morghan held the space for a few minutes longer, then let it fold together until it was gone, and she stood in the ordinary bedroom again.

'He's gone,' Lily said, then looked around at her brother and sister. 'Isn't he gone?'

Jimmy's rasping breathing had ceased.

'He's passed,' Morghan said quietly. 'From this world to the next.'

Laura burst into loud sobs.

. . .

'How did it go?' Grainne asked, meeting Morghan at the door and helping her off with her coat.

'It was an easy passing,' Morghan said. 'He held on until the youngest daughter was there, and then he slipped out and away.' She grinned suddenly, despite her fatigue. 'His cat came to meet him.'

'His cat?' Grainne raised an eyebrow.

'Kipper.'

'Kipper?'

'Mmm.'

'Just the cat?'

'No,' Morghan smiled. 'His wife too, and more family waiting back in the light.'

Grainne nodded then giggled. 'Kipper? Really?'

'I like the name,' Morghan said, and slipped an arm around Grainne's waist, kissed her cheek. 'Perhaps we need a cat named Kipper.'

'You're not serious, are you?' Grainne laughed, shaking her head.

'No, but if I ever do have the urge to get a cat, Kipper is a fine name.' Morghan stretched, yawned. It was full dark now. 'I'm craving a cup of tea,' she said. 'Where's Rue?'

'She went upstairs to read a story to Clarice. After that, she was going to her room.' Grainne paused. 'She really is very nervous.'

'Does that surprise us?' Morghan asked, still standing in the dim hallway, reaching again for Grainne, and resting her cheek on Grainne's warm hair.

Grainne shook her head. 'Not even a little,' she said. 'I think she is also feeling guilty for staying here. She didn't realise really, what was happening.'

'Did you tell her I am going with Selena?'

'Yes. She was greatly relieved.' Grainne looked up at Morghan. 'You're just doing it for that reason, though? Not because you think Selena really needs you along?'

'I don't think Selena really needs me along,' Morghan said. 'On the other hand, by her own admission, it has been a long while since she visited this particular place.'

Grainne paused. 'And how long has it been for you?'

'Much less time,' Morghan assured her. 'Do you remember Betty Thompson?'

Betty had crossed over just after the winter solstice, Grainne remembered. She nodded. 'She needed you to go there?'

'Yes. I found a shard of her there.' Morghan rubbed her face and yawned again.

'You're tired,' Grainne told her severely. 'Can Selena not wait until you've had some rest?'

'I'll be fine,' Morghan said. 'I just need that cup of tea.' She led Grainne down to the kitchen and lifted the kettle to fill. 'Every moment that Selena waits is another that Clover suffers.'

'That poor child,' Grainne said. 'What must it be like to have such a gift?'

They were silent a while as Morghan put the kettle on to boil and filled the teapot. She brought it to the table, with the biscuit tin.

'She'll find it hard, don't you think?' Grainne asked as though they'd never paused. 'To live like this as she grows.' She pursed her lips. 'Different perhaps if she'd been born here, but she wasn't.'

'Yes,' Morghan agreed. 'That thought has occurred to me

too, with some interest. But perhaps the reasons will become clear in time.'

'Or not,' Grainne said. 'You think Clover is the child in Rue's little jaunts back to her past life, don't you?'

'I do, yes,' Morghan said, pouring tea for them both. She held up her cup, letting the steam waft over her tired skin. She'd been up since five that morning, and it was good to sit down, enjoy a moment's quiet and peace with Grainne.

'She's seeing the past to know what to do for her now; that's what I think,' Grainne said. 'The better informed we are, the better we know how to act.'

'Yes,' Morghan agreed. 'I think that's a big part of it.'

'There's more, to your reckoning?'

Morghan sipped at her tea. 'I don't know what,' she said at last. 'But there's bound to be more, to my mind.' She shook her head a little. 'Dragons and wizards.'

'Dragon for protection,' Grainne said. 'If we go by experience.' She smiled at Morghan.

'Yes.' Morghan returned the smile. 'If we go by experience.'

'I wish I'd heard your conversation,' Grainne said. 'Pity you weren't wired to record it!'

Morghan laughed. 'If I'd known I'd be sitting in a car across from you, persuading a dragon that I could be trusted, then I would definitely have purchased a recording device beforehand.'

Grainne nodded, sobering. 'He was protecting the golden heart of the child.'

'Little Grainne, yes,' Morghan said quietly. 'Assuring himself that I would take good care of her.'

Grainne reached out and took Morghan's hand, held it.

'All of us are golden-hearted,' Grainne said, her voice low, musing. 'But Clover's heart is untarnished, so to speak. A very great treasure.'

Morghan was silent.

Grainne squeezed her hand. 'I'm glad you're going with Selena, even though I will worry, with you being so tired.'

MORGHAN STEPPED OUTSIDE INTO THE NIGHT. IT WRAPPED itself around her like a cloak and she stood on the terrace breathing it in, before lifting her lantern and crossing the lawn to the path through the woods. She'd decided earlier in the evening that she would go to the cave to accompany Selena.

There were two caves, a smaller, big enough only for one person, and another, much larger. Something told her that the larger would be the right choice for this night.

Morghan yawned, then let herself sink into her body, relaxing, becoming pleasantly alert to all that surrounded her.

Something rustled in the darkness beside the path, and she smiled.

'Good evening, little one,' she said to the creature.

The fresh air tasted good upon her tongue, and she thought about the next spoke of the year that was fast coming upon them. Beltane. Rue would be with them still, heading home soon after. They would have to do something special for her.

There was a light already in the cave when Morghan ducked her head and entered. She smiled at Ambrose.

'Grainne told you I would be coming here, did she?'

Ambrose fed another stick to the fire and grinned back. 'She did.' He patted his drum. 'I thought you might like the accompaniment.'

'I would indeed,' Morghan said, setting down her lantern and reaching a hand out to the wall of the cave to whisper a greeting and a blessing.

'I have come into your warmth to birth new visions,' she murmured. 'I hear the beating of your heart. Let me see in your honour.'

She came over to the fire, squatted down and took a handful of herbs from her bag, threw them on the fire, and watched as the fragrant smoke billowed.

On the far side of the fire, Ambrose picked up his drum. He started slow, picking out the heartbeat of rock and stone.

Morghan lifted her head, listened.

'Maxen,' Ambrose said.

She nodded, the notes from the flute rising and falling, silvery upon the night.

'I am honoured,' she said.

She rose and stood straight in the centre of the cave, closing her eyes, the flames from the fire safely off to one side. There was no need to sanctify the space; Morghan could easily feel that Ambrose had done so already. And on its own, used as such for so very, very long, the cave was a space between the worlds even without the formal rituals.

Pulling a fringed mask from the bag at her waist, Morghan slipped it on. Now the space around her fell to dimness, and she spread her arms wide, embracing it.

There she stood, placing herself on the Wheel, one foot in either world, suddenly timeless, Ambrose's drum low and hypnotic in the space around her.

Maxen's flute became the sound of Hawk's wings.

Beside Morghan, her wolf lifted his head, tensed his muscles to run.

Morghan stepped easily into the Wildwood and Hawk swooped down to grasp her in her talons, lifting her into the air for a moment before she put on her feathers and they became one, the beat of their wings like a song to Morghan's ears.

How she loved flying. How she loved to fly.

Below them, their keen eyes saw the black streak that was Wolf, running across the field, Snake at his side, great muscular body parting the grass in his wake.

Morghan opened her mouth and cried out in Hawk's voice, before they lowered their head, brought their wings down, and the ground grew closer until they stood upon it, woman and bird again, Hawk on Morghan's shoulder, the Otherworld breeze rustling her feathers, tugging loose a strand of Morghan's hair.

They waited for Wolf and Snake and when they arrived, Morghan went down the wide stone steps set into the ground and entered the maze. The walls rose high over her head, made of yellow stone, but she had been here before, had learnt the path between them.

The statue of the weeping woman brought her to a halt, as it always did. Morghan took an offering from her bag and dropped the twist of herbs into the woman's cupped hands.

'My blessings on you,' she whispered as she touched the cold stone hands for a moment. 'I weep with you; tears of compassion for the world seep from my eyes.' Morghan spoke with her head lowered, feeling the sweet ache of love for the world in her heart.

Then it was time to go on, to find her way through the maze and meet Selena on the other side of it.

At the gates to the City of Lost Souls.

32

SELENA SAT BESIDE THE WELL, THE AIR WARM AROUND HER. She knew that if she dipped a hand into the water of the well, it too would be warm, silky around her fingers, even while it was shaded by the oak that had grown beside it, planted there by Morghan.

And there was Morghan herself. Selena rose to meet her on the grassy lawn, embracing her wordlessly.

'We are well met,' Morghan said, speaking first.

Selena bowed her head. 'Thank you for accompanying me.'

'I will always be at your service,' Morghan said, smiling.

'Well,' Selena said, turning to look at the large wooden gates. 'There is no point tarrying, I expect.'

They put their hands to the gates together and pulled them open wide enough for them to slip through. They drifted shut behind them.

'I don't like this place,' Selena muttered. 'It is an abomination on the landscape.'

Morghan looked upwards, saw that Hawk rode the air currents above them, and higher still, the long-necked form of Crane was visible, cloud-coloured in the blueness of the sky.

She touched her hand to Wolf, who had resumed his place at her side.

'We do not walk alone through it,' Morghan said, although she spoke quietly, her voice a low murmur, for one did not speak loudly in this place.

One did not do anything to attract attention at all.

Snake slithered beside her as she stepped forward, forked tongue tasting the air.

'Do you know where we are going?' Morghan asked.

Selena shook her head. 'Clover would know, but I will not bring her to this place.'

Morghan shook her head, looking around at the cracked road, the rubbish that had blown into the gutter, the derelict buildings, their windows smashed, their walls covered with graffiti. The buildings might look on the verge of collapse, she knew, but they were not empty.

People lived in them. Shards of souls stuck in their misery.

'Remind me of her name,' Morghan said. 'The one we seek.'

'Rachel,' Selena answered. 'Her name is Rachel.' Selena shook her head, drawing up the image of Rachel Manners before her. She brought the young woman's face to mind well enough, closing her eyes for a moment and lifting her face to the still, tepid air of the city, as though she could sniff Rachel out. Rachel, who had been a young woman only just beginning to taste life, she thought. Just on the cusp of finding her true way into living.

'Are there trees in this place?' she asked, shaking her head slightly.

'I would be surprised if so,' Morghan answered.

'It is a city,' Selena said. 'Even cities have parks, do they not?' She looked to Hind, who had taken several steps forward, nose quivering.

'Hind will show us the way,' Selena said.

Morghan nodded, content to let Selena and her kin lead them. They had met the young woman, after all.

'I've not walked this way before,' she admitted in barely more than a whisper, as they headed deeper into the warren of streets. The road seemed to narrow, and Morghan listened to the sound of her boots upon the twisted asphalt of the road, wincing with each echoing step.

A man came to the doorway of an apartment building, and leaned against the entrance scratching his belly, looking at them. Morghan turned her gaze away from him and gathered the air around herself, drawing her aura inwards, holding it close so that she would not shine so brightly. A glance at Selena told her that Selena was doing the same.

Even their kin seemed dimmer in this place. Hind had her head down as she walked, and Snake had changed his colour to a dun brown.

Only Wolf still stalked alongside her, his eyes a fierce amber. Morghan rested a calming hand upon his shoulder.

Somewhere, from a high window, a woman screamed, then broke off abruptly.

'May your soul find rest,' Morghan murmured, sending

the blessing fluttering upwards on silver wings. 'May you seek wholeness and to leave this place.'

Selena glanced at her, and Morghan shook her head slightly.

'No,' she said. 'I do not know if it is possible for them to leave this Goddess-forsaken place, unless someone fetches them.'

'That would be the work of lifetimes, for someone to save all these souls,' Selena said, then gasped out a breath.

They stood at a crossroads, a traffic light hanging dim, broken, and swaying from its pole. This was not where Selena looked, however. She stared instead across the road, into the green of a city park, above which the sky hung, a dirty yellow orange smog.

'That is no park,' Morghan said. 'That is a jungle from someone's nightmare.'

'She is in there,' Selena said with dismay colouring her voice.

'You can feel her there?'

'I can.'

Then there was nothing for it, Morghan thought, and stepped out onto the road. Traffic in this place was non-existent, despite the roads. There was only a foul breeze, the jittering rustle of litter, and every now and then, the sound of movement from the buildings that surrounded them.

The park was shadow and twisted trees. Snake disappeared into the undergrowth while Morghan and Selena looked for a way through it.

'There,' Selena said, pointing to a vague path.

'May the Goddess bless and protect us,' Morghan muttered, ducking her head under a thick tree limb that looked as though it would be slimy to the touch, if she were to put her hand to it.

She had no intention of touching it.

Something chittered from the darkness and scurried away from them.

Better than scampering towards them, Selena thought, pressing onwards, following Hind as she lifted her hooves and stepped through the thick tangle of grass and roots.

'I can hear her,' Selena whispered, as they stepped with relief into the heart of the park and found that the growth thinned out, the trees stood further apart, the catching, snatching undergrowth returning to sharp-bladed grass.

'You can hear her?'

Selena nodded. 'She is crying.'

They picked up their pace, as much as they were able, and now Morghan could hear it too. The low sobs of a woman crying.

A woman who had been crying for some time, in confusion and without hope.

'There,' Morghan said, lifting her arm to point at the shadows under a tree whose trunk grew sideways, horizontal to the ground in a tangle of branches. 'Do you see her?'

Selena hurried forward, hands outstretched to the suffering woman. She fell onto her knees next to her.

'Rachel?'

The woman turned hollow eyes to her, parched, cracked lips moving. 'Help,' she said.

Selena nodded. 'I'm here to help. It's going to be all right.'

Rachel – for it was Rachel, despite the blood and dirt on

her face, the torn clothes, the dazed, desperate eyes – lifted a hand and touched her head with probing fingers.

'I'm hurt,' she said dully, then wrenched herself suddenly upwards. 'I've lost my boy.' She clutched at Selena's clothes. 'Help me – I've lost my baby.' Her gaze shifted from Selena, and she saw Morghan. 'Do you have my boy? He's only young. He needs me.'

'Hush, now,' Selena soothed. 'Let us see to you, and then I can take you to your son.'

Rachel's red-rimmed eyes widened. 'You have my baby?'

'We know where he is.' Selena said, her hands upon Rachel's shoulders, pushing back her hair that was stiff with blood.

'Is he...is he safe?' Rachel asked, and she touched her head again. 'I've been hurt. How did I get hurt?' Her eyes clouded with confusion, and she sobbed again, pushing Selena's hands away and cowering under the thick tree limb to scream once more.

Selena looked back at Morghan. 'We can't get her out of here when she's in this state.'

Morghan agreed. 'She'll bring everyone to look.' Morghan lifted her head and gazed around the dim jungle of the park.

'Apathy will perhaps keep the people away,' Selena said, hoping it might be true, fearing it would not be.

'It's not the people I'm worried about,' Morghan said softly, watching a shadow detach itself from a tree. It skulked in the dark interior of the park, and Morghan imagined she could see the flash of teeth in the vague shape of its head.

'I think we need to take her and get out of here,'

Morghan said, crouching down next to Selena while Wolf stood staring at the shadow moving slowly towards them, a low growl rumbling in his throat.

'How do we move her?' Selena asked, shaking her head.

'Like this,' Morghan replied, pressing a palm to the dead woman's eyes. For surely she was dead. The wound to her head was visible, and, Morghan thought, quite obviously non-survivable.

She drew Rachel's screams inside herself, tucking her pain around her own heart and letting it settle there a moment, her other hand going to steady herself on the ground.

'You shouldn't be doing that,' Selena hissed. 'How will you bear it?'

Morghan shook her head. When she spoke, it was with effort, her lips thick, her heart heavy with the borrowed grief. 'We need to move,' she said, breathing in the air like it was syrup.

Wolf pressed himself against her side, and Morghan allowed his heat to bring her comfort. She lifted her head, waited for the dizziness to subside, then scooped her arms under Rachel's spirit and lifted her, standing up.

Something howled in anger behind them, and Morghan turned.

'Come,' she said, squeezing the word around Rachel's sob in her throat.

Selena stood quickly, throwing a look in the direction of the thing that lurked not far away, teeth bared. She grasped Morghan's elbow, and wove a quick bubble of protection around them, ducking her head and retracing their steps, pulling Morghan along with her.

Morghan stumbled along, eyes blinded by tears borrowed from Rachel. She blinked them away, tried to focus, tried merely to carry the heaviness of grief and fear that was curled around her heart without being over-whelmed by it.

'Are you all right?' Selena hissed as Morghan stumbled again then righted herself.

Morghan nodded. 'She is very confused,' she whispered. 'I don't know that she understands what has happened to her.'

A twig cracked behind them, and Selena tugged Morghan to go faster. In Morghan's arms, Rachel's flimsy spirit bounced with each step, the blood dark on her head.

They broke free of the woods and crossed the empty intersection. Selena winced at how loudly their steps rang out in the silence of the place and she took a deep breath, ducking her head and thickening the bubble around them, hiding them from notice in a sort of reverse glamour.

They retraced their steps, down the narrow roads, around the rusting supermarket trolleys, the burnt-out cars. Selena gazed up at the windows of an apartment building, thinking she saw a pale smudge of a face watching them through the grimy glass, but if she had, it was soon gone, and she shivered, looking at the entrance instead, hoping that no one would appear to shriek at them.

It seemed an age before they reached the gates again. She looked at Morghan before pushing the gates open, but Morghan said nothing, did not return her gaze. She had retreated to some silent place inside herself, some part of her mind where Rachel's grief was a distant thing, felt only dimly.

It was an act of effort, however, to keep it at bay like this, to not let it swamp her, to hold it and give it space, but not to let it become her own.

Morghan breathed deeply, stepped with relief onto the grassy lawn that lay between the gated city and the maze.

'All right?' Selena asked.

Morghan nodded, carried Rachel's spirit the last few steps to the well, then almost fell to the ground, setting her down beside it.

Morghan bent over Rachel's prone body. Her hair had come loose from its knot at the back of her head and dark strands hung over her face so that Selena, coming to kneel beside her, could not see her expression.

'You have to give it back,' Selena said.

'She'll become hysterical again.'

'We will deal with that. You cannot continue to carry what is rightfully hers.'

Morghan closed her eyes. Once, she had done that for Grainne, carried a wounded shard of her, for her, for months, until Grainne had been strong enough to take her back and care for the child.

But this woman was not Grainne, and Rachel was safe now, out of that place. Morghan rested her palms on the spirit's chest, breathing her pain back into her.

The sensation of lightness was so sudden that Morghan rocked back on her heels, turning her face to the sky, then standing and stumbling over to the oak that grew there. She put her hands to the rough bark of the trunk and leaned against it until she'd recovered her equilibrium.

'Is she all right?' she asked, turning at last to see that Selena was kneeling beside Rachel, wringing a handkerchief in the water from the well and gently cleaning the poor soul.

'She is quiet at least,' Selena said. 'Perhaps in shock.'

'What are you going to do with her?' Morghan leaned her back against the tree and dug her fingers into Wolf's thick fur. There was a flash of feathers and Hawk landed upon a branch, her golden eyes looking at her then away toward Selena, and the woman she gently cared for.

'I don't know,' Selena said. 'Take her back to the forest, I expect.' She glanced over at Morghan. 'She needs some recovery time before moving on. Then I will call her kin to her, and she can pass on.'

Morghan looked at Rachel, lying unresponsive now on the grass, her eyes open, but staring unseeingly at the sky.

'Her husband knows what happened to her,' she said.

Selena dropped her hand that held the cloth and stared at Morghan. 'Are you sure?'

Morghan nodded toward the wound on Rachel's head. 'Someone did that, and I would be asking him about it. How it happened. It was no simple accident.'

'You could tell that when you held her pain? Was it him who did it?'

Morghan stroked Wolf, thinking. Hawk cocked her head at her, listening.

'It was very garbled. Her emotions were a great tangle.' Morghan paused, sorting through the impressions. She sighed, shifted on her feet.

Selena stared down at Rachel, who groaned suddenly and curled onto her side.

'You can just help her to move on,' Morghan said.

'Without finding out who did this?' Selena stroked

Rachel's hair. She'd washed most of the blood from it. 'I do not know that she will want to go.'

Morghan considered the question.

'We are spirit workers,' she said at last. 'Not detectives.'

'You would not pursue it?'

A small smile curved on Morghan's face. 'I never said that.'

Selena shook her head. 'Rachel has a child. He's only 18 months old.' She looked at Morghan.

'I don't think I can leave it alone.'

33

Rue heard the back door open, then close again, and crept from the shadows on the stairs, where she'd been sitting, waiting.

'Morghan?'

Morghan turned swiftly in the gloom and touched a hand to her heart. 'Rue,' she said. 'You gave me a start.'

'I'm sorry. I've been waiting, that's all.' She stood on the bottom step, one hand wrapped around the carved acorn that was atop the newel post. 'Is everything all right? Is Selena okay?'

Morghan dipped her head. 'Selena is perfectly well.'

The tightness in Rue's chest loosened a little. She closed her eyes a moment in relief. 'What...what did you do?'

Morghan hung up her cloak. It had not been cold outside, but the air was damp with falling dew. 'I am going to make a cup of tea,' she said. 'You can join me.' She lifted her head and listened briefly to the quiet of the house.

Everyone else was in bed. She thought longingly of her bed, of sleep.

But eating and drinking something would be a good idea, so she turned for the kitchen, Rue padding along behind her.

Morghan smiled. The tea things were set out, the teapot and a cup neatly beside the kettle. Grainne had put them there, for the Parkers left for their cottage straight after dinner every night. Her smile widened when she saw that the biscuit tin lay on the counter with them.

Rue pulled a chair out, wincing as it scraped along the floor. She sat down and knotted her fingers together, forcing herself to wait while Morghan put the kettle on and spooned tea into the pot.

'Do you want a cup?' Morghan asked, spoonful of tea leaves poised. It was a blend dried from Teresa's garden and she already knew it would soothe her tiredness.

'Um. Okay,' Rue said. 'Yes please.'

It would give her something to do with her hands.

Morghan tipped the leaves into the pot, picked up the kettle just before it boiled, and poured the water. She brought the things over to Mrs Parker's scrubbed kitchen table and sat down with a sigh.

Rue cleared her throat. Morghan's hair had come loose in a dark curtain across her shoulders, and there were shadows under her eyes. It made her look different, Rue thought. Softer. More vulnerable.

As if catching Rue's thoughts, Morghan gathered her hair into a twist and repinned it.

'I think I need to go home,' Rue said, blurting the words she'd been holding inside herself all evening, turning them over this way and that, coming to the inescapable fact that she believed them.

Morghan didn't answer straight away. She poured the tea and pushed one of the cups over to Rue.

'Clover won't be in so much pain now,' she said finally.

But Rue shook her head. 'I've been thinking about that,' she said. 'I want to be with her.' She looked down into her cup, at the amber gold liquid steaming there. 'She's my responsibility.'

Morghan leaned back in her chair, considering this. As it happened, she agreed with Rue. 'I think there is more you need to do here before you leave,' she said.

'More?' Rue asked, then she sighed, rubbed at her tired eyes. 'I know. I was only just getting started.'

'We haven't gotten to the crux of things yet,' Morghan said, taking a grateful sip of tea. She stretched out her legs under the table and rolled her shoulders, flexing the kinks out of them. It had been a long...she glanced at the clock on the wall...nineteen hours.

'You mean with Bryn?'

'That's exactly what I mean.'

Rue chewed on her lip. 'I was dreaming of her at home – who's to say that won't carry on?'

'Perhaps,' Morghan agreed. 'But there is something I've been building up to for you here, and I'd like you to do it before you go.'

Rue was silent for a moment. 'But I can go?' she asked. 'You won't be mad if I go early?'

Morghan laughed and dragged herself upright. 'No,' she said. 'I won't be mad. Your place is with your sister.'

'She said – Clover said – it was okay if I stayed, but I

think it would be better if I was with her anyway.' Rue frowned. 'Or is it all over? With Josh's mother and everything?'

Morghan contemplated this before answering. She thought of the set, serious look on Selena's face and shook her head. 'Hopefully Clover is no longer feeling Rachel's shock and pain, but it isn't over, no.'

'Then I'm going to go to her,' Rue said, every nerve in her body taut with the urge to get up right then and there and move, pack her things, fly home. She forced herself with an effort to sit still, relax.

'This last thing,' she asked. 'That you want me to do. What is it?'

Morghan yawned, reached for the biscuit tin. 'I want you to call Bryn to yourself, let her walk with you.'

Rue was silent, thinking about this. 'Is that even possible?' she asked finally.

'Yes, it is,' Morghan replied. 'And she has come to you already, has she not?'

'Yes,' Rue said slowly. 'She was with me when those two guys chased me.' For a brief moment, Rue was woozy with the memory of someone – Bryn, she now knew – taking over, keeping her safe.

But she didn't quite understand. 'What do you mean, let her walk with me?'

Morghan thought of Catrin. 'Let her teach you.'

'Teach me what, though?'

Leaning forward over the table, Morghan touched a finger to Rue's hand. 'All the things you haven't yet remembered,' she said.

Another long pause before Rue spoke. 'Is this, like,

normal?' she asked, then shook her head. 'I mean, can this sort of thing go on for everyone?'

Morghan considered the question. 'Yes,' she said. 'I think so, although perhaps to varying degrees, for not all of us come here with someone like Clover in our care. But all of us have spirit kin, whether they are our own past lives, or members of our soul family, or simply those who are our guardians. We ought to be open to our relationship with them.'

For some minutes, both drank their tea and ate several of the biscuits. Morghan got up to clear the things away. She yawned, thinking she would be glad to get to her bed.

Rue turned to her on their way from the kitchen. 'So,' she said. 'We'll do this thing later this morning, then?' She paused, a quickening of nervous excitement coursing through her. 'This calling Bryn to me?'

Morghan nodded. 'Yes,' she said. 'I think you're close enough to being ready for that. And I've a feeling Bryn is standing there simply waiting for the opportunity.'

They headed up the stairs, and Rue went to her room, where she sat on the side of her bed for a long time, staring out the window at the stars, wondering how often she'd looked at them from much the same viewpoint.

Bryn had looked up at these same stars, she thought. She'd roamed these woods, trod upon the same ground.

Was she really thinking about going home, Rue wondered, her hands gripping the blankets at her side? Was she really going to leave Wilde Grove and go home? Leave Morghan and Grainne, Clarice, Ambrose, and Teresa? Before she got the opportunity to dance at the stones with them at Beltane?

She shook her head because there was Clover and Selena. Even, she thought, if they didn't need her, were doing okay with her staying where she was, she thought that she might need them.

Rue sighed, changed wearily into her night clothes, and climbed into bed, lying on her side, still staring out at the view of treetops and stars outside her window.

Sleep overtook her with little warning, dragging her down into its depths and into its dreaming.

BRYN TUCKED THE STEMS OF MEADOWSWEET IN HER BASKET and swiped an arm across her forehead. It was hot this day, past the midsummer mark, the days grown hotter in the way they always did, bringing Bryn to think the season would never turn and that all there ever would be was these endless days of sweltering sun and harvesting.

She picked up the basket, scanning the green hillside meadow for more of the delicate frills of white flowers, then narrowed her eyes and searched instead for Rhian.

The child was nowhere to be seen, and a sudden panic welled up in Bryn. Had she not told Rhian not to wander off, but to play near?

'Rhian!' she called, standing still as a young deer to hear the answer.

The bees hummed on their own search for flowers. The breeze scratched a little in the grasses, and some insect somewhere set up a sawing drone.

But Rhian did not answer.

Bryn set down her basket, the sweat upon her skin cold now. She should not be worrying, she told herself. Rhian knew the area as well as any of them – perhaps better for she spent her days shying away from her tasks, playing instead, roaming the grounds, tagging along after Finn and the others as they minded the animals, a small silent shadow with eyes that watched everything.

'Rhian!' she cried again. The girl, who had been with them – with Bryn – two turns of the sun now, made no answer.

Perhaps she went back to the cluster of buildings that made up the Forest Grove, Bryn thought, for she knew well enough that the child often wandered away when bored.

Why then, this prickling sensation under her skin? Why then was her breath quickening? Bryn turned a full circle, hand shading her eyes, scanning the greenery for the small dark head that would be Rhian ducking and diving through the knots of shrubbery, parting the long grasses.

But the meadow was still, silent except for the buzzing and sawing of the insects.

The girl had gone into the woods. Bryn knew this as suddenly and as certainly as she knew her own name. Her hand went to the hag stone still worn around her neck and on impulse, she lifted it to her eye and turned in a circle, peering through it.

There. Bryn lowered the stone and looked at the trees. There was nothing to tell her that was where Rhian had entered the woods, and yet, she knew it was.

'Goddess guide me,' she whispered, and looked through the stone once more. Yes, she thought. The air wavered there, and Bryn knew with a shiver that Rhian had stepped not just into the woods that still grew like a brown and green cloak over the hills, but that the child had stepped into the other forest that grew here as well.

Rhian wandered the Wildwood.

For a moment, Bryn was undecided, the basket of meadowsweet forgotten at her feet. She squinted into the shadows of the woods.

Should she run back for help? Awel was adept at crossing the borders. She would help look for Rhian.

But Awel tended Wendyl, who was nearing her time of departure to the Summer Lands and would not wish to be disturbed.

'Do not stand dithering,' Bryn chastised herself, the sense of urgency making her pant, there in the sunshine. 'Fetch someone or go yourself.'

She would go herself, she decided, forcing limbs to move. And all at once, she was running, calling Rhian's name as she swept through the meadow and into the dimness of the woods.

There, she slowed, peering forwards, looking for signs of Rhian's passing.

It looked as it always did, the trees paying her no mind, bent upon their own tall, twiggy business. Bryn shook her head, for she knew she could wander these woods the whole day and not find Rhian.

Because this was not the Wildwood. These were the woods of the Grove, not of the Otherworld.

But she could find her way there, could she not?

It would only take a deep breath, a stepping, a passing over the border. Had she not been learning to do just this thing? Had not Awel been teaching her and the other younger ones to do this?

Bryn shook her head. There was no time for the preparations necessary, the cleansing, the offerings. She stepped across.

'Rhian!' she yelled.

She stood listening, one foot lifted onto her toes, poised to run in the direction of any sound that was not the chittering of insects, the laughing squabbling of birds, or the summer sighing of the trees themselves.

Nothing. There was nothing. Bryn lifted the stone to her eye again and scanned the woods. Perhaps she would be able to see Rhian through the stone, for it was said that looking through the hole in stones like these afforded a view of the Otherworld.

Something shimmered, close to the ground, a small, fading stream of mist, tinted blue, that seemed to hang suspended above the ground.

It was Rhian's path; Bryn knew as well as she knew anything.

She followed it, deeper into the woods until the sun did not blaze upon her head anymore but peeked instead from on high between leafy boughs.

'Rhian,' Bryn called, but it was barely more than a whisper, although the urgency inside her was still strong, grew in fact, with every step.

The wispy path took Bryn on a merry chase, until it ended between the roots of a large tree, who had been growing upon that spot for so long that its roots were the size of Bryn's thighs. Larger.

For a good long moment, Bryn thought there was nothing more to see, and she stood at the tree and gazed around.

The warm air pressed against her. She paddled a hand in it. Then looked down at the roots.

There was a hole between them. A fox or rabbit hole perhaps, and Bryn frowned. An animal was inside the hole; she could make out the dark brown of its pelt.

Bryn dropped to her knees and scrabbled frantically to reach for the creature wedged between the roots.

For it was no rabbit, nor fox neither.

She tugged Rhian out from the ground and heaved her into her lap.

34

Rhian sat in the grass, squinting at the greenness surrounding her. It was as though she sat in a basket, the blades of grass waving at the height of her head. She wriggled onto her knees and parted the grass in front of her, peering through for a glimpse of Bryn.

Bryn was further down the hill, the sun bright against the veil she wore covering her hair, and Rhian flopped back against the ground. She ought to be helping, she knew. The flowers had to be harvested before they wilted, their potency diminished.

But Rhian preferred her daydreaming to chores. She flung out her arms and tickled the grass.

Something moved, and she turned onto her side, sticking her elbow into the soft ground and resting her head on her palm. It would be an insect, she expected. Or perhaps, if she were extra lucky, a baby bunny, for she had seen them before in this place, their fur soft and brown, little tails bobbing as they ran away from her.

It was not a baby bunny that Rhian saw, but a rabbit, full grown. She stared at it, surprised to see that it looked back at her, dark eyes fixed upon her.

Rhian froze so as not to frighten the animal. She expected that it would go still also, but instead it took a hopping step towards her.

Enamoured, Rhian put out a hand to touch it.

The rabbit's nose quivered, but it did not move. Instead, it let Rhian touch it, run her fingers lightly over its soft fur.

Rhian gasped. She'd caught a baby rabbit once, by surprise rather than stealth, and had held it against her chest, hands tucked around it. She'd felt its heart beating so quickly that she'd been afraid for it, and sorry, and had let it go again.

This rabbit was twice the size of the baby, and it did not move, seemed instead to invite Rhian's touch.

What's your name? Rhian asked it silently, for she did not speak outside her own head.

The rabbit looked at her, then took two hopping steps away, before turning to regard her again with its luminous eyes. They were an amber brown, shades lighter than Rhian's own.

Rhian gazed at the rabbit and got slowly to her knees. Do you want me to follow you? she asked it.

The rabbit hopped another few steps. Four this time, then turned and looked back at Rhian.

Rhian crawled through the grass after it, and the rabbit moved again, hopping slowly, turning its head to check that she followed.

Rhian followed it out of the meadow and into the woods. She stood up and walked after it, barely aware that the trees grew taller here, that they hummed between themselves. She was used to that. She had not let Bryn discover it, but she skipped between the trees of the Grove and those of the Wildwood quite often, although usually without quite meaning to.

The rabbit leapt, and Rhian followed. It was cooler among the trees and the air was silky soft against the warm skin of her cheeks. She giggled silently when the rabbit, its fur the colour of bark, found a burrow between the roots of an ancient tree and looked at her again before diving down into it and disappearing.

Rhian leaned over the hole, her small hands on the tree roots to either side, and stared down into the darkness.

Except, it wasn't quite dark down there, she realised. And the hole was rather large. Large enough surely for her to squeeze down it, to see what the light was at the bottom.

She thought she saw a flicker of rabbit tail and nodded.

Wait for me, she called, and regarded the hole again, debating, then scooted her legs into it, and shimmied down into the not-quite-darkness.

Soil got in her hair, and some in her mouth, and Rhian wrinkled her nose, spat it out, then looked around.

The rabbit sat only a few steps away. It had waited for her, Rhian thought in delight. It occurred to her that she ought to be afraid, but she felt instead only a growing excitement.

Where do we go next? she whispered in her mind to the rabbit, looking around at the great expanse of world that existed under the roots of the old tree.

Rhian looked upwards, back the way she'd come, and there was the rabbit hole. There was a tree – the same one?

No, she decided. It must be a different one, its roots like great veins in the green flank of a hill, but between them was the hole.

The rabbit grunted and Rhian swung her attention back towards it, forgetting about the tree and gazing around again. They were in another meadow, but Rhian didn't recognise the flowers growing there, and there was no sign of Bryn.

The rabbit moved, and Rhian followed it, her head swivelling as she took in the view. They were headed for more trees, but for a moment Rhian was sure she'd seen something down the bottom of the hill. A great garden of some sort.

Who lived there, she wondered?

But the rabbit was going in a different direction, its bob tail bouncing, and Rhian turned reluctantly to follow it.

There was no path the way they were going, and Rhian wondered why not, if perhaps they were the only ones to ever come this way. She would have thought likely not – did not Awel teach Bryn and the others that there were few paths untrodden?

Rhian did not like lessons. Learning the names and uses of herbs bored her. She preferred to sit in the long grass and spin stories in her mind. Always she preferred to be outside, wandering among the trees, although this made Bryn cry out and chastise her mercilessly.

Rhian shook her head. As if she'd get lost. Bryn overreacted when she trailed home after some adventure, covered in burrs and mud. Bryn was always telling her she'd fall down some rabbit hole one day and break an ankle.

That made Rhian giggle, for hadn't she just tumbled

down a rabbit hole? Her ankles, however, were perfectly sturdy still and she ran after the rabbit, who had disappeared into yet more woods.

The trees made a tunnel from trunk and bough and Rhian ducked into it, trotting to keep up with the rabbit, who practically ignored her now, except to glance back if she fell behind. Rhian looked up at the trees, then stopped still to look again, not caring if the rabbit turned back to look and found her gaping at the trees instead of hurrying after.

In truth, however, it was not the trees themselves that Rhian stared at, although they were remarkable enough with their leaning trunks, their branches that reached out to intertwine over her head.

It was the animals that she gaped at, twisting her head first this way then that. There were hundreds of them, she thought.

A mouse stood on its hind legs upon a branch, its small round eyes returning Rhian's gaze. A deer spied on her from between two trees. She looked up. The branches were lined with birds.

She looked down, past the deer, saw creatures she knew only from tales told around the fire. Bear, wolf, badger, boar.

They were looking at her, standing as though they'd been waiting for her to pass, as if they'd heard word of the strange girl that would happen along their way that day, and decided to come see her for themselves.

Rhian inched along the tunnel of trees. Rabbit sat on hind legs waiting for her.

She was a strange girl, Rhian knew. Since the Fae had

given her over to the care of the priestesses, no one had known who she was or where she'd come from.

Rhian didn't know herself. She didn't remember anything from that time, as though she'd woken up that day on the bank of the stream, her mind as blank as a white winter sky.

There had been consternation among the priestesses, and even now, Bryn was the only one who didn't regard her with a question in their gaze.

Rhian thought of the garden she had looked down upon before following Rabbit down the hill in the other direction. Something about that place had struck a chord in her, she decided.

One day, she thought, she would come back, and go down there and see who lived there. Perhaps they knew something about herself.

Rabbit was turning again, to lead her onwards, and Rhian held out a hand and smiled at the animals lined up to look at her.

Hello, she thought to them all. Hello, hello, hello.

She did not speak the words out loud, for that was another thing that made everyone purse their lips at her. She could not talk. Her throat was mute, no words ever even wheezed their way out from her mouth.

She could understand plenty, though, and she knew as soon as Rabbit brought her to the door that she was supposed to open it and go inside.

They had left the strange trees behind, and entered a tunnel proper, that dug into a hillside and was lit by nothing that Rhian could see.

And now there was a door. Rhian wondered how far into

the Otherworld she had come – for surely that was where she was.

There was no fear prickling at her body. Only curiosity had her skin tingling under her shift and dress. She pushed the door open while the rabbit regarded her with its round, shiny eyes.

There was a chamber behind the door, and Rhian stepped fearlessly into it, letting the door swing closed behind her. Rabbit dashed in at the last moment and came to stand beside her.

Rhian stilled, gazing about the room, at the faces who looked back at her, for the room was filled with people.

They were men and women both, like and unlike those Rhian shared her days with, Bryn and the priestesses, Kennocha and Gitta, and the men, Finn, Calum, and the others.

She inched further into the room, curious. The people ringed the walls, and she stopped by one, her brows raised in delight as she touched his hand, marvelling over the darkness of his skin. She compared hers to it, but hers was light next to his hand. She grinned, excited over the difference.

Unafraid, Rhian walked around the room, touching the long robes of a woman here, the hand of a man there. Some, she could not tell if they were men or women, only that she was not afraid of them. In fact, she decided, she had always known these people, even if this was the first time she'd seen them.

Perhaps it had been in another lifetime, when she had been not Rhian, the small fosterling of the Forest Grove, but another, with another name and history. Or perhaps, it had been between lives, when she had lived in the Summer Lands.

She smiled up at one, and was greeted with a smile in return, eyes that crinkled in the corners with recognition. Rhian wanted to ask why they were there, but she had no voice with which to speak.

One of the people stepped forward and bent down to peer more closely at Rhian's face. He was old, she saw, his own face a map of paths and wrinkles, but she broke into a sunny smile at his inspection, for his eyes danced with laugher even while he touched his thumb to her forehead, then straightened and held out his hand for her to take.

'Come, my little one,' he said, the first words anyone had spoken. 'We have been waiting for you.'

She looked up at him, her small hand in his large one. His palm was warm. Rhian raised her eyebrows in a question.

'Just into the next room, my dear. It is time, you see.'

Rhian didn't see, or at least, not on the top of her mind where her thoughts flitted to and fro like a butterfly.

Perhaps deeper down, though. Perhaps deeper down she knew and even understood, for she followed him into the next room with no qualms to make her hesitate.

There was a fire in the next room, and over it a great cooking pot. Rhian sniffed the air but could not place the scent. It was no stew bubbling in the pot, she knew that for certain.

However, when a cup was filled from the pot and handed to her, she only looked at it for a moment before lifting it obediently to her mouth and drinking.

It was bitter, twisting her lips into a grimace of distaste and she thrust the cup back at the old wizard.

He smiled at her and patted her shoulder. 'We know it does taste bad,' he said. 'But it is necessary.'

Rhian stared up at him, frowning again, her question unspoken on her face. She glanced around at the others who had crowded into the room behind her.

'You are not to worry,' the man said, bending at the waist to look seriously at her. 'This is an agreement we made long ago.'

Rhian lifted her brow and gazed around at the others. Had she been one of them, of these people, before being born as a small, wordless girl?

'Tis true,' the wizard said. 'And the potion will set things in motion, for the time has come.'

Rhian nodded solemnly, as though she knew what he was talking about.

The old man, with his twinkling eyes and beard long and white in contrast to the dark skin of his face, nodded at her, then ushered her back into the other room. Rabbit waited at the door for her, and it was open again. Rhian gave the man a questioning look and he nodded at her.

'Time for you to return, Rhian, and quickly too,' he said. 'Rabbit will show you the way.'

Rhian wanted to say that she remembered the way perfectly well, but her tongue was still mute. She also wanted to ask what the herbs were that she had drunk, and what they would do, but her tongue was stubbornly silent. She gazed around at the gathering and nodded when they smiled at her, hands pressed together now over their hearts, as if in prayer to the Goddess herself.

Rhian bowed to them, making the gesture before she'd even known she intended to, but if felt good, and right. Then she was following Rabbit again, out the door and back into the tunnel, turning left even though an inquisitive part of her – the part for which Bryn was forever chastising her – wanted to turn in the other direction and explore where the tunnel would lead her.

But Rabbit grunted at her, hopping right back to her to stand on her hind legs, putting her front paws against Rhian's legs.

Delighted, Rhian reached out and stroked the animal's soft fur, touching her fingers to the long ears before Rabbit lowered herself to the ground again and led the way down the tunnel, back the way they'd come.

Rhian followed and was glad to be out of the strange light of the tunnel once they reached the trees again. She looked around for the animals, but they were gone, as though they'd come for a glimpse of her, and having had it, had returned to their own business.

She dawdled up the hill, bending to pluck up a blade of grass, pressing it between her fingers and putting it to her mouth, whistling shrilly through it then grinning. She dropped it as she reached the level where she could look down and see the faraway garden.

Rabbit grunted again, then made a squealing, whining sound, trying to get Rhian to hurry.

But Rhian gazed at the hint of garden, blurred as if from a trick of the light, she thought. But still, peering, she could make out hedgerows, and trees as graceful as they were ornamental.

It was as she took a couple steps in that direction, Rabbit

squealing frantically at her now, that Rhian felt suddenly sick to her stomach. She clutched at her belly, bending forward and throwing up on the grass. It was the herbs she had drunk, she thought, spinning woozily on her legs, unsteady and dizzy.

Rabbit pawed at her, urging her through the hole between the tree roots, back the way they'd come.

Rhian pressed her hands into the dirt, shuffling into the hole between the roots of the tree, her stomach churning, vision darkening.

35

RHIAN WAS A HEAVY WEIGHT IN HER ARMS. BRYN STAGGERED
out of the forest, barely aware that she was making a series
of bleating cries for help.

She ran, muscles burning, up the hillside and back to
the Forest Grove, her voice in her throat louder now, calling
out for someone, anyone to help her.

But when they came, Kennocha with her light eyes wide
with shock, Ula clucking her tongue, then falling silent at
the sight of Rhian, head dangling, dirt in the creases on her
face, they fell back, whispering to the Goddess, not knowing
what was happening.

Bryn carried Rhian to the wellspring and sank down on
her knees, lying the unresponsive girl on the ground.

'Does she breathe?' Ula asked, coming to her senses.

Bryn flung her head from side to side. She didn't know.
All she knew was that she had plucked Rhian from the hole
between the tree roots and the girl had lain as if dead in her
arms.

'She has dirt in her mouth, look,' Ula said, and Bryn looked, pushing Ula's hands away and scooping out the muck herself.

'Is it back in her throat, then?' Ula asked, leaning forward urgently.

Prying Rhian's mouth open, Bryn peered in, then shook her head. The soil had not gone so deep. Bryn could have sobbed with relief.

'She breathes,' Kennocha said, laying a hand on Rhian's chest. 'Look. She breathes.'

Bryn bent over the child, relief making her limbs weak. She held her close, felt the beating of Rhian's heart next to her own, then laid her back down, lifting her face to the sky.

'The Goddess blesses us,' she whispered.

'She's filthy as though she's been bathing in dirt,' Ula said, the sudden relief making her tongue sharp. 'What has she been up to now?'

Bryn shook her head. Why was Rhian still not waking?

'I found her inside a rabbit hole,' she said, her voice pitched higher than usual.

'In a rabbit hole?'

Bryn nodded, then looked to Kennocha. 'Run and get me a cloth.'

Kennocha nodded, got to her feet. Only a minute later she was back, holding out the linen to Bryn who took it and dipped it in the water of the well.

'Goddess protect this child,' Bryn whispered as she wiped dirt from around Rhian's nose.

'Goddess let her wake,' she muttered, wiping the soil from Rhian's face, neck, smoothing the cloth over her skin then wringing it out in the water.

When Rhian was clean again, Bryn looked down at her. 'She is sleeping,' she said, seeing the rise and fall of her chest.

'She is unconscious,' Ula corrected her. 'Take her to her bed; I will see what Awel has to say.'

Bryn looked up at her. 'Not Mother Wendyl?'

'Mother is not well enough,' Ula said, her face becoming suddenly drawn and apprehensive. 'She has not long for this world.'

'Has it been decided who will take her place?' Kennocha asked. Life without Mother Wendyl was unthinkable.

'The one from across the sea is ready finally to come.' Ula's voice trembled lightly, for the Priestess had long been promised to them, since their beginning, and now she was to come. Much change would likely come with her.

'If anyone needs me,' Bryn said, standing up with Rhian in her arms, 'I will be with Rhian, watching over her.' She did not this minute care that the promised priestess was coming, or that Mother Wendyl was passing.

She carried Rhian away without further speech and entered the sleeping quarters she shared with Kennocha, Brigit, and Mairenn. There was a small pallet next to her own that had been made for Rhian and Bryn lowered the child to it, then crawled onto her bed next to her, the better to keep watch.

It was dark, Bryn fallen asleep, when Mairenn shook her awake, a lantern in her hand that jittered with her trembling limb and made grotesque shadows on the walls.

'What is it?' Bryn asked sleepily, then snapped her eyes open to look down at Rhian, whom she had brought into her arms sometime during the night.

Rhian's eyes were open.

'Mother Wendyl has passed,' Mairenn whispered.

The words made no sense to Bryn, and she had to repeat them to herself. Mother Wendyl was dead?

'She has gone to the Summer Lands,' Rhian said. 'There to await her next life.'

Mairenn dropped the lantern, then hastily snatched it up to hold it in front of Rhian, her eyes wide.

Bryn sat up, staring also at the child in the bed next to her.

'You spoke,' she said, awe colouring her words.

Rhian looked momentarily confused, then opened her mouth again, wrapped her tongue around the sounds that had always escaped her so far.

'I can speak,' she said, hearing her voice outside her head for the first time.

'It is a miracle,' Mairenn whispered. She turned to go to Mother Wendyl, then remembered that that were without their mother priestess.

Bryn snatched Rhian up and hugged her tightly, bursting into overwhelmed tears.

'You can speak,' she said through the sobs. 'The Goddess has granted you your tongue.'

Rhian hugged Bryn back tightly, although she didn't know if it was the Goddess who had given her the power of speech. She thought it was the wizards instead, and the drink they had given her. Finally, she disentangled herself from Bryn and looked around.

'Why is it dark?' she asked. The day had been bright when last she looked, the sun barely past the noon point.

'You slept all afternoon,' Bryn said, looking at Mairenn with wide eyes.

Mairenn shook her head, setting her lantern down and lowering herself to her own bed only steps away. The other priestesses were gathered in Wendyl's room. Only Bryn had not been there, because of Rhian.

Rhian who could now speak. Whose first words had been of Mother Wendyl's waiting for her next life.

'Will she come back to us?' Mairenn asked, for her heart was heavy with the knowledge that she would miss the older priestess, who had acted as mother to them all.

'Who?' Bryn asked, her gaze on Rhian.

Mairenn shifted on her bed. 'Mother Wendyl, of course.' There were tears shining in her eyes.

'Oh,' Bryn said, then shook her head. 'Why do you ask her that?'

'Because she said Mother Wendyl is in the Summer Lands waiting for her next life.'

Bryn's head shake was impatient this time. 'Is that not what we all do after our deaths?'

Mairenn went to speak, but it was Rhian who got in first.

'No,' she said, the word firm, certain. 'Not to us, not as we are.'

Bryn, kneeling now, put her hands on Rhian's shoulders, still astounded at the sound of the girl's voice. 'How do you know that?' she demanded.

Rhian shook her head and looked down at her body, at her thin chest and belly, as though expecting to find the answer there somewhere. She looked back up at Bryn.

'I don't know,' she said. 'The knowledge is just there, as though there is a door.' She frowned, falling silent, remembering for some reason the rabbit. 'I followed a rabbit,' she said.

'A what?' Mairenn asked from where she was sitting on her bed, arms wrapped around her knees now to stop her trembling. It was a warm night, but she could not help her shivering.

'A rabbit,' Rhian repeated. 'She had fur that was soft and thick.'

'All rabbit fur is soft and thick. That does not explain how you can speak, and of such things.'

Rhian turned to Bryn. 'You believe me, don't you?'

Bryn did. 'I pulled you from a rabbit hole,' she said, her voice low as the lantern's light wavered, guttered, sprang back to life.

Mairenn was crying softly now. She wiped her eyes on the linen sheet of her bed. 'I will miss her,' she whispered.

'Miss who?' Bryn asked, her mind filled still with the fact that Rhian could speak.

And know things she shouldn't.

'Mother Wendyl, of course,' Mairenn said, drawing a blanket around her shoulders for comfort.

Bryn nodded, feeling a prickling of grief, then pushing it away. There would be time for that later. Right now, she must cast around for another question for Rhian.

She could only think of ones to which she did not know the answer – but then, surely, Rhian would not either?

Time would have to show her veracity.

'The new priestess, from across the sea,' she said in a half whisper. 'Is she like Mother Wendyl?' Bryn paused, thinking about the way Wendyl had welcomed her when she first arrived, homesick and more than a little frightened.

Wendyl had been as a mother, her hands and voice soft both, and quick to soothe.

'No,' Rhian said, speaking the knowledge from somewhere deep inside. She touched Bryn's cheeks, her own still creased from her hours of sleep. 'She has marks on her face here, like this.' Rhian traced a spiral pattern over her cheekbone.

'I've heard they still do that, over the sea,' Mairenn said from her bed, where her teeth chattered now, despite the blanket. The light from the lantern wobbled and a shadow climbed the wall, stretched there for a moment, then subsided.

Rhian closed her eyes and a vision rose in front of her. A deer, leading the priestess through the forest towards them.

'The Goddess herself brings her to us,' she whispered. 'And we will become true Priestesses of the Deer Mother.'

Mairenn stared at Rhian for a long moment, her tears forgotten, and then she unfolded herself from the bed and shrugged off the blanket.

'You'd best bring her to see Awel, and Gwynnett,' she said.

They were the two most senior priestesses.

Bryn nodded. She crawled from the bed and held out her hand to Rhian, who paused a moment before taking it and standing.

'You and I shall be often together,' she said to Bryn.

Bryn frowned back at her. 'We always are,' she said. 'Together. I have been taking care of you since the day the Shining Ones put you in my arms.'

Rhian nodded, but the knowing was still growing inside her. She touched a finger to Bryn's arm. 'You shall be my mother next,' she said. 'When the Grove is in flames.'

Bryn's blood turned cold inside her veins, and she looked over at Mairenn, who stood frozen, the lantern swinging in her hand.

'What did you say?' Bryn asked, her voice high with shock. 'What did you say about the Grove burning?'

Rhian blinked at her, withdrew her hand. She covered her eyes, but still there were flames behind them.

'It burns,' she said. 'Men come, and they throw sticks of fire at our houses.'

Mairenn was moving again, and she tugged on Bryn's arm. 'Come on,' she said. 'We must take her to Awel and Gwynnett.' She cast a fearful glance at Rhian. 'They will know what to do with her.' She pulled harder at Bryn. 'I thought it was a miracle,' she added. 'But perhaps it is more akin to a curse.'

RUE WOKE, THE TASTE OF THE DREAM STILL ON HER TONGUE. She rolled over in the bed and looked at the window, through which daylight strengthened.

She had slept in.

But for once, she didn't throw back the blankets and hurry into her clothes. Instead, she lay there frowning, looking at the remnants of the dream, tugging on the strings of it, trying to bring it back before it slipped away forever.

'Something about rabbits,' Rue muttered, then shifted onto her back and stared up at the ceiling, not seeing it at all but looking into the tatters of her dream and grimacing. Why did they slip away so?

There had been a rabbit, and Clover – but not Clover, the girl the Fae had given Bryn.

Rue closed her eyes.

Yes, that had been it. But the girl was Clover, Rue realised. And that had been what Clover meant when they'd spoken on the phone. Not who she was now, but who she was then.

Rue reached for more. What was it about the rabbit?

Clover had followed the animal down a rabbit hole. Rue shook her head. No, she thought. That was Alice in Wonderland. Not Clover in the Otherworld.

The words had Rue opening her eyes. Clover in the Otherworld. Yes. That had been it.

The Otherworld and a room full of wizards. Rue had seen it as though she'd been there, watching, an invisible observer.

They'd given her something to drink, and then she could speak.

The thought came to Rue, and she knew immediately that it was true. That was what had happened.

And speak she had, of things that had frightened Bryn and the other young priestess.

Rue's lips formed the words. 'You shall be my mother.'

She turned onto her side. Watched the light through the curtains.

'You shall be my mother,' Rue repeated. 'When the Grove burns.'

She shivered. Had that already happened?

Or was it yet to come?

And if it was possible for Bryn to one day be Rhian's mother, was it also possible for her to one day be her sister?

KATHERINE GENET

Just how long, Rue wondered, had she been looking after Clover?

Rue sat up and swung her legs out of the bed.

Lifetime after lifetime, she thought.

That's how long she and Clover had been together.

But for what purpose?

Rue closed her eyes.

Today, she thought, was her birthday. She was sixteen years old.

Opening her eyes, she looked down at herself. Sixteen years in this body, she thought.

Thousands of years old otherwise.

If not more. Did time exist in the same way, outside of flesh and blood?

Rue stood up, thinking of wizards and potions, and small girls who could see the future.

Could see far and wide.

She wanted to go home, she thought. Her place was with Clover.

And she would. She would go home and take her place back with her sister. Who had once been her daughter. Who had once been a child given into her arms by the Fae.

Rue reached for her clothes.

First though, before going home, there was something that she was going to do today.

She was going to let Morghan teach her how to call Bryn to her side. To guide her through this maze that was life.

That was lifetimes.

36

Tara, Dandy, and Selena sat in a huddle around the kitchen table.

'So, she's dead?' Tara squeezed her eyes shut, but the tears leaked out anyway. She sniffed. 'I can't believe it – I was just sitting here talking to her only two weeks ago.' She shook her head. 'At this very table.' Tara looked over at Dandy and Selena. 'I liked her. I thought we might end up friends. She loved bringing Josh here, loved the way it feels here in our home.' Tara shook her head, a fresh thought occurring to her. 'Josh,' she said. 'That poor little boy.'

Dandy reached out and grasped Tara's hand, wrapping her own around it and holding on.

'He's such a little joy,' Tara said, and the tears streaked her cheeks. 'Rachel loved him so much – what is he going to do without his mum?'

'What's he going to do without his dad?' Dandy asked, her voice grim, her eyes wet also. She looked at Selena. 'Because it was him, wasn't it?'

Selena shook her head. 'I don't know for sure. Morghan said just that it seemed so.'

Dandy nodded. 'There might have been another man in her life.'

Tara's eyes widened and she stared at Dandy. 'What? You never said.'

'I didn't know for sure,' Dandy said. 'It was just something in her reading. The cards showed the possibility of it, and she blushed when I pointed it out, but she didn't confirm it. There might have been someone, or she might just have been thinking it would be nice to have someone other than her husband.'

Selena sighed and shifted in her seat. 'If she was wanting to meet someone else, or already had, then it does complicate things.'

'It provides motive, you mean,' Tara said.

'Yes,' Selena agreed. 'That could be so.'

'But what do we do?' Dandy asked. 'We've spoken to the police – they didn't take us seriously.' She thought back to Sandy Rice sitting awkwardly at this very table, telling her and Tara that a handbag in a kitchen was not a clue to a murder.

The three sat silently for a while, grief heavy on their shoulders, each trying to puzzle the pieces into place.

'What makes me feel so much pain,' Tara said at last, 'is that no one is even paying attention to the fact that Rachel is missing.'

'That's because Mike Manners says she isn't,' Dandy said sourly.

'Well, we know better, don't we?' Selena said, and she got up from the table, moving with a sudden decisiveness, glad that Damien and Ebony had taken Clover out to shop for a birthday present for Rue.

'What are you going to do?' Tara asked, sniffing and wiping tears from her cheeks.

'I'm going to go down to the police station and report a missing person.' Selena stopped at the door. 'If we get them doing their job, then we can get on with ours.'

'What's our job?' Tara asked, confused.

Selena's answering smile was gentle. 'Mourning Rachel and singing her over.'

THEY SAT FOR FORTY MINUTES IN THE WAITING ROOM AT THE police station before someone came out to see them.

'Sorry to keep you waiting,' the officer said. 'Please, come this way and we can have a chat about what's going on.'

They filed into a small meeting room, with table and chairs. The walls were a pleasant colour, and there was a window with blinds half shuttered over it. Tara could see the supermarket next door through it and marvelled over the normality of the shoppers going in and out.

'I'm Sergeant Rose Griffith,' the officer said. 'You're here about Rachel Manners?' She frowned over the table at the three women lined up on the other side. Two older, one younger, all serious, while the younger's face was blotchy, as though she'd been crying.

'Yes,' Tara said.

'We spoke to Sandy Rice about her a week ago,' Dandy added.

Rose nodded. She'd done a quick search on her

computer and noted that Sandy had logged the interview in. And indicated no follow up necessary.

Rose eased herself into her seat. 'I saw Sandy's notes,' she said. 'You still have concerns about Mrs Manners?'

'Grave concerns,' Dandy said, scowling, as she always did when worried.

'Her husband changed his story,' Tara added.

Rose raised her eyebrows. She had no idea whether these women needed to be taken seriously.

But she had ten minutes for them. She'd listen with an open mind for that time.

'In what way?' she asked, reaching for her pen and the pad of paper she'd brought in with her.

Tara began. 'Well, he said she'd gone to her sister's to visit.' She huffed out a tense breath. 'Without her son – I'm her baby's caregiver.'

Rose nodded but made no judgement yet. Sometimes it was nice to take a break, even from your children.

'Then, just the other day, when we asked for a contact number for Rachel,' Tara said, 'Mike – Mr Manners – got very huffy with us and said she'd left and wasn't coming back.'

'Left without her son,' Dandy popped in there.

Tara shook her head. 'She wouldn't leave Josh, her boy. She loves him more than anything.'

Rose considered this, and the three faces drawn with worry in front of her.

'She's never even been late to pick Josh up,' Tara said. 'She's usually early, if anything. There's just no way I can see her leaving him.'

'How old is Josh?'

'Only eighteen months,' Tara replied.

'And when was the last time you saw Rachel Manners?' Rose asked, making a note of the boy's age.

'Two weeks ago, Wednesday,' Tara said promptly. 'She was supposed to pick Josh up at 12.30, and she never turned up.'

'Who did come to pick him up?'

'Well,' Tara said. 'No one. Rachel doesn't have a mobile phone, so I tried their home phone, but no one answered. Eventually, more than two hours later, I got hold of Mike Manners on his mobile.'

'And he came to get Josh?'

Tara nodded. 'Straight away.'

Dandy held up a hand. 'We forgot,' she said.

Tara looked questioningly at her.

'We forgot why Mike Manners said Rachel was late that day.' Dandy looked at Rose. 'He said she had a hair appointment that must have run late.' Dandy shook her head. 'Two hours late.'

'Hair appointments don't run two hours late,' Tara said, nodding. 'And when we mentioned that, he said she must have gone shopping afterwards.'

Rose frowned. 'So when did he say she'd gone to her sister's?'

Tara looked at Dandy. 'The next day, wasn't it? When he dropped Josh off?'

Dandy nodded.

Rose considered this before asking her next question. If the trip to the sister's place had been previously organised, then the husband would have known to collect his son at 12.30. On the other hand, she acknowledged, he may have just forgotten. It wasn't outside the realm of possibility.

But why, then, did he say his wife was getting her hair done? She may have been, of course, before going away, and she may have been expecting her husband to pick up the boy. And again, he forgot to and preferred not to admit it.

She looked at the line of women. 'When did you first try contacting Mr Manners instead of his wife?' she asked.

'Rachel,' Dandy said. 'Instead of Rachel.' She glanced at Tara, aware of Selena sitting silently beside her. 'We tried his number when we called the house and no one answered.' She shook her head. 'He didn't answer his mobile the first couple times we tried it.'

Rose made another note. 'He didn't pick up until 2.30? Is that right?'

'That sounds about right,' Tara said.

'Hmm.' Rose considered her options. Sandy had taken her notes back before the women had been told that Rachel had left for good. Did it change anything now that this had been said?

She sighed. 'It would be far better if it was Rachel's husband sitting here filing a missing person's report.'

'He's not going to do that,' Dandy said. 'We think he killed her.'

Rose's eyes widened, then a moment later, she narrowed them, shaking her head. 'Do you have any evidence of this? It pays to have evidence before making such an accusation.'

Dandy swallowed and leaned forward to look at Selena. She turned back to Rose.

'Did Sandy tell you where she'd met us before?'

Rose paused before answering, wondering where this

was going. 'No,' she said. 'You've been involved in a police matter before?'

Dandy ploughed on. 'Up in Opoho late last year. When a man was chased away just as he was going to break into a house there?'

Rose thought back, nodded, remembering the case. There'd been something unusual about it. She frowned, trying to remember what it was, then stilled when it came to her.

'The police were called before he went to break in,' she said slowly. 'By someone who couldn't have even known he was there.' A wave of gossip had swept through the station about it.

Dandy nodded. 'That was us,' she said. 'We called it in.'

'I don't understand,' Rose told her.

'Have you watched that new show Sensing Murder?' Dandy rubbed her hands together.

Rose nodded. 'No,' she said, and sighed inwardly. But she'd seen it in the TV Guide. Were these women suggesting that they were...psychic?

'It's a bit like that,' Dandy said. 'This situation. We know Rachel is dead because...' She paused, looked at Selena.

'Because we've seen her spirit,' Selena said, speaking for the first time.

Rose stared at them, face impassive. 'And did her spirit tell you her husband murdered her?'

Selena shook her head. 'No. She was too confused and upset.'

Rose set down her pen and leaned back in her chair. She shook her head. 'I don't know what to say.'

'Just say you'll look into it,' Tara said, leaning forward.

'Please. Go and talk to her husband. Rachel doesn't have a sister she can go and stay with.'

'Her family's Exclusive Brethren,' Dandy added. 'So, she was disowned by them when she left.'

'Perhaps her sister left too,' Rose said, her head still spinning from the assertion that these women had spoken to a spirit.

Dandy shook her head. 'I think she would have told me that.'

Rose held up a hand. 'Wait,' she said, and looked at Tara. 'I thought you were the child's caregiver?'

'I am,' Tara said.

Rose looked at the others. 'What are your relationships to Rachel Manners? How do you know her?'

'I did a tarot reading for her two days before she disappeared,' Dandy said. 'And the three of us share a house, which is where Tara looks after the kiddies, so we all have met Rachel. She was becoming something of a friend.'

Tara's mouth twisted in anguish.

Rose nodded dubiously. This just kept getting worse, she thought, and looked at Selena. 'What about you?' she asked. 'Are you the one who talked to Rachel's ghost?'

She'd spoken flippantly, but Selena decided to take the question at face value and nodded.

'I am,' she said.

Rose gathered up her pen and paper and stood up.

'What are you going to do?' Tara asked, alarmed. 'You're not just going to do nothing, are you?'

Rose tucked the pad of paper under her arm and thought about it. Yes, these women had gotten a bit wacky at the end there, but did they have a legitimate claim? And, as she well knew, wacky didn't mean wrong. She sighed again. If there was even a chance that was so, she needed to check it out.

'I'll go and speak to Mr Manners,' she said. 'What will happen after that, I don't know, but I will speak to him about his wife's whereabouts.'

Tara stood up, relief flooding through her body so that she had to grasp the table. 'Thank you,' she said. 'Thank you so much.'

'Hmm,' Rose said, looking at the other two women.

'Will you let us know what you find out?' Dandy asked.

'I'll contact you if I need to re-interview you,' Rose said, and she headed for the door.

Filing out of the police station, Tara looked at Selena. 'What do we do now?' she asked.

Selena shook her head. 'I don't think there's much more we can do when it comes to getting the police to investigate.'

'I think you're right there,' Dandy said. 'That women we just spoke to is close to not doing anything at all.' Dandy shook her head. 'I should have kept my big mouth shut, instead of opening it and making us come across as the biggest trio of flakes in town.'

Tara hugged Dandy. 'You only told the truth.' She let her go and squeezed her hand instead. 'I'm glad we decided to do this. And besides – what else could we have done?'

'Nothing, really, I suppose,' Dandy said, and looked at Selena. 'So, as Tara says, what do we do now?'

'Now?' Selena shook her head. 'Sergeant Rose Griffith will do her job, and we will do ours.'

Dandy's eyebrows rose almost to her hairline and a smile hovered around her lips.

'That sounds good,' she said. 'What is our job, again?'

They started walking toward Tara's car.

'Our job is to look after Rachel,' Selena said.

'We take care of the dead.'

37

'IT'S NOT THE FIRST TIME,' RUE SAID, STANDING AT THE stream with Morghan, marvelling at the fact that she'd once stood here as Bryn, the water around her calves then as it was now. For a moment, time seemed to fracture, and Rue stood where she was, the water cold on her legs, and stood there also as Bryn, the sun hot on her head, and then the moment passed, leaving Rue blinking, taking a deep breath.

'She's been like this before, that's what the dream told me.' Rue nodded, looking at Morghan to her left and Ambrose to her right. 'She couldn't speak, when the Fae first gave her to Bryn, but then, after she'd gone down the rabbit hole, and the wizards gave her something to drink, then she could.'

'And she was foretelling things?'

Rue nodded, frowning. 'She said something about the Grove burning.' Rue looked at Ambrose. 'I think it horrified everyone, her saying that.' She shivered with the thought that had occurred to her earlier. 'Has that already happened?' She shook her head. 'I mean, it's not going to happen now, is it?'

Ambrose considered it. 'I don't know,' he said. 'Our written records only go back so far. The original Hawthorn House burnt down, but I've no knowledge of any fire before or after that.' He smiled in a sort of bemused wonder. 'Foretelling things. A rare enough gift.'

'I don't think it was a welcome one, or at least not everyone thought so,' Rue said.

'Seers are surely rarely welcome when they foretell difficult things,' Morghan commented.

Rue turned her head, the burbling water around her legs forgotten. 'Seers?'

'Those who can see far.'

Rue dropped her chin. Thought about it.

'That's Clover, then.' She looked up at the far bank, seeing the Shining Ones again, leading the small child who was Rhian, and also Clover, by the hand. 'But why then, and why again now?'

'What do you mean?' Ambrose asked. He tilted his head towards the warming sun and closed his eyes, letting his spirit relax until it flowed out around him, and the edges of who he was and who everyone was around him blurred. He could feel the water, how alive it was, the pebbles and grit under his feet, the air against his skin, the trees at his back.

He felt all of it and was part of it. The great web of the world.

Rue thought about her question. 'Well,' she said. 'Her wizards, or whatever they were – are – they gave Rhian this drink, and it made her able to speak, and she could see things.' Rue closed her eyes, for she felt suddenly a rush of wellbeing, and she looked at Ambrose beside her, saw his face tipped back, a smile on his lips.

She swallowed. 'You're shining,' she said.

'I am at peace with the world,' Ambrose replied, straightening, opening his eyes to look at Rue. 'We do not know the purpose of Clover's gift,' he said.

'We only know to keep her safe,' Morghan added.

Rue turned to her. 'She's in danger?'

But Morghan shook her head. 'Her gift makes her vulnerable, that is all.' She put a hand on Rue's shoulder. 'Perhaps this is why she has you.'

'Has always had you,' Ambrose said.

'But I don't know how to keep her safe,' Rue said. 'Not like this, anyway. I barely managed to keep her fed and clothed.'

Morghan turned and stepped out of the water where they'd said their morning salutations to the world. She dried her feet and put her boots back on.

'Bryn will teach you,' she said.

Rue stood very still for a moment, feeling the truth of the words as it dawned on her. 'She has been already, hasn't she?'

It was Ambrose who replied, stepping also from the stream and donning his footwear. 'The dreams,' he said. 'That has been her doing, I think we can safely say that.' He reached out a hand to Rue and helped her from the water and handed her boots to her.

They stood, the three of them, facing each other for a moment, and then Rue nodded.

'I'm ready,' she said.

Morghan smiled at her. 'Yes,' she said. 'I know you are.'

Her smile widened. 'How has your dancing been coming along?'

Rue rolled her eyes then winced. 'Um, not bad, I suppose.' She lifted her gaze to Morghan's. 'That's not what we're going to do today, is it?'

'Not specifically,' Morghan answered. 'But the lack of self-consciousness you've been developing from it is needed today.'

'That's the bit I haven't quite got the knack of yet.'

Morghan laughed. 'Then what you're going to do now will just take a little longer.'

Rue's eyes widened. 'What am I going to do today?'

Ambrose was gathering up his drum. He straightened and nodded at Morghan who looked back at Rue.

'Come,' she said. 'Come to the beginning of the path.'

Rue wanted to ask more questions. What path? What was she supposed to be doing? Would she know how? What did dancing have to do with today?

But Morghan had turned her back and was walking between the trees, retracing their earlier steps, and with a quick glance at Ambrose who nodded encouragingly, Rue fell into step behind her.

She followed Morghan, and stumbled a step, that strange feeling of dislocation coming over her again.

Ambrose steadied her with a hand cupping her elbow. 'Are you all right?' He glanced ahead at Morghan, at her straight back, her dark hair that hung down in a long braid.

Rue nodded and turned to hurry after Morghan, keeping her eyes on the ground this time. It had been a fleeting sensation, but strong – that she had walked behind Morghan like this before.

As in, long, long before.

Rue concentrated on the woodland floor under her feet.

They came to a crossroads and Morghan stopped.

'This is where you will begin,' she said.

Rue looked around, saw nothing but the path branching through the trees, and nodded anyway.

Morghan smiled. 'It is your turn to learn something that I learnt many years ago now, taught it by Selena, who was taught in turn by Annwyn, the Lady of the Grove before her.'

Rue's eyes widened, and she felt a sort of awe ripple through her. 'Is it something for the Grove priestesses?'

'It is,' Morghan answered. 'But anyone can do it.' She paused. 'Once they know it can be done.'

Rue nodded, thinking she sort of understood that. She drew breath. 'Okay,' she said. 'What do I do?'

Morghan indicated the path with a wave of her hand. 'This path loops around in a wide circle through the trees. It has other paths branch off it, but I want you to walk the main one.'

'In a big circle?'

'Yes,' Morghan agreed. 'Because you are not walking to go anywhere, but because calling in your power is most easily done when you are in motion.'

'Calling in my power?'

'Indeed.'

Morghan glanced at Ambrose, who had unsheathed his drum from its carry bag and struck it now, finding its voice, listening to the beat it wanted to play, firm and low, the heartbeat of the woods.

Rue stood confused. Surely Morghan was going to give her more instructions?

Morghan was. She stepped over to Rue and turned her gently to face the path, then rested her palms on Rue's shoulders.

'Let yourself relax,' she said, and felt Rue take breath, let it slowly out. 'You will walk the path, your pace quick enough so that you forget yourself.'

Rue frowned but said nothing.

'As you walk,' Morghan resumed, 'you will call those who are your kin to walk with you.' She paused, her hands still in place on Rue's shoulders, but her eyes closed now. She let her spirit relax and the worlds turned around her, and she held them, and Rue within them.

'The world is alive,' she whispered near Rue's ear. 'It is larger than you ever imagined, and it has spirit. Everything has spirit. Hear the trees sing. Hear the wind sigh and laugh. Hear the secret stories of the stream. Hear the low murmuring of stone. Feel the lift of your own spirit. When you step forward, walk in the knowledge that all is alive around you. Everything dances, everything sings, everything dreams. We are all part of the great spin of the worlds. Walk the path and hear it all, feel it under your skin, in your heart, and call it to you. Call to you the ones who once you were, all the many shapes and sizes of you, and walk feeling them walk behind you, fanned out, so many, so fine. Stride the path until they are all there, and then walk the way longer, until it is just you and the ones who will stay to walk all paths with you.'

Ambrose's drum beat in time to Rue's heart, and she closed her eyes, feeling the sound of it inside her skin, feeling Morghan's touch on her shoulders, her whispered words swirling in the air around her head, falling upon her, melting into her.

And she walked. Stepping forward onto the path, she walked, following the way between the trees, the drumbeat coming with her, and she walked, barely knowing where she was or where she was going, and yet at the same time, she felt almost as though she could see everything, the path, the trees, the wind, the stars.

Rue strode along the path, her mind dazzled, and she stretched her arms out, imagining all her lifetimes falling into step with her. She almost wanted to turn her head, so strongly did she feel them gathering behind her.

She stumbled, and almost lost her grip on it all, almost came back to not seeing, to the ordinary path, but the woods wrapped their magic around her, and she straightened, stepped forward and flexed her spirit, her imagination again, and there they were, walking behind her, walking with her.

The path looped around, and she passed Ambrose, the beat of his drum growing stronger as she came nearer, passed him.

She barely gave him a glance, did not notice that Morghan wasn't standing with him.

Instead, her feet carried her along the path, her mind as loose and limber as her legs, and she walked around the looping path again, feeling the truth of Morghan's words, that the world was alive around her, that it shone, hummed, sang, danced. Her chest heaved with her breath, her heartbeat quickened with her steps, and her vision blurred, cleared, blurred again. She barely saw where she walked; she only felt those who walked with her.

And then there were only two, and Rue's steps slowed, and she turned to see Bryn smiling at her, Ram standing on the path beside her. Rue lifted her gaze and caught a glimpse of long wings circling the sky above.

'Are you really here?' Rue asked.

'I am as real as you,' Bryn replied, spreading her arms. 'Here in this space where we meet.'

Rue looked around them. 'What is this space?' she asked, then faltered. 'Did I make this happen?'

'You are dreaming awake,' Bryn said. 'You are seeing the world as it really is, spirit as well as flesh.'

Rue licked her lips, her mouth suddenly dry.

'Take a deep breath,' Bryn told her. 'Keep hold of it a little longer.'

Nodding, Rue breathed slow and deep. It was like seeing with her whole body, she decided. Not just her eyes.

'Yes,' Bryn agreed. 'Just like that.'

'I've been dreaming about you,' Rue said, looking at the other woman, her other self.

Bryn was short, sturdy, dark, her brown eyes dancing with humour. There were tattoos up and down her bare arms, and Rue wanted to lean closer, examine them to see what the designs were. But she stayed where she was, afraid to break the spell.

'I saw you pull Clover – I mean Rhian – from the rabbit hole,' she said.

'It wasn't really a rabbit hole,' Bryn answered.

Rue shook her head. 'No,' she agreed. 'It wasn't.' Another thought occurred to her.

'Thank you for saving my life,' she said. 'When those men were chasing me. It was you who saved me from them.' She looked at Bryn again, at the long staff the woman held. The tip was rounded. Not a spear, then.

'I was glad to be able to come to your aid,' Bryn said.

'Are you sure this is real?' Rue blurted the question, somewhere inside herself marvelling over the impossibility of what was happening.

Bryn smiled at her. 'I am sure.'

'But how?'

'Once you know you can do this, it can be done.'

Rue was silent. 'But why?' she asked at last. 'Why are you reaching out to me?'

'None of us are alone,' Bryn said, and touched a hand to Ram's thickly curling wool. 'I reach out so that you may not feel so, and so that you can remember, and be stronger for the remembering.'

'Remember what?'

Bryn nodded at Rue. 'Connection,' she said. 'The thread that binds us and our purpose.'

38

SELENA CHECKED IN ON CLOVER, POPPING HER HEAD AROUND the door to the playroom.

'Is she all right?' she whispered to Tara.

Tara, down on the floor helping Josh build a garage for his truck out of blocks, looked up.

Her face was pale and drawn with grief, Selena thought. Clover wasn't the only one this had taken a toll on.

It was affecting them all.

'She's doing better,' Tara said, also whispering. 'At least she isn't wrapped up on the couch watching Matilda for the hundredth time.'

Selena nodded and looked over to the little table where Clover sat bent over a piece of paper, a crayon in her hand.

'I'm going for a walk,' she said. 'I shan't be long, and I will take my phone with me in case you need me for any reason at all.' She was getting used to carrying the mobile phone with her, although she hoped, particularly this morning, that it would stay silent in her pocket.

Selena let herself out the back door. None of them used the big front entrance, it was always the back door in the kitchen that was more convenient. The air outside was cold, damp, and Selena was reminded again that it would be Samhain in less than two short weeks.

What would they do for it, she wondered, crossing the road in front of the house and slipping into the Botanic Gardens. It had rained overnight, and the trees dripped onto the jacket she wore.

Her lips curved in an unconscious smile. She'd worn her cloak one morning, coming to the gardens for a walk amongst her new tree friends, but it had made her too conspicuous in the eyes of the people she passed, and they'd all stared at her. It had been distracting, so now she kept to more regular clothes.

But perhaps she'd wear the cloak on Samhain.

How strange, she thought. She'd celebrated the season just a few short months ago in Wilde Grove before she'd left, and here it was again.

The Wheel turned, and she with it.

But these musings were not her purpose this chill morning.

Greeting the trees with a whispered hello or a touch of the fingertips as she walked, Selena made her way up the hill. She held her thoughts still so that they did not wander away from her, keeping her attention instead on her surroundings. The way the last of the rain dripped from the ferns, the way the big Pinus Radiata towered over her and yet were among the most approachable of the trees in the park, standing in their group of five, the smaller oaks humming along beside them.

Selena left the main garden and crossed the road to walk through the small piece of woodland to the gates of the Northern Cemetery.

It was a fitting place, she thought, to offer the prayers she wanted to.

And to check on Rachel.

There was one main path looping around the cemetery that sat upon the hillside, the graves lying feet first down the slope.

Selena walked the path, making her steps measured, unhurried, neither fast nor slow. She let herself relax further out of her head, sinking into her heart as she walked. Her eyelids fluttered, and she saw the graves, some so old that the weather had blurred the names on the headstones, and she saw the trees, to whom she thought this graveyard really belonged, for they grew between and around and in the graves, gathering the bones of the dead together, holding them close in their rooted embrace.

Ruru, the little brown native owl, landed on Selena's shoulder and she smiled a greeting at the small spirit.

She walked until she was seeing in spirit as well as with the eyes of her flesh. She saw the auras of the trees spreading like clouds from their branches. She heard the fluting of the birds, the skittering of the insects. She felt the crisscross of the web, connecting everything, humming with life.

She gathered the trees of the Wildwood around her as she walked, eyes unfocused, heart calm and untroubled, feet finding the path.

She walked in the cemetery, and she walked in the forest

of the Wildwood, and she sought the place where she had laid Rachel's spirit, hoping to give her rest, ease.

Rachel was no longer there, and Selena closed her eyes for a few steps, unsurprised.

Had she passed on? Selena meditated on the question. Had Rachel gone onwards in her soul's journey from this world to the next?

She shook her head, and the knowledge was certain inside her.

Rachel would not rest, she thought, could not rest. She was hurt, confused, fearful.

Selena began her second lap around the cemetery, face lifted to the drizzling sky, feeling the misty water on her cheeks like tears.

She sang now, as she walked, her voice rough, chanting the words of her prayer.

You are among now, our beloved dead
And our mother brings your bones home
to the cave of her heart,
Where the light is dim, but your bones, they are radiant.
Our Mother, she counts them one by one.
A wide curve of pelvis, that once cupped a child.
And something thinner but just as strong,
A forearm, that once held another.
Our Bone Mother, she strings those of yours that are smallest
Into a necklace to sit upon the ribbing of her chest.
Fingers, toes, ear bones, all the pieces that once
You were, she knits them back together
With dreams woven of silver and sun,
Here in the dimness of her cave, the quiet of her heart.
Fear not, my beloved, for

You will sing again,
You will fly, and walk,
And run,
And the curve of the world will hold you
And lead you over the horizon.
Run with the deer, my darling,
Your bones newly shined,
Run with the deer, my darling.
Follow Mother home.

Selena stopped under the largest of the trees, its branches spread overhead like a tent, the ground around her feet strewn with cones. She considered what to do next.

It was possible, she thought, that she could gather the Wildwood back around herself, and step through it into the Middleworld, and seek Rachel there, for that surely was where she wandered.

Would she be able to find her? Selena pondered this question. It had been Clover who had tracked Rachel before.

She couldn't ask Clover to do that again.

And what would she be able to offer Rachel, even if she did find her?

Selena shook her head. The rain was falling harder now, although she was dry under the tree's thick branches.

She would try, she decided. She would look again for Rachel.

Selena stepped out of the shelter of the tree and back onto the path, sinking again into the cemetery's atmosphere of still, sad beauty. Her feet walked the path, through the cemetery, through the Wildwood, her spirit spreading wide around her, heart seeking Rachel.

There were steps along the path behind her and Selena was brought rapidly back to her body as a man and his dog overtook her and continued along the way. The dog turned, head low, and gave her a lugubrious look before they reached a corner and were out of sight.

She couldn't do this here, Selena decided. Not if she needed to go deep. Walking while travelling was good, and it worked well, but it was awkward when others, strangers, walked the same path.

Briefly, Selena thought of Wilde Grove, and missed the paths and trails through the woods there. The paths and trails, and the caves, everything perfectly just so for the work she needed to do.

But she felt the pang of longing only briefly before pulling herself back from it. Yes, there were limitations here, but hadn't she just visited Wilde Grove, and hadn't she, while there, wanted to be back here?

Selena retraced her steps home with a smile on her face.

CLOVER HEARD SELENA'S STEPS IN THE ENTRANCEWAY AND ran over to tug the playroom door open.

'I got a picture for S'lena,' she said to Tara, who was reading a book to Danielle and Josh.

Clover got the door open. 'S'lena,' she called. Selena turned and smiled at her. 'I got a picture for ya.'

Selena nodded. 'That's lovely,' she said, taking the piece of paper and turning it the right way up to look at it. She examined the crayon drawing.

'Who is this?' she asked, showing Clover her picture and pointing to one of the figures.

Clover's mouth turned down. 'That's Josh's mama.'

Selena nodded. She'd rather thought so. Walking over to the stairs, she sat down on the next to bottom step and patted the spot next to her. Clover came and sat down, and they looked at the drawing together.

'She lookin' at Josh,' Clover said. 'She not screamin' anymore, though.'

'That's a very good thing,' Selena said. 'Is this her house?'

Clover leaned against Selena's arm and nodded. 'Where she used to live.'

Selena closed her eyes, letting the paper with its black and grey crayon drawing lie on her knees.

'She misses Josh,' Clover said sadly. 'I hear her tryna talk to him.'

Selena looked down at Clover and put an arm around her. 'Does she follow him here?' she asked.

Clover shook her head and shuddered. 'No, and I'm glad. That would be scary.'

Yes, Selena thought. It probably would be. 'She's at her house, then?'

Clover just nodded and they sat for a few minutes together on the step just thinking about it all.

'Is everything all right?' Tara asked, coming out of the playroom. Her face was drawn with worry.

But Selena nodded. 'Yes,' she said. 'Clover was just giving me a picture.'

'It Josh's mama,' Clover said to Tara. 'You can look if ya like.'

Selena held out the crayon drawing for Tara, who took it and looked at it, her frown growing deeper.

'Josh's mama gone home,' Clover said, climbing into Selena's lap. 'Not home where she s'posed to go, though, 'cross the sea an' all.' She looked up at Selena. 'Isn't that right?'

'That's right, darling,' Selena said. 'She's not gone there yet.'

'Where is she then?' Tara asked. She was rubbing her head now, unable to believe how this nightmare had happened. Finally, she pointed to the small figure in a bed. 'Is this Josh?' she asked.

'Yeah,' Clover said. 'At his house in bed.'

Tara nodded. That made sense.

'An' his mama lookin' in the window.' Clover rested her head against Selena's breast and sighed. 'I'm tired again,' she said.

Selena kissed the top of her head. 'I know you are, sweetheart. I know you are.'

'I wanna have a nap.'

'It's time for morning tea,' Tara said, letting the hand holding the picture fall.

'I not hungry,' Clover said. 'I tired.' She looked up at Selena. 'Rue comin' back soon?'

Selena nodded. 'She'll be here in just two sleeps.'

Clover was glad. She'd told Rue she had to stay, to see, but she was glad now that Rue was coming back. It would be better with Rue home. Rue always took care of her.

'Come on, sweetheart,' Selena said. 'I'll tuck you in for a nap, if you like.'

'Can I have Blackie?' Clover asked. Blackie was the stuffed blackbird Selena had brought back with her. Rue had finished it while she was away.

'Of course.'

Selena stood up and Clover held her hand, standing on the stairs. Selena looked at Tara and tried to smile.

Tara nodded back, but her eyes were still worried when she looked at Clover.

This was hard on the little girl. They had to do something for her. Tara looked again at the picture in her hand and hoped that Rose Griffith, the police officer they'd spoken to, was out there now, doing something about finding Rachel.

Her body, that was. Tara, gazing at the crayoned picture, thought she had a very good idea where Rachel's spirit was.

39

ROSE OPENED THE DOOR AND WENT RIGHT IN, PEERING around the old house.

'Mum,' she called out. 'It's me.'

She found her mother wrapped up in one of her Nan's crocheted afghans and watching television.

'Have you seen this, Rosie?'

Rose stepped around the coffee table to see what was on the screen and her mouth flattened.

'No,' she said. 'But I've heard it mentioned.'

'Yeah?' Kiri Hōhepa squinted up at her daughter for a moment, then looked back at the screen. 'They're good.'

'It's scripted,' Rose said. 'Has to be.'

But Kiri shook her head. 'Nah, love. You know better than that.' She settled back against the couch. 'I could be on it.'

'On Sensing Murder?' Rose was incredulous.

Kiri shrugged and grinned at her daughter. 'Yeah, too right, eh? They wouldn't let a fat old Māori lady like me go on it.' She sniffed. 'I could do it, I reckon.' She laughed. 'Wouldn't be so interesting though, watching me snore on screen.' She jiggled with laughter.

Rose pursed her lips. 'That's sort of why I'm here.'

Kiri raised her eyebrows, saw Rose was serious, then reached for the remote and turned the sound down on the TV. She wanted to watch the show, but she wanted to hear what her daughter needed even more.

Rose backed up a step, snatched up her mother's cup and clutched it to her chest. 'I'll make us a cup of tea, eh?'

But Kiri followed Rose into the kitchen and sat herself down at the small dining table at the far end, where she watched Rose with narrowed, thoughtful eyes.

'Something bothering you?' she asked at last, nodding her thanks when Rose brought the mugs of tea over and sat down.

Rose fiddled with a spoon, shrugged, then sighed. She put the spoon down and scratched her neck.

'Yeah, guess so,' she said.

'Well, spit it out then,' Kiri said, fishing the tea bag out of her cup.

'Okay, okay. So, I had these three women come in yesterday about a missing person.'

Kiri perked up. A missing person – perhaps she could do a Sensing Murder to find them. She nodded and gestured for Rose to carry on.

'Right. So, they've nothing to go on, really. The lady has probably just left her husband.'

'Who are these women, then?' Kiri asked.

Rose shook her head. 'One of them is the caregiver for the woman's child.' She paused.

'There's a kid?' Kiri asked. 'Where's the kid, then?'

'She left him with the father.'

Kiri put down her drink and stared at her daughter. 'She left her kid? Hine, do you know how many women would leave their tamariki behind?'

Rose shook her head. 'Not many.'

'Too right not many,' Kiri agreed. She took a sip of tea, hearing for a moment, the TV in the other room. 'But that's not why you're here, is it?'

'I come here every day,' Rose said.

Kiri grinned. 'Yeah, but today something is on your mind.'

Rose rolled her eyes, but she didn't tell her mother she was wrong.

'One of the women was the kiddie's caregiver,' she said instead, going back to the story. 'And the other gave the missing lady a tarot reading...'

'Did she say what cards turned up?' Kiri interrupted.

Rose shook her head. 'And the last of the three said she'd spoken to her ghost.'

Kiri gave a low whistle. 'Now,' she said. 'I'd like to meet those two.'

'Sure, Mum,' Rose said, clenching her hands on the top of the old Formica table. 'I'll organise a merry get-together for us all. It'll be fun.'

Kiri ignored her. 'What did you tell them after that?'

Rose shrugged. 'I should be used to that sort of thing – there's you, after all – but they really took me by surprise. I ended the interview.'

'Did you say you were going to look into the missing woman?'

'We don't know she's missing.'

Kiri waggled her head from side to side. 'Did you tell them you'd find out if the woman was missing or if she just hated her husband and kid?'

'Yeah,' Rose said, relaxing her hands and resisting the urge to rest her head in them. 'Yeah, I did.'

Kiri nodded. 'Good girl. When you going to go visit this fella?' She closed her eyes for a moment, withdrawing to test the air around the guy. 'Can you get someone to go with you?'

'Nah. Probably not,' Rose said. 'It's not the husband who's reported her missing, so it's low priority.'

Kiri grunted. 'You staying the night, then?'

Rose nodded. 'I thought I would, yeah.'

'That's good, then.' Kiri got up and padded out of the room. 'Let's watch the rest of the show. This lady on it, she's real good. Got a good line to the dead.'

ROSE KNEW THE DRILL. SHE GOT UP EARLY, SHIVERING, THE house cold, draughty. She wished she could afford to get the place properly insulated for her mother.

Kiri was still asleep, the blankets tucked tightly around her neck, her long hair with its streaks of grey spread over the pillow. Rose sat down gingerly on the side of the bed, pen and notebook at the ready. She touched her mother's face.

'Tell me what you see,' she said, speaking around the lump in her throat that always turned up when they did this. No matter that she'd been doing this all her life with her mother, that lump in her throat and the prickling sensation in her skin was always there. She shifted her feet on the floor and cleared her throat, touched Kiri's face again, and spoke a little louder.

'Tell me what you see.'

Kiri's eyes moved under their lids, and she smacked her lips together.

'There's a little boy crying for his mama,' she said, her voice thick with sleep. 'He crying and crying and she not hearing him. She far far away.'

Rose closed her eyes. 'How far away?' she asked.

Kiri moved her bulk in the bed, sniffing, but her eyes stayed closed and under the lids, they roamed back and forth, back and forth, searching.

'She gone where he can't find her. Even when she stands over him, he can't find her. Little boy crying. She crying. Everyone 'cept *him* crying.'

Rose paused from writing her mother's words down. 'Him?'

Kiri, still sleeping, curled her lip in contempt. 'Him. Nasty man. Gone and taken her away from her bubba. No māmā should be taken away from their pēpi.'

Pēpi was baby, Rose knew, and she wrote down the words with a heavy heart. Her mother was telling her the woman was dead, she knew it.

When she went around to Mike Manners's house later that morning, she would likely be speaking to someone who had killed his wife.

'Mr Manners?'

He looked dismissively down at the woman on the

doorstep. 'Do I know you? You need to make an appointment first. I don't take people off the street.'

Behind him, a child yelled.

'Listen,' Mike said. 'You have to go. Give me a call, make an appointment, and I can see you during working hours, all right?'

Rose shook her head, held up her Police Identity Card. 'I'm police, Mr Manners,' she said. 'Can I come in and have a word?'

The baby cried out again.

Mike glanced back into the house, then turned to Rose again. 'You're not in uniform.'

Rose didn't answer.

'Look,' Mike sighed. 'Is this about Rachel?' he asked. 'That day care woman called you, didn't she?'

Rose stayed impassive. 'If we could go inside and have a word, Mr Manners.' The baby was crying now. 'I think your son needs you.'

'So it is that annoying woman – she called you, didn't she?' Mike turned and walked down the hallway to the kitchen, leaving the door open for the policewoman to follow him or not.

Josh was in his highchair, his bowl of cereal overturned on the floor. Mike pressed his lips together to make himself stay silent and scooped the bowl off the floor. There were cornflakes everywhere.

'You'd better be quick,' Mike said, getting a paper towel and swiping ineffectually at the mess while Josh set up howling again. 'I have to take him to day care.' He threw the paper towel in the rubbish and grabbed a tea towel to wipe the milk from Josh's face and hands before pulling him out of the highchair and making the effort to bounce him on his hip.

'This is the day care run by the woman you just said was annoying?' Rose asked, looking around the kitchen. There was an air of neglect about the room. Dishes in the sink, dried food on the table where it hadn't been wiped down properly.

She saw a handbag on the sideboard and raised an eyebrow at it. Rachel's?

'Yes, that's her,' Mike shushed Josh in his arms, and he quietened, turning his small sweet mouth down and staring at Rose. 'I haven't had time to look for anyone else, and Josh likes her well enough.'

'Is this your wife's handbag?' Rose asked, plucking up the blue vinyl bag and snapping it open.

'Hey, you can't just go looking in that,' Mike said, snatching it off her. He tucked it under his arm. 'She left a lot of her things behind.' He sniffed. 'Shouldn't you be wearing a uniform?'

Rose lifted her lips in an entirely fake smile. 'No,' she said. 'I'm in the criminal investigation department.'

It gave her a great deal of satisfaction to tell him so, and she watched as he paled slightly.

Which he should, she thought. There had been a wallet in that handbag – she'd seen it just before he'd whipped it away from her. One of those old gold mesh ones that had been popular way back in the '80s.

And while it was pretty normal for a woman to have more than one handbag she used, Rose considered whether it was also usual for a woman to have more than one purse for her money and cards.

She thought not.

'Shall we go into the living room, Mr Manners, so that the little one can play while we chat?'

Mike opened his mouth, then closed it again and nodded. 'Only for a few minutes though. I have to get Josh to day care, and I've got an appointment first thing this morning.' He turned into the front room, which was actually his office, rather than the living room, but there were a few toys for Josh on the floor, and Mike decided he felt better in here than he would sitting perched on the edge of the couch with his knees around his ears.

He put the kid on the floor and Josh promptly grabbed his toy digger and sat down with it on his lap.

Mike slid into his seat behind his desk and waved at the other chair.

Rose sat down and stared at him. She'd already decided how to go about this.

Start with the basics. Some history.

Dates. Times. Movement.

'Mr Manners,' she said. 'How long have you and your wife been married?'

'Two years.'

Rose straightened in surprise. 'That's not very long.'

Mike Manners shrugged.

'How did you meet?'

Mike's mouth tightened. 'Do I have to answer these questions?'

Rose shook her head. 'No, but if you don't, then I'll be asking for you to come down to the station with me, and there you will have to.'

It wasn't strictly true, but Rose made her face bland and patient and waited him out.

Finally, Mike sighed. 'Rachel was my first wife's cousin,' he said. 'We met through her.'

'What was your first wife's name?'

'Susan.'

Rose nodded, getting out her notebook and turned to a blank page, pausing only a moment over the one she'd written on that morning, recording her mother's sleeping words.

'Rachel came from an Exclusive Brethren family, is that correct?'

'Yes.'

'When did she leave?'

Mike sat forward. 'Listen,' he said. 'What's this got to do with anything? She's left me, that's all. Done a bunk with a new boyfriend or something.'

'Rachel has a boyfriend?' This was interesting, Rose thought. No one had mentioned this so far.

Mike collapsed back against his chair and rubbed at his face. The jilted husband.

'I don't know, really. I considered the possibility,' he said. 'She'd been acting different the last couple months. I thought it could be another bloke.'

'And did you ask her about it?'

Mike considered Rose before he answered. 'No,' he said finally.

Rose was quick with her next question.

'Why not?'

'I decided it wasn't likely after all. You gotta understand – Rachel was a bit of a sad girl. Probably from being kicked out of her family. She wasn't worldly. No one would be interested in her.'

'You were.'

Mike stared at Rose before shrugging. 'She was real sweet when we first got together.'

Rose paused. Decided she couldn't afford to go down that path. Mike was already looking at his watch.

'When did you last see your wife, Mr Manners?' she asked instead.

'Wednesday morning two weeks ago, before she took Josh to day care.'

'Before she left?'

'That's what I said. I had a business meeting out of the house, so if she came back, I didn't see her.'

'You told Tara Cross that Rachel had a hair appointment that day.'

Mike rubbed his face. 'Yeah,' he said. 'She did. That's what she said.' He looked toward the door, wishing the policewoman would leave.

'Then you said Rachel had gone to stay with her sister.'

'Yeah, because it wasn't any of that Tara's business.' Mike glanced at the door again, this time wishing he could leave.

'But really, Rachel had left you.' Rose nodded. 'Which would explain why you weren't expecting to pick up Josh that day.'

Mike dragged his gaze back into the room. 'I was out all day. First I heard of any of it, was when Tara Cross rang and said that Rachel hadn't come to get him.' He glanced at Josh, who was sitting on the floor still hugging his digger.

'Do you mind telling me where you were that day, Mr. Manners?'

'I bloody do, actually,' Mike said.

'You said you had a meeting?' Rose was unperturbed. On the surface.

'Several.' Mike looked at the other wall, stared out the window.

Rose paused. She wasn't going to get the details from him, she could tell. He'd refuse, and she couldn't make him.

'Where do you think your wife has gone, Mr Manners?'

'No idea,' he said.

Rose stared at him. 'Do you miss her, Mike?' she asked.

Finally, he looked back at her. 'I do, actually,' he said.

Rose nodded, looking at the little boy sitting silently on the carpet with his toy truck. She thought that was practically the first truthful thing Mike Manners had told her.

40

RUE BURST INTO TEARS.

Everyone was there, at the airport, waving madly to get her attention as she walked off the plane and into the building.

'Rue!' Clover bounced up and down, then couldn't wait any longer and breaking free from Selena's hand, she tore across the floor to her sister.

'Rue,' she said. 'I missed you!'

Rue crouched down, dropping her backpack to the ground and opened her arms to hug Clover tight.

'I missed you too, Clover Bee,' she said. 'I'm sorry you had to go through everything without me.'

Clover stood back and touched the tears on Rue's face. 'Is okay,' she said. 'S'lena helped.' She wrinkled her nose. 'Did you see?'

Rue stood up and picked up her bag, then swooped Clover into her arms. They were in everyone's way.

'See what?' she asked.

Clover put her palms on Rue's cheek and peered into her eyes. 'You did, din't ya?'

Rue nodded. She reckoned she knew what Clover was on about. 'Yes,' she said. 'I saw.'

'Good.' Clover was emphatic. 'I don' know it all, what you seen, but was 'portant.'

Rue kissed Clover on the cheek and wiped her tears away with the back of her hand. 'Yeah,' she said. 'It was important.'

She beamed at everyone, letting Clover slip back down to the ground so she could hug them all.

'I can't believe you all came to meet me,' she said, wrapping her arms around Damien and squeezing him tight.

'I think you grew while you were away,' Damien said, stepping back to examine her before passing her onto the next in line.

'We brought both cars so we could all fit,' Tara said, letting her own tears fall even as she laughed. 'No one wanted to miss out on seeing you as soon as possible.'

Ebony punched her lightly on the shoulder while Suze and Sophie beamed at her.

'Didn't think you could just sneak back home, did ya?' Ebony asked.

Rue shook her head, grinning like a fool, and Ebony flung her arms around her.

'Wow do we have so much to catch up on,' she whispered before letting Rue go again.

Rue, overwhelmed, nodded, and greeted Natalie, then Dandy, before getting finally to Selena. She held Selena tight.

'I'm sorry,' she whispered. 'I couldn't stay away any longer. I know you wanted me to.'

Selena shook her head even as she still held Rue tightly to her. 'Morghan told me you discovered what you needed to.' She gave Rue another squeeze, then looked at her, at the tears tracking down Rue's face again.

'You did well,' she said. 'So very well.'

Rue closed her eyes and nodded, then gave Selena a shaky smile. 'It's just the beginning, I think,' she said, then looked at Clover, who stood looking up at her with her big blue eyes.

Rue sniffed, snatched Clover up again. 'Come on everyone,' she said. 'I want to go home.'

'SURPRISE!' TARA SAID, WHEN RUE PILED INTO THE KITCHEN behind everyone.

'We made you birthday stuff!' Clover crowed, climbing up to the table to stand over the cake Natalie had baked.

Rue shook her head in wonder. 'You guys,' she said. 'You went to so much trouble.'

Dandy wrapped an arm around Rue's shoulders and kissed her head. 'Nothing is too much trouble for you, my dear,' she said. 'Happy birthday. We're glad we didn't have to miss it entirely.'

'Yep,' Ebony added. 'Any excuse for a party, you know.'

Suze and Sophie grinned at her, nodding.

Rue twisted the ring on her finger and looked at Selena, swallowing.

Selena smiled back.

'Come on!' Clover said, waving her hands. 'Light the candles, Nat'lie, so Rue can blow 'em out!'

'The cake is beautiful,' Rue said, walking over to the table on legs that were a little unsteady.

'Natalie made it,' Damien said, grinning proudly at her.

Natalie blushed, pleased. She was still getting used to being part of this odd but wonderful new family. 'It's a chocolate gateaux.' She swallowed, offered her next words nervously. 'I remembered you said the best birthday cake your mum had ever gotten you was a chocolate gateaux.'

Rue looked at her.

'I wanted your mum to be remembered, while we're all together.' Natalie grimaced. 'If it wasn't for her, none of us would be here.'

Rue took a breath, looked back at the cake, tears coming back to her eyes.

'Thank you,' she said. 'That means so much.' She looked around the room and sniffed even as she laughed in wonder. 'I love you all so much,' she said.

Clover nodded from her chair at the head of the table. 'We love you too, Rue.'

Rue looked at the pretty chocolatey confection. 'It's the most beautiful cake I've ever seen.'

'Is got sixteen candles, Rue,' Clover said. 'Light 'em, and blow 'em out, and don' forget to wish.' She nodded seriously. Rue had taught her all about making birthday wishes, and hadn't all the ones she'd made come true?

They had, she thought, looking around the room at her family.

'I'll light them,' Damien said, springing into action, and pulling a lighter from his pocket.

A moment later, Rue was in front of the cake taking a breath to blow out the candles.

'Don' forget to make a wish,' Clover told her.

Rue shook her head. 'I have everything I need.' But she closed her eyes for a moment and made a wish before blowing the candles out.

Everyone cheered and sang happy birthday to her, then Clover sidled up and climbed on her lap.

'What you wish for?' she asked in a whisper.

'Isn't that supposed to be a secret?' Rue said.

But Clover shook her head. 'I wanna know. You not s'posed to keep secrets from me.'

Rue laughed, because every year that she'd managed to make herself a birthday cake since Clover was old enough to talk, she'd had to spill the secret of her wish.

Each year, it had been the same thing, to be safe.

Until this year.

'I wished to always be here for you, Clover,' she said.

Clover gazed at her, eyes wide in their fringe of blonde lashes. 'Always?'

'Yeah.'

Clover nodded.

Selena picked up the knife to slice the cake. She cut a piece for everyone, Natalie holding out plates for her to put them on.

'Who's the extra one for?' Damien asked. He looked toward the door. 'We expecting someone else?'

Selena shook her head. 'This last piece is for Beatrix,' she said.

'Mum?' Rue asked.

Selena smiled at her. 'Yes,' she said. 'To honour and

thank your mother, because the dead live on, and Natalie was right – without Beatrix, none of us would be here, and I am so thankful that we all were.'

There was silence for a moment, then Damien held up his slice of cake. 'To Beatrix,' he said.

'To Beatrix,' everyone echoed.

'To Mama,' Clover crowed.

LATER, RUE SAT BACK ON HER BED, EXHAUSTED, CLOVER sleeping in the crook of her arm. She watched Ebony prowling around her room. Sophie and Suze had gone home, promises to meet up again soon on their lips.

'What's it like?' Rue asked. 'Working at Beacon?'

Ebony shook her head, eyes shining. 'It's awesome,' she said. 'Meg's fantastic, and she's teaching me everything about the stock – all about the crystals and what not, so that I don't sound like a complete moron when I'm talking to a customer.' She paused, came to a standstill in front of the window, the late afternoon light dimming around her head.

'I'm not going back,' she said.

'Back where?' Rue asked, confused. 'You just said you loved it at Beacon.'

Ebony shook her head. 'Not to Beacon. To school. I'm not going back to school.'

'What?'

'I've almost convinced Meg to let me stay on full time.' Ebony beamed. 'I'm not going back to school, I'm telling you.'

Rue was amazed. 'Is your mum all right with that?'

Ebony shrugged. 'She's not real pleased, but she knows

me well enough – there wasn't anything useful I could learn at school for what I want to do.' Ebony came over and sat on the bed, one leg jigging up and down.

'What about you?' she asked.

'What do you mean, what about me?' Rue said.

'You're going back?'

'To school?' Rue thought about it. 'I guess so. I mean, I hadn't thought not to.'

'But what for?' Ebony asked. 'You want to be a priestess, right?'

Rue thought about everything that had happened in the last few weeks. She'd promised to tell Ebony about all of it when she wasn't so tired.

'Yeah, but no one's going to pay me to do that,' she said at last, looking down at Clover, who was curled up to her side.

Ebony flung herself backwards on the bed and stared up at the ceiling. 'Yeah. That's what I figured out too.' She looked over at Rue. 'I mean, I want to do the ghost busting and all – and I will, I'm sure of it – but it's not like you can charge people for helping spirits pass over.' She wrinkled her nose. 'Doesn't sound ethical to charge for that, you know?'

Ebony went on before Rue could drag up an answer. 'And I don't reckon you'd have a steady stream of work, either.' She pursed her lips. 'But now I have a job at Beacon, which is extra double cool, and I can do all the rest on the side, you know?'

She rolled over onto her side. 'You're still going to do some of it with me, right?'

Rue wound a blonde curl of Clover's around a finger,

thinking about it. 'Yeah,' she said. 'Of course. But when it comes to work, I still really want to do something with fashion design, so I'll go back to school next term.' She smoothed Clover's hair down. 'And when I finish school, I'll do the fashion design course at the polytechnic.'

'But doesn't all the stuff Selena is teaching you – and whatever you learnt at Wilde Grove – make you want to do something more?' Ebony shook her head. 'I don't know – something more in line with it?'

Rue thought about that. 'I'm not certain,' she said at last. 'I'll definitely learn and practice more, but the most important thing to me is making sure Clover is okay.' She remembered the vision of Bryn pulling Rhian from the rabbit hole, and Mairenn asking if Rhian's seeing was a blessing or a curse.

'Well, that's taken care of, at least,' Ebony said. 'You've got five people out there who would probably throw themselves in front of a moving vehicle to keep the kiddo safe.'

Rue nodded. Closed her eyes.

If she had her way, she thought, there'd never be a car to throw themselves in front of to begin with.

It was late enough now, the sun down, the day done. Rue had made it through to bedtime – or close enough, she thought. Jet lag had had her wanting to go to sleep when Clover had napped beside her, but she'd forced herself to stay awake.

It was nice to be home, she decided, taking in the sight of all her familiar things. It had been a shame to come home early from Wilde Grove, because she thought there was probably so much more that Morghan could have taught her; but all the same, she was back where she belonged.

Clover was tucked into the bed watching her get ready. She'd decided she didn't want to sleep in her own room, and Rue hadn't had the heart to make her.

'Be like before,' Clover had said.

Except the bed was bigger and Rue slept better these days than she ever had then.

She came and sat down on the covers now.

'What you doin'?' Clover asked. 'Aren't you comin' to sleep?'

'In a minute,' Rue answered. There was something she wanted to do first, or check, rather.

She wanted to make sure Bryn was still around.

There wasn't the space in the room to walk around and around like she had at Wilde Grove, but Rue had another idea. She wasn't confident it would work, but she figured there was nothing to lose by trying it. She reached under her pillow for the gift Damien had given her.

'I wanna listen too,' Clover said immediately.

'You can't,' Rue said. 'It only works with headphones.'

Clover flopped back down under the covers with a groan. 'Fine,' she said.

Rue laughed. 'Okay, okay. I'll use the CD player.' There was a small one on top of her desk so she could listen to music, if she wanted. She crossed the room to it, checked which CD was already in it, hesitated a moment, then shrugged and hit play.

There was a clear area of floor between the bed and the

desk, and Rue stood there, letting her body loosen, and closed her eyes.

'What ya goin' to do?' Clover asked.

'Dance,' Rue said.

And she did, awkwardly at first, aware of Clover sitting cross-legged on the bed, and then, gradually, just as had happened at the stone circle, she got more comfortable, and forgot she wasn't alone. The room became bigger around her, and her movements fluid, and she concentrated on her steps, and all the space there was inside her, and outside her, and her spirit expanded to fill it, and wellbeing flooded through her, chasing away the fatigue, the worry, all the business of the day, until there was just her and the music and the dance and the swirling, spinning universe.

And Bryn, dancing with her.

41

There was a knock at the door.

'I'll get it,' Damien said. 'And then I gotta fly.'

He pulled the door open to see two women standing there. 'Heya,' he said. 'Help ya?'

Rose cleared her throat. 'Is Tara Cross at home?'

Damien opened the door wider. 'Yeah, sure. You wanna come in? I'll get her for you.'

'Thanks,' Rose said briefly, wanting to stick her elbow into her mother's side, stop her goggling at the guy who'd answered the door. 'Is this some sort of boarding house?' she asked.

'Nah,' Damien said. 'Though it's big enough.' He led them through into the kitchen and scratched his head. 'Ah, you can take a seat here, I guess. I'll go get Tara.'

Rose looked around the room, trying not to meet her mother's eyes as the guy who answered the door disappeared out somewhere into the rest of the house.

'Look at this place,' Kiri said.

'Yeah,' Rose answered, wondering why she was feeling so sour about all of this. 'You think it's hygienic to prepare food with this many plants around?'

Kiri raised an eyebrow at her daughter, who had been disgruntled ever since she'd agreed to this visit.

'Most foods are plants, aroha,' she said, pulling out a chair and sitting down.

Rose just sniffed and stayed standing. She linked her hands in front of her, then put them behind her back. Then on her hips. Then, finally, crossed them in front of her chest.

'Oh,' Tara said, coming into the room, seeing her visitors.

'You right, Tara?' Damien asked. The visitors looked harmless enough, or at least the elder did. He returned her smile.

'Yes, thank you, Damien.' Tara took a breath. 'This is Sergeant Rose Griffith, and...' She gave an inquiring look.

'And her mother,' Kiri said, suppressing the laughter that wanted to bubble inside her at Rose's expression.

Rose looked like she'd been sucking on a lemon.

'Kiri Hōhepa,' Rose said, introducing her mother reluctantly. She wanted to leave, take her mother home. Really, she thought, how could she do her job when she was dragging her mum around with her?

Although actually, it had been Kiri who had dragged her there. And Rose reminded herself that it was the weekend, and this was not a formal police visit. She shifted, still uncomfortable.

'You're the police officer looking into Rachel's disappearance?' Damien asked, his eyes going wide.

'Yes,' Rose said shortly, cutting him off before he could

ask why she had her mother with him. 'But I'm, ah, not here in my official capacity.'

'You got that right,' Kiri giggled. 'She doesn't take me with her when she's being a proper detective.'

Damien laughed. 'Right, nice to meet you – I gotta get to work.' He waved a hand and slipped out to his car.

'Nice boy,' Kiri said, and looked at Tara. 'He your fella?'

Tara shook her head. 'Heavens, no.'

Kiri nodded, looked at Rose. 'You should ask him out.'

'Mum!' Rose gaped at her mother, cheeks turning beet red.

'Um.' Tara didn't know what to do. 'Damien's seeing someone, I'm sorry,' she said, thinking of Natalie. 'Er, can I get you a cup of tea, or coffee?'

Rose fell on the offer with relief. 'A cup of coffee would be great, thanks,' she said. She cleared her throat. 'Are the others here? The two who came to the station with you?' She felt like she was fumbling her words and sent her mother a glaring look.

Kiri stared placidly back at her then turned to Tara. 'I'll have a nice hot cuppa, thanks. Just a teabag in a mug will do me.'

Tara nodded, looked at Rose. 'They're here. I'll put the jug on and get them.'

She slipped out of the kitchen and knocked quietly on the door to Dandy's sitting room.

'Come in,' Dandy called.

Tara edged open the door and looked in. 'That police-woman is here,' she said then paused. 'With her mother.'

Dandy sat straighter on the couch in her little sitting room. She put the newspaper down.

'With her mother?'

Tara nodded. 'They want to talk to us. The three of us, I mean – you, me, and Selena.'

'Is Selena home?'

'I think so.'

Dandy stood up. 'In that case, what are we keeping them waiting for?' She shook her head, bemused. 'Her mother, did you say?'

Tara nodded and went in search of Selena.

THEY SAT RANGED AROUND THE KITCHEN TABLE, ALL THE introductions made. Rose cleared her throat.

'I'm sorry to be interrupting your Saturday morning,' she said.

'But I made her bring me here,' Kiri interrupted.

'We're pleased you came,' Dandy said. She leaned forward a little over the table. 'And frankly very curious.'

Rose nodded. 'I can understand that,' she said, and cleared her throat again.

'Which of you said she'd spoken to the missing woman's spirit?' Kiri asked, interrupting again. She could see that Rose was floundering. This wasn't the sort of police work she was used to.

There was a moment's stunned silence around the table.

'That would be me,' Selena said.

Kiri nodded slowly. 'Her kiddie's crying for her. I seen him. But she's far away, can't get back to him.'

Selena regarded Kiri for a moment, then nodded. 'That's right,' she said.

'She's dead,' Kiri said flatly.

'Yes,' Selena agreed. 'I'm afraid she is.'

Kiri sniffed. 'My Rose is going to find out what that husband did with her body, but we need to talk about what to do about the rest of her.'

Selena flicked a glance at Rose Griffith, whose cheeks were a dusky pink as she stared down at her hands, fingers knotted together where they lay on the table.

'That's good,' Selena said. 'I brought her back from the place where she'd become stuck.' She shivered slightly at the memory, and grief for Rachel weighed heavily on her heart. 'The shock sent her there.'

Kiri nodded, picked up her mug and sipped the tea. It was good, not a teabag but some sort of loose leaf herbal stuff put in a pot. It was tasty.

'Where is she now, then?'

Selena shook her head, aware that Rose, Tara, and Dandy were listening to the conversation, their heads going back and forth as though watching a tennis game.

'I calmed and tended her as well as I could, but I couldn't keep her.'

'She wouldn't cross?'

'No.'

Kiri hurrumphed. 'Not surprising, is it? Not when she's been murdered and her little one left with the fella who did the murdering.' She pointed with her chin at Rose. 'That's where you come in, hine.'

'You believe us then?' Tara asked. 'That something's happened to Rachel? Something bad?'

Rose untangled her fingers and rubbed her palms against her thighs. She nodded, sighed.

'Mum has the gift of sight,' she said. 'If she says the

woman is dead, then the woman is dead.' She gave a tight, one-shouldered shrug.

Tara squeezed her eyes shut to hold back the sudden tears. 'We knew she was – I'm just so relieved you're going to do something to find her.' She paused, drew out a tissue from her pocket and wiped her eyes. 'What will happen to Josh?'

'That's jumping the gun,' Rose said. 'I have to find evidence, build a case.' She paused. 'Find Rachel.'

Dandy was frowning. 'Isn't there some way we can discover where her body is?' She gazed around the table. 'All our talents, and we can't do that?'

'I haven't started to look, yet,' Rose said grimly. 'But I'll find her, don't you worry.'

'What have you discovered so far?' Tara asked. 'About her husband?' She grimaced. 'It's so hard having to interact with him when he drops Josh off and picks him up.'

'He's not the chatty kind though, is he?' Dandy asked.

Tara shook her head. 'No, he barely says a word to me.' She looked at Rose. 'He must know I've talked to you.'

'He does,' Rose agreed. 'But good childcare is a precious thing, and he needs you.'

'I guess he doesn't think he'll get caught, either,' Dandy said.

They were all silent, with that thought.

Tara turned to Selena. 'You found Rue and Clover,' she said. 'You found where Beatrix was buried.'

Selena nodded. 'But I had a very close bond with Beatrix. That was what showed me the way.'

'You been watching Sensing Murder?' Kiri asked. 'It's that show on the telly.'

'I've watched it,' Dandy said. 'They're good.'

'We could try,' Kiri said, nodding.

'Or you could let me do some police work,' Rose told her.

'What about both?' Tara said quickly.

Kiri smiled widely. 'You're right. All of us together, we could find the poor girl's body.' She thought for a moment. 'You got anything of hers? Rachel's?' She was looking at Tara.

'Um.' Tara considered the question. 'I've only got things that Josh plays with. Nothing of Rachel's.' She held the tissue tightly.

Kiri turned to her daughter. 'You're gonna have to get me something of hers.'

Rose stared back. 'What? Just go get something?'

'Won't you be getting a search warrant, or whatever?'

'I have to find just cause first.' Rose shook her head. This whole discussion was getting off track. She spread her hands out on the table. 'Right,' trying to corral it back in. 'Let's see where we are.'

'Good plan,' Dandy said.

'Hmm.' Rose took a breath, gave her mother a warning glance, and started talking. 'I'd like to know a few things.' She looked at Dandy. 'Getting a tarot reading sounds like a pretty personal thing. Did Rachel tell you anything about what was going on in her life?'

Dandy nodded, glad she could contribute something. 'Yes,' she said. 'We had quite the chat, and there were her cards, of course. They were quite revealing too.'

Rose held up a hand and got out her notebook and pen.

This wasn't a strictly official visit, or even a loosely official visit, but she was still going to take notes.

'Right,' Dandy said when Rose nodded at her. 'Well, she'd decided to leave her husband, I think.'

'She said so?' Rose asked.

'Not in so many words,' Dandy admitted. 'But she was definitely thinking about it.' She tapped a finger on the table. 'What you have to realise about when people come to get readings, is that there are three main reasons why they do.' She held up a hand and ticked them off on her fingers.

'First, they want to see if there's something exciting ahead of them. Second, they want to clarify which path they ought to be taking. Or third – and this one was Rachel's, I believe – is that they're looking for permission to do something.'

Rose nodded, her pen poised. 'What do you think Rachel wanted permission for? To leave her husband?'

'Yes.'

'She told me she'd decided to,' Tara said. 'On Wednesday, the morning I last saw her.'

Rose turned immediately to Tara. 'She did? Tell me what she said. What was her demeanour?'

Tara reached for another tissue, pinched it between her fingers. Shook her head. 'I don't know,' she said helplessly. 'She was talking about why she'd had to leave her family – she wanted to be a dancer, but they're not allowed to listen to music.'

Kiri interrupted. 'What? Who's not allowed to listen to music?'

'Her family is Exclusive Brethren,' Tara said. 'No music, or anything like it, apparently.' She sniffed and mopped at her eyes again. 'So, she told me that, and that she was leaving Mike, but then she changed her mind about saying anything else and got up and said goodbye to Josh, told him to be a good boy, and left.'

Rose thought for a moment about asking Tara if, when Rachel had said goodbye to her son, it had sounded as if she wasn't coming back, but a glance around the table told her it would be a question immediately refuted.

Everyone at the table thought Rachel was dead.

She shook her head slightly. No, she corrected.

Everyone knew Rachel was dead.

'When I spoke to him on Friday,' Rose said instead, 'Mike Manners indicated that he'd thought for a while that there might be another man in Rachel's life. Would you agree?' She looked at Tara, then Dandy.

'Perhaps more the possibility of one,' Dandy said, frowning slightly and remembering the cards. 'I think she'd realised that there was a whole world out there that she had never experienced before.'

Rose put down her notebook and nodded. 'I did a bit of background research after visiting Mike Manners.' She shook her head. 'Rachel left the Brethren when she'd just turned seventeen, around two and a half years ago, and went to live with the only family she had on the outside, a woman named Susan Manners.'

'Susan Manners?' Selena asked.

'But that's...' Tara shook her head.

'Yes,' Rose said. 'Her cousin was her husband's first wife.' She checked her notes, even though she remembered perfectly well what they said. 'Susan died two years ago from heart failure.'

There was a disbelieving silence. Dandy broke it.

'If Ebony was here, she'd be asking if Mike killed this Susan lady too.'

'Rachel must have been already pregnant when her cousin died,' Tara said, shaking her head and leaning over the table. 'Josh is eighteen months old.'

'Did she live with them the whole time?' Selena asked. 'It may not be as bad as it sounds.'

'Oh,' Kiri said. 'It's as bad as it sounds. She never moved out, did she, Rose? She lived with 'em the whole time.'

Rose nodded. 'It's a bit weird,' she admitted.

'And when she wanted, finally, to leave,' Dandy said. 'He killed her.' She looked around the table.

'Perhaps,' Rose said after a beat, deciding she had to offer the voice of reason, considering that they had no evidence whatsoever.

Or none, at least, of the sort she could take to the rest of the guys at the station.

Kiri shifted in her chair and looked around the table at these women she'd just met. The house was a bit big and fancy, but the three women seemed all right. She focused in on the English one.

The one who could see spirits.

'I reckon while Rose here finds our poor lady's body, we gotta take care of her spirit.'

Selena nodded, but it was Rose who spoke, shaking her head.

'I wish I had a place to start.'

Kiri looked at her, thought for a moment, then nodded. 'We'll dream the answer for you.'

Tara's eyebrows rose. 'Dream it?'

'That's how it works for me,' Kiri said, not without a degree of chagrin. If it was different, if she didn't have to be asleep to get her best results, maybe she could have a shot of getting on that show.

'Dream incubation,' Selena said. She looked across the table at Kiri and nodded, smiling. 'People have been doing it for millennia.'

'But what is it?' Tara asked again. She picked up her cup, saw it was empty, and held it anyway. Poor Josh, she kept thinking. What would happen to him?

'We should try it,' Selena said before answering Tara's question. 'It's fairly simple. Before going to sleep, we ask a question, hold an intention.'

'Ask who a question?' It was Dandy who spoke, mostly for Tara's benefit. She herself hadn't heard the fancy term for it, but she knew her dreams had often provided answers to the knots in her life.

'The atua,' Kiri answered. 'The spirits. Ancestors.'

'Yes,' Selena agreed. 'Exactly.'

42

RUE HANDED THE FLOWERS TO CLOVER WHO BURIED HER FACE in them and sniffed.

'Smell good?' Rue asked and smiled when Clover grinned up at her and nodded.

'They're made of fabric,' Rue said, shaking her head.

'They still smell good,' Clover insisted, touching her fingers to the cloth petals that she and Rue had made the night before. Rue had done most of the making, but Clover thought she had helped lots.

'An' the cakes,' she said.

Rue nodded and knelt down on the picnic blanket with the nylon backing they'd brought and spread out on the grass so they could sit down. She dipped into her backpack and got out the container she'd put the muffins in.

'What are they again?' Clover asked, sitting down too and crowding closer.

'Poppy seed,' Rue said.

Clover nodded. 'They good. Mama will like 'em.' She

looked up at Rue. 'She like 'em? Even though she gone 'cross the river?'

'She'll like them,' Rue agreed. 'Are you going to give her the flowers?'

Clover picked the three flowers made from fabric scraps again and nodded. She checked with Rue. 'Just put 'em here?'

'Just like that,' Rue said and watched as Clover took each flower and carefully laid it on the little patch of garden behind the plaque with their mother's name on it.

'For you, Mama,' Clover said. 'Cos we love ya.'

Rue nodded, took out one of the poppy seed muffins and passed it to Clover.

'This one for her too?' Clover asked.

'Yes,' Rue said. 'That one's for Mum.'

'She don' got a plate.'

Rue shook her head. 'That's okay. You can just put it next to the flowers.'

Clover did exactly that, then sat back and surveyed her handiwork. 'Why we give her cake, Rue?'

'Because we love her,' Rue said. 'We share what we have with her, because she still exists, and we know that. She is still part of our lives.' Rue reached out and touched Clover on the arm. 'We honour her,' she said. 'We are sharing our wealth with her because she helped bring it to us.' Rue knew she sounded just like Selena and Morghan, but she didn't care because what she said was true. She knew that for certain now.

'She brought S'lena to us.'

'Yep.'

Clover stood up, moved, then sat back down again, this

time on Rue's lap. She twisted around to look at Rue. 'Do we eat our cake now?'

Rue laughed. 'Of course,' she said.

Clover took a muffin out of the container and passed it to Rue, then got the last for herself.

'They good,' she said, her mouth full. She swallowed, nodded. 'Mama like 'em too, I bet.'

'I'm sure she does.'

Clover frowned, brushing crumbs of her hands. 'Rue,' she said. 'Does Mama have a mama too?'

Rue stilled. 'You know what?' she said at last. 'She must have. Everyone has a mother.'

'Where she, then?'

'That is a good question.'

Clover crawled off Rue's lap to adjust the position of one of the flowers, then turned to look at Rue, her brow wrinkled with sudden worry.

'She not like Josh's mama, is she?'

'What do you mean?'

Clover shrugged awkwardly. 'You know. Wanderin'.'

Rue shook her head. 'I don't even know who she was,' Rue said, trying to think what she did know about her grandmother. 'I don't know any of our relatives.'

'Lots of people wanderin',' Clover said, the poppy seed muffin feeling like a hard lump in her stomach now. 'I heard Josh's mum real loud, but there be others.' She looked at the tiny grave. 'We should leave 'em cake too.'

Silent, Rue thought about this. 'We can't leave cake for everyone,' she said.

'Why not?' Clover asked.

'Well, because we don't know who they are?'

393

Clover wrinkled her nose. 'We can just say is for ev'ry-one. We don' have to know who is for.'

Rue supposed Clover was right.

Standing up, Clover peered into Rue's face, and touched her hair, holding onto a thick strand. 'We give offrin's to the fairies, an' to the house, an' to Mama, we can give 'em to all the other dead people too, can't we?' She frowned. 'We can sing for 'em, right?'

Rue took Clover's hands in hers and held them. 'Right,' she said, and she was thinking of Bryn, who was, in Rue's time, dead, but yet lived still.

'We can honour them all,' she said. 'If that's what you want.'

Clover nodded, her small face serious.

Rue hugged her, bringing her suddenly squealing onto her lap and squeezing her tight, closing her eyes as she did so, and seeing there behind her lids a white dragon, wings spread, rising into the sky. She kissed the top of Clover's head.

'Dragons,' she murmured. 'Rams, rabbits.' She shook her head, but she was smiling. 'Come on,' she said. 'It's getting cold, let's get back.'

RUE RAISED HER EYEBROWS AT THE STRANGE CAR IN THE driveway and opened the back door, Clover's hand in hers.

Tara was baking something.

'Whose is the car out there?' Rue asked.

'Hi Rue,' Tara said. 'It belongs to Rose, the police officer who's helping us find Josh's mum.' She nodded with her head, her hands covered in flour from kneading dough. 'They're through there, with Selena.'

Clover ran to the door that led to the rest of the house, Rue on her heels.

'Hello girls,' Selena said, smiling and leaning down to hug Clover whose arms were wrapped around her legs. She straightened and introduced the strangers.

'Rue, Clover, these are our new friends, Kiri and her daughter Rose.'

Rue nodded at them. 'Pleased to meet you,' she said, then looked back at Selena, confused. Hadn't Tara just said that Rose was a policewoman? Helping to find Rachel? This didn't look like police work.

'What are you all doing?'

It was obvious they were doing something. One of the narrow hall tables that stood against the wall of the wide entranceway had been cleared of the miscellaneous bric-a-brac that had accumulated on it. Clover's books, mostly.

'We are making an altar for the dead,' Selena said.

Clover's eyes widened. 'We was just talkin' 'bout that,' she said.

Rue nodded, a lump in her throat. 'Clover and I went to see Mum,' she said, then looked awkwardly over at the two new people. 'Our mum died when Clover was born. We were visiting her grave.'

'We gave her poppy cakes,' Clover said.

'Poppy seed,' Rue corrected her. 'Muffins.'

Clover shrugged. 'I think she liked 'em.'

'What a wonderful idea,' Kiri said, beaming down at the little girl. She was cute as a button. 'I bet she liked 'em real well.'

Rue looked back to Selena. 'This is weird,' she said.

'In what way?' Selena placed a small bowl on the table and emptied a tiny bottle of sea water into it from her stash of such things up in her attic room.

'Clover's right,' Rue told her. 'We really were just talking about it.' She smiled shyly at Kiri, who was arranging a vase of fern leaves and dried flowers. Rue recognised some of the flowers Tara and Natalie had dried over the summer.

'Clover asked about Josh's mum, see? And about our grandmother – who we don't know anything about.' Rue shook her head. 'It just kind of tumbled from there. All the forgotten dead.'

Rose spoke up. 'Josh's mum isn't forgotten.' She didn't add that perhaps the woman wasn't even dead, because that would be pointless. She thought of her mother's words the other morning. *Gone and taken her away from her bubba.*

'No, she's not,' Selena said. 'We will remember her, and we will sing for her, and all the other hungry mothers out there.'

'Hungry mothers?' the words made Rue want to shiver, but she forced herself to stay still, to stand straighter, if anything. For a moment, she felt Bryn standing just behind her.

'Yeah,' Kiri answered. 'All the mothers who died still yearning.' She paused a moment, her large hands delicately holding the stem of a dried rose. 'Too many of them,' she said, and shook her head.

Clover frowned. 'Wha' does yearnin' mean?'

Kiri smiled down at her. 'Means they died still with pain in their hearts.'

'Why were they painful?' Clover wanted to know.

'Maybe they died before their pēpi was grown.'

'Like Josh's mum,' Rue interrupted.

'Just like that,' Kiri agreed. 'Or perhaps they couldn't keep their bubbies safe and that hurt them, or perhaps they couldn't even have a pēpi. That can hurt a woman's heart, if she wanted to be a mother and couldn't.'

Rue was quiet a moment, taking it in while Clover nodded at Kiri. 'Can I help?' she said.

Selena nodded. 'If you want to find something to represent your grandmother – both of them, and all the women before them in your family line, then you may, and feel free to put it on the altar.

'Will it help?' Rue asked, her voice almost a whisper. 'Will it really help?'

'It will help us, with our grief,' Selena said. 'And it will help them, if they are lost, for our love and our songs will reach them, and perhaps even lead them onwards.'

'That's really how it works?' Rue asked, taking Clover's hand when she reached for her.

Rose paused too, not that she was doing much, just passing her mother the dried flowers. Did it really work that way?

'Yes,' Selena said. 'That's really how it works. We provide solace for ourselves and them. We sing of our grief and love and joy and it blesses us, and them.'

Rue nodded. 'Then we'll find something, won't we, Clover? And join in.'

Clover's face was serious. 'Josh's mama still cryin' for him.'

Selena nodded. 'Her heart is hurt.'

'And she'll be worried, I reckon,' Kiri said, and looked

over at Rose. 'You have to find her. I'd be hurting hard too, if the fella who killed me still had care of my bubba.'

They were all silent for a good long minute after that, thinking of the pain of such a thing.

'Are you going to find her?' Rue asked Rose at last. 'You're police, right? Are you in charge of looking for her?'

Rose hesitated before answering, knowing that there was no official investigation yet. She took a breath, nodded.

'I am,' she said. First thing tomorrow, she was going to make sure there was a case officially opened.

She stood back and looked at the altar they'd made. It didn't look like much, yet. 'I think we need a picture of Rachel,' she said.

'An' our mama,' Clover said. 'She wa' hungry.' Clover looked up at Selena, who nodded.

'She was.'

'But you found us, and she went 'cross the river to the next place.'

Kiri's eyebrows rose, listening the child she'd just met. 'This sounds like a good story,' she said.

'No' a story,' Clover said. 'Is true.' Her small face puckered with outrage.

'That's not what she means, Clover,' Rue said.

'Nah, sure isn't,' Kiri agreed. 'Meant only that it's something I wanna hear more about.'

'Oh.' Clover's face smoothed out. 'Kay, then.'

Rose touched her mother's arm. 'I think we ought to get going, don't you?'

Kiri sighed, looked at Clover. 'You tell me all about it next time?' she asked.

'When you comin' back?' Clover said.

Kiri straightened, considered the question, glanced at Selena.

It was Selena who spoke first, sensing that Kiri didn't want to be rude, pushing for another visit. She smiled across at her.

'We need to come together again to compare our dreamings,' she said.

Kiri nodded. 'And we'll do that tonight, right?'

'Dreamings?' Rue asked, looking from one to another. What was this new thing going on?

'Yes,' Selena said. 'We're going to dream intentionally tonight, see if we can't get something to help Rose here find Rachel.'

'Find Rachel?' Rue asked.

Selena winced. 'Her body.'

'Right.' Understanding dawned. She shook her head slightly. Dream intentionally.

Once, she would have thought that was just the weirdest thing.

Now, it seemed practically normal.

43

'Oh, this is awesome,' Ebony said, rubbing her hands together. She stuck an elbow in Rue's side and grinned at her. 'I mean, isn't it?'

Rue shook her head. 'We're looking for the body of a murdered woman. How is that awesome?'

'Ah, we're going to dream where she is?' Ebony said, and she rolled her eyes. 'Of course it's really shitty about Rachel, but we're going to help her, right?' She nodded. 'And the way we're going to help her is definitely awesome.'

'You, my dear,' Dandy said to Ebony. 'Are incorrigible.'

Ebony gave Dandy a wide smile. 'I don't even know what that means.' She finally sobered and held a hand up. 'All right,' she said. 'I'm over my enthusiasm. I'm ready to acknowledge that this is serious stuff.' She took a breath and shook her head. 'Someone has been hurt, and that's real bad.'

'So,' Damien said. 'What's our intention, then? What we're supposed to hold as we go to sleep?'

'We're going to dream as many particulars as possible of Rachel's...' Dandy cast about helplessly for the right term.

'Her murder,' Ebony said, who felt no such qualms about being blunt.

Dandy sighed, reached over and took Tara's hands. There were tears on Tara's cheeks, and she grasped Dandy's hand gratefully.

'That's not going to make for a cheerful night,' Damien said.

'Not at all,' Selena agreed. 'But we must look after our dead.'

'She's our dead?'

Selena nodded. 'She was part of our lives, even if only peripherally. And we are generous to all dead.'

'Our hungry mothers,' Rue added.

'Yes,' Selena agreed.

But Ebony was shaking her head. 'Hungry mothers sounds so gruesome,' she said.

'I don't think there's anything that isn't gruesome about dying with pain in your heart,' Natalie said, glad that the pain in her own had eased considerably. She leaned against Damien, who put his arm around her.

Rue fiddled with the fraying seam of her jeans. 'What about those who just die, you know, naturally.'

'What about them?' Dandy asked gently, trying to find out what Rue needed.

Rue shrugged. 'Well, do we just ignore them?'

'Those that love them will mourn them,' Selena told her.

'How?' Rue wasn't sure why she was asking this. She sat up a little straighter. 'Like, when Mum died, there was her funeral, and that was it. Everything was kind of expected to go back to normal after that.'

Not that anything was normal afterwards, but no one had seemed to have any time for the grief she'd felt then. She hadn't known what to do with it.

'What do we do with it?' she asked. 'All the grief? The missing the person?'

Dandy sighed. 'It's a good question. Most of us don't know what to do with our grief these days, do we?'

Rue ducked her head down, looked at her knees.

'Rachel's the first person I've known who died,' Ebony said, then looked at Tara's face. 'And I never even met her.'

'What about in your family?' Selena asked.

But Ebony shook her head. 'All grandparents, aunts, uncles, and so on alive and accounted for.' She leaned forward and propped her chin on a hand. 'Although I suppose my grandparents are you know, due.' She wrinkled her nose. 'My Grandad Harry is ninety-four.' She groaned. 'Now I've got this sudden urge to go visit him and Gran.'

'Do they live close?' Damien asked.

Ebony nodded.

'It's a good idea,' Selena said. 'They'll be enriched by your company, and you'll be enriched by theirs.'

Ebony considered this. 'Yeah,' she said. 'I think I will. I think I'll start visiting them, regularly perhaps.'

'But what about Rachel?' Tara asked, bringing them back on track.

Selena nodded. 'Yes,' she said. 'It's getting late. Let's talk about dreaming.' She gazed around the circle of friends in her living room, marvelling over their loveliness. All of them were gathered there to honour the bonds they'd forged between them, and to seek to ease the torment of another.

She was proud of them all.

And blessed to be among them, she thought.

'So,' she said. 'Tonight we will seek the guidance of our souls and their companions through our dreams.'

No one spoke. Selena's words fell upon them as if they had weight. Damien glanced at Natalie, and she was pale but nodding. He looked over to see Tara, whose eyes were red, but her mouth had a determined set to it.

He turned back to listen to Selena.

'The force behind our dreams wants to help us,' Selena was saying. 'Our kin, our gods, our own souls can speak to us through our dreaming, and we can turn around and ask them for what we want to know. Think of the dream almost as a living thing. It is a real place.'

She smiled at them. 'And I know you've all been learning to remember your dreams.'

'Which is no easy thing,' Damien muttered.

Selena shook her head. 'No,' she said. 'It isn't. But even a fragment can be useful. Even the echo of a dream can guide you.' She spread her hands. 'But tonight, we will go to the land of our dreaming carrying an intention with us.'

Ebony resisted rubbing her hands together in glee, reminding herself of the seriousness of their quest.

'Isn't it going to be kind of horrible, though?' she couldn't resist asking. 'I mean, we want to dream where a dead body is.' She looked around the circle, shrugged. 'Sorry, but that's what we're really talking about doing, right? We want to see what this bastard Mike did, where he put his wife after he killed her. Sounds like we're asking for nightmares.'

'Have you changed your mind, Ebony?' Dandy asked.

Ebony shook her head. 'Nope, but I'm just making sure we all know what we're going to go to sleep asking to see.'

Selena, who sat next to Ebony, took her hand, then reached for Natalie's on her other side. In a minute, everyone was holding hands.

'Although what we will go seeking in the land of our dreams is not pleasant, nor a fun diversion,' she said, 'we don't go there alone – we go there together, and also with our kin. We go there to do this because it is necessary, because the strength of our caring for one who has become lost is greater than our fear.'

There was silence around the room as Selena's words sank in.

'Yes,' Dandy said. 'Well put.'

Tara nodded, drawing in a deep breath. 'So,' she said. 'Tell us how to do this.'

Selena checked with everyone else, got their nodding agreement.

'We're fortunate,' she said. 'I've heard that group dreaming can be very powerful.'

Damien spoke up. 'The Māori believe that the wairua – the soul – leaves the body and travels in dreams, and what happens then is often an omen, one way or another.'

Selena nodded. 'I agree with you, then. I think we travel from our bodies in many dreams.'

'Is that what we're going to try tonight?' Tara asked. 'Travelling from our bodies?'

'It's what we do often during the night, so this will be

little different in this way. But tonight we're going to ask our dreams a very specific question,' Selena said. 'The question is important. It needs to be clear and unambiguous, so that our dream can meet us on the terms of the question.'

'What do you mean?' Ebony asked.

Selena thought about it, shifted slightly in her chair. It was dark outside the windows, the night having drawn its cloak around them. Inside the room, only the lamps were on, throwing their warm light like a net over the group.

'In general,' she said, 'when we do dream incubation, we ask a question that is relevant to our lives, that is open ended rather than requiring only a yes or no answer, and is a question that we're willing to listen to the answer to.'

'Why would you ask a question and then not listen to the answer?' Ebony scoffed.

But Selena shook her head. 'You'd be surprised,' she said. 'There is something about an asked question that makes us vulnerable. When we begin asking questions of our lives, the answers usually prompt us to change and grow, and we all know that change can be unsettling.'

Natalie ducked her head and looked at her hands. Yes, she thought. Selena was right.

'So,' Selena continued. 'We will ask a question knowing we must be brave enough to accept the answer.' She shook her head. 'It is only a little different for us here tonight, because we're coming together to ask about someone other than ourselves, but the principle remains the same.'

'So, what should our question be?' Dandy asked.

'What happened to Rachel?' Ebony suggested.

'Where is Rachel's body?' Tara asked, closing her eyes.

'Our question must come from the heart,' Selena said.

She touched her chest. 'If we are heartfelt in our expression, then we are more likely to receive a helpful response.'

'I think you can be sure this is heartfelt,' Tara said, knotting her hands together. 'I can't bear the thought of little Josh left with his father when the man did such a thing.'

Selena nodded, thought about what Tara had said. 'Perhaps this can be your question, then,' she said.

'What do you mean?' Tara asked.

'Are we going to have different questions?' Damien said.

Selena held up a hand. She looked at Tara. 'You knew Rachel the best of all of us,' she said. 'You have the closest bond with her son. Perhaps you could ask something along the lines of *what is most important for me to know for Josh's wellbeing?*'

'I could ask that?' Tara said.

'Yes,' Selena replied. 'In fact, perhaps that would be a good thing. Because we are concerned about Josh, are we not?'

There were nods all around.

'Okay,' Ebony said. 'What should I ask my dream?' She wrinkled her nose, thinking about it. 'I think I'm going to go straight for the main issue. *Where is Rachel's body?*' She nodded. 'Yep. That's the one I want to know, and I'm not going to look away.' She gazed around the circle. 'That is the question we most want to answer, right?'

'I say we give it a go,' Damien said, stretching, then looking at Natalie. 'What about you, are you going to be okay with that one?'

Natalie felt pale just thinking about it. She couldn't imagine going looking for a dead body, even in her dreams, but she nodded anyway. 'I want to help,' she said. If that was even slightly possible – and she knew from her own dreams that it was – then she wasn't going to shirk the responsibility. This dream incubation didn't just work in situations like this. Selena had taught her to ask questions of her dreaming self, kind of like they were her own, tailor-made self-help. 'We're all in this together, right?'

Selena smiled at her. 'Take Bear with you,' she said. 'Bear will bolster your spirit.'

Natalie thought of all the dreams and imaginings she'd had with Bear by her side and nodded. She always felt safer when Bear was with her.

Selena had another thought. 'We should all call upon our kin as we go to our beds tonight.'

'And thanks to our little seer, we know who they are,' Dandy said.

Rue's eyes widened. 'Why did you call her that?'

Surprised, Dandy frowned at Rue. 'Call who what?'

'Call Clover a seer.'

'Oh,' Dandy was discombobulated for a moment by the question. 'Because that's what she is, isn't she?'

Rue subsided, nodding. 'Yeah,' she said. 'The word just caught me by surprise, that's all.' She rubbed at her head. There was so much going on, she thought. Clover and Rhian and Bryn, and then this Rachel business.

And something in this night's conversation had brought up how she'd felt when her mother died. Rue thought about she and Clover at their mother's graveside. How they'd decided to honour her, and all the other mothers out there.

'Are you all right, dear?' Dandy asked her.

Rue nodded. 'Just a bit tired still, I guess,' she said.

'You know,' Ebony mused. 'This brings me to something

I want to know.' She held up a hand and grinned. 'No, don't groan, everyone, I'm being serious.'

Damien snickered.

'So, since Clover can see things – she saw Rachel's what, spirit, right?' Ebony paused for a moment to reflect on how absolutely wonderful it was to be able to say such things out loud, then continued. 'How come she can't see the body as well?'

'I'm glad she can't, for crying out loud,' Tara said, horrified. 'She's three years old, Ebony, and you want her to see a murdered woman?'

Ebony shook her head. 'No,' she said. 'I guess not, when you put it like that.' But still, she looked hopefully at Selena.

'It's easier for Clover to see the spirit rather than the body,' Selena said calmly. 'The body has no life attached to it anymore, whereas the soul lives on.'

Ebony nodded. 'Yeah,' she said. 'That makes sense.'

Selena stood up, smoothed down her skirt. 'All right,' she said. 'Let's set our intention as a group, shall we? It's getting late.' She checked with Ebony. 'You're staying here tonight, aren't you?'

Ebony nodded. Damien had moved into the flat over the garage, which meant there was now another guest room in the house. Which she was more than happy to take advantage of.

They gathered in a circle, hands linked to match their shared purpose.

'Tonight,' Selena said. 'Tonight, we come together in our desire to aid Rachel Manners and her small child Josh. We are grieving for her, we feel the hole she has left in our lives, and we mourn the fact that she will never reach the potential she had here on this earth in this lifetime.'

Selena nodded slightly to herself. 'We know that Rachel lives on, as we all do, and we are comforted by this fact, but still our hearts are pained, still tears come to our eyes, still we would wish her back here, amongst us.'

Tara closed her eyes, feeling her heart like a fist in her chest.

'Tonight,' Selena continued, 'we come together here to ask for guidance. We wish to know how we can help Rachel to rest, how we can ease her fears over her son, where we can find her physical remains, so that the person who violated her sacred life may be disallowed from repeating his mistake.'

The words seemed to remain in the air between them for a long moment, and then each in the circle stood straighter, breathed deeply, and took the task into themselves.

44

'YOU RIGHT?' KIRI ASKED, LOOKING ROSE OVER. SHE SEEMED a bit peaky.

Rose nodded, then shook her head. 'I don't know how I got into this,' she said.

Kiri tugged on a strand of Rose's hair, just as she'd done when her daughter was small.

'Rosie, love,' she said. 'When are you going to accept this?'

Rose gazed up at the ceiling in frustration. 'I do accept it,' she said. 'I just can't reconcile it.'

'What do you mean?'

Rose looked pleadingly at her mother. 'It's like walking in two different worlds. There's no room for woo woo in my job, and yet when I'm at home, everywhere I look there's woo.'

'But it's true,' Kiri said, still confused. 'It's real and true.'

'I know.' Rose drooped over the table in her mother's dining area and put her head in her hands. 'That just makes it harder.' She peered at Kiri. 'If I told anyone about this at work, I'd be the laughing stock of the station.' She grimaced. 'I'd probably be fired.'

'But it's a gift, aroha.'

Rose fell silent. She knew it was a gift. Hadn't her mum helped heaps of their family? Every time someone lost something, or needed some advice – was this guy a good fella? Was this girl going astray? – They came and asked Kiri.

It was a gift.

Rose sat up again, shook her head. 'You know what?' she said. 'Fuck it. Fuck them. It is real. This does work.'

Kiri nodded across the table. 'That's my girl,' she said.

'I've just worked hard, that's all. You know I have.' Rose spread her fingers out, looking at her hands, not really seeing them, seeing instead all the years she'd spent getting to where she was now.

'You find this girl, love, and you gonna be a hero.'

Rose looked across at Kiri. 'And when they asked how I found out where she was? What do I say then?'

Kiri heaved her shoulders in a shrug. 'What's wrong with the truth?'

Rose only narrowly managed to stop herself from rolling her eyes.

'And the conversation comes back to me being a laughing stock.'

'Nah,' Kiri said. 'They can't laugh if you deliver the goods.'

Rose sighed. Perhaps her mum had a point. 'You think we can?'

'It's not just us trying,' Kiri said. 'There's them too.'

'Yeah.' Rose went to make another cup of tea. It would make her have to get up during the night to pee, but maybe that wasn't a bad thing. She needed to remember her dreams, anyway and waking up during the night would help.

She spoke with careful casualness as she filled the jug and switched it on.

'What do you think of them, anyway?'

Kiri grinned. She'd been hoping for this question. 'I liked 'em. That Selena, you can tell the river runs deep through her.'

'The river?'

Kiri shrugged again. 'Yeah. The river of spirit, on the way to the sea.'

Rose lifted an eyebrow. A river, she thought, and funnily enough, it seemed to fit.

'And the little girl,' Kiri said, musing upon Rose's question. 'She's got some far-seeing eyes.'

'Do you think it's true, then?' Rose asked.

Kiri looked at her, shocked. 'Couldn't you feel the kiddie? Rose, you're my girl, you got some of the gift, I know you did. All the women in our line did. From mother to daughter.'

Rose flicked off the jug before it could reach a boil and poured water over the teabag in her cup. She got Kiri's cup too and refreshed it.

'Yeah,' she said reluctantly. 'There was something about her.'

Kiri nodded. 'The waters run extra deep in that one. It didn't surprise me one little bit that she could feel something had happened to her friend's mum.'

Rose sat back down at the table. 'It's an awful story, isn't it?'

Kiri nodded, drawing her cup across the table. 'A sad one.' She leaned back. 'But we're doing our bit, Rosie. We're doing our bit.'

ROSE WOKE DURING THE NIGHT, JUST LIKE SHE'D KNOWN SHE would after that last cup of tea. The room was dark and quiet, and she sat there on the edge of her bed blinking, face turned blindly toward the window.

She could still hear it, she thought, not fully awake.

The sound of the sea.

Nodding. That was right. The sound of the sea. Rose closed her eyes again, searching for the weft and warp of her dream, gathering up the thread of it.

She'd been at the beach, she thought.

Ah, but which beach?

She saw water again, behind her eyelids, drawing the dream closer again. At the beach, she could hear the waves crashing against rock.

And she was looking through the stone, looking through the hole in the stone at the water, at the tide coming in.

Rose swayed where she sat, eyes closed, letting the dream come back to her.

The crash and pour of the waves. Looking through the rock as though it was a window. On the beach, cliffs rising around her, a woman, standing watching the tide come in, twigs in her hair, dirt on her face.

And Rose uttered the words she'd cried out in her

dream. That's what had really woken her up. The cry on her lips.

Watch out!

The tide was coming in. Sweeping up the narrow beach. Waves coming through the hole where Rose watched, looking.

Seeing.

Rose let out a breath, opened her eyes, and looked at the lighter square of window in the bedroom she'd slept in as a kid. It was raining outside. She could hear it against the glass, the roof. The alarm clock glowed on the bedside table. Almost five in the morning.

Slowly, she got up off the bed, and went to the bathroom, relieved herself, then tiptoed into her mother's room.

Kiri was muffled in her blankets, the way she'd always slept, for as long as Rose could remember.

Rose sat down on the edge of the bed. She clicked on the dim lamp, looked at Kiri, who didn't move, then picked up the pen and notebook she'd put there the night before.

Her hands were shaking, she realised, and she gripped the pen tighter, smoothed a knuckle across the page turned mustard yellow from the lamp. It had her notes from her visit to Michael Manners on it. She stared at the words for a long moment, then flipped to a clean page.

When she touched her mother's face, it was with the tips of her fingers, lightly.

'Tell me what you see,' she said.

Kiri sniffed, frowned in her sleep.

'Tell me what you see,' Rose repeated.

Kiri's eyes roamed around under their lids.

'Tide's coming in,' she said, her voice thick with sleep.

Rose wanted to ask another question, but she kept quiet. She'd been doing this since she was a kid, knew how it worked.

'Tide's coming in and the girl, she's waiting till the last moment to go through the tunnel. That's the game they used to play. Her an' him.'

Rose, frowning slightly, wrote down each of her mother's words. Then waited for more.

But it was several minutes before Kiri spoke again. 'Someone pulled a tree down on her, and the tide's going in and out.' She fell silent.

Rose touched her face again, asked what she saw, but Kiri just turned slightly in the bed and repeated her first words.

'Tide's goin' in and out.'

Rose waited, but there was nothing more. Kiri began to snore gently, and Rose stood up, notebook still tucked in her hand.

She went back to her room, pulled on a dressing gown and tugged thick socks onto her cold feet, then padded through to the kitchen. There was no way she was going back to sleep.

Instead, she made a mug of coffee and sat down at the table to think about her dream, and her mother's words.

They'd been seeing the same thing.

She was certain of it.

SELENA LOOKED DOWN AT HER FEET. THERE WAS SAND between her toes, cold as though it had just rained, or night had just passed. She wriggled her toes and watched the coarse grains of sand coat her skin.

Then there was the sound of water, waves coming to shore, and Selena looked up, saw the water rushing up the beach towards her and stepped backwards before she could help herself, flinging out a hand to touch something cold and solid.

Turning, she gasped, shocked to find herself hemmed in by tall cliffs behind her.

'We used to come here all the time,' a voice to her right said.

Selena spun on her bare feet and found Rachel standing ankle deep in the running waves.

'Where are we?' Selena said, regaining her balance and watching the waves with their frills of froth dragging the sand back with them as they retreated, spinning around Rachel's legs and trying to take her with them.

'We called it our place,' Rachel said, ignoring the question. She lifted her chin and gazed around. Selena did the same, estimating that it must be some time just after dawn as the sun rode low in the sky behind a curtain of clouds. She shivered again, unable to stop herself. Perhaps on a bright sunny day, this place would be amazing, she thought, with its towering cliffs cupping the deep crescent of sand.

The tide was coming in, the waves reaching up to Rachel's knees now.

'You and who?' Selena asked, tasting salt on her tongue. 'You and Mike?'

But Rachel ignored her, staring out towards the horizon instead, and the sun lifting itself out of the ocean.

The waves spread their wet fingers towards Selena, and

she found herself with her back pressed against the cold sandstone behind her. Did the beach disappear altogether with the high tide? There was a rock to her side, jutting out from the sand and for a moment, Selena thought of climbing its sharp flank to stand above the water.

But the rock was not high, and she closed her eyes instead, reminding herself that she was dreaming.

She was dreaming, just as she'd asked to.

Another wave came in with a rushing booming that echoed in the amphitheatre created by the cliffs. The dawn darkened, clouds thickening over the sun.

Rachel stared out at them, the water up around her thighs now.

'We would come here early in the morning when the tide was right,' Rachel said, her voice dreamy over the crashing of the waves.

Selena closed her eyes. The water washed around her toes, then retreated, sucking at the sand between them.

'It must have been lovely,' Selena croaked. She forced her eyes open to discover that the water was up to Rachel's waist now and that Rachel had turned to look at her, face pale, eyes dark smudges.

'It was terrifying,' Rachel said, and Selena heard her perfectly well above the roaring of the ocean. 'It was frightening and exhilarating, waiting till the last moment to leave, watching the tide come in.'

Selena nodded, all too aware of how terrifying it was. The next wave rose around her ankles, trying to tug her back into the sea with it.

'Is this where you are?' she asked, her skin coated with salty spume.

Rachel lifted her face to look to the right, up at the cliffs, and Selena turned to follow her gaze.

There was nothing to see but cliff and sky, and the next wave jerked her attention back to the beach. Except there was nothing left of the beach; the tide was in, the sand covered, the rock standing in a rushing swirl of water.

And Rachel, standing out in the sea, the water under her arms, clasping her tightly around her chest. She looked back at Selena, hair wet and bedraggled, tangled with sticks and leaves, just her shoulders and head visible above the waves.

Selena wanted to call out to her, beg her to wade back to the shallows, but her tongue was stuck to the roof of her mouth, and when she finally gained breath, Rachel was gone, under the waves, out to sea, or just gone.

This is a dream, Selena reminded herself as another wave hit her, reaching up her legs even as she pressed back against the cold cliff.

Just a dream. She could leave if she wanted to.

She could wake up.

And she did, throwing back the blankets on her bed and sitting up gasping.

It was dark in her bedroom, and Selena groped to turn the lamp on beside the bed, then looked at the clock. Five in the morning. She sat on the mattress, concentrating on her breathing.

A hot shower, she thought. She needed a hot shower to wash the salt away.

45

RUE OPENED HER EYES TO THE DARKNESS OF HER BEDROOM and lay there for a moment, disoriented. Where was she?

She'd been dreaming, but not about Rachel. Rue frowned. She'd been supposed to dream about Rachel, holding the question and intention inside her as she went to sleep, but she must have done it wrong, she thought, because it hadn't been Rachel she'd dreamt of, tucked in the big bed, Clover next to her.

It had been Beatrix. Her mother.

She'd been back at the house on the street opposite where Dandy had lived. Sitting on the couch next to her mother, her hand on her mother's pregnant belly, feeling the baby kick.

They'd both been laughing.

Clover had been a strong baby.

Rue touched Clover's hair, felt the soft curliness of it. Her mother had been so surprised to find herself pregnant, and she'd worried that Rue would be upset by the news. She hadn't been though, Rue remembered, she'd been happy for both of them. A little sister would be fun.

They'd both known it would be a girl. Rue didn't remember how, why, or when they had decided that the child growing in Beatrix's womb was a girl, but they'd always spoken of it as she, and her.

Rue closed her eyes and wrapped herself around Clover's warm little body. She'd been supposed to dream of Rachel, but she'd dreamt of her own mother instead. Her tears seeped into the pillow underneath her head.

Clover stirred, reached up a sleepy hand and touched Rue's face.

'Why you cryin'?'

Rue shook her head. Of course Clover had woken up to ask her this. Clover always knew when she was upset about something.

'I miss Mum,' she said, and flashed suddenly on the memory of Bryn's mother folding the holey stone into her hands.

Clover was nodding. 'I miss her too,' she said.

'You never even got to meet her,' Rue said, sniffing.

'Did too,' Clover said, sounding perfectly awake now. She snuggled closer to Rue. 'Used to come see me.'

For a moment, Rue was confused. 'Who used to come see you?'

'Mama,' Clover said. 'When I was in my cot. She'd come smile at me and sing me a song.'

Rue felt Clover's small shoulders shrug. 'But now she's gone where she's s'posed to go, and I got you.'

'You've always had me.'

Clover wound her arms around Rue's neck and kissed

her on the cheek. 'And we got S'lena an' Tara an' Damien and Dandy.'

Yes, Rue thought, and everything was much better since they'd come into their lives. Because of them, she'd been able to let go of the stress and the fear, and now she was being looked after.

'Our mum was a good mum,' she whispered.

Little fingers groped her face again. 'You still cryin'?'

'Little bit,' Rue said.

'Is okay,' Clover said. And then, as if she'd only just remembered, 'did you dream 'bout Rachel?'

'How do you know we were all going to dream about her?'

Clover shrugged. 'Heard you thinkin' it, I s'pose.'

Rue shook her head. 'Well, I didn't dream of her. I dreamt about Mum instead.' Laughing on the old couch, picking out names.

'Is alright,' Clover said. 'S'lena dreamt of her. An' the other lady.' She shivered and burrowed closer to Rue. 'Don' wanna think 'bout it, Rue. Don' wanna hear Josh's mum cryin'.'

Rue scooped Clover into her arms. 'You don't have to,' she said. 'The others will find her and make everything okay.'

Clover nodded against Rue's chest, and they lay like that as the morning lightened outside the window.

Selena was in the kitchen, sitting at the big table there, hands wrapped around a gently steaming teacup. She looked up as Rue entered the room. Clover had gone to find Tara.

'Good morning, Selena,' Rue said. It was still dim outside, the sun rising later now that it was nearing Samhain.

'Good morning, Rue,' Selena said. 'Did you sleep well?'

Rue nodded. She had, despite the dreams. 'I didn't dream of Rachel,' she said, sliding onto a chair opposite Selena.

Selena raised her eyebrows, sensing there was more that Rue wanted to say.

Rue looked down at her hands. 'I dreamt of my mother instead,' she said. 'We were sitting on the couch in the house we used to live in, and she was pregnant, and I was feeling the baby kick and we were deciding on names.'

Selena looked across the table at Rue with sympathy. 'I imagine this has all brought up the memories of your loss.'

Rue nodded, twinging her fingers together. 'I cried for months,' she said. 'After Mum died. I cried every day for eight months.' She knew that; she'd counted.

'Of course you did,' Selena said. 'You'd lost your mother.'

'Everything changed after she was gone.' Rue shifted slightly in her chair. No one else was in the kitchen with them, it was just her and Selena, the day still very young. 'I remember when I went back to school, one of my teachers demanded to know why I had been away for the last four days.' Rue swallowed around the knot of grief in her throat. 'I had to stand up in front of the class and say that my mother had died and that was why I'd been absent.'

Selena smiled sadly at Rue. 'That must have made it all the more difficult.'

Rue shrugged. 'Then the story went around the school that Mum had killed herself.' She shook her head. 'I don't know why everyone thought that, but it made it real hard. I was either contaminated by it in everyone's eyes and avoided, or I was questioned, asked for gory details.' Rue blew out a big breath. 'I've never told anyone that before,' she said.

Selena reached across the table and took Rue's hands in hers. 'That's a big thing to hold inside yourself,' she said. 'Take another deep breath and let it go.'

Rue nodded. Her first deep breath had been spontaneous, but this one she did deliberately, breathing in until it felt as though her whole chest had been filled, and then letting it out in a rush of relief.

'That's good,' Selena nodded. 'And thank you for trusting me with what you went through back then.'

'It feels good to tell you,' Rue said. Her hands were still in Selena's. 'I guess this Rachel business has brought it all up for me.' She gave a strangled laugh.

'Take another deep breath,' Selena said.

Rue did. 'The only good thing at the time was Clover,' she said. 'I loved her because Mum and I had before she was even born. But I was sad for her too, you know? I was sad for both of us.'

'You were grieving,' Selena said.

'I don't know why I'm telling you this,' Rue said, and she sniffed, blew out another breath, shaking her head. 'It's all gone and past, you know? I never told anyone at the time. There wasn't anyone to tell, really.'

'It's good that you're saying it now,' Selena said. 'Giving our grief words helps us.'

The door opened and Tara came in, Clover at her side freshly washed and dressed.

'Oh,' Tara said, stopping when she saw Selena holding onto Rue's hands over the table. 'We're not disturbing you, are we?'

But Selena shook her head. 'No,' she said, noticing Tara's red-rimmed eyes. 'We were talking about grief, and the importance of giving it words.'

Tara frowned while Clover climbed up onto the chair next to Rue.

'Words?' Tara asked. 'What do you mean?'

Selena gave Rue's fingers a last squeeze then sat back. 'There's something about our emotions,' she said. 'We deal with them better when we put them into words.' She paused for a moment, thinking about it, checking herself. 'I think that language is very important for humans.'

'I don't follow,' Tara said, going to turn the jug on. She'd already decided she needed a good strong cup of coffee on this particular morning.

'We process things better, our experiences and our emotions, if we put them into words for ourselves,' Selena said. 'Emotions especially, are something it's easy to feel steamrolled by. They often feel overwhelming, which is why putting them into words gives us both understanding and a tiny sliver of distance from them, letting us acknowledge them and maybe even make some choices about them.'

Tara was still shaking her head. 'I'm not sure I understand what you're saying.'

Selena smiled. 'Let me give you an example, then. You are feeling grief for Rachel, are you not?'

Tara put the jug down. 'I don't know,' she said. 'Is that what it is? I'm very upset, and can't stop thinking how terrible it is, what's happened.' Her eyes welled up again and she ducked her head.

'That's grief,' Selena said. 'You've suffered a loss, and in terrible circumstances.'

Tara nodded. Inside her chest, everything churned together, and she looked at her coffee, suddenly craving something much sweeter. 'I feel an awful mess,' she said.

'We do so often feel messy in our feelings,' Selena said. 'That's when talking to ourselves about them, describing them, helps. Say to yourself that you're grieving. That you're upset and angry because something terrible and sad has happened.'

Tara looked at Selena, then nodded. 'Do I need to say that out loud?'

Selena smiled, shook her head. 'Clearly inside you head will be fine.'

Rue, listening from her seat at the table, Clover next to her holding her hand in one of hers and drawing a picture with the other, frowned slightly. She thought she might try what Selena was suggesting. Perhaps it would help the knot inside her.

I'm grieving too, she said to herself, somewhat in surprise. *I feel the loss of my mother again, because she died when I still needed her.*

Rue shook her head, bemused. The knot inside was looser, as though she'd done a little bit of magic, just by giving herself the words to say what she was going through.

'It works,' she said. 'I sort of explained to myself what I was feeling, going through, and I guess, I guess I feel more in control now.' Rue shook her head. She didn't think control was the right word, but she wasn't sure what would be. 'Space,' she said suddenly. 'I feel like there's more space for it, and it won't run me over.'

Selena beamed at her.

Tara looked at Selena. 'Is this sort of like what everyone says – what doesn't kill you only makes you stronger?'

Selena's eyes widened and she shook her head. 'Good gracious no,' she said. 'I don't hold with that at all. What gives us strength, and the strength to get through difficult things, is a deep and stable foundation.'

'A foundation?' Tara frowned.

'Indeed,' Selena said. 'The calmness and assurance that comes with knowing that this life is not our only existence, that we can direct our own thoughts, that they do not have to run amok inside our heads, that we can speak to ourselves of what we feel, and give space to and realise our responses, and that we are not alone as we walk through this life, that there are unseen presences that will guide and console us.' She smiled. 'The human spirit is strong and resilient and beautiful. We need to build our foundations on remembering how to be this way, that it is our natural state, and so institute habits and practices in our lives to facilitate this.' She paused. 'And when we have been wounded, to tend to our wounds with generosity and compassion for ourselves.'

Tara nodded silently, thinking now about Natalie, who had rebuilt her life on ground firm enough for her to stand on, who had learnt a different way of approaching the world, and was thriving because of it.

'I'm grieving,' Tara said. 'I'm grieving because I've lost someone I was growing to consider a friend. My heart hurts because of the way in which I've lost her, and because of my fear for her son.'

She closed her eyes, leaning against the kitchen counter. 'I feel a little calmer,' she said. 'Just saying all that out loud has calmed me a bit. Like it's not some bogeyman, but something I can understand and give space to.'

Selena nodded. 'Just keep doing it,' she said. 'Putting into words what you're feeling and why.' She looked over at Rue.

'It helps,' she said.

46

THE MORNING HAD GROWN AND NOW EVERYONE WAS THERE.

Even Josh. Tara looked over at him playing in the corner with Clover. His father had called and begged her to take him, just for a couple hours, he said.

Tara hadn't been able to say no.

'Is it all right, do you think,' she asked Selena now. 'Josh being here?'

Selena nodded, but it was Kiri who answered. 'Feels right to me,' she said. 'It's his mum, after all.'

'I worry he'll...hear us talking about her.' Tara drew in a slow breath and steadied herself. 'I'm worried because he is a precious child and my heart aches for him,' she said out loud, with a glance at Selena. Then, feeling calmer, she watched Clover and Josh for a moment. 'What are you building?' she asked.

Clover glanced back at her. 'Bones,' she said.

Tara heard the answer with a shock.

'What do you mean, bones?' Damien asked. He was

sitting on the arm of the couch, next to Natalie. The huge living room was full with everyone there.

Rose looked at the little girl with interest. It had already been established that Clover, to use Kiri's words, was one whose eyes hadn't adjusted to being human yet.

Clover looked over at Damien. 'We building Josh's mama's skellington.'

'Her skeleton?' Rue asked. This was weird, even for Clover.

But Clover just shrugged. 'Put the bones in the cave and they grow new bones.' She frowned, looked over at Selena. 'That right?'

Selena considered it for a moment. 'Perhaps,' she said. 'If the cave is that of the Bone Mother.'

'The Bone Mother?' Dandy asked. 'That's a new one to me.'

'She's a winter goddess,' Selena said. 'A nurturer of the dead, collecting their bones together, she brings them into the warmth and care of her cave.'

'Her womb,' Kiri said, nodding sagely.

'Yes,' Selena said with a wide smile. 'Her womb. That is exactly so.'

'I don't get it,' Damien said. 'I thought the dead like, went to the Summer Isles. Where does this winter goddess fit in?'

'There are many stories, and many parts to the truth, to understanding,' Selena said. 'The Bone Mother gathers the pieces of ourselves together and cradles us until we are whole again, knitted back together in the dark safety of her womb.'

She glanced at Rue. 'Morghan told me a story from the

work she does with the dying, while I was there.' She smiled apologetically at Kiri and Rose.

'Morghan is a death worker – she helps those dying both in preparing them for the great journey they are about to undertake, and holding space for them as they transition, even accompanying them part of the way, if necessary.'

Kiri turned to her daughter, astonishment on her face. 'That is some good and necessary work,' she said to Selena.

'It certainly is,' Selena agreed. 'Part of it, Morghan explained to me, is often helping the person's soul to heal before they even begin dying. Bringing back any shards of their souls that have splintered off from trauma or shock, and knitting them back together.'

'Like the Bone Mother,' Rue said. 'Like you did for Josh's mother.'

Selena nodded. 'Yes, like Morghan and I did for Rachel.'

Kiri nodded. She and Rose had heard that story. Selena and this Morghan lady had been brave, she reckoned, creeping through a place like the City of Lost Souls.

'In the instance that Morghan told me about,' Selena said, 'she was helping one such soul, and said she ended up cradling them in her arms for a significant time.'

'Their body, you mean?' Damien asked.

But Selena shook her head. 'No,' she said. 'Their spirit. It needed that one simple thing, to be held as a loving mother holds her child, to be safe in her embrace.' Selena fell silent for a moment. 'One thing we can do for Rachel,' she said. 'While Rose is looking for her remains, is to hold her spirit in our arms, in our Bone Mother embrace. We will hold her in love and compassion, like we need to do for all those we have loved and known who have passed onwards.'

Rue looked over at Clover, whose fair curls bounced about her shoulders as she passed blocks to Josh, and helped him arrange them in some esoteric pattern only they could decipher.

She thought about their mother, about holding her in such an embrace. It had never occurred to her before, to put it like this. To hold her mother, her own beloved dead, in her arms. Always, she had wanted her mother's arms back around her. Always, she had thought about it from her perspective, what she needed and wanted. But perhaps, it would help to do it the other way around.

She imagined it, holding her mother in some dark, warm cave where everything came back together, was remade, made anew. She met her mother there and held her, tenderly, love welling from her heart.

Tears came to her eyes, but they were not tears of despair, but rather of joy, for her mother lived on, every small piece of her still there, still part of her, for her mother remembered everything, Rue realised. And the reaching out to hold her mother in this way made Rue's heart less heavy, helped it heal it in some way she couldn't explain to herself, but as though in the giving of the gift of her embrace, she had received a gift in return.

Tara was nodding too, her eyes damp again, closed, looking inwards where she stood in the dimness of a cave shaped like a womb, opening her arms to Rachel, drawing her to her, holding her. Without asking for anything, she simply held her.

'When someone is lost,' Selena said. 'We look for them, and bring them home. If we cannot find them, we make ourselves their home so that they will find us in their darkness and know our comfort.' She looked over at Josh, playing quietly with Clover.

'Now,' Selena said. 'Our dreams. How did we do?' She grimaced a little at her own.

'I didn't dream of Rachel,' Rue said apologetically. She shook her head, looked down in her lap. 'I dreamt about my mum instead. Sorry.'

There was a slight pause, that Ebony decided quickly to fill.

She looked over at Rue. 'I dreamt about the day you and I went to the beach looking for a stone with a hole in it, do you remember?'

Rue nodded. 'Of course. That was the day before I left.'

'Yeah,' Ebony said. 'That's right.' She shrugged and lifted her hands. 'Anyway, that's what I dreamt about – walking down that beach, looking for a stone with a hole in it for the water to come through.'

'For the water to come through?' Rue asked.

'I don't know what that meant,' Ebony said. 'But that's what we were doing. Looking for a hole in a stone for water to come through. It's like some sort of riddle.'

'I dreamt of water as well,' Rose said, turning to look at Ebony. 'I was looking through a stone with a hole in it, at the tide coming in.' She turned to Selena. 'There were cliffs all about me too.'

'And what did I have to say?' Kiri asked for the benefit of everyone else.

Rose answered promptly. 'Tide's coming in; that's what you said. Tide's coming in and someone had pulled down a tree to cover her.'

Selena's eyebrows rose and she closed her eyes, thinking about what Kiri had said in her state of knowing.

'It's really worked, hasn't it?' Ebony said, awe in her voice. 'I mean, this dream incubation thing – it's really worked. That's three of us who dreamt of water, of the beach.'

'Make that four,' Damien said.

'Five,' Dandy added. 'I dreamt of walking down a lot of steps. Steep, stone steps, and at the bottom was just a lot of seawater.' She shuddered lightly. 'I did not want to get to the bottom of the steps.' She paused a moment. 'The steps were covered in branches. Twigs. A real mess.'

Damien shook his head. 'I didn't see anything in my dream,' he said. 'It was as though I was blind or something.' He paused, thought about the dream he'd brought back from the night. 'But I could hear something, the ocean, waves coming in, going out, coming in.'

'Six,' Natalie said, licking her lips. 'I dreamt I was sweeping the sand on a beach with a branch. Just sweeping and sweeping.'

'I dreamt of being on a beach too,' Selena said. 'It was actually quite awful. I didn't like it there. The beach was just a small moon of sand with high cliffs all around and the tide was coming in, until there was no beach left.' She shook her head. 'Rachel was there with me, telling me that this was their favourite place to come.'

'Well, that's it, then,' Dandy said. 'She's at some beach somewhere.'

'Which one?' Ebony asked. She looked over at Tara. 'We haven't heard about your dream, yet,' she said. 'You were going to ask a different question, though, weren't you?'

KATHERINE GENET

Before Tara could open her mouth to answer, however, Ebony looked over at Selena. 'This is so cool,' she said. 'This dream incubation thing. Could we do it for anything?'

'People have always used their dreams to search out answers for issues they're having,' Selena said. 'You can ask anything of them, and your dreams will attempt to tell you what you need to know.'

Ebony laughed. 'So, we do come here with a user manual, then.' She was delighted by the thought and reckoned immediately to experiment with it. As far as she was concerned, they'd had an amazing result, to have all dreamt of the beach. She turned back to Tara.

'So, what did you dream?'

Tara gazed over at Josh, who had tired of playing with the blocks and was lying on the floor on his back reading to himself from a small cardboard book. She shook her head, realising suddenly that the book Josh held was about a trip to the beach.

Coincidence? She didn't know.

'I asked to dream about what I needed to know for Josh's wellbeing,' she said.

'What did your dreams tell you?' Kiri asked. It seemed horribly tough for the little guy to lose his mother, and by his father's hand.

Tara shook her head slightly, leaning forward in her chair. 'I dreamed I was cooking,' she said. 'Making lunches. Snacks.' She lifted her hands. 'So, I didn't dream anything, really. I was just making endless amounts of food.' She pressed her lips together in a dissatisfied line.

'You were providing nourishment,' Selena said. 'Looking after his physical needs.'

'Interesting it was lunch and snacks,' Rue said, then looked around at everyone, and nodded. 'Rather than breakfast and dinner, if you know what I mean?'

'Right,' Kiri said. 'So maybe your dream is saying you're not going to be the one who takes the little guy in.'

Tara frowned. 'You mean, if his father gets caught?' She glanced at Rose. 'When his father is arrested for this, I mean. What will happen to him then?'

Rose spoke in a low voice, even though she knew Josh probably wasn't paying them the slightest attention and wouldn't understand the words anyway.

'He'll go under the care of a social worker, who will likely approach his extended family.'

'The ones who are Brethren, you mean?' Dandy asked.

'Who won't let him listen to music,' Tara added. She'd rather keep him than have him go somewhere he couldn't dance and sing, or even watch his favourite DVD. But, she reminded herself, Rue was right about the dream. She hadn't been making breakfast in it. Or dinner. Just lunch and snacks. She sighed. It would be hard not to want to do more for him.

'We have to find Rachel first,' Natalie reminded them, leaning against Damien's solid warmth.

'Yes,' Dandy said, and she looked around the circle at everyone. 'So, a beach, I think we're quite clear on that.' She pursed her lips.

'Which beach, though?' Ebony asked. 'There are lots of them around here.' She looked at Rue. 'We were at Aramoana Beach that day. Maybe there?'

'It has cliffs,' Rue added.

But Selena shook her head. 'Aramoana is a long beach,

though, isn't it? The one I dreamt of was quite small. I was cupped by cliffs.'

'And what's with the stone with a hole,' Ebony asked. 'Looking through at water, a hole the water could go through and all that.'

Rose was busy thinking, tapping her fingers on her thigh. She shook her head. 'I need to think about this, look at some maps, see if Mike Manners owns property anywhere else, near a beach, for example.'

But Damien was shaking his head. 'I got it,' he said. 'I know which beach.'

47

ROSE PARKED HER CAR AND GOT OUT, THE WIND WHIPPING UP
the hill from the sea and blowing her hair into her face.
Impatiently, she pulled a hair elastic from her wrist and tied
it back out of the way.

'Where do we look, do you reckon?' Damien asked. He'd
insisted on coming with Rose as soon as he'd realised Rose
wasn't going to get any of her fellow officers on the job
with her.

Not an official investigation yet, Rose had said.

Rose stood looking out to sea now. She shook her head.
'It's a long way down to the water,' she said.

'He coulda killed her down there,' Damien replied,
catching on quick. He looked at the path that led down the
hill to Tunnel Beach and decided that Rachel had to have
been alive if she went down there with him, because it was a
bit of a hike if you were carrying a dead weight.

He winced at the thought.

'If she'd gone into the water, wouldn't she have turned

up by now?' he asked, turning to look along the top of the grassy paddocks that were part of the farm the path to the beach led through. He wrinkled his nose, leaning a hand on the car as he thought about it.

'I don't know much about currents and so on,' Rose said regretfully.

Damien contemplated the view again. 'He coulda chucked her off the cliff,' he said, pointing. 'Within view of the hole in the rock we dreamt about.'

They walked down the path a way, looked down at the jutting peninsula that ended in an arch over the water, a great hole through which the surf rushed.

'You'd have to be bloody keen,' Rose said. 'Be easy to go over with her.'

Damien was nodding before she'd even finished her sentence. 'I agree,' he said. 'And it was probably during the day, right? That he got rid of her?'

Rose mused upon this. 'He was late picking Josh up, and he wasn't answering his phone. So, yeah, I'd say you were right. Unless he went back out at night to put her somewhere.'

'Not here, then,' Damien said. 'I wouldn't come here lugging a heavy weight at night. I'd end up going for a swan dive too.'

They turned back for the path, walked up again to the car, looked around.

'This is a farm,' Damien said.

Rose nodded. 'What are you thinking?'

Damien shrugged. 'Lots of stands of trees and what not see? Didn't your mum say someone had pulled a tree down over her?'

Rose surveyed the paddock and nodded, an eerie certainty creeping into her bones. 'And it's not as though the farmer goes poking about under them, is it?' Rose said.

'Not at this time of the year,' Damien added. 'Not until lambing, and even then.' He shrugged. 'Some of that elder over there, look – it's been cut down and left in piles for years, from the looks of it.' He squinted. 'We should go closer.'

Damien glanced at Rose. 'Didn't we all dream of branches? And those of us who saw Rachel in our dreams said she had twigs in her hair.'

Rose nodded. 'This place makes sense.' She pointed to the piles of downed elder and thought of all the things you could hide under there.

'We'll drive up to it,' she said. 'Do you think someone would notice a car driving through the gate into the paddock over there?'

'Probably not, or at least, they wouldn't pay it any attention. If you're here, you're looking down at the water, walking down to the beach.'

As if to underscore Damien's words, a car pulled up and a couple got out, already oohing and aahing over the view, walking past them without a second glance.

'See?' Damien shrugged.

Rose nodded, and they got back in the car. 'Let's go see, then.'

She put her seat belt on, then paused.

'Alright?' Damien asked after a minute.

'I think we're going to find her,' Rose said. 'And it's a horrible thing.'

'Yeah,' Damien said. 'Which is why we're going to find her, and then you're going to put her husband behind bars.'

That was true, Rose thought, cheering up slightly at the idea.

Damien opened the farm gate, jumped back in the car. But Rose didn't drive through.

'What's going on?' Damien asked.

Rose shook her head. 'We should walk down,' she said. 'Are those tracks? In the grass, look – going down to that woodpile?' She backed away from the gate and parked over to the side, out of the way. 'Just in case she's there, and there are tyre tracks.'

'It's rained a fair bit since then,' Damien said.

But Rose shrugged. 'Better to be careful.'

That was fair enough, Damien thought, as they got out of the car and walked through the open gate. Damien closed it behind them, not quite knowing why he did. For a bit of privacy, perhaps. It wasn't every day you went looking for human remains.

His throat was dry as they walked down into the paddock.

'That one,' Rose said, pointing to the nearest. 'You could drive right to it.' She didn't need to add how convenient that would be.

The big piles of downed trees were left scattered about the paddock like unlit bonfires. She thought that the farmer probably didn't use this paddock much. It was smaller than the others, and there was a rusting old Land Rover sitting on flat tyres behind the pile of wood they were making for.

'I'm surprised that all this junk is here,' Damien said, waving a hand at the rusting vehicle, the old piles of tree cuttings. 'Especially when there are tourists walking right nearby.'

Rose shrugged. Her attention was focused on the large dome of branches that had been half-heartedly stacked and left there probably twenty years ago. They'd morphed since then into their own entity, and, she thought, an excellent place to hide a body, if you could get it inside the structure.

Rachel had been on the smaller side. 160 centimetres, 55 kilograms, or thereabouts, Rose thought, from descriptions of her. She skirted the faint marks in the grass that led down into the paddock, noting them with interest, since they seemed to have been made recently. When she lifted her head and gazed around the paddock, she nodded. This one had been pretty much abandoned, so why, she asked herself, were there tracks, even faint ones, in the grass?

'Can you see anything?' Damien asked when they reached the woodpile and skirted around it. He found that he was almost afraid to look properly and was glancing off to look at the ocean instead, or the abandoned Land Rover, or anywhere really, except inside the tangle of elder tree branches. 'I think I can smell something.' He cleared his throat.

Whoever had cut these trees down needn't have bothered, he thought distantly. The trees themselves had sprung up again, creating even more of a tangle next to the pile of old branches that was at least as tall as he was.

'Good place for rabbits and the like,' he said.

Rose didn't answer. She was squatted down, peering into the crisscross pile of branches, her hand across her nose. She'd found a place where you could squeeze in a body, if you were determined.

If you weren't squeamish.

She stood up slowly, limbs almost creaking. She could hear the rush and suck of waves beneath them on the beach, and Rose lifted her face to the wan light of the sky and closed her eyes.

Damien looked over at her, saw her stiff-legged stance, her clenched hands, and knew she'd found something.

Rachel.

'Are you alright?' he asked, but his voice sounded thin against the backdrop of the sea, whose roar seemed to grow louder inside his head.

Rose lowered her face and opened her eyes. She looked across at Damien and nodded.

'Did you find her?'

She nodded again.

Damien felt himself pale. 'Should I...should I come over and look too?'

Rose closed her eyes again, thought of her mother. *Little boy crying,* she'd said, speaking from that place inside her that was more awake when the rest of her slept. *Little boy crying. She's crying. Everyone except* him *crying.*

Rose snapped her eyes open, looked at Damien, shook her head. 'I need to call the station,' she said. 'You can go back to the car, just don't walk on those tracks.' She reached into her pocket for her mobile phone, flipped the lid, and pressed the buttons to make the call.

Damien watched Rose for a moment, then nodded and walked back up to the gate, which he opened slowly, as though suddenly he were an old man.

He left it open.

When he reached the car, he turned back to look at

Rose, standing with her phone pressed to her ear, her other hand gesturing in the air as she told whoever was on the other end what she'd found.

Rachel, Damien thought. They'd found Rachel.

He'd never paid much attention to Rachel. She was just Josh's mum, and sometimes he was still rushing out for work when she arrived, Josh in his pushchair, Rachel looking around the kitchen and the rest of the house with eyes that seemed greedy for it.

Tara had told him once that Rachel never really wanted to leave, that she seemed to savour every moment she spent in Windswitch House, soaking up the atmosphere.

And now, she was lying face in the dirt under an old pile of woods, twigs tangled in her hair. Damien pressed his hands to the cold metal of Rose's car and shook his head.

Her body was, he reminded himself. Her spirit roamed, not free, but snagged by the circumstances of her death, of her need to make sure her child was okay.

Damien turned his face towards the sea, then looked back at Rose, saw that she'd put her phone away and was standing beside the woodpile, chin tucked down, hands in her pockets, the wind tugging at loose strands of her black hair.

In a few minutes, he knew, this area would be swamped with police, scene of crimes officers, detectives.

Thank all the Gods, he thought, that Tara could look after Josh and the little kid wouldn't have to go to strangers straight away. Damien had the idea that Mike Manners would soon be paid a very uncomfortable visit by a couple of police officers, handcuffs jangling.

Good, he thought.

Rose toiled her way up the hill. Soon, she knew, when everyone else arrived, she'd be energised, eager to collect evidence, to begin building the case. Right now, though, she was only filled with grief for the young woman who had been thrown away, broken and discarded, and why? Because she dared to have dreams for herself?

'You okay?' Damien asked.

Rose shook her head. 'Not really.'

They stood silently for a minute.

Damien looked at the sea, the sky, the green grass, cleared his throat, lifted his voice.

'Kia hora te marino, kia whakapapa pounamu te moana, kia tere kārohirohi i mua i tō huarahi.'

Next to him, Rose nodded, her eyes damp as she translated. 'May peace be widespread, may the sea glisten like greenstone, and may the shimmer of light guide you on your way.'

They stood there a moment longer, side by side, faces to the wind.

Rose spoke first. 'I can't run you back yet,' she said. 'We should have brought two cars.' She couldn't fathom why they hadn't.

But Damien shook his head. 'I'll be right,' he said. 'I'll just walk down to the beach for a while.' He gazed down at the bit of land that jutted out into the water, the sea rolling through the archway of stone. 'This was somewhere special to them.' He shook his head. 'Why'd he bring her here?'

Rose folded her arms over her chest, hugged herself. 'A shred of decent feeling, perhaps?'

'Or maybe he just remembered the woodpiles.' Damien

turned to look at Rose. 'What's the likelihood of finding her here if you know, we hadn't dreamt about it?'

That was a good question, Rose thought, looking down the paddock where Rachel lay beneath the tumble of branches and twigs. 'Not good,' she said at last. 'No one goes into the paddock; everyone is busy following the path to the beach instead. And even if they did?' She winced. 'She was well tucked in there.'

That brought them to silence again, the wind picking up, bringing the sound of waves closer as if they broke upon the green grass of the paddock instead of down below upon the rocks.

'They're coming,' Rose said, hearing the cars.

'I'll get out of the way for a while,' Damien said.

Rose nodded. 'Give me half an hour, then I'll take you home.' She paused. 'Will you give my mum a lift home after that?' She shook her head. 'I'm going to be busy the rest of the day.'

Damien lifted a hand. 'No worries,' he said.

By the time he was dipping his head to walk through the man-made tunnel through to the beach, Damien knew that up above him, Rose was leading her colleagues down to the woodpile, showing them where Rachel was.

They'd found her, he thought, stepping onto the cold, damp sand of the narrow beach and looking around at the high cliffs.

They'd found her, he thought. They'd dreamt of her and found her, but he shook his head, nonetheless. He didn't think he'd ever come back to this beach, no matter how impressive it was.

For him, it would always be haunted now.

48

CLOVER LOOKED UP, HER FACE ALERT, FROWNING.

'What is it?' Rue asked. They were still in the living room, everyone together, except for Damien and Rose. Rue let her hands drop to her lap, the dress she'd been putting the finishing touches on falling in a puddle. She glanced at Ebony, who had been pretending to read a magazine and who now stared back at her, eyes wide.

'Josh's mama,' Clover said, getting up and going over to Tara, who had Josh asleep on her lap, his skin flushed with sleep, little chest rising and falling.

Rue put the dress she was sewing aside slowly, carefully, her gaze on Clover.

'What about her?'

Clover shook her head, smiled at Tara. 'She found now.' Clover looked at Selena.

None of them had felt like leaving the big room where they could sit together, pretending to be busy, but really just waiting for news from Damien and Rose.

A mobile phone warbled and for a moment no one moved.

Tara pulled her phone from her pocket. 'It's Damien,' she said, glancing over at Natalie, who sat pale-faced next to Rue and Ebony on the couch.

Natalie took a breath, nodded. 'Answer it,' she said.

Tara flipped the phone open, put it to her ear.

'Damien,' she said, and listened for a minute. She cleared her throat, said goodbye, and looked down at Josh, kissed his forehead.

'Have they found her, then?' Kiri asked. She was in an armchair, calm, knowing her daughter would find the poor woman. 'They've found Rachel?'

Tara sniffed, squeezed her eyes shut and tried not to move too much. She didn't want to disturb Josh. She took a watery breath, aware that everyone was watching her and waiting.

'At Tunnel Beach,' she said. 'Under a woodpile in a paddock there.'

Selena lowered her head. 'It's good she's been found.'

'Josh's mama real happy now,' Clover said.

'Oh my god,' Ebony said suddenly. 'Can you feel that?'

Rue's skin prickled and like everyone else in the room, she froze.

'What is it?' she whispered a moment later.

'It's Rachel,' Selena said.

There was a pressure in the room, a sense of something being opened, someone stepping through, someone they couldn't see.

But they could certainly feel her.

'What does she want?' Natalie asked.

'She wanna give Josh a kiss,' Clover said. She was smiling, because Josh's mama wasn't screaming and crying anymore. Instead, she was beautiful, her happiness making her glow. Clover watched Rachel as she looked at her son.

Rachel turned her head, gazed back at her.

'She gonna be sad to leave Josh,' Clover said.

Selena reached for Clover, put her arms around her. She couldn't see Rachel except with her inner vision, but the feeling of her presence was very strong.

'But she glad too,' Clover said, staring up into Rachel's face, then turning to look seriously at Selena.

'You gotta make the light for her now,' she said.

'The what?' Selena asked, surprised.

'She ready to go, she says. You gotta make the light.'

Kiri nodded. 'She's ready.'

'Make the light?' Ebony said. She was on the edge of her seat and looked at Selena. 'Like we did at Sophie's house?'

Selena nodded, understanding dawning.

'What about Josh?' Tara asked.

'She can't stay with him, love,' Dandy said.

Clover watched as Rachel bent over and stroked her small friend's hair, put her lips to his forehead and kissed him, then stood back up and looked expectantly around her.

'She lookin' for the light,' Clover said.

'But what about Josh?' Tara repeated. She could feel something standing in the room with them, perhaps even in front of her, and her heart raced. She panted the question, feeling the pressure of Rachel's presence.

'He is going to be all right,' Selena said. She stood up

and patted Clover on the shoulder, then stepped across the room to where Kiri sat.

'Will you help?' she asked.

Kiri beamed. 'This is turning out to be quite some day.' She got herself to her feet and took Selena's outstretched hand.

'I'm doing it too,' Ebony said, and crossed the room to take Selena's other hand.

Selena nodded, then closed her eyes. Widening her senses, she took the faintest step to the side and the world's spirit aspect opened up to her.

Rue stood up as well, joined the circle, along with Dandy and Natalie. Soon, everyone except Tara, who still held Josh in her arms, stood together around the room, closing their eyes the better to see.

Rue calmed her heart with deep breaths, Clover standing in front of her, leaning against her legs. She remembered Morghan's lesson on top of everything that Selena had taught her and envisioned the room around her. There was the couch, she thought – felt – and there was the little table with its miniature chair that Clover used when she was drawing and colouring. There was the big front window, which looked out onto a strip of grass and the hedge. If she followed the hedge, she'd get to the road, and Clover's lion sitting on its pedestal at the gate, watching over the house.

She felt the house rise around her, felt its walls, floors, the rooms above her, the rooms beside her. The statue in the entranceway, the spirit of the house.

And she felt Rachel. Felt her presence so strongly it took her breath away.

Was this what it was like for Clover all the time, she thought? This short step to the side so that the world opened up, everything in it so much deeper and wider, so wild with information.

Yes, she thought, looking at Rachel who gazed down at Josh.

This was what it was like for Clover all the time. She'd been born being able to see everything in the world, unable to dial it down, or switch it off.

Rue shook her head. How could someone live like this? All the time, all of this. Sensing everything at once. Seeing everything behind everything just at a turn of the head, just for the looking.

It was a wonder, Rue thought, that Clover managed anything close to a normal life. She looked down, where Clover leaned against her, and knew that what kept her sister from wandering off and getting lost, was herself.

It was her.

It was Selena and Tara, and Dandy, and Damien, and Natalie too, now.

But it was her, Rue, most of all.

She felt a presence at her back, a comforting, strengthening presence, and knew that Bryn was there, steadfast, her companion and guide. The one who would strengthen her when she faltered, who would help her navigate, who would help her always with Clover.

Steadfast in life, Rue thought, and in death. She breathed slowly, her lips curving up in a smile.

Her vision filled with golden white light, and she knew that while she'd been wandering off down her own paths, the others had been bringing their intention to life.

She looked and saw Rachel, glowing with light, place a hand on her son's head, then turn, gaze brightening as if she saw someone or something she recognised, was glad for, and then she stepped through somewhere Rue couldn't see, and the light closed around her until she was gone, leaving the room with just an echo that sounded of love.

'We did it,' Ebony said, and let go of the other's hands to dance a little jig on the carpet. 'We really did it!'

'That was cool,' Kiri admitted. 'You guys are like battery packs or something. Really amped up the energy.' She shook her head. 'She crossed over, didn't she? Crossed over right in front of us.'

'She got what she needed,' Dandy said. 'That's what happened.' She looked over at Kiri and nodded. 'Your girl found her, and she knew everything would fall into place from then on, so she passed over.'

Tara shook her head. 'What about Josh, though?' It was the question she kept asking. She licked her lips. 'Damien said he reckoned that Mike might be a bit late picking Josh up.'

'Rosie will be taking him to the station,' Kiri said. 'For a formal interview.' She rubbed her hands together in satisfaction.

'Will they charge him?' Natalie asked.

Kiri shrugged. 'Hope so,' she said. 'Will depend on what evidence they find.'

Tara looked horrified. 'You mean he might not be arrested?' She held Josh more tightly. 'He might come and get Josh? I thought Damien was just being smart.'

. . .

IT WAS ANOTHER HOUR BEFORE ROSE AND DAMIEN PULLED UP outside the house. Tara swept the door open and all but pulled them inside.

'What's going on?' she asked. 'What's going to happen to Josh?'

Rose held up a hand. She looked simultaneously elated and exhausted. 'Will Josh be all right with you for the next few days, if necessary? You're a registered foster carer, right?' she asked.

'Yes,' Tara answered quickly. 'Definitely. Both Selena and I am. What's happening to Mike?' Josh was in the playroom with Clover and Rue and Ebony; they were watching a movie.

Not Matilda, thank goodness. Tara thought she'd be very happy if she never had to see that movie ever again.

'He's being questioned right now,' Rose answered.

'And his place is being searched,' Damien added. He looked at Rose. 'Isn't that right?'

She nodded. 'Officers will be going through it with a fine-toothed comb. But it's going to take a while to put everything together. There's a lot of work yet.' She hugged herself. 'In fact, it's really only just starting.'

Tara nodded. 'But will Mike be coming to get Josh today?'

Rose couldn't say, not with any certainty. 'It will depend on the interview and the search. He might be detained, or we might have to cut him loose.'

Tara's eyes widened and she shook her head. 'Will I have to give him Josh if that happens?'

'Yes,' Rose said. 'I'm afraid so.' She glanced at Damien and pursed her lips. 'But I don't think it's going to go down like that.' She nodded at Damien. 'That handbag you saw? In the kitchen? I got a look at it, and it had a purse in it. If that has Rachel's bank cards and so on in it, then there's probably cause to keep hold of Mike right there.'

'She wouldn't go anywhere without her bag,' Damien agreed, then beamed as Natalie came into the kitchen. 'You're still here.'

She nodded. 'Did you get him?' she asked Rose, going over to Damien and letting him put his arm around her.

'We're working on it,' Rose said. She looked back at Tara. 'If we do detain Mike, then you'll be having a visit from Child Services.'

Tara nodded. 'We have a pretty good relationship with them, now, so we can keep Josh with us for as long as necessary.'

Rose nodded, glad. 'I'd better get back to it,' she said and nodded at Damien. 'You'll take Mum home for me?'

'You betcha,' Damien said.

Natalie smiled. 'She's having the time of her life with Selena and Dandy, I think,' she said. 'They're in the living room talking about all manner of things I don't have the slightest clue about.'

Rose nodded, sparing a moment to be glad her mother had found some like-minded new friends. The thought surprised her, and she paused.

Friends, she thought. Were this lot new friends?

She decided that maybe they were.

'I have to get going,' she said, and looked at Damien. 'Thanks for coming with me.'

He nodded seriously. 'I'm glad I could,' he said. 'And don't worry about Kiri. I'll get her home no problem.'

Rose nodded again, lifted a hand in a wave, and slipped out the door.

'I can't believe it,' Tara said, sitting down at the table. 'It's like a dream.' She gave a little laugh when she heard what she'd said. For hadn't they dreamt where Rachel could be found? And she had been found, and Tara had been in the room when her spirit turned up. She'd felt Rachel lean over Josh, had felt her as clearly as she'd ever felt anything in her life.

'What do you think will happen to Josh when all this is done?' Natalie asked. She went to switch the electric jug on. A pot of chamomile tea would be just the thing.

'They'll see if any of his family will take him,' Tara said, resting her head on a hand. 'That's what usually happens.'

'Yes,' Natalie said. 'But aren't Rachel's family part of that religious group?' She glanced at Damien. 'What are they called?'

'Exclusive Brethren,' Damien said.

'Doesn't matter,' Tara said. 'If they'll take him and love him, then that's where he'll be placed.' She straightened, smiled wanly.

'I just want him to be safe,' she said. 'Safe and loved.'

Natalie nodded, holding the jug. She looked at Tara and Damien and drew breath.

'That's what we all want,' she said.

'To be safe and loved.'

49

'IT'S THE SEASON FOR IT,' EBONY SAID, SHRINKING LOWER INTO her jacket. The day was dark, as though the sun hadn't been able to summon the energy to rise far or fast.

Rue tipped her head back and looked through the bare branches of the trees towards the sky. It was shrouded in clouds.

'It's going to rain,' she said, then sighed. 'I miss you at school, you know.'

Ebony grinned at her. 'Yeah,' she said. 'Must be hellishly dull without me there.'

Rue rolled her eyes and laughed. 'Okay, I asked for that.' They walked along the path through the gardens, then turned to head up into the Rhododendron Dell where the rhododendrons were over a hundred years old, large with graceful and curving trunks. To Rue, they looked as though they were dancing.

She thought Morghan would like them.

'Are you annoyed you had to come back early?' Sophie

asked, shoving her hands deeper into her pockets. 'I wish I could go travelling already. And to a place with such a long history – where they're still living it.'

Rue shook her head. 'We'll go back,' she said. 'Some day. And I learnt plenty while I was there to keep me busy practicing it for a long time.' She paused, peered through the tangle of bush. On the other side of the trees, she thought, was Windswitch House, and her family. And Clover.

'Besides,' she added. 'I learnt the most important thing.'

She could feel Bryn's presence at her back. The light sensation of her there, like a shadow.

'What was that?' Suze asked.

Rue turned onto the new path and reached out a hand to touch the sinuous trunk of a rhododendron. She thought for a moment she could feel it vibrating beneath her hand. On a breath, she widened her senses, feeling her friends around her, the good strong weight of their energy, and Bryn too, coming just a little more into focus.

And beyond that, beyond the trees, she could feel Clover, the bright beacon of her sister's light, shining away.

Just, she thought, probing at it, just shining away.

A light that bright, she thought, was bound to attract more than a few moths. Rue looked at her friends and smiled.

'I learnt how much it means to be Clover's guardian,' she said.

Suze frowned and asked the question before anyone else could. 'What do you mean by guardian? Isn't that Selena, now?'

But Rue shook her head. 'It's always been my job.'

'Yeah,' Ebony said. 'But you can hand it over now, right?'

'Wrong.' They'd stopped on the path, standing in a group, in a circle, but now Rue turned and resumed walking. She spoke back over her shoulder, as much to Bryn as to the others.

'Clover will always be my responsibility,' she said.

'But she's going to be grown up one day,' Sophie said, confused.

Rue shook her head. 'Grown up, sure – but how is she going to get on?'

'She gets on fine,' Ebony said. 'She's one of the most well-balanced kids I've ever met.' She paused. 'Especially having, you know, grown up the first few years the way she did.'

'She is,' Rue said.

'Which is down to you,' Ebony said. 'But Soph's right. Clover's going to be a big girl one day. She's not going to need looking after.'

Rue stopped again and looked at Ebony. 'Isn't she?' she said. 'Can you see her holding down a job? Entering the rush of the modern world?' Rue shook her head.

'Huh,' Ebony said, head down, considering it. She looked at Rue and grinned. 'You might be onto something,' she said, with a glance at the others. 'Can you imagine Clover – her first job at McDonald's – *would you like to know your animal kin with your fries*?' She snorted.

Rue shook her head, but she was laughing too. 'We joke,' she said. 'But that's really how it would be.' She lifted her shoulders in a shrug. 'I just think she's going to need a bit of support, that's all.'

'I'll give her a job,' Ebony said. 'At Beacon.'

'Beacon's not your shop,' Sophie said.

But Ebony just sniffed. 'It will be one day. Besides, that's not the point. Clover can come read cards at Beacon. That would suit her, right?'

Rue guessed it might if anything were to.

Suze frowned at her. 'But you're still going to have your own life, right? I mean, Clover has Selena and everyone; we could all do with so much support. She doesn't need you to sacrifice everything for her.'

'It won't be any sacrifice I'm not willing to give,' Rue said, thinking of Bryn, and the white dragon. Protectors.

'That's good,' Suze said. 'I'd hate to think you were going to you know, shut yourself away from having your own life.' She blew out a breath. 'Like dating, or getting a job that you really want, or something.'

Rue didn't laugh. She stuck her hands deep in her pockets and started walking again. She didn't think it was worth arguing with Suze or the others.

Dating, she thought, would definitely take a back seat. Any guy she dated would have to be extraordinary. So far, she didn't have her eye on anyone.

She knew what she planned to do for a job, though, and it involved building her own business. She knew what she wanted.

She was just going to make sure Clover was always there.

Always okay. Shining away.

They crossed out of the Botanic Gardens, through the woods and into the cemetery.

'Right,' Rue said, looking around at the old graves sitting shadowed in the day's gloom. 'You still want to do this?'

'Are you sure about doing it here?' Sophie asked, also

gazing around at the graves. 'I mean, I don't want to call up the wrong spirits, you know?'

Rue shook her head. 'This is the only place I can think of where we're not likely to run into someone.' She wanted to teach them what Morghan had shown her, how to walk in power.

'Yeah,' Ebony said. 'Because it's a cemetery. I'm kinda with Soph, now that we're here.' She looked up at the sky, which was heavy with dark clouds. 'It's definitely going to rain.'

'Then we'd better hurry up,' Suze said, ever practical. 'I say we just go for it. The dead will stay in their graves.'

'Their spirits aren't even here,' Rue said. Then she remembered how Clover had always hated this place. 'Most of them, that is,' she amended.

'Whatever,' Ebony said on a sigh. 'Let's just do it.'

But Rue was thinking. 'There's something we could do first,' she said. 'So that you know, we don't have to worry about conjuring an entourage of ghosts when we do it.'

'An entourage of ghosts?' Ebony asked with raised brow. 'That's pretty good.' She blinked. 'If it weren't so spooky.'

'You love spooky.'

Ebony was forced to admit that generally, she did. 'True,' she said. 'What's your trick for getting them to stay put, then?'

Rue rolled her shoulders, considering it. They could do it. Would it make a difference?

Maybe.

She opened the little bag Grainne had made and took out one of the miniature herb bundles and held it up.

The four girls had made them just a few days before.

'What do we do with them?' Suze asked.

'We walk the path,' Rue said. 'And bless the graves.'

Sophie got out her own herb bundle. 'That will work?'

'Why wouldn't it?' Rue said.

'True enough,' Ebony agreed. 'I say we do it.' She shook her head. 'Real Halloween-y business, too. Suits the time of the year.' For a moment, she thought about Rachel, and everything that had gone on there, everything that was still going on.

'Samhain,' Rue said, as if reading her thoughts. She remembered the story Selena had told them. 'The time of the Bone Mother and the Beloved Dead.'

The four were silent for a moment, pausing to let Rue's words sink in, then they rustled about lighting the fragrant herbs. They'd made them with Selena, using herbs to honour the season.

Lavender, so that the dead should be remembered.

Rosemary, so that the dead could be spoken to.

Lemon Balm, for the dead are immortal.

Comfrey, to ease the grief of loss.

'What do we say?' Suze asked.

'Whatever feels right,' Rue said. 'You can just think it, if you don't want to say it out loud.'

Suze nodded. She thought she might feel more comfortable just thinking it, then was suddenly cross with herself. What was wrong with speaking to the dead?

After all, when this was done, their plan was to call in their own dead to walk with them.

Suze's mouth was suddenly dry. Not really their dead, she reminded herself. But those who they'd once been, and still were, time being the twisty thing it was, and those who walked with them in support and guidance.

It didn't sound so bad, when she put it like that.

'I'm ready,' she said out loud, her little herb bundle smoking nicely in the damp air.

'Let's do it then,' Ebony said.

They split naturally, two to each side of the path, holding the herbs so that their smoke drifted over the graves.

'May the Bone Mother hold you in her embrace,' Rue said. 'Every bone counted, every bone remembered.'

Sophie nodded, behind her. She had learnt a new story recently, and it came to her now. It was an old Samoyed tale, about a great hero, who could not be brought back to life a third time. Thus, his bones were gathered together and taken to the Bone Woman, who lived deep in a cave, attended by bone people and guarded by monsters.

The Bone Woman took the hero's bones and burnt them to ashes. That night, she laid out the ashes and slept on them, and in three days' time, the hero was once more restored to life.

Now, in the cemetery, letting her smoke drift over the old graves, some of which had subsided over the years, the concrete coverings cracking to show a glimpse of dark earth underneath, Sophie thought about the story, about being nurtured back to life in the Bone Woman's cave. She wondered if three days was the span of time it took a spirit to make the crossing to the Summer Isles.

Possibly, she thought. Possibly.

She cleared her throat. 'May the Bone Mother take your precious bones and bring you back to life,' she said.

They walked slowly along the path, looping back in a circle to where they began, and when the four reached the spot from where they'd started, they stood there a while, wide-eyed, thoughtful.

'We made a circle,' Ebony said at last, trying to find the words.

Rue nodded. 'A wheel,' she added.

'The circle of life, and death, and life again,' Sophie said.

Suze nodded. 'Ashes to ashes, dust to dust, the ground is fertile, and we live on.' She looked down at her hands, thinking of the bones under her skin.

Ebony looked up as the first cold, heavy drops of rain began to fall.

'I feel like we've done enough for today,' she said. She gazed around the cemetery, turning grey and green with the premature darkness of the day. 'I feel...'

'Like we just did something big,' Sophie said.

'Even if it wasn't what we were planning,' Suze added.

Rue nodded. 'I agree,' she said. 'We...sang to the bones, I guess.' She looked around. 'I feel like I need to leave something.' She took a breath. 'An offering. To...close the ritual.'

For it had been a ritual they had done, without quite intending it. They'd woven a spell over the cemetery, a song of living and dying and rising again.

Rue walked over to a tree growing strong a tall on its diet of bones, and bent down, putting the last bit of her herb bundle at its roots.

'For guarding the dead,' she said. 'For taking their bones and bringing them back to life.' She stood and looked at the others. Nodded.

Ebony took her place, laid her herbs, no longer smouldering, on the ground next to Rue's.

'Take me into your earth,' she whispered. 'Grow me strong. Give me life.'

She straightened. Gave up her place to Suze.

'Take all the dead to your breast, Mother,' Suze said. 'Feed them life.' She stood back, looking surprised.

Sophie stepped forward, hearing the rain upon the branches above her, on the ground around, on the graves. She laid her herbs down in the small pile.

'We enter your bone cave,' she said, thinking again of the story. 'And once more we live again.'

They stood together then, in the rain, looking out over the hillside of graves, knowing that each held a life that had been snuffed out, then in the darkness, in the fertile ground, had travelled far and come back again.

Come back to the wide, wide world.

Had never really left it.

50

'BUT DON'T YOU THINK THIS IS TOO MUCH FOR A SMALL child?' Tara asked. 'Especially one as perceptive as Clover?'

Selena smiled at her. 'Of any of us, Clover sees the most clearly. She knows the indestructibility of the spirit. This celebration of that is perhaps even more for her than for any of us.'

Tara shook her head. 'I don't understand.'

Selena placed the chair under the long table. 'Clover sees life and death wherever she looks, for that is the Wheel, the dance of our souls.' She gestured at the table they'd brought out of the kitchen into the long, wide entrance hall, and extended to its true length. 'Tonight,' she said. 'We celebrate this. We honour a view of the world that Clover sees every day of her life.'

'It gives me the shivers,' Tara admitted. 'I mean, it's a different way of thinking about everything that I'm still getting used to.' She paused, shook her head, thinking of Rachel. 'Death, I mean. This is the first time I've had to really think about it. Definitely the first time I've been confronted with it like this.'

'Well,' Selena said. 'Let's hope it's also the last time. Murder at the hands of anyone, let alone someone you trusted, is not the way anyone wants to pass.'

They were silent for a moment. Tara nodded, a lump in her throat.

'That day,' she said. 'When she came to say goodbye to Josh...' Tara shook her head slowly, wonder smoothing out her face. 'It was...amazing. Maybe the most astonishing thing I've ever experienced.'

She'd experienced a lot of mind-boggling things since Selena and Clover had come into her life, but the encounter with Rachel – she'd felt it, she'd felt Rachel's presence, almost even seen her.

It was something she'd never forget. Not for as long as she lived, and for some reason she couldn't quite find the words for inside her mind, she felt changed from it.

Nothing, she thought, would ever be quite the same again.

Now, however, she nodded. 'Okay,' she said. 'You're right. This isn't morbid at all, what we're planning to do. That's what I would have thought, if someone had told me about it before I met you. But I know better now.'

Selena moved around the table and drew Tara into a hug. 'You're doing brilliantly,' she said. 'Throwing all the windows and doors open, seeing how big the world really is.' Selena stood back and looked at Tara. 'I'm proud of you,' she said. 'So very proud.'

. . .

RUE SAT IN HER CHAIR BY THE WINDOW, STARING OUTSIDE. IT was surprisingly clear out there, the clouds vanished from the sky, leaving it a clear, empty, and pale blue.

Ebony, sprawled on Rue's bed, looked over at her. 'Penny for 'em,' she said.

Rue turned and looked at her. 'What?'

'Penny for your thoughts,' Ebony said, enunciating slowly and clearly while she grinned.

'Oh,' Rue said, and squinted. 'That's about what, twenty cents in today's currency?' She wrinkled her nose. 'You're a bit cheap.'

'I made a value judgement,' Ebony said. 'As to how much your thoughts might be worth.'

Rue laughed. 'I was thinking about Bryn,' she said.

'All right, then,' Ebony said, rolling over to look properly at her friend. 'I bid way too low.'

Rue just nodded, stared out the window again. 'I want to know the rest of her story, you know? About what happened with Rhian, and whether she made more, what would you call them?' She looked questioningly over at Ebony.

Ebony shrugged. 'Prophecies?' she said. 'Isn't that what seers do? Foretell things.'

'Whoa, that gives me goosebumps for some reason,' Rue said.

'Don't know why. You do have first-hand experience of it with Clover.'

Rue rubbed at her arms where the hair was standing on end. 'True, I suppose,' she said.

'But?' Ebony stretched out, rested her head on her hand and looked at Rue. She'd only worked a half day, and the Samhain celebration, or ritual, or whatever it was, would start soon, when dusk began falling. Clover was in her room, napping.

Rue had lost the thread. 'But what?'

Ebony shook her head. 'You want to know the rest of Bryn and Rhian's story. But... I sense a but there.'

'Maybe,' Rue said. 'I feel like I got what I needed, for now at least. Some insight into, not just who Clover is, and what she is, but who I am as well.'

'Her guardian,' Ebony said.

Rue nodded, grateful that Ebony got it. 'Her guardian, yeah.'

'And for all practical purposes, always have been,' Ebony added.

'This is going to sound weird,' Rue said, rolling her eyes at Ebony's sudden smirk. 'But I don't know how else to put it.'

'I'm good with weird.'

Rue nodded and touched a hand lightly to her head. 'It's not just in my head.' She frowned.

Ebony waited for her to find the words for what she wanted to say. She thought it would be more than twenty cents worth for sure.

'Definitely going to sound weird,' Rue said with a wry smile. 'I feel like my mind isn't just in my head anymore.'

Ebony raised her eyebrows but said nothing.

'I feel like it's in my chest as well, maybe even in my legs and arms.' Rue paused, shook her head. 'And I feel like it's kinda outside myself too. I am not explaining this well at all.'

'It's interesting though,' Ebony said. 'And I think I might know what you mean anyway, because hasn't Selena been teaching us to get out of our heads and into our hearts? And whenever I do that, I feel like...' She cast around for the words. 'Like the world is suddenly bigger.'

Rue nodded. 'That's it exactly. The world is bigger. And now that I know Bryn, it's like I can feel her out there in that world, and wow, that makes it even bigger still, you know? Because it's not just here and now in material and spirit, it's then and there as well.' She shook her head again, took a breath and blew it out. 'There's so much to it,' she said. 'The world. It's so big and so much more interesting and beautiful than I ever imagined.'

She paused. 'And that's why I don't feel impatient to learn more of the story, right? Why it feels okay to just let the rest come as it will in dreams or whatever. Because I can feel Bryn there, and she's satisfied that I've got the main thing. And just having her out there, standing on a hill in the distance of my mind or spirit or whatever, sometimes moving close to stand with me, but otherwise just out there in the world that's so huge, it's enough.'

Rue subsided. Looked at Ebony, who nodded.

'I get it,' she said. 'It's like there's no rush, because there's space and time for everything.'

'Yeah.'

The bedroom door rattled, then pushed open and Clover stuck her head around it.

'I waked up,' she said.

'So you did,' Rue told her.

Clover sidled over, pressed her hands on Rue's leg. 'Is it time yet?' she said. 'For the feast?'

Rue shook her head. 'Not yet. We have to wait until it's just starting to get dark.'

Clover thought about this and frowned. 'Then can I have a biscuit, and can we go feed the ducks?' She gave Rue a very serious look. 'It give us something to do when we waitin'.'

Rue laughed, looked over at Ebony who was already sitting up.

'You bet,' she said. 'Let's go give those ducks some afternoon tea.'

THEY WERE BACK AS THE SUN BEGAN ITS SLIDE TOWARDS THE western horizon. In the entrance foyer, they stopped and stared.

'Wow,' Ebony breathed. 'It's beautiful.'

Rue shook her head. 'Tara and Natalie outdid themselves.' She looked down at Clover who stared wide-eyed at the table decorations. 'Don't you think so?'

Clover nodded, gazing at the sprays of evergreens fastened together with white ribbon.

Rue touched her on the shoulder. 'Let's go get washed and dressed.'

Their clothes were hanging waiting in Rue's wardrobe. Ebony had put hers there when she arrived, and Rue opened the wardrobe door and they stood, the three of them, in a silent row for a moment.

'You're an amazing sewer,' Ebony said at last.

Rue nodded. She'd been inspired when she got home from the UK and had made Ebony trousers and a tunic that looked a lot like what Morghan wore. She smiled down at Clover.

'You like yours?' she asked.

Clover nodded.

Rue took out the small, simple dress and held it up. 'Let's get it on you, then,' she said.

Clover nodded again, looking at the white dress with the symbols Rue had embroidered on it, also in white.

'I not gonna get it dirty,' she said, but her voice was dubious.

Rue laughed. 'It's okay,' she said. We'll tuck a napkin on you when it's time to eat.'

Ebony was already dressed and did a swirl in front of the mirror. 'I'm going to get you to make all my clothes from now on,' she said, admiring her reflection.

'Sure,' Rue said. 'It'll be the start of my new business.' She grinned at her friend. 'You do look amazing,' she said.

When Clover was dressed and dancing about the room, Rue got changed herself, drawing on her own white dress, also embroidered. She touched her fingers to the Celtic knot symbol she'd fashioned, above which there was a deer head, whose antlers turned into tree branches.

She nodded to herself, thinking of Bryn, and the dream she'd had of her arriving at the Forest Grove.

Running with the deer, the other girl had said.

Rue hoped she'd one day learn what that meant.

'Ready?' Ebony asked. 'You look fantastic.'

Rue nodded. 'We all do,' she said. And they did, the three of them dressed in white, as Selena had suggested.

'We shine like stars,' Clover said, and in the dimming room, in their white clothes, it was almost as if they did.

51

'I CAN'T BELIEVE WE'RE DOING THIS,' ROSE SAID EVEN AS SHE herded Kiri to the car.

'I like 'em,' Kiri said, settling herself in the passenger's seat and waiting for Rose to get in the driver's side.

'That's cos they're as spooky as you.'

Kiri grinned at her daughter. 'Wasn't just them and me who dreamt where the poor girl was.'

Rose pressed her lips together and started the car. When she'd pulled out on the road for the short drive to Windswitch House, she shook her head. 'Well, I feel like I glow in the dark, wearing all white.'

Kiri chortled with laughter. 'I like the reason for the white,' she said when she'd finished laughing. 'It being a celebration makes sense to me.'

'Just because there's method to madness, doesn't mean there isn't madness.'

Kiri just shook her head and smiled into the dusk that was settling over the city like a gauzy blanket.

'Awesome,' Damien said, opening the door for them when they got to the house. 'You made it! Come in, come in.'

Kiri stepped into the house that closed around her like a welcoming hug. For a big house, she thought, it was incredibly friendly feeling. Not at all stiff and grand and intimidating like she'd thought it would be the first time she'd set foot in it.

'Wouldn't miss it,' she said and nudged Rose. 'Would we, hine?'

Rose shook her head and looked at Damien, seeing in his suddenly serious expression the echo of the day they'd gone looking together for Rachel. He touched her upper arm gently and she leaned in to touch their noses and foreheads together in the traditional hongi greeting.

Damien smiled at her, then greeted Kiri the same way.

'Nau mai,' he said, welcoming them. 'Haere mai.'

'ALL SPIRITS SHINE IN THE DARKNESS,' SELENA SAID, LOOKING around the table where they all stood behind their chairs.

There were three empty chairs.

'That's why we shinin' too, in our white clothes,' Clover piped up to say.

Selena smiled at her. 'Yes,' she said. 'We shine too, and we come together on this Samhain night of the year to greet and honour those who have passed through the valley into the land of the dead.' She put her hands on the back of her chair.

'Long may they live,' she said.

Around the table, everyone echoed her.

'Long may they live.'

Selena nodded. 'We will sit down and eat in their honour. We will toast them, giving them our blessings for their journey. We will remember them, for they are our beloved dead and we have set places for them at our table so that they will know our love and feel our welcome on this night of celebration for them.'

She drew breath. 'We remember them,' she said.

'We remember them,' Rue and Ebony echoed.

'We acknowledge their journey with love.'

There were nods around the table.

'We bless them and are blessed in return, for they are souls like us, and one day we will make the same journey, for this is the Wheel of life, the turning of seasons, the weaving of the worlds.'

Selena smiled at her loved friends. 'Let us sit now and serve each other. Let us rejoice in our departed friends and our ancestors, for who they are, we will one day be.'

In a rather awed silence, everyone took their places at the table. Beside Rue, there was an empty chair, and a place setting. She looked at it for a moment, then served a helping of food onto the plate.

Picking up her glass, she held it up in a toast. 'To Beatrix,' she said, and smiled at Clover. 'To her next adventure.'

Everyone joined the toast.

Tara cleared her throat. There was an empty chair beside her also. She held up her glass.

'To Rachel,' she said. 'May you continue your journey with a light heart.'

There was a murmur around the table as everyone wished Rachel well.

The chair at the end of the table, opposite Selena, was

also empty, except when Selena looked at it, she didn't see it as vacant.

'To our beloved ancestors,' she said, holding her glass in a toast. 'To those who walked the worlds before us, who continue on their path, who bless us in our memory and knowledge of them. To those who still come to check on us, or who walk at our side, their support often unseen, but always there.'

This time, each person around the table held up their glasses in a silent toast, Selena's words sinking deep into them, through their skin, into their hearts.

It was Clover who broke the spell. She held up her cup, careful not to slosh the fizzy lemonade in it.

'To wizards and dragons,' she said, giggling. 'An' to Josh's mama, and my mama, and to Rue who she was before, an' me who I was before, and ev'ryone who they was before.'

Satisfied, she took a sip from her cup, set it carefully down on the table, then plumped back down on her chair.

'Well put,' Kiri said. 'I couldn't have said it better myself.' She nodded. 'Kia tau ngā manaakitanga a te mea ngaro ki runga ki tēnā, ki tēnā o tātou.'

She looked expectantly at Damien, who, she'd discovered, was relearning his native language.

'Ah,' Damien said, thinking fast. He held up his glass. 'Let the strength and life force of our ancestors be with each and every one of us.'

Kiri grinned. 'Well done, boy.'

The rest of the meal was eaten quietly, with numerous glances at the empty chairs, which weren't really empty at all. Rue felt truly like her mother sat beside her, and for a moment, tears glistened in her eyes.

'I love you, Mum,' she whispered quietly, then smiled and carried on eating, glad she sat at this table with Clover beside her, with these friends surrounding her, with those who had gone before her taking turns to sit with them. She looked across the table to where Ebony sat casting thoughtful glances at the empty chair nearest her.

Perhaps she was seeing the woman in the sprigged dress, Rue thought, remembering Ebony's fleeting vision from that day at the beach. After all, everyone had ancestors, did they not? Everyone had guides, and guardians, and other lives.

Even Ebony. Rue grinned and Ebony looked at her, grinning back. Rue wished that Suze and Sophie had been able to come, but their parents had been against it, neither girl having been willing to lie to their families about the reason for the evening.

When the meal was eaten, Ebony and Rue rose quietly and cleared the plates, carrying them without fuss into the kitchen, where later, when the ritual was done, they would wash and dry them.

But the evening wasn't over yet. Selena rose and gathered everyone together, leading them outside into the darkened day.

Damien lit the fire, a job that he had taken for his own, finding and splitting the wood for the brazier and building it carefully, ready for his lit match.

The flames leapt upwards.

'Where I used to live,' Selena said, 'we would dance now. We would gather together and dance, our movements weaving the worlds together, our song turning the Wheel.'

She smiled around the circle, which had grown now to include Natalie, Ebony, Rose, and Kiri.

The light, Selena thought, the light of the beacons was spreading.

'But here we do not have the space to dance together. Instead, we will do a ritual of release.' She nodded to herself. 'But first,' she said. 'May we call the quarters?'

This would gather them into sacred space, plant them firmly within the warp and weft of the world.

Damien started. 'May there be peace in the east,' he said. 'May there be peace in the south.

'May there be peace in the west.

'May there be peace in the north.'

Rue closed her eyes. On the other side of the world, it was Beltane, and she'd been meant to dance with Morghan and Grainne and Ambrose at the stone circle to celebrate the day.

What a thing that would have been, she thought.

A small hand slipped into hers and she opened her eyes to smile down at Clover.

'I can see your ram,' Clover whispered. She looked around the circle. 'I can see your animal kins,' she said, and pointed at Ebony. 'Your elephunt is here.' She blinked and looked at the ground beside herself. 'My rabbits is here too.' Her kin stared up at her with shiny dark eyes.

Selena smiled at Clover and nodded. She had stepped into the half space, straddling the worlds, and she could see them too. Hind stood beside her, smooth flank trembling slightly. Beside Clover, a large rabbit gazed up at the girl, and yes, there was Rue's ram.

And Ebony's elephant, a large shadow behind her in the dancing light from the fire.

The newcomers had their kin with them too. An eel lay twined around Rose's legs, while beside Kiri stood an Arctic Fox, its fur a brilliant white in the dusk.

'We call and greet the spirits of the east,' Selena said. 'Be with us this night of the ancestors.' Ruru, the small spirit owl, came to land on her shoulder. 'Spirits of air, those of wing and light, hollow bone, bless us with your presence.'

Dandy cleared her throat. 'We call and greet the spirits of the south,' she said. 'Spirits of earth, of the rabbit who burrows, the worm who tunnels, bless us with your presence.'

Tara took a small step forward, and her cheeks glowed in the firelight.

'We call and greet the spirits of the west,' she said, thinking of the great oceans that surrounded their island home. 'Spirits of water, the eel who finds his way from river to ocean, bless us with your presence.'

It was Rue's turn, and she held Clover's hand tighter.

'We call and greet the spirits of the north,' she said. 'Spirits of fire, of the phoenix, who dies in a blaze of flames only to return to life again, bless us with your presence.'

For a moment, she felt great wings rise behind her and glanced again at Clover, who looked back at her with wide eyes, feeling it too, the vast, strong presence of a dragon who gleamed the colour of the moon against the sky.

'This night,' Selena said, 'we release the sorrow that walks with us when we think of those who we have lost, and in these flames, transmute it to joy. Joy that we have loved and been loved in return, that we have walked with our kin, that we have been held by our mothers, that we have held our children, that we have had the blessing of friendship, companionship of body and heart. That we have known mother and father, brother, sister, friend, and that although we have lost many, it is only temporary, for those who walked this earth still walk the path of life, and we are filled with love for them, and they are filled with love for us.'

She closed her eyes and breathed in the warm air from the fire. 'We do not lose those whom we love. They walk still, our beloved dead.'

Selena stepped nearer the fire and folded her hands over her heart, then lifted them to the sky. 'Those who I have loved, and lost. Stephanie, my mother, Annwyn, my teacher, all the others of my lifetime. Here is my sadness, turned to joy, for you live still, in my heart, and in the next world, just a breath away.'

She stepped back, and with a nod, Rue took her place, drawing in a great, shuddering breath. Clover came with her, hands already tucked against her heart as Selena had held hers. Together, Rue and Clover lifted their hands to the flames and the sky.

'For our mother, Beatrix,' Rue said. 'For Rachel, for our grandmothers and fathers who we never met, for all those gone before us, who live where we do not often see, here is our joy. Here is our sadness, turned for a moment to joy that you lived and breathed and live still.'

Clover nodded beside her. 'I can see you,' she said. 'I can see you if I look far 'nuff.'

They went around the circle, offering their sadness and their joy.

Tara took her turn, tears streaming down her face. She touched her heart, sent her love to the fire, to the sky, to the place where she could barely reach, where Rachel walked now.

'Let my continuing friendship be a joy to you,' she said, tasting tears upon her lips. 'Let my pain at your passing be for this moment, a joy at our meeting. Live well, my friend. I shall think now of you dancing, whenever I think of you.'

LATER, TARA STOOD IN THE KITCHEN. KIRI AND ROSE HAD gone home, Damien had gone back to Natalie's place with her, and everyone else was in bed. Tara looked around at the room, at her plants and her books and her mixing bowls and bottles of herbs.

Tara thought of little Josh, gone now to live with Rachel's family. She herself had put Josh into his grandmother's arms, watching as the woman wept tears of love and joy and sorrow over the child.

He would be all right, Tara thought. He would be okay. As would, she acknowledged, his mother.

They would all be just fine.

RUE WAS IN BED, CLOVER TUCKED BESIDE HER SNORING gently, exhausted from the day. She touched her sister's small cheek then lay back and closed her eyes.

She smiled into the darkness, because for just a moment, something had settled across them. A white wing, she thought, gathering them into its scaled and feathered embrace.

Inside her, the world spread out, expansive. Full of her kin, and full of magic.

PRAYER OF THE WILDWOOD

Long may you live, our Beloved Dead,
Long may you live.
We remember you.
We remember you.
We acknowledge your journey with
    love.
We bless you and are blessed in
    return,
for you are souls like us
and one day we will make the same
    journey,
for this is the wheel of life,
the turning of seasons,
the weaving of worlds.

ABOUT THE AUTHOR

Katherine has been walking the Pagan path for thirty years, with her first book published in her home country of New Zealand while in her twenties, on the subject of dreams. She spent several years writing and teaching about dream-work and working as a psychic before turning to novel-writing, studying creative writing at university while raising her children and facing chronic illness.

Since then, she has published more than twenty long and short novels. She writes under various pen names in more than one genre.

Now, with the Wilde Grove series, she is writing close to her heart about what she loves best. She is a Spiritworker and polytheistic Pagan.

Katherine lives in the South Island of New Zealand with her wife Valerie. She is a mother and grandmother.

BV - #0103 - 100223 - C0 - 216/138/27 - PB - 9781991177926 - Matt Lamination